MY SALVATION

STELLA BRIE

1st Edition: September 2020 ISBN: 978-1-7357715-7-1

2nd Edition: February 2024 ISBN: 979-8-9897738-6-2

Cover Design: Sarah Kil www.sarahkilcreativestudio.com

Editing: Proofs by Polly www.proofsbypolly.com

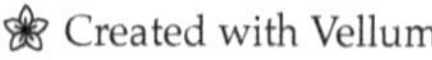 Created with Vellum

PLAYLIST

"Praying" - Kesha

"Need A Favor" - Jelly Roll

"Small Town Stars" - Molly Kate Kestner & The Monroes

"I Won't Give Up" - Kelly Clarkson

"Leave A Light On" - Tom Walker

"In My Blood" - The Veronicas

"I Need Your Love (feat. Ellie Goulding)" - Calvin Harris

"Love I'm Given" - Ellie Goulding

Playlists for all my books can be found on

youtube @authorstellabrie

This book is a Why Choose romance, which means the heroine does not have to choose between male interests. The story includes references to past abuse, work place shootings, and other sensitive topics. Please take care of yourself and read at your own discretion. If unsure, please do not read. Recommended for 18+ due to mature content.

To my husband… the man of my dreams.
Just a paragraph later. Love you!

My head is pounding, and the past is nothing but a black wave threatening to crash down on me at any minute. Yet, I refuse to give up. I can't. All I can do is sing at the top of my lungs to every song on the radio, play the travel games of my childhood, and deploy all the coping techniques given to me by my therapist. It's an exhausting battle, but the cage holding my demons back is intact, and I'm still on the road.

Every year on this dark anniversary, I usually hide in my bed, avoiding the present and giving in to the past. Memories play like a never-ending record, from beginning to end, as if they can only be played in sequential order. I relive the nightmare over and over, compelled to examine every word and action, mentally marking what I could have said or done to prevent my perfect life from crashing down around me.

Ultimately, guilt—a truly insidious bully—takes over and beats me down. He fills my thoughts with despair until escape becomes necessary. Alcohol saves me, muffling the accusing words falling like acid rain from his treacherous lips.

In the end, nothing matters. Collin is dead, along with my friends and colleagues, their families filled with hate and grief.

The stark awareness of these truths sobers me. On the third day, everything gets shoved back into its cage for another year. I once again become the calm, controlled woman and doctor facing the world.

But not this year. The first travel doctor screwed up royally, and my agency promised our clients they'd have another doctor on-site immediately. So, here I am, driving today and tomorrow, on the same two days I dread every year.

The gas tank hovers a hair above empty, so I pull off at the next exit. After filling up and grabbing a snack, I pop a pill for my head and get back on the road.

Welcome to Montana announces the picturesque sign as I pass over the state line, and I can't help but sigh in relief. It's been a long day of driving, but thankfully, it's almost over. Most of the drive from Colorado through Wyoming was scenic with mountains and wildlife, but the last hour has been the land of nothing, flat roads that seemingly go on forever, or at least as far as the eye can see.

Twenty minutes later, I pull into the parking lot of the hotel where I'm staying for the night, turn off the vehicle, and peel my hands from the steering wheel. I made it. The smallest feeling of victory washes over me. When I started the drive, I wasn't sure I could make it out of the state without falling apart, but I did. The battle isn't over, but the first day is done, and I'm still functioning like a normal human being. I flex my hands to get the circulation going again before picking up my phone and texting my mom.

> Kate: Stopping for the night in Billings.
> Love you.

I step out of the SUV and into the chilly night air, pausing to stretch out the kinks and crack my back. Then I grab my coat and overnight bag before walking into the lobby. It's your average hotel with basic amenities like Wi-Fi, but the attached restaurant is the reason I booked it.

Check-in is swift and soon I'm entering my room.

Setting my bag on the luggage rack, I head to the bathroom to freshen up. The tired reflection in the mirror makes me wrinkle my nose. Strands of blond hair have fallen out of its holder and my once immaculate ponytail is sagging. Grabbing the brush, I quickly fix it, then reach into my bag for my toothbrush.

So much has changed in the last three years. My cool blond, slightly wavy hair is much longer than the short, sleek bob I used to have when I worked at the hospital. My face, previously soft and glowing with youth and hope, reflects both the passage of time and my ongoing battles with the past. Now it's leaner and harder, the lines deeper.

Today's anniversary shows heavily in my shadowed green eyes, as well as the dark circles sitting underneath.

My phone pings, bringing me back to the present. I dismiss my thoughts and rinse my mouth. Raising my phone, I read my mom's text.

> Mom: Be safe. I love you and remember, I'm here if you need anything tonight. Any time.

I smile. She worries so much. I'm lucky to have her. All my life she's been my rock, but never more so than the last few years. My dad's always been absent, but my mom more than made up for it, encouraging me to go for my dreams and never give up. In my younger years, I used her support like a laser to hone my focus and achieve my perfect life.

Being the top of my class ensured I was accepted to my chosen university, an internship at a top five hospital led to a premier job, and of course, the cherry on top, a handsome husband who shared my love of medicine. And when it all came crashing down and I was drowning, her support became the steel I used to reconstruct my life.

Lately, she worries about me being too closed off from the rest of the world. I shake my head. While I'm not happy, I'm living and moving forward the only way I know how.

Needing to escape my thoughts, I head downstairs to eat. The hotel is almost empty, with only a couple of people scattered here and there. It's not surprising considering it's seven o'clock on a Tuesday night. I beeline for the restaurant and find an empty stool.

The bar itself is simple, with a plain pinewood bartop and green vinyl barstools circling it. An older gentleman with grey hair stands behind the bar polishing a glass.

"Hi, I'm Bob. What can I get you, Miss?" he inquires.

"Do you have a menu?"

"Here you go. Just let me know when you're ready to order," Bob tells me, placing a menu and cocktail napkin in front of me before walking away to tend to another customer.

The menu is limited, but I'm starving after having left early and driven all day. Lunch was a long time ago. A waitress walks by with a burger in her hand.

"I'm ready," I call out to Bob.

"Great, what would you like to order?"

"I'll take the burger, medium, with ketchup, mayo, pickle, onion, and a side of fries. What do you have on tap?"

A long list of beers rolls out of his mouth.

I raise an eyebrow and motion to the taps. "That's quite the variety. I'll have the Prickly Pear pale ale, please."

"Yep," he agrees with a grin. "On the weekend, ranch hands come to town for a bit of fun, and the selection draws them here. Let me get your beer and put in your order."

When he walks away, I pick up my phone and check my email. Quick taps delete most of them. I save the ones from favorite authors announcing new releases and a couple account items. An email with the subject line "Tomorrow's Meeting" makes me pause.

Dr. Michaels,

Thank you for jumping in so quickly to replace Dr. Foster. I'll meet you at the practice at noon tomorrow to conduct a walk-through, introduce you to the staff, and give you the keys. If anything comes up, please call me. Cell: 555-133-4712.

Lev Coleman

Hmmm, Lev.

An interesting name. I try to picture a face to go with the name. An old cowboy comes to mind with a weathered face and whipcord body, lean from years of ranching in the Montana winters. Old, worn cowboy boots and a ten-gallon hat completes the image. I know it's a stereotype, but that's what pops into my head. Laughing softly, I look up as Bob places my beer down in front of me.

"Thank you," I tell him, taking a long drink. A couple of these and I might be able to sleep for an hour or two before the nightmares start.

"Burger will be right out," he informs me, walking away once more to take someone else's order.

While I wait, I scroll through my social feeds. Collin's smiling face jumps out at me and my breath stalls painfully in my lungs. It's one of those "remember this post from years ago" type of things. Given my usual drunken anniversary state, I'd completely forgotten these reminders sometimes pop up from the past, or I would have stayed offline today.

Four years ago, I had a completely different life. The memory of that day floods my mind. It was such a good day. Absolutely perfect. I snapped the picture just a couple of days before the incident. Collin and I took a day off to go to the beach. He was splashing through the waves, his face beaming, sandy-brown hair blowing in its usual messy style, and icy-blue eyes crinkling... I couldn't help but try and capture the pure happiness in his face.

Happy Birthday to my McDreamy. @DrCollinKennedy May this

day bring you adventure and surprise. I couldn't imagine my life without you and cannot wait to celebrate tonight! Love, your McNerdy.

Such a simple message, yet so complicated in hindsight. The comments below the post are a stark reminder of the events of the day and something I can't handle, so I quickly close the app and shove it all into the cage in my mind.

My burger arrives and I shift my focus entirely, forcing myself to let everything else go. Taking a big bite, I practically moan at the taste. It easily wins the Best Burger award. Another surprise for this unassuming little hotel and restaurant.

"How's the food?" Bob asks.

"Delicious. Best burger I've had in a long time," I declare after swallowing my bite.

"Not surprising. Montana's known for its beef, straight from the cattle ranches nearby."

"It's incredible. Would you mind bringing me another beer?" I ask, scarfing down another bite and some fries.

"Sure, just a sec." He shuffles over to pull another beer for me. "Here you go. Let me know if you need anything else." With a smile, he sets it down and leaves me to eat.

After inhaling most of the burger, I slow down to finish the rest. The opening day game for the Texas Rangers is playing on the TV. I'm not a huge baseball fan, but I'll watch a few games every once in a while. Thirty minutes later, I glance at my watch. It's only eight-thirty, but I've been up since five this morning, and I'm physically and mentally exhausted. I signal Bob, thank him for the meal, and pay the check.

In my room, I change into an old T-shirt with the Stanford School of Medicine logo on it. It's eight years old, the cotton well-worn from repeated wear, and by far, the most comfortable sleeping attire I own. Soft jersey lounge pants complete my outfit for bed. After brushing my teeth and hair, I leave the bathroom door open, the bright light spilling into the room. I don't want to wake in the dark.

My tablet is lying on the bed. Snatching it up, I can't help but open the app and scroll down to see his smiling face one more time. Tracing my finger over his features, my eyes burn with tears, but I refuse to let them fall. They don't do any good. I close the tablet and drift off to sleep a few minutes later.

AN ALERT POPS UP ON MY PHONE, "CODE BLACK." I FREEZE. IT means there's terrorist activity in the hospital and all patients and personnel need to evacuate. Phones ping up and down the hallway. Hospital personnel start shepherding people toward the stairs and safety. Once the patients are gone, I turn with the rest of the staff to follow, but I hear someone shout my name.

"Where is Dr. Michaels!? Dr. Kate Michaels? Tell me where she is, or I'm going to fucking kill all of you. Do you want to die? No? Tell me where she is, and I might let you go."

I stop. Who is that?

Turning around, I head back toward the nurses' station. As I get closer, I hear him repeat, "Tell me where she is right now, or I'll start shooting."

A steady voice in the crowd tries to reason with the gunman. "I'm sure we can find Dr. Michaels. Why don't you let these people go? I'll stay with you, then you and I can check each of the rooms on this floor."

Oh my god, that's Collin. No, no, no.

I run toward the crowd standing together at the end of the hall. Stepping out from behind the gunman, I see Collin's eyes widen. His hand raises as if to stop me.

The gunman, seeing the gesture, panics and shoots Collin.

"Collin!" I cry out.

The gunman whips around at the sound of my voice. The mixture of glee and menace in his voice is terrifying when he orders me to stand in front of him. "Dr. Michaels, we've all been waiting for you. Get over here."

I hold up my hands, slide in front of the gunman, and drop down to check on Collin. Gunshot to the abdomen. My heart races as I try to think.

"Stand up!" the gunman shouts, waving the gun in my face, and I'm startled to see it's David Carson's dad. "Get up right now. You will answer for David's death! For my son's death." His voice is filled with anguish and grief.

I stare at him, then glance back down at Collin. Blood is running in a steady stream from his abdomen to the floor. Roaring fills my ears as my mind immediately switches to doctor mode.

Stop the bleeding.

I tear off my doctor's coat, ball it up, and push down on Collin's stomach. My hands check his pulse and reach for his eyes to check his pupils. I flinch as two more gunshots ring out. Screams erupt. Thud. Thud. *Two bodies fall to the floor beside me.*

Mr. Carson screams at me, "I told you to stand up! If you don't, I'll shoot everyone here. If you care about these innocent people, you'll stand up immediately."

If I stand up, Collin will bleed out. If I don't stand up, another person will be shot and possibly die.

I'm trying to figure out what to do when I see trembling hands lean over and press down on the coat. A shaky voice tells me, "I'll take over, Dr. Michaels. I won't let go of Collin. I promise." Looking up, I see Lindsey, an oncology nurse, nod at me as she puts pressure on Collin's wound. Silently thanking her, I blink and slowly stand to face Mr. Carson.

"Mr. Carson, please don't shoot anyone else. We can talk about David's death—"

Pop! Pop! Pop!

My body slams backward when the bullets hit me. As I lie there, waiting for death, more shots are fired.

In the early morning hours, I wake with a cry, breath frozen and tears streaming down my face, my mind racing to escape the images of bodies, blood, and gunshots bombarding my brain. My fingers automatically find the three points of impact on my torso. There's no blood, only scars to tell the story of my past.

My vision darkens. An image of Collin's smiling face from the beach morphs into an image of him lying on the floor of the hospital, bleeding to death.

Inhaling sharply, I pull in as much air as possible, hold it for a second, then exhale. Again. Breathe in. Hold. Breathe out. I lie there trying to some find semblance of control. Eventually, the panic subsides and my breathing steadies.

But my mind is chaos. To pull it back from the abyss, I recite every one of the two hundred and six bones in the body, then follow it with the two hundred distinct types of cells. By the time I finish the second list, my mind is back in the present.

A myriad of emotions swirl inside me… love, guilt, anger, and grief. But it's the guilt more than anything that destroys my peace, so I get up and jump in the shower. If I can't find a bottle and oblivion, I might as well start the day.

The hotel offers a free buffet starting at seven. I'm down there on the dot to grab coffee and breakfast. My appetite is fairly nonexistent, but I still portion out a spoonful of scrambled eggs and a slice of toast. Thankful for this piece of normalcy, I sit at a table by the window, and let the sun chase away the darkness lingering in my thoughts.

Eager to get back on the road, I finish up and head toward the front desk. With a click of a button, I remotely start the SUV while I check out. I can't stand the cold, and while it might be March, it's still winter in Montana. It takes the desk clerk a few minutes to print the receipt, so I take the time to check traffic. The map app displays only green from here to my destination, which is a relief. The clerk smiles and hands me the printout.

Freaking A, it's cold!

The brisk air causes me to inhale sharply when I step outside.

Rushing to the vehicle, I throw my overnight bag in the back seat and hop in. My new "temporary" home is about three hours away in a tiny town nestled between Bozeman and Helena called Lockeland Valley, Montana. I'm hoping to get in around eleven and take a quick tour of the town before meeting Lev at the practice.

Chapter Two

KATE

Entering the city limits, a sign tells me the population of Lockeland Valley is 24,337. Temporarily 24,338, of course. I'm not sure I've ever lived in a town this small. I'm guessing everyone knows everyone, which could be good or bad. Too many people feel like they have something to say about me, but maybe if I keep my head down and focus on my patients, I won't pop up on their radar.

I pass the town's hospital and note its location. I'll have to go by tomorrow and establish my temporary privileges in case one of my patients needs attention.

Reaching Main Street, I take a left and drive through the small downtown area. There are several restaurants, a couple clothing boutiques, a mercantile store, an ice cream parlor, and a few other miscellaneous shops. I was expecting a rural atmosphere, but the town is decidedly upscale and stylish. This might not be too bad for a city girl like me.

Finding a parking spot, I pull in and pick up my phone to text my mom, letting her know I've made it safely to Lockeland Valley. I then glance at my watch and note I have a little over half an hour before I have to be at the practice, which gives me just enough time to stroll through downtown. There are a few people out, but not many.

The shop windows are well-stocked with spring merchandise and there are a variety restaurants with an eclectic mix of menus. After walking up one side of town and back down to my vehicle, I realize I have about fifteen minutes to get to the practice. It should be close to here, but I'm not sure of its exact location. I map the address and realize my new workplace is about a half-mile to the east. Normally, I'd walk over, but Lev is supposed to take me to my new "home" afterward, and I'm not sure if it's close to the practice or not.

Nerves hit me. You'd think I'd get used to the unknown. As a traveling doctor, I move every few months, but new places make me nervous. Plus, there's always the chance someone will recognize me from the news. Besides the police and reporters—who I ignored—nobody ever asked me about the events of that day. People tend to take the TV commentary and use it to determine my guilt, and when that happens, I'm "suddenly" reassigned. If only I could stay in the same place at least for a few months.

My GPS pings my arrival, and I take a few deep breaths after I park. Staring at the building, I'm floored. It's in an absolutely gorgeous two-story modern farmhouse. Enormous windows sit cased in black siding, capped with a black, metal roof. It's breathtaking and totally unexpected, considering most practices are in plain brick office-type buildings. I wonder if all doctor offices in Lockeland Valley are this nice.

Opening the door, I step into a large waiting area. Several individuals turn to check me out. Smiling at them, I close the door and move to the counter on my left. Two ladies are giggling and blushing as they talk to the man standing with them. One's younger, maybe around twenty years old, and the other is significantly older with grey hair. Maybe fifty?

My gaze drifts to the man and I swallow hard. He's a little over six feet with a dark complexion and black hair cut in a military-style, shaved close on the sides and thicker on top. His arms, crossed in front of his wide chest, bulge with muscle while dark ink wraps around his massive biceps. Worn jeans and a black T-shirt are practically molded to his body. Hard, muscular, and fit. And hot. Seriously hot. I don't think I've seen a body… Actually, I don't think I've seen a *man* like this except in the movies.

As I'm checking him out, his head turns, and piercing dark green eyes catches mine. He quirks an eyebrow, and the two ladies look over to see who's stolen his attention.

With a firm smile, I introduce myself. "Hello, I'm Dr. Kate Michaels, the replacement while Dr. Bradford is out." I pause and study their faces to see if they recognize me. While most people don't, the few who have recognized me have always caused trouble. Thankfully, these three just seem surprised to see me.

"I thought we were getting a male doctor?" the young woman asks with a bewildered expression on her face.

The older lady glances over and rolls her eyes. Holding out her hand to shake, she states, "I'm Paula, and this is Brittany. We manage the office and billing. Welcome to Lockeland Valley."

After shaking her hand, I smile at Brittany, then turn my attention to the man staring intently at me.

"Lev Coleman?" I ask, taking a wild guess.

"Yes, I'm Lev. Nice to meet you," he rumbles, holding out his hand. As I gaze into his eyes, I'm surprised by the warmth in them. He might look like the epitome of a hard-core soldier, but his eyes tell the truth of his nature, and all I feel is the urge to step a little closer.

His large hand firmly grips mine as he continues speaking. "My brothers and I are trying to keep Thayer's, err… Dr. Bradford's, practice going until he is back on his feet. Let's go into his office and talk, then I can give you a tour and show you where you'll be staying."

As he releases my hand, I notice it's tingling, and I frown.

Shaking off the sensation, I grip the strap of my purse and follow him back to the office.

When we reach the hallway, Brittany rushes up to us. "Wait! What do I tell the patients?"

"The patients in the waiting room?" I ask, turning around to survey them. "Are they not here for another doctor or the nurse?"

"We don't have another doctor in this practice," she drawls slowly. "And if we send them to another doctor in town, they might not return."

"Is there a nurse here?"

"Yeah, Sarah's in the back," she answers without moving to get her.

"Wonderful. Can you go get her for me?"

Brittany hesitates for a second, but after glancing at Paula and Lev, she does as I ask and walks back to find Sarah. She returns two minutes later with a tiny but beautiful platinum blond-haired woman.

"Hi, Dr. Michaels, I'm Sarah," she introduces herself. "I've been Dr. Bradford's nurse for the last three years, and I'm thrilled you're here to help while he's out."

"Sarah, it's nice to meet you. I'm hoping we can use your knowledge and expertise for a minute?" Drawing her closer, I explain, "Apparently, we have patients scheduled for this afternoon. I don't really want to inconvenience anyone, but I'm not prepared to see all these patients today. Ideally, I like to study a patient's history prior to their visit, unless it's not possible due to urgency or illness. Would you mind identifying those who have an urgent need and those who can possibly wait until tomorrow or next week?" I ask. "Once you have a final list, we'll regroup and review their charts together so I can get your thoughts on their medical histories."

"Absolutely," she responds, approval shining in her eyes.

Turning around, I walk over to the waiting area and address the room. "Ladies and gentlemen, and little kids." I smile and wait until I have their attention. "I'm Dr. Kate Michaels, and I'll be your physician while Dr. Bradford recovers. Unfortunately, there's been a bit of a mix-up. As you can see, I've just arrived, and I haven't had time to study your medical history. If your issue is urgent or this is the only day you can take off from work or get a babysitter, I'm happy to take care of you today. There will be about a thirty-minute delay, but we should be able to see you. If your visit is not urgent and you have flexibility in your schedule, we'd like to ask you to reschedule for tomorrow or another day more convenient for you. We appreciate your support and patience as we transition the practice. If you can reschedule, please see Brittany at the front desk. If you need to keep your appointment, please see Sarah, and we'll get you back to a room shortly. Thank you."

Brittany flounces off while Sarah smiles and steps over to speak to the crowd forming on her left. Lev stares at me for a second, then nods his head as if I passed some unknown test. He motions to the hallway, and I follow him back to Dr. Bradford's office.

I almost whistle upon entering because this is so much nicer than the ones I'm usually given to use. Thick, built-in shelving, painted dark grey, covers the wall behind the desk. Each shelf is full of pictures, medical tomes, and other odds and ends. A large desk, in a natural light wood, sits directly in front of the shelving and presents a sharp contrast to the dark backdrop. The desk has a tablet, laptop, pens, and notepads on it, and in front of the desk, two camel-colored leather swivel chairs sit side by side. In the corner, opposite where I'm standing, is a gold bar cart with a few bottles of whiskey on top, including a very nice 25-year-old Macallan if I'm not mistaken.

This is definitely a man's office. It should feel dark or dreary, but it only feels masculine with touches of warmth here and there. It makes me wonder about the man himself. Did he decorate the office, or did he pay someone to do it?

A throat clears, and I turn my attention back to Lev. His

expression is bleak as his gaze moves across the room, stopping on individual pictures or pieces. Memories play in his eyes, but when they turn back to me, he wipes the melancholy expression off his face. Given the sensitivity of the situation, I sit in one of the swivel chairs and motion for him to take the other. Tall as he is, his knees brush mine and I scoot back a little to give him some room.

He studies me for a few seconds. "You handled that situation really well," he praises. "With consideration and compassion, but also with a firm hand. I'm impressed."

"Thank you. Unfortunately, I often find myself in this situation. The staff doesn't know what to do, so they fall into their regular routines. It's fine. We'll figure it out and get a temporary system in place to help things run smoothly. However, it doesn't leave us much time to walk through things right now. What are the essentials I need to know today, and what can wait until later?" I question with a glance at my watch.

Lev hands me a piece of paper with instructions typed on it. "Here's the security code for the practice, and the security code for your apartment. The apartment is upstairs, and I'll walk through it with you in a second. My brothers and I have power of attorney, so we'll pay the bills and manage all the necessary business-related items. As long as you can manage the medical practice part of it, we should be fine. Anything that comes up, you can call me, Shaw, or Lowell. I've put all our numbers on that sheet. Shaw's a rancher and hard to get ahold of during the day, but he's available at night. Lowell's a writer and can be available any time, although you may have to ring him more than once because he tends to live in his own world. Daytime is best for me. I own the bar down the street called The Black and Gold. I practically live there, so if you need something or just want to come in for a drink, drop on by."

We talk through a few other essential items before he leads me to the rear of the practice and up a set of stairs. At the top of the landing are a door and keypad. He asks me to punch in the apartment security code. Squeezing past him to get to the landing, I feel every line of his hard body brush up against mine, and tingles race down my body. I close my eyes for a microsecond and savor the shivery feeling; it's been a long time since I felt anything physical.

After taking a slow, deep breath, I turn to face the keypad. In the tight space, my butt grazes against his front, and he inhales sharply. I quickly type in the code and wait for the green light per the instructions in my hand. Once the light on the keyboard is green, I open the door and hear him exhale slowly behind me. My body feels jittery, like a live wire, and it takes a moment to clear my cloudy thoughts.

"I'm sorry, could you repeat that?"

He smiles knowingly and gives me the instructions again. "When you get inside, enter the second code, or an alarm will trigger. I've already entered it this time."

I make a quick note on my "cheat sheet." Finally calm enough to look around, I see a beautiful apartment. A living room is situated off to the left in front of a large bank of windows, which lets in a tremendous amount of light. A comfortable couch sits before the tall fireplace, which is wrapped in white shiplap with a TV above it. To my right, in the kitchen, is a massive black island covered in a white marble slab, with eight barstools situated around it. I can't help but run my hands over the sleek marble in appreciation.

The kitchen has all the amenities and aesthetics of my dream kitchen: white shaker cabinets to the ceiling, gold drawer pulls, and gorgeous state-of-the-art appliances, including a gas stove. It tempts me to pull out my very dusty cookbook.

Lev gives me a quick tour of the bedroom and bathroom—also gorgeous—then asks for the keys to my vehicle so he can bring up my luggage.

When I hand them over, I briefly squeeze his hand. "I'm very sorry your friend, Dr. Bradford, had such a terrible accident. If there's anything I can do to help, beyond managing the practice, please let me know."

His thumb strokes across my hand for a second while his dark green eyes study me. "Thank you." Tossing the keys from one hand to the other, he heads downstairs, leaving me to follow.

"Mine is the black Range Rover," I call out to him. "Bags are in the back seat and trunk area. Thank you for bringing my luggage in, and for all the information. If I need anything, I'll be sure to call."

He stops and turns to face me.

Even though I'd just held his hand, my hand automatically reaches out for his. Biting my lip, I can't believe I just did that, but it's too late to take it back now.

Lev regards my hand for a second, then reaches out. As his hand clasps mine, he gives me a small, secretive smile. "You're a pleasant surprise, Dr. Michaels. I'm looking forward to getting to know you. Don't forget to come visit me at the bar. Drinks are on me. Also, before I forget, we stocked up your fridge, so you should be fine for a day or two." With those words, he goes out to get my luggage.

I stand there for a second, holding my tingling hand.

What in the world has gotten into me?

Chapter Three

LEV

After setting Dr. Kate Michaels' bags in her new apartment, I head home. While she looks like the picture in her file, it doesn't come close to capturing just how stunning she is in person. Blond hair, green eyes, and a tall, athletic body. Normally, I would have been in full flirt mode, but the shadows in her eyes stopped me.

A woman like her is usually brimming with confidence, not secrets. Kate's smile was brief, almost tentative, and her eyes were full of wariness, as if she was waiting for us to reject her. But it was the air of sadness and pain wrapped around her that made me want to pull her into my arms and protect her.

Frowning, I shake my head at the thought, then run through the details of her file in my head. Nothing in her background raised a red flag and her references were excellent. Yet, instincts honed in the military are urging me to dig deeper. But I don't like prying. Maybe I'll discuss it with Shaw and Lowell and get their opinion.

Eagle's Nest, the sign announcing the name of our ranch, stands tall at the entrance of our long driveway. Tension eases when I hear the rumble of metal under my tires as I cross the cattle guard. All I want to do tonight is relax and have dinner at home with my brothers. The last few weeks have been exhausting, running from home to hospital to work and sometimes to the practice. For once, we're on the same schedule.

We'll eat early, then go to the hospital and visit with Thayer for a bit. They say talking to him while he's in a coma helps. The last few nights, we told him about the difficulties we've had finding a new travel doctor to cover his practice. Tonight, I'll enjoy telling him about the delightful Dr. Michaels, who's so easily taken charge of his staff. Thayer Bradford hates people messing with his ordered life. I grin. Maybe it'll bug him enough that he'll get his ass in gear and wake up.

Pulling up to the garage, I see several other vehicles parked inside, including a dark green Ford F250 heavy-duty pickup truck stamped with the Eagle's Nest logo, and a sleek black Aston Martin SUV. Good. We're all home.

Closing the garage, I head into the house to start dinner. It's quiet downstairs, which tells me Shaw and Lowell are in their rooms. Going outside to the back deck, I get the grill going. After it's lit, I pull the steaks that have been marinating all day out of the refrigerator and place them on the counter. Then I quickly prep the vegetables with a little garlic, salt, pepper, olive oil, and parmesan cheese, and throw them in the oven. Quickly slicing and buttering a loaf of bread, I put it on a sheet pan to go in last minute.

The bottle of Malbec calls my name, and I pour it into the decanter before setting it on the table for Lowell and me. Shaw typically drinks beer or bourbon, so he can get his own.

It's a simple meal, but there's something soothing about making dinner for my family. When I got out of the Army, I wasn't sure what skills I had to offer the world, but my passion for food has been constant. From choosing the right ingredients to preparing new versions of an old favorite, it's a world I can get lost in for hours at a time. I probably would have ignored it and gone to work for Shaw on the ranch if it hadn't been for them encouraging me to open my first restaurant.

The timer buzzes, and I quickly finish setting the table. Then I text Shaw and Lowell to let them know dinner will be ready in ten minutes. Once the bread is in the oven, I head out to the grill and throw the steaks on for a couple of minutes on each side until they are seared perfectly with a medium rare center. Back inside, I set the platter of steaks down in the center of the dining table before grabbing the vegetables and bread.

Picking up my phone, I sit down and text Lowell again. When he's in writing mode, it can take three or four texts for him to pull his head out of his fictitious world.

Shaw should be walking in right about… now. Shaw enters the room quietly with a beer in his hand and thirty seconds to spare.

For such a big man, Shaw's stealth is impressive. It can be startling to find him suddenly standing beside or behind you. Most never even notice when he enters the room. A skill that came in handy in more operations than I can count.

While we wait for Lowell, Shaw sits and studies me for a minute. He takes a drink of his beer and sets it down, turning his attention fully on me. I return his stare with a shake of my head. Damn man has a nose for intel. I haven't said a word, but he knows something is up. He'll wait until Lowell is here though.

Piercing a steak, I place it on my plate before handing him the fork to do the same. Adding vegetables and a piece of bread, I pick up my phone to text Lowell a third time, but surprisingly, he walks in just as I start typing the message.

His clothes are rumpled and his hair is sticking out every-where. Given his usual fastidious nature, it tells me he was deep in the zone. I'm kind of surprised he came down, but that usually means he hasn't eaten all day and the need for food is pulling him into the real world.

Lowell sits down, grabs the decanter, and pours a glass of wine. After taking a big drink, he fills his plate, then glances at me and Shaw. His eyes narrow and he sits up straighter. While he rarely expresses much emotion himself, Lowell is as good as Shaw at reading people and situations.

"Go ahead, or it'll get cold," I tell them, my mouth full as I take a few bites. "It's nothing urgent or bad."

Silence reigns for a few minutes.

Once I've appeased some of my hunger, I fill them in on my day, keeping to the facts. "Dr. Michaels arrived this afternoon. Unfortunately, a few patients were scheduled without our knowledge, so we only had a few minutes to go through the basics before she had to jump in with both feet. I handed her the codes, made sure she could operate the keypads, and gave her a tour of the apartment."

With his usual blank face, Shaw digests the information. "So, what's your read on her? Can she do the job? Is she going to work out?"

Not wanting to color their feelings toward her, I debate how much information to give them. "She's already handled herself well. Her calm management of the patient mix-up showed me her leadership ability. Overall, she seems to be a competent doctor who will take care of everything until Thayer is back on his feet."

This is a tremendous relief for us, as the last travel doctor sexually harassed the staff and caused a huge uproar before we caught on to what was happening. He won't be doing that to anyone else ever again. We made sure the agency fired him and filed official complaints with the state licensing board. Unfortunately, it made us leery to ask the agency to assign another physician, but we didn't have time to find one on our own. We made the request, but this time, we completed our own background check on Dr. Michaels before agreeing to the placement.

Shaw raises an eyebrow. He knows I'm holding back but cannot figure out what it is. Lowell simply leans back in his chair, waiting for me to spill my guts.

Rubbing my jaw, I think about how I should describe Kate. "She's beautiful, but she's full of pain or sadness or something. I think you or Lowell could probably read her better. She doesn't look like she's slept in days, and while that could be due to the last-minute travel, I don't think it is." Her green eyes were haunted. "I don't remember anything in her background file coming back as unusual, but I want to go through it again. Maybe we should dig deeper?"

"We completed an employment-level background check on her. References, past positions, degrees, licensing, and financials. We can go deeper. Do you think your gut is telling you she's hiding something that could become a problem for us?" Shaw probes intently.

"Yes and no," I try to explain. "Yes, I think she's full of secrets. Definitely hiding something, but I'm not sure it will impact the practice. In doctor… mode… for lack of a better word, she's strong and capable. I'd normally stay out of a person's personal life, but to be completely honest with you, I'm drawn to her. She tugs at me in a way I can't explain."

Shaw stares at me for a second, then swivels his gaze to Lowell to communicate silently with him for a minute. Those two always seem to instinctively know the right move to make.

"Let's hold off on a deeper background check for now," Lowell murmurs while rapidly tapping on his phone. "In the meantime, I'm planning to go by the practice tomorrow. Someone placed an order for supplies this afternoon. I assumed it was Sarah, but with your gut tingling, we should confirm."

Relieved to have more attention on the situation, I return mine to my steak. Maybe she had a bad break up or something. I really hope I'm overreacting though, because for the first time in a long while, someone has caught my attention.

Finishing our dinner, we quickly clean up and leave to visit Thayer in the hospital. Although he's in a coma, we talk to him about Dr. Michaels and how well the practice is doing. We also take a few minutes to speak to his doctor, who informs us that the swelling around his brain is receding, which is excellent news. They still don't know when he'll wake up, but this is progress. Nothing we can do but wait and see.

We all head home after, and yawning, I undress and slide into bed, my mind instantly filling with the beautiful Dr. Michaels.

I wonder how the rest of her day went.

There was definitely a spark between us. I chuckle as I think about how many times she reached out to shake my hand.

My body stirs when my thoughts wander to the moment at the top of the stairs, how it felt to have her lush cheeks brushing against me when she turned to face the keypad. It made me want to push her up against the wall and press into her so she could feel every inch of me. My hips move restlessly as I imagine all the possibilities. Eventually, I fall asleep, still feeling her tight body against mine.

Chapter Four

KATE

The remainder of my first day passed pretty quickly. Sarah and I kept things running smoothly and efficiently. After we treated the few remaining patients, she walked me through the layout of the practice, from the patient rooms to the supply room.

After giving me a quick tutorial on the system they use for entering patient information, which I was thankfully familiar with, we were finally able to review the charts for the patients scheduled for tomorrow.

It's late when I finally shove her out the door and wearily climb the stairs to my new home. Although exhausted, I can't help but feel grateful for the busy day that kept my demons in their cage. Surrounded by strangers with medical issues helps me stay in the real world. Now I just want a hot bath, some wine, a light supper, and hopefully a few hours of sleep before the nightmares start.

After keying in the codes, I enter and kick off my shoes. The suitcases stare at me, but I'm too tired to unpack tonight. My small overnight bag has the essentials I need right now. With a quick twist, I tie my hair up, grab my stuff, then walk straight to the bathroom to dump some bubble bath in the tub and start filling it. Heading to the kitchen, I open a bottle of Malbec, pour a glass, and pad back to the bathroom. It's almost full and steam has fogged up the chrome taps. Stripping down, I turn off the water and get in.

Hmmm, that feels good.

Sore muscles loosen as the heat works its magic. The only movement I make for the next twenty minutes is when I raise my glass. My taste buds are humming with appreciation at the delicious wine and I make a mental note to take a picture of the label.

Whoever stocked the wine in this apartment has superb taste.

As my body relaxes, my mind drifts over the events of the last couple days. I never would have chosen to travel and work on these two anniversary days, but I'm sort of proud of myself. While my body is sore from both driving and the intense battle of keeping everything at bay, I can't help but feel victorious for remaining lucid and sober. Sounds terribly simple, but to me, it's a miracle. I honestly didn't think I could make it through an anniversary without numbing myself, but I did. Not only did I make it, but I was also productive for the first time in years. A hard-earned win. My win. Sleep might be scarce, but this victory makes me think I might be... or at least, might *feel* normal again someday.

The practice and patients are wonderful. I really like Sarah. She operates with professionalism, but also with an empathy and compassion that's hard to find in some nurses. She reminds me of the girlfriends I used to have before they all drifted away. It's been lonely the last few years. I miss sharing things with others and laughing with them.

I haven't let myself get close to anyone since the hospital. Maybe it's time to let my fears go and find a friend. Maybe Sarah or someone else here. It's been over three years. I bite my bottom lip. I need more than just myself and the occasional visit from my mom.

Tall, dark, and handsome enters my mind, and my entire

body tingles. I forgot what it felt like to be attracted to someone, but it's more than his physical appearance. He's like the sun. The warmth he exudes makes me want to step into his arms until all the frozen pieces of me thaw.

Surely he's not single? Although Lev doesn't strike me as the sort of man who would flirt if he was taken. When I look at him, words like honor and chivalry come to mind. Along with laughter and fun.

But was it flirting? I think back to the moments we were together and realize he was just being nice.

Sleepy, I pull the plug and get out. Wrapping a towel around me, I stroll into the bedroom to get into my pajamas. *Brr.* It's cold, so I pull on fuzzy socks, a pair of flannel pants, and a long-sleeve T-shirt.

My stomach growls and I head to the kitchen to scrounge something up. Lev did say the kitchen was stocked, and when I glance into the pantry and fridge, I find a few basics like bread, milk, and cheese. Grilled cheese sounds perfect. Plus, cheese goes with wine, right? Pouring another glass, I pick up my phone and snap a picture of the wine label so I can pick up some more later.

After dinner, I grab my tablet to binge some Netflix in bed, but I don't make it past the first episode.

I SIT THERE IN THE HARD WOODEN PEW, STARING AT THE PICTURE OF Dr. Collin Kennedy, beloved husband, son, brother, and friend. It's such a good photo of him. Smiling. Alive. His parents fill the seats next to me and his sister sits on the other side of them. Both his mother and sister cry delicate tears beneath their beautiful couture, black veils, while his father radiates sadness and quiet disapproval. Collin's friends, significantly fewer than this time last year, sit scattered behind us.

The eulogies have been said and the hymns sung. All that's left is for us to go up and visit with him one last time. The procession led by his best friend, Mark, begins. As they go by, some touch Collin's arm, others say a few words, but all say their goodbyes. Next, his family goes up, his mom breaking down as she leans over to kiss his forehead.

Then it's my turn. My body is shaking. God, I don't know if I can do this, but I must, because I need to say goodbye, not just to Collin, but to this period in my life. As I walk up to the casket, memories flash by. How we met, our first date, when he told me he loved me, finishing our medical residencies, our wedding, when he saved my life, when he told me he hated me, when he hurt me... All the important moments.

I stand at the casket, staring down. His face is calm at first, beautiful, just like the start of our life. He isn't much older than when we first met. I wait for him to sit up and smile at me, tell me it's all a colossal joke and not to worry because he'll always love me.

But it doesn't happen. While I stand there, a hole opens up and blood pours out of the side of his head, signaling his escape from me and this life. Icy-blue eyes open and fill with hate as a gruesome smile stretches across his face.

"This is your fault," he says. "I'm dead because of you. You ruined my life, and I'll never let you go."

I stare at him in horror. There he is... the man of my nightmares. Straightening my spine, I turn and walk away.

He is dead. Dead. Dead. Dead. Dead. I keep repeating it to myself as I walk out of the church and get into the limo.

"HE IS DEAD!" I SCREAM AS I WAKE UP, MY HEART POUNDING. GUILT lies thick on my tongue, but so does relief. I don't know which is worse.

I get up, turn on the light, and then lie back down. Sleep is far away as I think about Collin's birthday and the day after, when he died. If I had made different choices, would he still be dead? Would we still be together? Even after all this time, I can't help but wonder how one decision destroyed my perfect life.

Chapter Five

KATE

Friday rolls around and I blow out a huge sigh of relief. We have a full roster of patients lined up, but if I can get through today, I'll be able to unpack and settle into my new life here.

Picking up the next patient's file, I walk into my office to review it before the appointment and find a stranger sitting at my desk. A very handsome stranger, with a sexy smile and beautiful grey eyes framed with black glasses, but still a stranger.

"Can I help you?" I ask.

Grey eyes move from the computer to me with laser focus. Absolutely silent, he sits there studying me. Uneasy, I slide toward the door to call for Sarah or Paula when his words halt me.

"How did you get into this computer?" he demands.

"Excuse me? I'm not sure that is any of your business, Mr....?" I inject, trying to at least get a name. Failing to get a reply, I politely introduce myself. "My name is Dr. Michaels, and you are?"

Removing his glasses, he runs a hand across his face, then gives me a hard analytical stare, like he's trying to figure out the best method to interrogate me. Now I'm getting nervous. Why do I feel like he's going to frog-march me into the next room and torture me for information?

Waterboarding is illegal, right?

It's time to get reinforcements. Thankfully, Sarah walks into the room.

"Have you seen Mr. Henry's chart… Oh, hello, Lowell. How are you today?" she asks, eyes moving from me to him.

Lowell. Lev mentioned him yesterday. Kind of intense for a writer.

Lowell glances at Sarah, and his eyes warm up a tiny bit. "I'm fine, thank you. Do you know who has access to this computer?" he questions her.

"Dr. Bradford and I," she responds. "Why?"

"Have you accessed it recently?"

"Yes," she answers, crossing her arms with irritation. "I ordered supplies yesterday after Dr. Michaels noticed we were getting low on a few key items."

He jots a quick note on the pad beside the laptop. Tension eases from his shoulders. Yet, when he looks up, his gaze is no less intense, as if he's trying to drill into my soul. I cross my arms to ward him off.

I turn to Sarah and raise my eyebrows. She shrugs her shoulders in return.

My patience deserts me. "Excuse me, Lowell, is it? Would you mind leaving the room so Sarah and I can discuss our next patient?"

"Go ahead. I won't bother you," he replies, almost absently, his focus on the laptop.

"I'm sure you've heard of doctor-patient confidentiality? We cannot discuss a patient with you in the room. It's time for you to leave. You're welcome to take the laptop with you, as I doubt Sarah needs it today, but we have a lot of patients to see, and you're causing a delay."

He says nothing. All his focus is on the computer.

Frowning, I motion to Sarah, then to the laptop.

"Dr. Michaels is correct. I won't need the laptop for the rest of the day. Let me help you get it in the bag so you can take it with you." She walks over to grab the messenger bag and places it on the desk. Shutting the laptop, she slides it and the cord in the bag.

Then I walk over to the desk, take hold of his arm, and help him stand. As he stands, I realize how tall he is compared to me. Wow, he must be 6'5" to my 5'9". It makes me feel petite.

What are they feeding the men around here?

He seems slightly amused as he stares down at me but says nothing.

Grabbing the coat from the chair, I hold it out to him. "Is this yours?"

When he nods his head, I hand it to him. Sarah puts the bag in his arms, then we walk him to the door. Once he's through the door, we close it and listen. When we hear him walk away, we turn to each other and burst out laughing.

"Did you see his face?" she crows. "Priceless."

Laughing, I agree. "Thank goodness you were here. He didn't introduce himself, and I wasn't sure what to do. Plus, he kept staring at me," I add. "Once you said his name, I remembered Lev giving me a list of his contacts that included his brothers, Lowell and Shaw."

"They're not brothers in that sense," she explains. "They were in the Army together, and I guess it made them as close as brothers. All four of them, including Thayer, live together on their ranch outside of town, like a family."

"Well, Lowell is definitely interesting. I thought he was going to torture me for information," I admit, laughing.

"That could still happen. Rumor is, they were all in a special forces unit assigned to some of the most dangerous places in the world," she tells me, shrugging. "I could see Lowell interrogating someone."

I could too. "Well, I'm glad he's on our side. At least, I think he's on our side. I have to say, after meeting those two, I cannot wait to see what Shaw and Dr. Bradford are like. You may not realize it, since you have lived your entire life in Montana, but the real world doesn't grow men like they do here."

Sarah rolls with laughter. "We're definitely spoiled, but when you have been around them all your life, they can be boring. I dream of a sophisticated city man who will fly me to Paris to wine and dine me. One who doesn't wear boots or cowboy hats and appreciates going to museums and fine art exhibits."

"Hmmm, it might be tough to find that man in Montana, but I have faith in you." I smile at her hopeful expression. "Now, let's go through Mr. Henry's chart and get ready for his appointment."

Chapter Six

LOWELL

WITH SILENT COMMUNICATION AND A FEW HAND SIGNALS, THEY HAD the computer in the bag and me out the door in two minutes. I've seen military units with years of training operate with less efficiency and focus than those two. Chuckling, I text Lev to find out where he is right now.

Entering The Black and Gold a couple minutes later, I walk toward Lev's office in the back. He's in there, talking to Courtney, his manager. As I wait for them to finish, I watch her lean over him to view a set of papers, her arm on the back of his chair. The angle of her body suggests a closeness, beyond employer and employee, to anyone who might see them. It's a lie, but one she sells well. She glances up and smiles softly at me, which I return with a raised brow. While she's a beautiful woman, I have no interest in what she's offering. She narrows her eyes at me and scoots closer to Lev.

Lev sees me, then leans back and smiles at Courtney. "Thanks, I appreciate you bringing this to my attention. Let's regroup at three p.m. and discuss it with the team." He waits for her to understand that's her cue to leave.

Courtney's hand moves from the top of the chair down to his

arm, and she squeezes it before slowly gathering the papers together.

Lev turns to me. "So, what did you think of—" He stops when I silently tell him to wait until Courtney leaves.

We both turn and stare at her. She glances from me to Lev and huffs.

"Please shut the door on your way out," Lev says quietly. He winces when the door slams.

"She's going to be a problem," I warn him, shaking my head at her antics. "Find her a position in another one of your restaurants, preferably one you don't actively manage, before she can do any damage."

Lev runs his hands through his hair. He doesn't question my assessment, but I'm afraid he'll put if off until it's too late. He likes to see the best in people. I shrug when he doesn't respond. We'll deal with it together later, I guess. Back to the topic at hand.

I smile, which causes Lev to immediately go into worry mode. *Humph.* I guess I don't smile much if that is his reaction. Clearing my throat, I tell him about my visit to the practice this morning and my meeting with the determined but delectable Dr. Kate Michaels.

He laughs at my story. "I can't believe they ganged up on you and won! I've seen grown men run from your stony face."

"Their tactics were impressive. I was so amused, it didn't even occur to me to stop them until I was out the door and down the hall. I could even hear them laughing like loons behind the door."

"I like her even more after this story," he says, then stops laughing. "What did you think? Did you get a good read?"

"She's beautiful, professional, and polite on the surface. She and Sarah are developing a close relationship, so she doesn't seem to have any issues with women. She isn't afraid to stand up for herself, but she got uneasy when she was alone with me in the room. That could be my demeanor though, as I was staring at her, trying to figure her out. She has powerful walls up and is surprisingly hard to read."

As I think about it, I can't remember the last time I had a hard time reading someone. Intriguing. "She has black circles under her eyes and looks like she hasn't had a decent night's sleep in a few days. I didn't see the pain you mentioned, but you don't build walls that strong without a reason. From a business perspective, I think the practice is in expert hands. From a personal perspective, I can see how you especially might be drawn to help her."

Lev studies my face for a second. "Maybe not just me. You sound intrigued. Is it the puzzle, or the woman?"

"Both," I admit, glancing at my watch. "I have a call with my editor soon. I'll see you at home. Also, I'll let Shaw know my thoughts when I see him later tonight. Don't forget to think about Courtney. You need to solve that issue sooner, not later."

Opening the door, I walk out and almost bump into Courtney in the hall, obviously listening at the door. Giving her the same flat stare I used to give soldiers in the Army, I let her know I'm not amused.

Chapter Seven

KATE

After a relaxing weekend getting acclimated to my new home and picking up necessary supplies, I feel a hundred times better, and now that the anniversary of Collin's death has passed, I'm sleeping again. Five hours at least each night.

The roster is light today. Six patients total. I wonder if this is the usual pace or if it's an anomaly.

"Sarah, are these all of the patients scheduled for today?"

"We typically leave a few spots open on Mondays so we can add in any walk-ins. People who have hurt themselves or gotten sick over the weekend usually help fill our Mondays," she explains.

"Very efficient," I say thoughtfully as I try to think of any other practice using this process, but come up empty. It's a very patient-first mentality. "Well, let's get the first individual back and see what the day brings us."

Sarah and I quickly take care of the morning patients. We had one walk-in from a nearby cattle ranch who had cut up his hand pretty badly after getting it tangled in a roll of barbwire, but nothing a tetanus shot, some stitches, and a round of antibiotics couldn't fix. He was the last patient of the morning, and it's now lunchtime.

I place a palm on each side of the doorframe, lean forward, and stretch my shoulders and back. Hunched over cleaning and suturing the rancher's hand for the last thirty minutes took a toll. Closing my eyes, I stretch my arms up high, and groan at how good this feels as it elongates my body and spine.

Hmmm, better.

When I open my eyes, Lowell is standing in front of me, his gaze skimming the small strip of skin where my shirt had risen. I quickly lower my arms, and his eyes rise to meet mine.

"Don't stop on my account," he murmurs, his eyes a slate grey.

Irritated at the desire sparking in his eyes, I can't help my icy response. "Hello, Lowell. Are you here to see Sarah about the supplies, or do you need something else?"

"Actually, I came to apologize to you and Sarah." He smiles. "And to tell you how impressed I was with your smooth moves in kicking me out of your office."

An apology?! And oh my goodness, is that a smile?

Yep, a genuine smile, and it's a good one. It makes him seem approachable. Maybe even... No. Lev is charming. Lowell is intense. Even when he smiles, you still feel the intensity behind it. It's like he focuses all his attention on you. It makes me want to blurt out my secrets, but I press my lips together, refusing to fall for his tactics.

Being the center of his focus is unnerving, but strangely, it's surprisingly sexual too. It makes me wonder what it would be like to have all that intensity in bed. Would the orgasms be more powerful? What would he focus on first...

"Kate? Are you okay?" he questions with a bit of a smirk.

It's almost as if he can read my mind. "Sorry, I was just thinking about... lunch." Heat flares across my cheeks. "I'm hungry."

"Yes, I can tell," he replies huskily. "Good thing I brought lunch for everyone." He pulls his hands from behind his back to show me.

"Lunch is always welcome." I smile and step back into the hallway. "Let me grab the team." Once I'm out of eyesight, I fan my heated cheeks, trying to get them to cool down.

We all sit down for lunch, and I watch Lowell, trying to figure him out. It's obvious he abhors small talk, but at the same time, he makes sure to ask everyone about their lives. You can almost see the wheels turning in his head when they answer too, like every piece of information gleaned are bits of data for him to examine and hoard.

I silently laugh. It's a bit of an interrogation, really, although I don't think he means it that way. Maybe it's the writer in him. The need to dig into people's lives to understand their motivations and desires. He simply asks, and with very little resistance the staff is giving him information. Not just the facts, but their emotions too. It's terrifying and makes me want to run far away.

Brittany is talking about her upcoming marriage and honeymoon, but he must feel my eyes on him because he turns his attention to me. "You should ask Dr. Michaels about going to San Francisco for your honeymoon. I believe you are from there, correct?"

I blink, but quickly realize he probably read about me in the agency's background check.

"Yes, I'd be happy to tell you about San Francisco, Brittany," I reply, lying through my teeth. I don't even want to think about San Francisco, much less talk about happy honeymoon spots to visit in that city, but I don't want him—or anyone, really—to know how much I hate that city and all its memories.

"Thanks, Dr. Michaels, but I think we want to go to Hawaii," Brittany chirps, smoothing down her blouse and puffing out her chest a bit. "My fiancé wants to see me in a bikini for our honeymoon."

"Hawaii is wonderful and the perfect place," I assure her, relieved I don't have to walk down memory lane. "Well, this has been fun, but we have a patient arriving in about ten minutes.

I'm going to review their chart. Thank you, Lowell, for a lovely lunch. Apology accepted."

"My pleasure," he replies quietly. Aware that I seem upset about something, but not exactly sure what prompted it, I'm sure he'll leave and dissect every bit of conversation from the past few minutes. "I'm heading out to write a few more chapters, but I'll see you later."

Finishing with my patients early, I walk over to Lev's bar to grab dinner and a glass of wine. While I was only with Lev for a few minutes the other day, something about him puts me at ease.

Lev seems like he would be a good friend, and I could use one of those. A wry smile flashes across my lips at the thought. My mind can't help but tack on benefits to that friend thought. I'm attracted to him, but I have a feeling friendliness is just part of his nature. Who knows if he's even single.

Would I even know what to do on a date? Since Collin died three years ago, I haven't been on any dates, and he and I had been together for seven years prior to his death. For the last ten years of my life, there has only been Collin. Before him, I dated a little in college, but with my class load, it was tough.

Grabbing the brass handle, I pull open the door to The Black and Gold. An old, renovated factory, it's huge inside, with exposed duct work and pipes lining the incredibly tall ceilings. Brick laid in a herringbone pattern covers the floor lending additional charm to the place. Light wood tables and black chairs fill the space and pull it all together. To the right of the entry is a beautiful, polished wood bar.

Lev is standing behind the taps, laughing while he pours a beer. *Mmm.* That man sure packs a physical punch. Stretched tightly across his broad shoulders is a black T-shirt with "The Black & Gold" on it. Jeans complete his ensemble, the denim molded comfortably to his body, telling me he wears them often.

When he spots me, he motions me over and steps out from behind the bar.

"Well, hello, Dr. Michaels," his voice husky as he greets me. "How are things going at the practice?"

"Kate, please. It's going well. I thought I'd come by and see this bar of yours and get dinner and a glass of wine."

He immediately pulls me over to a barstool at the corner of the bar. "Absolutely. Sit here and I'll grab you a menu. Do you want red or white?"

"Red," I answer as I sit down and put my tingling hand in my lap. Yep, tingles. One touch and tingles. My mind wanders, thinking of what his touch would do to the rest of my body, and it's such a tantalizing thought.

He pours a glass of wine and brings it to me. "Here. Try this red blend. It's from a new winery down the road. Very smooth, a bit dry, fruit-forward. Tell me what you think."

Taking a sip, I'm surprised this wine came out of Montana. It's better than most California wines on the market. "Delicious. I usually like a good Malbec, and this blend is like a close sister. Did you say this came out of a winery near here? Can you text me the address? I'd like to go and pick up some. Maybe do a tasting."

"Why don't we go together? I received that bottle from my supplier, but I'd love to visit and taste their other wines to see if they have anything else worth offering to my customers," he suggests.

Go together... Did he just ask me out on a date, or a friend-ship-only road trip? Sigh, I can't tell. "Going together" could be anything.

"Sure, that sounds like fun," I tell him, and I mean it because I know it will be a lot of fun, even if it's not a date.

Cocking his head to the side, he studies me for a second, then winks. "Great, it's a date. Look at the menu, and I'll be right back. Specials are on the back."

I sit there, stunned.

Could it be that easy? A date. I have a date.

Smiling, I pick up the menu, but I'm interrupted when a gruff voice chuckles and leans over to speak to me. "Damn, that boy is smooth. Reminds me of myself in my younger days."

Turning toward the man beside me, my mouth drops open. He's exactly what I pictured a cowboy from Montana would look like. Lean frame, tanned and weathered face, dark hair, and brown eyes. With the well-worn prerequisite boots and cowboy hat.

Smiling, I hold out my hand. "I'm Dr. Kate Michaels. It's nice to meet you. He was a bit smooth, wasn't he? Maybe he needs a little competition. I've always wanted to flirt with a genuine cowboy. What do you say?"

The older man's eyebrows rise high and he lets out a loud laugh. "Nice to meet you, Dr. Michaels. I'm Hank Guthrie," he says, gently shaking my hand.

"Hank, it's nice to meet you too. Please call me Kate. What's good to eat here?"

"Well, now, seeing as how I own a cattle ranch and Lev gets his beef from me, I'd be a fool if I didn't recommend the steak. Although, the spaghetti and meatballs are really my favorite," he whispers, winking at me.

I laugh, and as I go to reply, Lev comes back and eyes the two of us.

"Hank, are you flirting with my girl?"

"If I was younger, I'd give you a run for your money," Hank promptly informs him. "Beautiful woman like her, and smart too? She'd never settle for your playboy ways when she could have a hardworking man like me treating her like a queen."

Lev laughs. "Hell, I guess I'm lucky you're just an old fart now, huh?"

"'Old fart!?' See if I give you the good beef in the next ship-ment," he grumbles, scowling at Lev before turning back to me. "See how he treats his elders? You may want to rethink that date. Maybe you should pick Lowell or Shaw to go on a date with instead of Lev. They know how to show a man respect."

I shake my head in mock agreement. "I'll think about it. Manners are important. If he doesn't have any…" Trailing off in disappointment, I can barely contain my laughter.

With a chuckle, Hank eases off the stool. "It was good to meet you, Dr. Michaels."

"Call me Kate," I remind him.

"Kate, I'll see you around. Lev, you treat this girl right." Hank shakes Lev's hand, then strolls out of the bar.

Lev crosses his arms. "I'm gone for five minutes and you're already flirting with someone else?"

Crossing my arms in response, I lean back and raise an eyebrow. "Your girl?"

His forest-green eyes twinkle as he leans over the bar. "I would love to claim you right now, but I'll settle for a date or two before we get to that stage. No need to rush into things." A slow smile spreads across his face. "What can I get you for dinner?"

Blushing, I stare at him. I want to laugh like it's a joke, but his eyes are intently serious, and the sound gets stuck in my throat. That's ridiculous, right?

Licking my lips, I answer, "I have it on good authority the spaghetti and meatballs are the best. Is that correct?"

"We make our meatballs with lamb, beef, and pork, and the pasta from scratch. It's one of our best dishes," he promises me. "I'll put in an order, and we can talk about our first date when I get back."

A date. As I think about it, I wonder what the hell I'm doing. The last time I cared about someone, I became trapped in my worst nightmare. Do I really want to go through that again? Hell no. Sweat beads on my forehead just thinking about it, but the other half of me aches with the need to trust someone again. To hold them in my arms and be held by them. I eye his long arms and massive muscles. His hug would encompass my entire body.

I don't have to love or marry him. It's just a date. Easy peasy, right? Fun. Nothing serious.

Settling everything in my mind, I watch him return. The man walks like he is prowling through a jungle. A sensual predator that makes me feel like prey until I see the warmth and laughter spilling from his green eyes.

"Your dinner will be out soon." Leaning over the bar, he searches my eyes for a second, as if he can see the conflict raging inside me. "How about dinner for our first date? Friday, seven p.m.?"

First date? "That sounds good, but I thought we were going to a winery?"

"The winery is far enough away that we would need to spend the night, and I don't think we're ready for that yet, do you?"

Yet? He's already planning on spending the night?

"Nope, not ready for that yet," I fervently agree. I want to smack myself when I realize I just used the word yet. By the smile on his face, he definitely caught it. "I think you should know, I haven't been on a date in a very long time."

He winks. "Don't worry. I've been told I'm a fabulous date."

What a flirt! "Ha, Hank was right. You're a playboy," I tease him.

"My playboy ways are far behind me." He looks at me seriously, then turns when the waiter comes with my dinner. "Just in time. Here you go, the best spaghetti and meatballs you'll ever eat."

"Bold words. You must think a lot of your chef," I remark, taking a bite. *Freaking A.* Flavor bursts across my mouth. "And you would be right. This is amazing. Your chef is spectacular. I should date him, or at least give him a big kiss. Any man who can cook food this good knows the way to my heart."

His eyes lock on my mouth. "Would you like to give me a kiss now, or after you finish your dinner?"

"What?"

We haven't even been on a date and he's asking me for a kiss? I take another bite.

Damn, this is good.

"I'm the chef. I didn't cook it tonight, but it's my recipe. So, although we're already going on a date, I'll gladly accept a kiss tonight." His eyes move to my lips again as I lick them clean.

I stare at him for a second. "Why are we going to a restaurant for our date if you can cook this good?"

He hesitates for a second but then leans over the bar to murmur, "Honestly? I'm not sure I could keep my hands off you if we're alone in your apartment or my house, but I don't want to start that way with you. I want to get to know you, and I want you to feel more certain about me."

Staring into his dark eyes, I think about it for a second. He's right. I'm intensely attracted to this man, but I'm not ready to take it to the next level, so I nod in agreement.

"You're right. Our first date should be out in public. If the first date goes well, we'll see where the second date happens," I tease him. Unsure where this boldness is coming from, I can't help but blush at the thought of us two together.

His eyes darken, as if he is thinking of the possibilities, then someone calls out his name. Lev goes to deal with an issue in the kitchen while I finish the meal. The empty plate makes me groan. I definitely ate too much, but damn, that was worth it. He returns and I ask him for the bill.

"It's on the house."

Uncomfortable with the idea, I shake my head. "No, please don't. This isn't a date. I'd like to pay for my own meal."

He studies the look of determination on my face and realizes this is important to me. Going over to the register, he prints out a bill and sets it down.

"Thank you," I say quietly, handing him my card.

He charges me and returns with the receipt for me to sign, which I do. Instead of handing it to him, I crook my finger, silently urging him closer. He leans over the bar, and the subtle hint of musk and man surrounds me and I know the scent is going to linger in my mind long after I'm gone. With careful precision, I place my lips on his cheek, savoring the contact for a few precious seconds, then draw back.

"Thank you for dinner," I tell him huskily. "The meal was delicious. I can't wait for our date."

Chapter Eight

KATE

When the last patient walks out the door Thursday afternoon, I eye Sarah for a long minute. The rest of the staff is leaving now, but we usually stay later to prep the practice for the next day.

"Do you have a second?" I ask, biting my lip. Sarah's confidence and easy banter around men tells me she's perfect for what I need.

"What's up? Did someone call for a walk-in?" she drawls as she walks around the corner.

"I'm hoping you can help me. I have a date tomorrow night and I don't know what to wear. The last time I dated was in college. Over ten years ago. I'm so nervous. At this point, I'm seriously wondering why I agreed to go, but I did. And I want to look good." The words rush out of my mouth, barely giving her time to respond. "Do you have some time tonight or tomorrow at lunch to browse through my closet?"

She looks at me in disbelief. "Ten years? Wow. One day soon, we'll have a girls' night so you can explain to me how someone as beautiful as you hasn't gone on a date in TEN YEARS?!"

I wince. "Long story, filled with love and hate. One day, I'll tell you, but honestly, I'm tired of living in the past, so not today.

Will you help me?" Maybe I should bribe her. "I'll provide food, wine, or whatever you need."

"Deal. Dinner and drinks. Tonight." She winks. "Lucky for you, I come cheap."

Picking up my phone, I search and find a Thai place nearby. "How about the Thai place down the street? Is it good?"

"Jasmine's great. I'll have Pad Kee Mao with shrimp, please."

"That's my favorite too. I'll get two orders and some dumplings." I call in the order. "I've got plenty of wine at my place. I think Lev stocked it, and he's got superb taste."

Sarah finalizes her reports and pulls the files for tomorrow's patients. After getting a rundown of each one, we wrap up the prep and head to my apartment.

Walking in, she looks around in amazement. "This is gorgeous!" she exclaims. "I knew there was an apartment up here, but I thought it was a plain old bachelor pad, not this gorgeous place. I'm soooo jealous. Do you mind if I take a peek?"

Waving my hand, I motion for her to go ahead. "Do you want red or white?"

"White, please. Is there a Sauvignon Blanc or something tarty?" Sarah asks.

"Tarty."

I laugh as I pour each of us a glass of Sauvignon Blanc. It's from Chile, and while my favorites are usually from New Zealand, Lev's picks have been spot-on. He must get a lot of samples from his vendors. Taking a sip, I moan in appreciation.

Hmm... crisp and only slightly tarty.

It's perfect. My phone pings with a text from the delivery service. Sweeping up the tip, I head down to get the food. The young man hands me a warm bag full of savory smells, and I head back upstairs. It takes me little time to set the table.

Sarah returns from her tour. "This place is incredible. It gives me so many ideas for redecorating my place. Hmm, that smells good."

"Do you need silverware? Or do you use chopsticks?" I ask, motioning to the two options.

She picks up a pair of chopsticks. "These work for me."

"Me too." I set her carton in front of her and the dumplings in the middle of the table. Dumping the soy sauce into a little dish, I set it by the dumplings.

Unable to wait, I dive into the Pad Kee Mao. The rich spicy flavor hits my tongue from the first bite. "Wow, this is probably the best Thai I've had outside of San Francisco." Memories try to creep in, but I quickly block them.

"Did you live in San Francisco long?" she asks as she picks up her wine and takes a drink. "Hmm, you were right. This wine is delish!"

"Every wine I've tried so far has been amazing. I'll have to ask Lev to help me replenish his stash here," I reply slowly, contemplating the best way to answer the first question in a way that won't lead to a plethora of others. "I went to Stanford Medical School, and when I graduated, I settled in San Francisco for my residency and then my first job. I was there for about seven years."

Her eyebrows raise. "Stanford, wow. That's a fantastic medical school. I can't even imagine."

Sometimes, when I allow myself to think back, it seems unreal to me too. "It was definitely my dream. Thankfully, I got a scholarship, or I never could have afforded it." Not wanting to get too deep into the past, I change the subject. "So, tell me, how long you have known Lev?"

"Lev? You didn't tell me your date is with Lev!" Sarah grins and fans herself. "Spill." She holds up a shrimp and takes a bite while she waits for me to answer.

Girl talk. It's been so long since I had a friend to talk to that I freeze for a second. The things I used to take for granted. This simple moment brings so many emotions to the surface. The ever-present guilt, fear, gratitude... and so much more that I can't even explain what it means to have someone to chat with about my date. I'm excited, but I can't help the tinge of worry that skates down my spine. What will happen when Sarah finds out about my past?

She nudges me. "You okay?"

With a forced chuckle, I nod. "Sorry, brain freeze." Details rapidly spill from my mouth, telling her about my visit to his restaurant. "That man is seriously attractive. I'm talking toe-curling, can-barely-breathe-because-it's-so-intense attraction, which is why we're going to dinner. In public." A thought occurs to me. "Does he date a lot?"

"He's not a playboy if that's what you're asking. From what I hear around town, he dates, but he's not a heartbreaker. Lev is incredibly fun and an overall good guy," she reassures me. "He moved here with Shaw, Lowell, and Thayer about three years ago, when they all got out of the Army. Well, Shaw was from Lockeland Valley, so I guess he just moved back home."

She shrugs. "Shaw shocked everyone when he returned, including me. We went to high school together, but he was three years ahead and outside my circles. Captain of the football team, All-American, dated the head cheerleader, straight-A student... Basically, the town's hero. We all thought he would go off to college and have a big football career, but after high school, he joined the Army, and we didn't see him much for the next fourteen years. They live on Shaw's family ranch outside of town. All of them are outstanding men. They date and have fun, but honestly, I've never heard anyone speak badly about any of them."

"They all live together? I remember you telling me that before, but I must have forgotten. That seems odd for four grown men."

She waves a hand. "It doesn't seem odd to me. Shaw's family ran a large operation, and he inherited all of it when his dad died. The house itself has ten bedrooms, so it's not like they don't have enough room. Wait until you go out there. It's incredible. We used to go to pool parties at his house when we were in high school, and they were a blast." She takes a sip of wine. "Now, back to Lev. You said dinner?"

Shaw. Besides Thayer of course, the only one I haven't met. I glance at Sarah and nod. "He said we're going to Helena. I don't know what to wear. If we were in San Francisco, I'd probably throw on a little black dress to be safe, but I wasn't sure if that was a good idea for a first date." I pause, feeling myself blush. "Honestly, for some reason, I kind of want to wow his socks off."

Her eyes light up. "Okay!" Sarah exclaims, throwing down her napkin. "Let's go find a va-va-voom outfit that will bring him to his knees."

A giggle escapes me. "I'm not sure this mythical outfit exists."

We walk down the hall, and I pull open the closet doors and stand back. She immediately dives into its depths.

"Hmm, okay. Maybe you weren't kidding. Your clothes are more geared to conservative professional than hot dates, but I think we can work with some of the items." She thinks for a moment. "It's still kind of cold out. That narrows it down to a dress and boots or pants."

She pulls several items until four different outfits are lying on the bed. A dark green sweater dress, a pair of tight-fitting black pants with a blazer and a red bodysuit top, dark jeans with a dressy burgundy blouse, and a black wrap dress.

"These are all good contenders. Try them on, and we'll give them a rating and see which one works."

Automatically grabbing the black wrap dress, I change and do a twirl.

Her nose wrinkles. "I give it a six. Nice dress, but doesn't say date, much less sexy. Next!"

I put on the dark jeans and burgundy blouse next.

"Hmm, keep this one in mind for your winery date. Gorgeous, but a little casual for your first date," she suggests.

I agree and put on the dark green sweater dress. It has a deep vee that shows off my breasts, skims closely to my body, and ends mid-thigh. I turn in a circle.

"Wow. Ten out of ten. Who knew you were hiding that body in your scrubs? This is definitely a sexy date night dress. Do you want to try on the last outfit or go with this one?" she asks, holding up the last outfit.

I think about it for a second. I love the red bodysuit, but I'm going to hold off. Shaking my head, I tell her, "It doesn't really feel like it's meant for a date with Lev. Lowell, maybe, but not Lev." My eyes widen as I hear what I just said. "I mean, if I was having a date with Lowell, but I'm not."

Where the hell did that come from?

She stares at me for a second, then bursts out laughing. "You have a thing for Lowell too? Damn, girl."

Blushing, I groan and throw up my hands. "I do. It's so weird. I haven't dated a single person in years, and now I like two men. Not just two random men, but friends. I mean, seriously?! What are the freaking odds?" I shake my head in disbelief. "I can't help it though. Lev is hot, but it's more than his physical appearance. He exudes this incredible warmth and sense of adventure. Lowell is an attractive man but cool and restrained, and his mind intrigues me. But I don't have a date with Lowell. I have a date with Lev. He asked me out first. And you can't date friends. It's like an unspoken rule." Brushing off the thought, I smooth down the dress and stare into the mirror. "So, let's go with the sweater dress."

"It's okay to date more than one person, you know. It might be tougher with friends, but just be honest about your attraction. They each bring out a different side of you. Lowell is probably more like your own personality, and Lev is a bit of an opposite." She shrugs. "Don't sweat it. Go out with Lev and see what happens."

Thinking about it for a second, I have to agree. It's one date. "We're not exclusive. I get it, but I want to be cognizant of the fact that they're friends. I don't think I'd want the man I'm dating to also be dating my best friend, and I can't imagine they would want to date the same woman."

"You'd be surprised," she murmurs. "Okay, so that's the dress. You have the knee-high, black heeled boots to pair with it. I'd add some dangly gold earrings and a long necklace. Done!"

"Thanks so much." Impulsively, I lean down and hug her. "I really appreciate it. Not just the outfit, but the background information and advice too."

Sarah returns the hug, then yawns. "Sorry. It's been a long day." She walks over to the front door. "That's what friends are for, right? Okay, I'm out of here. Thanks for dinner and the wine. We'll definitely have to plan a proper girls' night out soon. I'm going to want to hear all about this date."

Turning my head to the left, then to the right, I scrutinize my make-up. Green eyes pop against the creamy tint of my skin. Knowing the dress would bring out the color, I played up my eyes more than usual. I can't remember the last time I wore this much make-up.

Slipping into the bedroom, I dress, then stand in front of the mirror. I love this outfit. The dress and boots emphasize my long legs, and the clingy fabric makes my curves stand out more than usual. I feel sexy. Going over to the dresser again, I add a spritz of perfume and grab my clutch just as he knocks on the door.

I take a deep breath and open the door. Stunned, I stare at the sight in front of me. Tall, dark, and handsome doesn't even begin to describe Lev. He's sin incarnate in his black jeans, black button-down, and charcoal grey blazer. As my eyes travel from his feet to his face, it hits me that I'm going on a date with him. In the past, I've always gone for the boy-next-door type of guy. Not tall, dark, and hunky.

Heat crosses my cheeks when I finally stare into his forest-green eyes.

He steps inside and leans in to kiss me on the cheek. "You're so damn beautiful. And you smell as good as you look." He chuckles. "It's a good thing we're going out to dinner tonight. Just thinking about you makes my heart race." He grabs my hand and holds it to his chest so I can feel the truth for myself.

Sucking in my breath, I hold my hand there and peer up at him. How do I even respond to that?

"Breathe," he commands me. His other hand moves to cup my cheek.

I hadn't even realized I'd been holding my breath. I slowly exhale. "You're beautiful too. Handsome." Well, that was lame, but damn it, this man short-circuits every thought in my brain.

Still holding my hand, he pulls me out the door to the black pickup sitting in the driveway. "Thank you, sweetheart. Let's go."

Not once during the entire drive does he let go. The smooth slide of his thumb across the top of my hand sends tingles up my arm. During the forty-minute drive to Helena, we talk about each other's week. I tell him about Sarah coming over last night for dinner and wine.

"Both Sarah and I love your wine choices. To be honest, your reserve is almost depleted." I grin. "I'm happy to stock it back up, but I might need your help to pick out the best wines."

He lifts a shoulder. "Drink all of it. I can always bring by more. A lot of them were samples from vendors I thought were excellent." He squeezes my hand. "It will give me an excuse to come by your place and cook you dinner one night."

"We haven't even finished this date yet," I remind him softly, although I can't help the smile that curves my lips at his words.

"I already know I want a second date," he responds firmly.

Stunned, I stare at him for a second to see if he is serious. His eyes meet mine and the resolve in their depths convinces me. My nervousness disappears. This is going to be a good date.

We reach the restaurant, and he hands the keys to the valet, then walks around to open my door. With his large hand at my back, he escorts me inside.

The host greets him by his first name and smiles. "Hello, Lev. We have a private booth reserved in the back, as requested."

She hands our coats over to be checked, then slips the ticket into Lev's palm. With a sweep of her hand and another smile, we follow her back to the booth. Several people stop us along the way to say hello to Lev, curiosity burning in their eyes, and he briefly introduces me but keeps us moving.

He must come here a lot.

A roaring fire in the center of the room lends a cozy feeling to the entire place, which is further enhanced by the wood encasing the fireplace, but there's nothing rustic about this place. The upscale atmosphere is understated elegance.

We finally get to our table, and I realize just what the hostess meant by a private booth. A curved, camel leather sofa is tucked into an alcove with a screen to shut off the rest of the dining area. Very romantic. Thanking the hostess, Lev motions for me to slide in first, then he scoots in after me. I move to the center to give him some more room. The man is a giant sitting in this booth.

"You're popular. Come here often?" I ask tentatively, now slightly worried this is just a run-of-the-mill date for him. Biting my lip, I wait for his answer.

With a pleased expression on his face, he reaches out and gently eases my lip from between my teeth. "I own this restaurant, and two others in Helena," he explains. "I'm here a lot on business. My customers tend to visit all three, so I've gotten to know a few of them."

"You own this restaurant, the bar, and two others?"

He shrugs and tilts his head in consideration. "I love food and entertaining people. Seeing the satisfaction they get from eating a good meal, celebrating their most important milestones, and meeting the friends and family they bring with them. It's the best job, and I love it."

Hearing this helps me understand another side of him. One

that is serious about business and success, but more for the joy it brings himself and others rather than the prestige and money.

"I don't know you very well, but I noticed when we first met that you exude this incredible warmth and joy of life. It draws me like a flame, and I'm sure your success comes just as much from people drawn to you as they are to the delicious food and ambiance."

Leaning back, his green eyes stare intently into mine while his fingers play with mine. "Thank you. It means a lot to me that you see the man, not the success."

"Honey, you're a hard man to miss," I tease him. My stomach growls, and I feel myself blush. "Please excuse me."

With a laugh, he presses a menu into my hand. "I'd better feed you, or this will be the worst first date ever."

Snickering at the thought of my worst date ever, I shake my head. "This date is already better than my worst first date. Any recommendations for me?"

"This is a story I think I need to hear," he says, pointing to the specials on the back of the menu. "These are my favorites… the lamb chops, the ginger-glazed Mahi Mahi, and the crab-stuffed filet mignon."

Those were the same three dishes calling my name. "It's so hard to choose. I wish my stomach was big enough for all three."

"How do you like your steak?"

"Medium rare, on the rare side."

"What about wine? Red? A Malbec?"

Baffled, I nod in agreement.

He motions for the server and asks for a couple glasses of the Malbec, then proceeds to order the rest.

"Hi Andrew, thanks for waiting on us tonight. We're going to mix it up with a 'create your own' platter. We'll take one crab-stuffed filet, medium rare, and one of the ginger-glazed Mahi-Mahi." He raises an eyebrow. "Why don't we each pick a side and share those too?"

Loving the idea of a smorgasbord, I quickly glance back at my menu. "Hmmm, how about the parmesan risotto?"

He nods approvingly. "Great. We'll take one parmesan risotto and one grilled asparagus. And two lamb chops. Not the entire dish, just the chops. And a couple of extra plates so we can split everything," he says as he finishes ordering. "All good with you?"

"Not having to choose? Absolutely. I love it. Maybe I should date more restaurant owners," I jokingly add.

"No, you don't have to choose." He gives me a brief, serious look before he grins.

"I'm not sure I can eat half, but I can't wait to taste it all."

He nods and turns back to Andrew to hand him the menus. "Thanks, Andrew." His hand automatically reaches for mine again. "Now, tell me about your worst first date."

With a laugh, I launch into the story. "It was my first date in college. I had been crushing on this guy, Rob, in school. Every day, I'd flirt with him in class. He would flirt back, but the semester was almost over before he finally asked me out. Excited, I spent all day getting my hair and nails done, and at least an hour picking out the perfect outfit. He was about twenty minutes late picking me up, but he came to my door, so I quickly brushed it off.

"When we walk out to his car, he opens the back door for me to get in. Confused, I look in the front and notice a woman sitting in the driver's seat. I get in the rear, and he sits beside me. He tells me to ignore the woman in the front seat. He proceeds to explain that he doesn't have a driver's license, so he asked his mom to drive us. I'm almost dying at this point. We're in college, and his mom is our chauffeur?! I'm not sure what to think at this point, but I decide to make the most of it."

Lev's eyes widen. "Seriously?"

"Wait, it gets better. Or worse. We get to the restaurant, and his mom sits at the table with us! I introduce myself, but just as I begin to ask her questions, Rob taps me on the arm and reminds me to ignore her. I'm flabbergasted. How do you ignore someone sitting right there? She orders dinner but says nothing. The situation is weird and uncomfortable. At this point, I don't know what to do. Rob, however, doesn't seem to have the same problem. He spends the entire dinner talking about himself. I can't get a word in, and just mimic his mom and sit there quietly eating. Finally, we finish dinner, and Rob turns to his mom and tells her we will be outside while she pays the bill!"

I'm almost crying with laughter now. "When we get in the car, he asks where I want to go next. I tell him I have to work in the morning and need to get to bed early. With a shrug, he leans over to kiss me. With his mom in the front seat. I wouldn't let him. When we get back to the dorm, he refuses to walk me to my door because he's mad that I didn't kiss him. It was literally the worst date ever."

Lev is practically on the floor laughing. "How old were you?"

"Eighteen or nineteen. We were sophomores in college. Can you believe it?" I tell him, wiping a tear from my eye. "That was my worst first date. Nobody has ever topped it."

"Well, I'll try for one of your best first dates, since the award for worst is taken," he replies with a husky laugh.

Our food arrives, and we dig into the feast. Putting a little portion of each item on my plate, I start with the lamb chop first. They're incredibly juicy and perfectly cooked. Delicious.

He asks about the practice and whether I'm enjoying Montana. I tell him about getting lost on the country roads, my aversion to the frigid weather, and how despite all that, I can see why people love living here. It's beautiful, there's room to breathe, and it feels like a place where I can make genuine friends.

"Sarah tells me you moved here three years ago. With Shaw, Lowell, and Thayer?" I take a bite of the fish.

He nods. "We were in the Army together. Same unit. Going through what we did together, we became as close as brothers.

Well, Lowell and I were already close, because we grew up together in Chicago. When we were twelve years old, we were placed in the same foster home. The couple was older. The man was a retired Army sergeant, and the lady a housewife. Their only son, who had also been in the military, had died, and they didn't have any family left. They wanted to foster a couple of kids, and the city placed Lowell and me with them. It turned out to be the best day of our lives."

His smile reflects his deep affection for them. "When Lowell and I turned eighteen, we joined the Army. Lowell was smart enough to get a scholarship to any school, but he didn't want me joining the Army without him." He chuckles. "For the first six years, we weren't even stationed together, but we took unique paths, did well, and rose through the ranks. Both of us were offered a position with a special operations force, and we took it. That's where we met Shaw and Thayer." He pauses for a second as the server comes by to check on us.

"I would like another glass of wine, please."

Andrew glances at me. "Yes, ma'am. Lev, would you like another?"

"No, I'm driving. Please refill my water though?" Lev asks him.

Grabbing a pitcher, Andrew refills our waters and goes to order my wine.

"You were in a special operations force? Like the SEALs?"

"SEALs are a Navy special operations force. We were in the Army, but yes," he replies. He places his arm along the back of the booth.

"How long were you in the Army?"

His fingers brush lightly against my shoulder, but I can tell from the distance in his eyes that he's thinking about the past. "From the time we joined until we retired, Lowell, Shaw, and I were in it for fourteen years. Thayer was in for six."

I contemplate asking about them all living together, but I don't want to seem nosy or that I've been gossiping about him.

Lev had been watching the thoughts flit across my face. "You want to know why we all live together, don't you?" he asks.

I bite my lip. "I don't want to pry though, believe me, so if it is not something you want to discuss, that's fine with me."

A small smile plays on Lev's lips. "We all went through some intense times during the years we served in the special operations force. We lived together and ate together in down times and during operations. The intensity and close proximity to death made us into brothers. Our lives in each other's hands. I'm not sure we even know how to operate without each other anymore. When Shaw's dad died, he inherited the ranch, and we all decided it was time to get out and start a new life. At first, Shaw needed our help to get the ranch in order, so it made sense just to move in together. We never left."

Thinking it through for a second, I get it. After all, I, more than most people, know how traumatic situations can shape a relationship. For them, it had forged their brotherhood in fire. For me, it had twisted my relationship with Collin into shards of ice that drew blood at will.

Softly, I tell him, "I understand."

He peers into my eyes and sees the truth of my statement along with the feelings it stirred up. Frowning, he reaches for my hand and squeezes. "I didn't mean to bring up bad memories. Do you want to talk about it?"

That's the last thing I want to do. "No, I don't." I shake my head as I push away the thoughts clamoring for attention. With a lightness I don't feel, I pat my stomach. "The food was delicious, but I'm stuffed." Pushing away my plate, I set down my napkin and motion with my hand. "If you'll excuse me for a second, I need to use the restroom."

Standing up, he lets me out, but he's studying me intently.

Schooling my features into a pool of blankness, I squeeze his hand to reassure him. "I'll be right back."

Stop letting the past ruin your life, I order myself, scowling fiercely at the reflection in the bathroom mirror.

Chin up, I wash and dry my hands and return to the table.

"I…"

"Just…"

"You first," he tells me.

"I just want to say I'm sorry for cutting you off, especially after you shared yourself with me. It's just that I'm not ready to talk about my past yet. Maybe never," I explain.

His eyes soften. "Sweetheart, you don't have to explain anything to me," he states firmly. "If, or when you're ready to talk about it, I'll be here, okay?"

Internally chiding myself, I look down at my lap. He's being so nice about things, but what if he doesn't really feel that way? Maybe this date wasn't such a good idea.

Lev puts a hand under my chin and raises my face so he can search my eyes. "Kate…?"

"Dammit, our first date was going so well, and I feel like I ruined it," I blurt out, irritated that I let the past get to me.

Laughter follows my words. "Believe me, there's no way that could happen. I want to get to know the real you, not the fake show you put on for others, and I want you to get to know the real me. Believe me, after being in the Army, I have quite a few ghosts of my own poking up from the past. We all just manage, however we can, to get through to the next day. I've had a wonderful time tonight, and if I get a kiss at the end of the night, it will be a perfect first date."

Narrowing my eyes, I scan his smiling face. Sincerity shines out of his eyes. I can't really deny the "fake show," but the fact that he can see it tells me he pays way more attention to me than I thought. What is he going to see tomorrow?

I notice it's late. We've been here for several hours. His words echo through my mind, and I lick my lips in anticipation. When I glance up, he's staring down at them. Then he leans over, angling his head…

"I'll just leave this check right here," Andrew stutters, hastily dropping the bill on the table.

Groaning, Lev straightens. "So close. Let me settle with Andrew, and we'll get out of here."

He pulls out some bills for Andrew's tip and signs a receipt for the meal. As he is the owner, he doesn't pay, but he explains that they use it for accounting purposes.

Reaching for my hand, he helps me out of the booth and grabs our coats on the way out. While we wait for the valet, he wraps his arms around me from behind to help combat the cold. He's so warm. It's like having a cozy fire at my back. His body feels good against mine. *Hmm.* I've always felt tall at 5'9", but even with heels, he towers over me.

On the way back to Lockeland Valley, all I can think about is kissing him. My eyes are drawn to his lips again and again. A tiny flash of emotion stops my thoughts though. Besides the peck on the cheek I gave him on Monday, I haven't kissed a man in years. It's stupid, but I'm nervous. Biting my lip, I wonder if I'll be any good. Do I even remember how to kiss?

We arrive at my apartment in the blink of an eye, and Lev shuts off the SUV before coming around to help me out. Walking into the practice, he follows me up the stairs and into the apartment.

His eyes trace my features, my nervousness apparent. "I had a wonderful time tonight. One of the best first dates ever."

"Thank you for a wonderful meal and evening." I step closer to him.

His hands cup my elbows, pulling me closer. "I'd love to see you again."

"Me too." Another step toward him.

He seems to read the hesitation in my face and nods. "I'll call you this week." Then his hands release me and he steps back.

"Lev, wait," I reply huskily, gripping his coat and pulling him close once more. "I…" Losing the words, I tug his head down and brush my lips softly over his.

Mmm, soft, but so firm too.

My thoughts scatter as I tug his pouty bottom lip between

mine and suck lightly on it. Pulling my mouth away, I stare at his plump lips. Maybe just one more… but this time, he breaks.

Wrapping his arms around me, he pulls me in tight and deepens our kiss. His tongue traces my lips, asking for entry, and I can't help but open for him, accepting his playful strokes. Moaning, my hands slide under his jacket. Kissing him is like kissing the sun, and I rub up against him. His warmth spreads throughout my body, melting the ice around my heart.

I had forgotten how it felt to be desired, and I don't want to stop. Kissing him, my need grows fast, like a fire out of control. It's been so long. Pressing into him, the urge to surrender is nearly overwhelming. Finally, I turn my head to the side to gulp in some much-needed air.

His mouth doesn't stop though. It skims from my mouth along my cheek to my ear. Then his lips tug on my lobe before continuing down my neck. Shivering, I gasp as he hits the middle of my neck, a hot point for me. When he hears my response, his hips jerk forward, and I feel his desire pressed up against me. A breathless moan escapes.

The sound seems to send a jolt through him, and he pulls his mouth away. He lightly rests his forehead on mine and works on slowing his breathing.

When he glances up, his eyes are dark green pools of desire, making my fingers clench in his hair.

He gives me a heated smile and says huskily, "Sweetheart, this is exactly why we went out tonight instead of having our first date here. I've wanted you since the first time I saw you, and I could so easily get lost in you. But I want to take it slow, so I'm going to say good night."

Floored, it takes me a minute to catch on. "What if I want you to stay?" My voice is but a whisper in the darkened room, but there's not one tremor. All my nervousness is gone now.

At my words, he closes his eyes and takes a deep breath. When they open, they're filled with determination. "You don't, not yet, not completely. When you're ready, without a single doubt, you'll know it, and I'll know it. For now, we'll take it slow."

He takes my hand and places it against his racing heart, ending the night the same way we started it. "Slow is good. Just think of all the things we can do together first." He gives me a wicked smile and soft, lingering kiss. "Thank you for an incredible first date. Good night and sweet dreams." Taking another deep breath, he releases me. Then he walks over to the alarm, sets it, and walks out the door.

With him gone, I flop down on the couch. When I thought about the date, I imagined warmth and laughter. Never did I imagine it would be the kind of date where you start wondering where it could lead before it's really begun. Lev is warm, funny, sexy, smart, loyal, and so much more than I thought him to be. It sounds like a good thing, but I'm not sure I want something that could disrupt the very foundation I've struggled to build the last few years.

A bell from my past tolls, reminding me how I felt when I met Collin. And how he changed. I would never have thought he could be so cruel.

Maybe I'm not ready. I stare at the stars through the window. Or maybe I'm getting ahead of myself. I press my lips together to savor the feel of desire still lingering on them and head to bed.

Chapter Nine

KATE

Lev texts me early the next morning and asks for a second date. He's definitely in pursuit, and my body tingles just thinking about our first date, the kiss, and all the things we can do as we take things slow.

I groan. He's right, I'm not ready emotionally, but damn, our chemistry is unbelievable, and I find myself unable to resist the temptation to see him again. So I say yes.

Monday at lunch, Sarah grills me about the date. I quietly tell her the dress was a huge success, the date was incredible, and we're going out again soon.

In turn, Sarah tells me all about her crappy date for the weekend with another ranch hand. Swearing them off for good, she threatens to quit the practice and move to a big city so she can find her sophisticated dream man.

Laughing, I tell her I like the men in Montana.

By Wednesday, I'm definitely missing Lev. My phone pings at lunch with a text from him.

> Lev: Sweetheart, why don't you come up to the bar tonight so I can see your beautiful face? My treat for dinner.

Kate: Would love to see you too. How
about six?

Lev: Six works. See you then and be careful. If
you want to walk, I'll bring you home afterward.

I'm permanently wearing a smile the rest of the day. Sarah just laughs.

After the practice closes, I go upstairs to get ready. Throwing on dark jeans and a black sweater, I grab my keys and walk over to The Black and Gold. Lev is behind the bar talking to a beautiful blond woman when I enter. She has her arm slung around him while they stare down at a piece of paper.

Hmm, that's cozy. We're not exclusive, but the thought of Lev also dating someone he works with is hard to swallow.

When he looks up and sees me, a broad smile crosses his face, and he motions to the seat at the end of the bar. He holds up a hand to indicate he needs five minutes. I take off my coat and sit down.

The bartender comes over and leans over to smile at me. "What can I get you, doll?" he asks with a flirtatious smile.

I scan the list of beers on tap and order the IPA. He applauds my choice and goes to pour my beer. Lev comes up to him and says a few words and takes the full glass from him. He walks around the bar to place it front of me, then pulls me up out of my seat.

What is he doing?

Lev's arms wrap tightly around me in a giant hug, and it feels so damn good. I bury my nose in his neck and inhale, imprinting the smell of him into my memory.

Easing back to peer into my eyes, he continues to hold me. "Hello, sweetheart," he says, smiling. "I couldn't get you off my mind."

Returning his smile, I reach up and rub my hand across his jaw. "Hmm, hello to you too." I swallow, unable to be as free with my words as him. "I might have thought about you once or twice."

With a frown, he leans down and whispers in my ear, "Only once or twice? I must be losing my touch in my old age." Blowing in my ear, he makes me shiver.

Flushing, I tease him back. "Well, it was only a kiss. Surely you can make a better impression?"

With a low groan, he removes his hands from my body. "You win. I still need to walk, and if I think about the possibilities, that will become exceedingly difficult. And I also need to be here for another hour."

Laughing, I sit down and order a burger and fries. Shaking his head, he goes off to enter my order.

"I don't believe we've met," a cool voice says to me from behind. I turn around on the stool and stare at the blond I saw earlier.

"You're right, we haven't met. I'm Dr. Kate Michaels," I tell her, holding out my hand.

Her hand briefly touches mine. "Ah, right, you're the doctor who's covering for Thayer," she says. "I heard Lowell mention you the other day. I'm Courtney Miller, manager for The Black and Gold, and a very close friend of Lev's, if you know what I mean."

"Nice to meet you," I reply, although that's not what I'm thinking. "Are you from around here?"

"No, I grew up in Bozeman, but I've been with Lev since he opened this bar. You know, we should hang out sometime. I could even set you up with my brother, and we could double date," she says in a tone as fake as the tan on her body, subtly implying her date would be Lev.

Unwilling to play games, I simply state the truth. "I'm already dating someone but thank you for the offer." My eyes drift to Lev behind the bar.

Her hands fist, making me tense. She opens her mouth to say something more, but Lev comes up behind me.

"Nice to meet you, and welcome to Lockeland Valley," she says with a glance toward Lev, then walks away.

"Your burger will be right up," Lev murmurs, his lips nuzzling my ear.

Uncomfortable, I open my mouth to say something but pause for a second. While I don't see him dating Courtney now, maybe he dated her in the past and she has lingering feelings. I want to ask him about it, but we've only been on one date.

He turns the stool around and reaches for my hand. Sitting down beside me, his fingers play with mine while we chat about the various types of beer on tap and the ones he recommends.

My burger arrives, along with one for him, and we eat and talk about our schedules. He explains that his is hectic, especially with Thayer in the hospital. He usually spends Monday and Wednesday at The Black and Gold. Tuesdays and Thursdays, he visits his restaurants in Helena. The weekend is up in the air, depending on what is going on, but all three go together to the hospital on Sundays to visit Thayer.

I ask him about Thayer's prognosis.

He explains the swelling in his brain is going down and they've treated the inflammation around his spine, but the doctor isn't clear about the extent of the damage. Once Thayer wakes up from the coma, he'll run more tests.

"How did the accident happen?" I ask.

"Thayer has this need to push his physical limits to test his boundaries. This time, he went too far. While he's an expert skier, he decided dusk was the perfect time to take the double black diamond ski trail at a reckless speed and collided with a tree," Lev says with a note of anger in his voice. "It could cost him his life, or at the very least, the freedom he values so highly."

"Concentrate on getting him to wake from the coma first," I tell him. "Make sure to talk to him when you're visiting. Coma patients respond to voice stimuli, and it can make a difference in getting them to wake up sooner."

His finger reaches up and tucks a piece of my hair behind my ear. "I'm thankful he's alive, but it pisses me off to see him this way. You're right. The only thing that matters is him waking up."

Once we finish our meal, Lev goes to grab his coat so he can walk me home. When we leave, Courtney is staring out the window at us.

It takes minutes to reach my apartment, and without asking, I lead the way upstairs. The second we get in the door, he grabs my hand and turns me around, pressing me up against the door. He reaches out to take my other hand, bringing both of them above my head and leans his hard body into mine.

My green eyes stare into his, simply waiting for the kiss I know is coming. Full lips tease mine, brushing softly, nibbling, and licking until they open for him. Unlike last night, he controls the tempo with lingering kisses that have no sense of time or urgency in them, just a slow dance of our mouths.

Minutes or hours later, he lifts his lips from mine and says huskily, "All I could think about this week was kissing you again."

His eyes blaze with heat, telling me his words are true. His lips find mine over and over. My body shifts to get closer to his. Eventually, he leaves my lips and makes his way back over to that spot on my neck. Kissing, sucking, licking it, my back arches, and I gasp as heat spreads throughout my body.

"I want to touch you," I tell him, pulling my hands free. The man has muscles on top of muscles and all I want to do is feel them. My fingers try to trace them through his clothes, but it's not enough. I need to feel his skin, the warmth that radiates from his body. Reaching out, I unbutton his shirt and impatiently push it aside.

Finally reaching my goal, I place my hands on his body, and heat seeps into my hands, as if he's my own personal sun. His harsh exhale tells me my touch feels good. My hands skim over the surface, marveling at the perfection. There's not one point of softness on his chest. I glide over every inch of his warm brown skin, from his hard pecs to the hard lines of his eight-pack abs. The sheer dedication it must take to achieve and maintain this body... It's anatomy at its finest. My fingers follow each line until I reach the trail leading down to his belt.

Propping his arm above my head, he inhales sharply and stares down at me, cheeks streaked with passion, and when I continue my soft caresses over his lower stomach, below his belly button, his body automatically presses into me.

"God, you feel so good," I rasp, unable to look away from his intense stare.

His mouth takes mine, hard and greedy this time. Reaching down, he lifts me up and pulls me in tight, making sure I feel every inch of him. Our bodies grind together in raw need.

Closer, I think.

Wrapping my legs around him, I center his cock and lift into him, meeting his next thrust.

OMG, that feels so good.

It's been so long since I felt a man against me. I know it wouldn't take much to push me over the edge. With that thought, I do it again and again.

"Fuck, sweetheart. Hold on. I think we should even this up a bit," he says, his hands skimming the hem of my sweater.

Air hits my stomach and I grab the hem for a second to stall him. *Shit!* I didn't think about someone seeing me naked yet. So stupid. I don't know why it didn't occur to me. Swallowing, my heart pounds loudly in my ears. How do I tell him I've been shot?

"Lev, wait... I've got some scars, and they're not pretty."

Studying my face for a second, he realizes I'm worried about showing him my chest. "What? Seriously? Sweetheart, have you seen mine? My body's filled with scars from both my childhood and stint in the Army. Scars don't bother me."

Honestly, I hadn't even noticed, too caught up in all the skin and muscles on display. Leaning back, I scan his body and find several scars—a few from a knife or other sharp object, several round cigarette burns, and even a bullet wound.

He reaches up to his chest and taps on one. "Got knifed here." His hand moves to a spot on his shoulder where he has several lines of scars. "A barbed wire wrapped around my shoulder here. That was damn painful." He continues to point out various scars on his body until the tension in me eases a bit.

After studying his scars and reading his face, I decide to get it over with quickly and yank off my sweater, leaning into the light so he can see the past.

"Beautiful," he rasps, his eyes riveted to my breasts, encased in black see-through lace. His eyes travel to the two scars on my chest and the one on my stomach. Slowly, he reaches out and traces his fingers over them. "You were shot? At close range." His voice tightens with anger. "Who the hell shot you?"

"A gunman came to the hospital where I was working."

His scowl is dark and menacing.

Self-conscious, I'm bringing my hands up to cover my scars when he reaches out and stops me.

With a shake of his head, the fierce expression fades a little. "Fuck, sweetheart. You're beautiful. I'm just trying to wrap my mind around you being shot. With the placement, you're damn lucky to be alive."

His strong arms lift me high until pouty lips can easily reach the top two scars on my chest, the tops of my breasts, and the scar on my stomach. Warmth follows every caress until I'm blazing with emotions.

Lifting his head, he stares into my eyes. Anger, relief, and desire swirl through them. He closes his eyes for a second, and when he opens them again, the anger has been pushed back until they only burn with desire. Relief pours through me.

With deliberate intent, his hand reaches out to cup my breast, lightly caressing my nipple through the lace. With a quick twist, he unclasps my bra and my breasts spill out. His thumb reaches out to caress the nearest tip. Fire races through me. I gasp at the sensation, then I lean against the door and arch my back, wanting him to continue. He takes my breast into his huge hand and traces the outside, deliberately narrowing his circles and driving me crazy until he gets to the center. Taking my nipple in his fingers, he lightly pinches and rolls it.

"More," I demand.

Grasping my body, he pushes us tighter against the door to free both his hands. With our hips melded together, he tilts his head back to watch my face while his hands reach out to cup my breasts.

Frowning, I move restlessly, needing more than a soft caress.

"So impatient," he admonishes me, followed by a soft chuckle.

Reaching out with his thumbs and fingers, he finally grasps each nipple. Heat pools between my legs when he rolls and tugs on them with increasing pressure, and my hands tighten on his hard biceps, trying to hold on against the wave of desire threatening to take me under. This is bringing me so close to the edge.

My breaths come faster, and he knowingly watches me but doesn't stop. Faster and faster, his fingers move between rolling, pinching, and tugging while his body grinds into me.

My hands trail mindlessly across his body. Everywhere I touch, muscles tighten in response. I'm on the edge and burning up. Just a little faster. I move my hips frantically up and down to create enough friction to come. There. Heat flashes through me and I throw my arms tightly around his neck.

"Lev!" I cry out. My orgasm hits and darkness caresses the edge of my vision. I pulse softly against him, riding each wave rolling out from my core.

"I've got you, sweetheart," his voice is gruff like sandpaper. Muscled arms pull me closer, holding me tight, until even the little tremors are gone.

With a contented sigh, I open my eyes and lean my head back to stare at him. It's been such a long time since I felt desire, and my body is quiet and content in the aftermath.

His eyes are dark green, almost black, and his lips find mine in a hard kiss, telling me he's still on edge. "You're so beautiful when you fall apart."

"Thank you." Blushing, I kiss him back.

Shaking his head, he steps back from the door so I can drop my legs.

Wobbly, I cling to him until I'm steady, but almost cry at the loss of him next to me.

Stroking his hands down my body, he gathers me in close and holds me tightly for a few minutes. He's so quiet that I'm sure he's having regrets.

Running my hands nervously across his shoulders, I start to ask about taking care of him. "Would you like to…?"

He pulls back with a frown. Two fingers cover my mouth to stop the words. "Hush, I'm fine and can take care of myself later," he states firmly. "Watching you come for me was so fucking beautiful, I'm just taking a moment to savor it. To remember your face and the way I feel. I want every detail burned into my memory."

Tears spring to my eyes at his words, but I turn my gaze away, not wanting him to see them. "It was incredible."

With deft movements, he picks my sweater up off the floor and pulls it over my head. Once it's on, he picks me up and swings me around, then plops a kiss on my lips. After a few more kisses, he goes home, promising to text tomorrow.

Chapter Ten

KATE

On Friday, I'm having lunch with Sarah when Lowell comes striding into the break room, his face set in a scowl.

"I need your help," he snaps.

We both raise our eyebrows at his tone.

He takes one look at our faces, sighs impatiently, and starts over. "Hello, ladies. Sorry for barging in like this, but I'm wondering if I could talk to you both about your plans for Saturday. I'm scheduled to hold a signing event at a bookstore in Bozeman, and both my PA and agent cannot make it. While the bookstore can supply someone to help with the books and setup, they cannot be with me one hundred percent of the time. I usually have one or two of my own people to help keep things flowing smoothly. Would you be available on Saturday to help me out? I know this isn't your problem, but neither Lev nor Shaw can assist this weekend, and I don't have anyone else to ask."

Sarah shakes her head. "Sorry, I can't make it, Lowell. It's my Granny's seventy-fifth birthday this weekend, and we're throwing her an enormous party. I can ask around, if you'd like?"

"I understand," he says, then pushes his glasses up on his

nose and turns a half-pleading, half-demanding gaze toward me. "Kate?"

Tilting my head, I study him for a second. His normally impeccable façade is showing small signs of his irritation and impatience at this disruption to his orderly life. His hair is sticking up as if his hands have been running through it repeatedly, his leg is constantly twitching, and his voice is even more clipped than usual.

Lev is working an event at one of his restaurants this weekend, which leaves me free. "I'd be happy to help, Lowell." I'm not sure if this is a good or bad idea, but spending time with him outside of the clinic might give me some insight into why I find him so intriguing.

"Really?" he asks, sounding surprised. "Thank you. I'll text you the details. This is very kind of you." He abruptly turns around and heads out the door.

Sarah gives me an exaggerated wink. "So kind of you to help Lowell."

"We'll see."

Pulling out black pants, a dark grey blazer, and a green silk button-down blouse, I get dressed. My hair is already pulled back in a sleek ponytail, and my make-up is minimal. Slipping diamond studs into my ears, a quick spritz of perfume, and I'm almost ready to go. I hear Lowell knocking on the door as I grab both my black heels and short black boots.

Opening the door, I smile when I see he and I almost match. Except his shirt is white, not green. "I'm almost ready. Do you think my boots will be okay for the event, or do I need to wear something a little dressier?" I hold up both pairs of shoes.

"Hello, Kate. You look perfect, and boots will be fine."

I murmur a thank you for his compliment, then pull on my boots, smooth down my tapered pants, and grab my coat and purse. Lowell punches in the code to the alarm, and we head out.

He opens the door to a very nice, black luxury SUV. It's gorgeous, and seems a bit unlike Lowell.

"Gorgeous vehicle. Is this new to the market?" I get into the passenger seat, and it hugs my body like a cockpit. The sleek camel-colored dash holds a large touch-screen, displaying the latest in technology. My hands caress the luxurious leather, and I can't help but sniff. "It smells brand new. Have you had it long? How does it drive?"

"I bought it a month ago. It was a present for myself after I finished my last series," he replies. "It drives like a dream. The handling and control are top-notch. Are you a car enthusiast?"

"I wouldn't say enthusiast, but I like to drive nice cars. After seeing this one, I think I want to trade in mine." I laugh, but I'm only half-joking. I bought the Range Rover when I accepted my first job seven or eight years ago.

"I'll come by sometime, and you can drive it to see if you like how it handles," he offers.

"Deal. Now, let's talk about this event. What do you need me to do today?"

"If you reach into the side pocket of your door, you'll find a large envelope. My PA felt the contents would be the most useful for you. It contains a schedule for the event, the primary contacts for the bookstore, and a checklist so you can make sure they don't forget anything like extra markers, pics of how the signage should be set up, and a few other details." He motions to the door.

I pull the items out of the envelope and scan through the information. It seems straightforward. There's a name tag in the bag. Using one of the markers, I write KATE MICHAELS on it, then attach it to my blazer. I put the pictures in my pocket for easy access. Everything else, I drop back into the envelope for now.

"You have a great PA," I tell him, admiring the sheer organization of the information. "It's all laid out for me to follow."

"Lisa's very organized," he agrees. "I'll be sure to let her know you appreciate her preparation."

Not wanting to let him down, I take the time to study the information. Twenty minutes later, we're parking at a large bookstore. With my instructions in hand, I follow Lowell into the store. We're about a half-hour early, which gives us plenty of time to check everything out and correct any potential issues. I ask for Cheryl and Dale, and the clerk points us to the rear of the store. Walking to the back, we see a sizeable area with a podium and table cordoned off for the event. The lady looks up as we arrive and, recognizing Lowell, comes right over.

"Hello, you must be Lowell. Welcome to Carl's Book Nook. I'm Cheryl, and that is Dale over there, finishing up the books," she says, welcoming us.

"Hello, Cheryl. It's nice to meet you. This is Kate Michaels. She'll be assisting me today. My PA, Lisa, who you spoke to on the phone is out," he explains, introducing me. His eyes scan the setup and nod approvingly.

"Hello, Cheryl. Nice to meet you," I jump in quickly. "I've got a checklist from his PA and a few other items, which should help us finish quickly. I would like to chat a bit about the signage because I think there is a piece missing." I pull out the pictures from my pocket to show her.

Once we're ready to go, I give Lowell a thumbs-up. He's speaking to a few fans who have arrived early, but nods at my gesture.

Completing my final walk-through, I snatch a book from the pile and read the blurb. Military thriller. Fits him perfectly.

"Ladies and gentlemen, welcome to Carl's Book Nook. I'm Cheryl, this is Dale. If you need anything, just let us know. Now, we'll bring out Lowell Monroe, the New York Times and USA Today bestselling author known for his military and political thrillers. Lowell recently released *Mission Control*, the last book in his Robert Newman series." She waits while the crowd applauds. "He will read a chapter from the book, then we'll commence with the signing. Refreshments are available in the back of the room. Thank you and enjoy!"

The crowd applauds when Lowell steps up to the podium. "Thank you," he says. "It's always tough finishing a series because you come to rely on the characters' ability to tell their own story. This is my favorite series to date, and I hope you'll be pleased with how it ends. Chapter One."

Lowell's voice is deep and strong, perfect for reading to a crowd, and it flows over me, making me shiver. As he speaks, his military experience comes through to the audience, and the action packed into the opening chapter becomes even more believable. His intelligence in conveying that knowledge to others is apparent as he confidently captures the audience and brings them into his world.

After reading a couple of chapters, he takes a few questions from the crowd. After he wraps up, Cheryl provides instructions to the audience on how to pick up a signed copy of their book. If they didn't pre-order, they can still purchase the book and Lowell will be happy to sign a copy for them.

About an hour and fifteen minutes later, Lowell signs a book for the last person in line. Looking at Cheryl, I ask her what happens next, and she explains that she and her staff will take care of putting the store back in order. I ask to purchase a copy of the series, and she calls Dale over to pull them from the shelves and pack them up for me. After paying, I pick up the bag and head to the front of the store, where Lowell is studying his book display and talking to Lisa on the phone.

"Kate handled things beautifully and says to tell you thank you for all the instructions and pictures," he is telling her when I walk up. His gaze falls to the bag in my hand and he frowns. "Lisa, I've got to go. We'll talk more next week. Go get some rest." He hangs up the phone. "Did you purchase my books? I would have given you some of my own copies."

"Just contributing to your bestseller status," I tease him. "Seriously, I love a good book, and this series sounds exciting."

Shaking his head, he gives me one of his penetrating stares where he is trying to figure out my nefarious motives or angle, and I roll my eyes. His flare in response. Taking a firm grip on my elbow, he steers me outside and into the vehicle. Once he is in the driver's seat, he turns to me.

"Would you at least let me buy you dinner for helping out today?" he asks, his tone full of exasperation.

Laughing at the expression on his face, I agree to dinner. "Yes, I'm starving. What do you have in mind?"

"I know a great little place that serves authentic Spanish tapas and paella," he says with a turn of the key. "Does that sound good?"

I put on my seat belt and nod.

Lowell eases the SUV into traffic, and fifteen minutes later, we're parking in front of a small brick building with a beautiful courtyard and fountain. Lowell comes around to help me out of the vehicle, and with a hand lightly on my back, he escorts me into the restaurant. I shiver. These light touches of his are driving me crazy, making me crave more and more from him.

"Mr. Lowell, it's so good to see you," exclaims the lady at the front desk. "We're quiet tonight, which means we can probably seat you at your favorite table."

Lowell smiles. "That will be perfect, Maria, thank you."

Guiding me to the left, I notice a large fireplace with several tables around it. We sit at the one on the right side, and Maria sets down menus in front of us.

The place is full of couples, candles, and an overall coziness. This is a very romantic place. I squirm a bit, thinking of Lev. Lowell hasn't asked me out on a date. This is just a thank you dinner, right?

Ignoring the vibe, I turn to Lowell. "So, how good is the paella here? They seem to have several variations on the menu, but the seafood one sounds the best."

"It's excellent. The owners are from Spain," he replies. "Would you like something to drink?"

"Mmm, I'll have a glass of the red Sangria." Licking my lips in anticipation of the drink, I can almost taste it. It's hard to find good Sangria.

Lowell stares down at my lips for a second, then quickly shifts his eyes back to mine. "Sangria it is," he says curtly. Shifting a bit, he puts down the menu and takes a long drink of water. When the waiter comes by, he gives him our order.

"How did you go from the Army to writing thrillers?"

He lifts one elegant shoulder. "I was in the intelligence branch in the Army. Predicting millions of scenarios with a limited set of variables to find the best actionable intel was my job. When I got out, I realized it was similar to creating a story. I begin with a few variables and a lot of potential scenarios that eventually get whittled down until I can tell a cohesive but action-packed story."

"Well, you seem to love it, and guessing by tonight's audience, you're very successful at it. Tell me about the first book you wrote."

He tells me about all the trouble he ran into because it too closely resembled a classified scenario he had led while he was in the Army. I listen to him explain his frustration with how he had to twist the plot around to present a completely plausible but entirely unique story before they would allow him to publish it. Fascinated by his involvement in real-life intelligence plots, I can only assume his IQ is exceedingly high. It's amazing the stuff his brain comes up with for his stories.

"Lev told me you joined the Army because of him, but it sounds like it was the perfect challenging environment for you?"

He admits the Army was a perfect fit. "Listening to Sarge, my foster father, talk about how the Army provided him with control and direction was appealing to me. My life prior to Sarge's home was a series of unstable environments where I had no choices of my own." Long fingers carefully straighten the fork by his plate. "Joining the Army had the added benefit of also cementing my brotherhood with Lev. Discovering I was good at intelligence work gave me the direction and purpose I'd searched for my whole life."

It's interesting how much Sarge changed both Lev and Lowell's life. "Are they still alive? Sarge and his wife?"

He immediately shakes his head. "Sarge and Clara passed shortly after we got out of the service. I miss them both, but I have Lev and the others." For the first time, his eyes look away from mine.

Thankfully, the food arrives, and we both dig in. With a mock groan, I thank him for introducing me to this wonderful restaurant. The paella is divine. Licking my lips, I reach out to try my Sangria.

"Seriously, I would have come to Montana sooner if I had known there was such excellent food here." I tell him all about the restaurants I've tried since I stepped into Montana, but my favorites so far have been Lev's bar and the Thai place down the street from my apartment.

Lowell watches me intently. "You seem to have a lot in common with Lev," he says, making me pause. "He loves food too. I believe you two have been dating?"

Well, that explains tonight. Lowell knows I've been dating Lev. This is clearly a thank you for helping today, not a date. I'm glad he knows though. I don't want to hide anything from either of them, but I can't help the twinge of disappointment I feel, which is silly because he hasn't even asked me on a date.

Reaching out to tuck a piece of hair behind my ear, he murmurs, "This can be both a thank you and a date, can't it? Lev knows we're out tonight. As brothers, we don't really keep secrets from each other."

Stunned, I stare at him for a second. I'm not sure if I should agree it's a date, but I definitely don't agree with them sharing personal details about me.

"It's fine that you two are transparent with each other, but

I'm not sure I want you sharing personal details about me. What exactly is he telling you?" I'm now a little pissed at them both. "And no, I don't believe this is a date. I like to be asked out, not have it assumed that I would be fine in going along with a half-hearted attempt where I have to wonder whether it is a date or not."

Lowell reads the irritation and confusion in my face and grimaces. His grey eyes are bright and direct behind his black-framed glasses. "I apologize. You're right. We'll keep this as a thank you dinner, but to be clear, I intend on asking you out for a date when I take you home tonight. I know you're dating Lev, and he's aware of my interest in you. He has only told me you have gone on a few dates, but he hasn't shared any intimate details with me. We have too much integrity and respect for you and each other to share those types of details," he says, sounding both apologetic and offended at the same time.

Seeing the sincerity in his eyes, I believe him, and I can only offer him the same. "Thank you for the explanation. I like you, Lowell. You intrigue me with your incredible intelligence and absolute confidence. Although sometimes you can be abrupt to the point where I question whether we can get along." I take a deep breath. "But I'm not sure I'm really the type to date several men at once. You two are close, like family, and I don't even know how that would work. The last thing I want to do is come between you two."

"It makes me happy to know you and Lev are together. I don't want that to end. He would feel the same. To be honest, we usually have completely different tastes in women, but there's something about you that intrigues me. It has from the first moment I met you in your office. I don't know what it is, but I believe it's worth pursuing. We might go out on a date and decide we're better off as friends. I don't know, think about it, take some time to talk to Lev, and let me know later. I'm not going anywhere."

Thoughts buzzing, I give him my reluctant agreement. I'm

still not sure how this would work, but he's right, I need some time to think, and I haven't heard Lev's opinion yet.

Driving home, I watch Lowell tap his fingers on the steering wheel. He appears to be deep in thought. When we arrive, he walks me up to the apartment and stares down at me for a few seconds.

"Thank you for dinner, and for sharing your world with me. You're an intriguing man, Mr. Monroe," I tease him.

Smiling slightly, he acknowledges the compliment. "Thank you for helping me out of a jam today. Your assistance was invaluable and helped me concentrate on the event. I appreciate it greatly. I enjoyed our dinner and the frank conversation. Most people are not direct with me as you are, which makes me stop and examine myself and my actions more than I want. To be absolutely clear… I would love to take you on a date, a romantic date, where we can explore this interest between us. Please discuss it with Lev and let me know." Taking my chin, he nudges my face to the side to place a firm kiss on my cheek. His eyes are unreadable when he pulls back, and with an abrupt turn, he walks down the steps.

Shutting the door, I lean on it and think about the day. That man is irritating, intriguing, and confusing as hell. I'm not even sure if he's sexually attracted to me or if I'm just another puzzle he wants to solve.

Rubbing my temples to ease the strain, I know I need to talk to Lev, but I need time to think about whether I want to date them both. I can barely handle the emotions stirring inside me with Lev. Everything is incredibly intense between us and I'm already worried about falling for him. Adding another to the mix could be disastrous.

Chapter Eleven

LOWELL

Besides being beautiful and poised, Kate both challenges and fascinates me. Her ability to pull more information out of me in one dinner than Vanessa had known the whole time we were together is remarkable. She's also engaging and insightful. I don't think I've mentioned my foster father in years, and yet all I wanted to do was share more of my past with her.

I can't help but break down the day into microscopic pieces, because relying strictly on attraction leads to impractical and emotional decisions. In some ways, Kate and I flow together nicely. Kate helped tremendously with the event, jumping in to help with whatever tasks needed doing. She didn't mind hauling books or searching out mundane items like paper or markers. Plus, she didn't complain, and she didn't even come near me when I was signing or talking to fans. In the past, other women often ended up bored and whiny or territorial, wanting to stake their claim in front of others.

The best part of the entire evening was when Kate had the nerve to dress me down for not asking her on a date. I smirk just thinking about it. I'm so used to other women jumping at the chance to link their name with a bestselling author, it didn't even occur to me to formally ask Kate out on a date. I assumed an offer of dinner was a date, and one with all the privileges a date would entail, including a kiss at the end of the night.

I wince at both my arrogance and the complete absence of the kiss I wanted. Although, I don't get the feeling Kate even realizes I desire her. If she lets me take her out on a date, I need to step up my game.

Pulling into the garage, I pick up my phone to text Lev.

> Lowell: Asked Kate on a date. She's aware we both want to date her but is not sure how to handle it. She'll want to chat with you about it.

He's still in Helena at one of his restaurants, but he texts me back quickly.

> Lev: Understood. I like Kate, and I think she'll be good for you, Lowell. But if she doesn't want to date us both, I'm not backing away from her.

I nod in agreement, although he can't see it.

> Lowell: I understand and agree.

Chapter Twelve

KATE

Lev and Lowell are all I think about for the entire week. The idea of dating them both is tempting and hard to ignore. I keep telling myself that people date more than one guy all the time, but casual dating has never been an option for me. In college, I barely had the time to date, and once I met Collin, he was it for me.

My phone pings and I see a text with a pic of a new dish Lev is working on for one of his Helena restaurants, a smoked trout chowder. I smile every time I receive something from him. He loves to share his day with me. I love it too. It feels good. Normal. And I need normal.

He's not the only one texting me though. While my conversations with Lowell are more reserved, he's charming and smart and easily pulls me into the kind of discussions I rarely have with others. Books, travel, cars, the topics are varied but always interesting, like the man himself. He's a night owl too and chatting with him in the dark is quickly becoming my favorite way to end my day. All the anxiety I usually feel before bed is slowly ebbing away.

Before I do anything, I need to have a serious discussion with Lev. I texted him earlier in the week to see if he could make time for something important. After switching his schedule around, he told me to come by The Black and Gold around eight on Thursday, and he would have some time to talk. I decide to eat a small dinner at home first, then walk up to the bar to have a glass of wine.

Around seven forty-five, I walk over to The Black and Gold. Entering, I immediately head to my usual seat at the bar and text Lev that I'm here. Courtney is behind the bar and strolls over to speak to me.

"Well, hello, Dr. Michaels. Lev's slammed tonight. Why don't you come back another time?" she drawls, anger simmering in her eyes.

"Hello, Courtney. I'd like a Malbec, please," I simply order, ignoring her words completely.

She stares at me for a second, then strides over and grabs a glass. Pouring the Malbec, she brings it back and slams it down on the bar, spilling a few drops.

"Thank you," I murmur. After taking a sip, I lean back in my chair, silent, unwilling to deal with her. I don't know if Lev is dating her too, but I refuse to get in a catfight over a man. Although, given her attitude, I'm bringing this up with Lev tonight. I won't come to the bar if I have to see the other woman all the time. It may be hypocritical of me since I'm here to talk to him about dating Lowell, but I can't stand the thought of him dating someone else, especially someone like Courtney. How do I tell him that and ask to date Lowell?

Tapping the bar in thought, I jump when an arm slides around my shoulders and turn to see Lev's green eyes staring down at me.

"Hello, sweetheart. Why don't you grab your wine and come with me?"

Once I have the wine in one hand, he takes the other and pulls me out of my chair. Grabbing my coat and purse, he strides toward the stairs in the back and I raise an eyebrow. I didn't even know this place had an upstairs. At the top of the stairs, a door greets us with "ROOF" labeled on it. He flips a couple of switches and steps through it. Soft, white string lights come on, illuminating the space, and I see a full rooftop bar with little gas fire pits and tables everywhere. It's enchanting.

"This is incredible." I smile as I turn in a circle. "I'm definitely coming here when it gets warm."

He pulls me over to a small alcove with a lounge area and a small gas fireplace. With a flip of another switch, the small fire pit roars to life. He sets my glass down and wraps my coat around me. It's not cold out, as it is the end of April, but it's still chilly.

Large hands carefully tuck my coat around my neck before tugging me in closer to meet his lips. It's a slow, languorous kiss but filled with enough heat to tell me how much he missed me this week. I wrap my arms around his big body and melt into his warmth, the tension coiled inside me easing. He's the sun I've been missing all week.

He slowly pulls his lips from mine, but he doesn't move away. "I'm not sure I should tell you how much I've missed you this week, but I have. A lot." His large hand runs up and down my spine. "Damn, sweetheart, you feel so good. We should probably sit down and talk because if I kiss you again, once isn't going to be enough."

With a sigh, I ease out of his arms. The cold rushes in, replacing the heat of him against my body, and I can't help but clench my teeth against the need to burrow in close again. Fortunately, the cold also brings a little clarity and focus back to me. I sit on the sofa and wait for him to join me.

When he sits, he reaches over and pulls my hand into his lap, his thumb rubbing lightly while he waits for me to start the conversation.

I take a sip of liquid courage, then begin. "I'm not sure how to start this conversation, so I'll probably blunder through it. I've never been one to date around, not even in college. In fact, I've barely dated at all, much less more than one person, but Lowell asked me out on a date. And I want to go, but I'm enjoying this... thing between us... and I don't want to stop dating you, but I also can't stop thinking about going out with him."

Words rush out of my mouth in a jumbled mess, but having got it all out, I suddenly stop. I wait for him to say something, but he doesn't. His serious face tells me nothing. Lowell assured me Lev knew. Maybe he's surprised I want to go out with Lowell.

The silence gets to me. Worried about what he's thinking, I start filling the quiet with more words. "Lowell said you guys already spoke about it and it would be fine for us to date, but I want to hear what you think about it. Truly think about it. I like you, Lev, probably more than I should, especially since I'm not even sure if I'm capable of more. You're my priority, not Lowell." I pause.

He leans closer. "Lowell and I don't have any secrets. We may not share everything in our lives, especially personal moments, but we don't hide things from each other either. We did talk about you, and I'm good with you dating us both as long as it's what you want too. It's not a competition. Lowell and I are brothers. I appreciate you coming to me first before telling Lowell. It means a lot to me. My biggest concern is your uncertainty. Sweetheart, I'm not sure why you think you aren't capable of more, but it's clear that there are some things in your past that you're working through. We can cross that bridge when we come to it. I'm not in any hurry," he says quietly, raising my hand to give it a kiss.

I swallow. This man and his words. They wrap around me in such a way that I can't help but believe in a future. "This is going to sound contrary but how can you be fine with me dating someone else?" Anxiety races through me as I tackle the subject of Lev and Courtney. "I can't stand the thought of you dating Courtney. I know we're not exclusive, but seeing her arm wrapped around you or thinking about you two on a date kind of eats me up inside. I'm not even sure I want to come to the bar when she's here." I stare at him in disbelief. "How are you not jealous at the thought of me dating Lowell?"

He straightens and turns fully to face me, nearly vibrating with anger. "Whoa. First, I'm not dating Courtney. Who told you we were dating? Did she say that to you?"

Did she?

Thinking back, I realize she only implied they were dating without actually stating they were. "Not in so many words. I think she meant for me to take it that way, but she didn't say you were dating. Maybe I misunderstood." Doubt clouds my voice. She seems to cling to him a lot. Wouldn't he ease away if he didn't feel the same way? I look down at my pale hand in his darker one.

Reading between the lines, Lev takes my other hand in his and turns me so I'm facing him directly. "Just to be very clear, I'm not dating Courtney, and I have no interest in ever dating Courtney. She's the manager of The Black and Gold, that's it. Something I'll make very clear to her," he states adamantly. "I'm only interested in dating you, nobody else. Just thinking of you makes my day a hundred times better. When I have nightmares about the Army, I bring up your smiling face on my phone and it soothes me. Hell, half the time I run around smiling like a goofy bastard, and the other half of the time I'm hard as a rock thinking about the next time I can be with you."

With tears in my eyes, I realize how much this man is starting to care for me. At some point soon, I need to tell him about my past and see if he still wants to be with me, but not yet. I want to enjoy this time with him a little longer.

With a tremulous smile, I nod. "Thank you for clearing that up. I know I'm asking for something that I'm not sure I can give to you in return. I don't want you to date anyone else." My brows furrow. "I'm still confused about how this will work with you and Lowell, and why it doesn't matter to you if I date him?"

"It's not that it doesn't matter, but I want you both to be happy. Lowell and I share bonds that can't be broken. Not only do we share a past and foster parents, but being in the same unit meant we often faced death together. Once you put your life in another man's hands, you must trust in him, completely. That he will be there at your back, no matter what. That kind of bond changes how you view him and the world. Things like jealousy take a back seat. When you're with him, you're with him, and vice versa with me. Just be yourself, be honest with us both, and let us worry about anything else."

Examining his eyes, I see his utmost belief in their bond and the conviction that things will be fine. Still conflicted, I give him my agreement.

"I'll be completely honest with you, both of you. If this gets serious between us, there are things about my past you should know, but I'm not ready to talk about them yet."

He doesn't even hesitate when he responds. "I'm already starting to get serious about you, Kate." His eyes search mine. "But I'll wait until you're ready."

Again, with the words, and the reassurance I so desperately need to hear. Unable to help myself, I lean forward and find his lips with mine. I can't give him the same, but I want him to know how much his words mean to me. How much he means to me.

Chapter Thirteen

KATE

After Lev walked me home last night, I couldn't help but text Lowell, who immediately asked me out for tonight. Originally, I thought I'd be a ball of anxiety about going out with someone besides Lev, but I'm sort of giddy about it. It feels like I'm going out with someone I've had a crush on for a while.

"Okay, what is the deal with you? Ever since you walked in this morning, you've had a permanent smile on your face," Sarah asks in a teasing voice. After a quick glance around, she drops into a whisper. "Did you and Lev finally decide going slow is for old people?"

With an exasperated shake of my head, I lean in close and reveal the secret I've been holding onto, "I have a date with Lowell tonight." Stepping back, I nervously wait for her to respond.

"WHAT?! Lowell?" she screams.

My nose wrinkles at her reaction, but I can't help the grin that takes over. "Yes. Lowell."

"Does Lev know?"

I give her an incredulous look. "Of course! We talked about it, and he's fine with me dating Lowell too."

"Damn, girl. I knew you had chemistry with Lowell, but I

didn't think you were the type to date two men. I'm so glad you decided to just go for it," she says with a nod. "Although, I'm envious. Two successful, sexy men. Almost a harem. I had a harem once. Best damn summer of my life."

"What are you talking about?" I eye the blissful expression on her face. "Isn't a harem like a man with multiple wives type of thing? You know, like in those romance books?"

"Sort of, but the opposite. I'm talking about a reverse harem. One woman and multiple partners—usually male, but not necessarily—who are solely dedicated to her. She dates or loves them all, but she's the only female they want." She taps her chin as she thinks about that scenario for a second. "I guess the more acceptable term is a polyamorous relationship, but I just love how naughty the term reverse harem sounds."

Sarah goes on to explain that it's more common than most people know, especially around Lockeland Valley. Although men only slightly outnumber women in Montana, it always feels like there's a shortage of women.

"Did your guys ever get jealous? And I'm not even talking about sex yet. Wait, are we talking group sex too?" Just thinking about all the possibilities makes me want to hyperventilate. I've never had sex with more than one guy at a time. Not even as an experiment in college.

"Honestly, they can get jealous. Mainly if one of my guys felt left out or I hadn't seen one of them in a while. They would get into it with each other. I just let them deal with all their issues and figure it out." She shrugs, thinking back. "Regarding sex, it was a-MA-zing. Seriously. Because there is more than one, it's like having a man who is always happy to see you and willing to put the time and effort into putting a smile on your face. And group sex? Oh, hell yes. Yummy."

Stunned, I stand there for a second. I feel like the most naïve woman on the planet. Now I wish I had experimented more in the past. Pictures flash through my mind of Lev, Lowell, and me. Lev is sunshine and passion, and Lowell is icy and controlled. I can't picture the two of them together in my bed, but I can picture myself in each of theirs. Tingles race up and down my spine at the thought.

"So, where are you guys going?" Sarah asks, interrupting the lust train in my brain. "Do you need help finding something to wear?"

"Not only is it a surprise, but Lowell actually sent me a dress to wear." Sarah turns to me like *WTH*? "I know, right? It's a gorgeous dress. Deep red, floor-length, with slits to the thighs on both sides. Spaghetti straps with a vee in the front and almost no back. It's very, very sexy." I'm breathless just thinking about what that dress means.

"Wow, I've never had a guy buy me a dress for a date. I'm not sure whether to be excited or worried for you," she says, but the touch of envy in her voice tells me she would definitely be excited if it happened to her.

"I can't believe I was worried about whether or not he was even attracted to me," I muse.

Sarah smirks. "He's definitely interested in you. Have fun tonight, and I can't wait to hear about your date on Monday."

She grabs her things and leaves while I lock up the practice. Going upstairs, I decide I have enough time to pull together a look sexy enough to match that dress.

TUCKING ONE LAST CURL BEHIND MY SHOULDER, I STEP BACK AND survey the results. I'm not sure where we're going, but only a blown-out, sexy hairstyle fits this dress. My make-up is minimal and neutral, except for my painted, deep red pouty lips, designed to match the dress.

The silk cascades down my tall body and skims my every curve, and I can't help but move to the mirror to see its effect. Thankfully, the dress fits snug on top, or else my breasts would be in danger of popping out. Just in case, I add some double-sided tape to the insides to make sure it stays in place. When I swish from left to right and back, the bottom half of the dress follows the movement, flowing around me. The slits, while high at the very top of my thighs, are cut so well, they don't expose me even when I'm twirling. The whole dress fits like a dream. Lowell must have been paying way more attention to my body than I originally thought.

Hearing his knock, I slip my feet into strappy gold heels and grab the matching clutch. Smiling, I open the door to a very well-dressed Lowell wearing a custom-tailored black suit and white shirt with a black tie striped with red lines to match my dress. Seeing him in that suit, I'm suddenly very thankful he sent me this dress. The man is polished perfection.

"Thank you for the dress. It fits beautifully." I slowly twirl around so he can see it from all angles.

His eyes take in every detail, from my hair to my toes, lingering a second on my breasts and the slits at the top of my thighs. Clearing his throat, he reaches for my hand, brings it to his lips, and gives me a soft kiss on the inside of my wrist. "You're stunning." His husky voice makes my toes curl. "Are you ready to go?"

I dip my head and hand him my clutch to hold while I grab my short, black faux fur cape from the closet. Draping it over my shoulders, I take the clutch back and follow him out the door.

"Mr. Mysterious, care to tell me where we're going tonight?"

"The Montana Club. For dinner." He glances over at me with a speculative look. "And tango dancing."

"What if I don't know how to tango?" I tease, lightly questioning his decision.

"They give lessons the first half-hour, then you dance the second half, and of course, I'll be here to lead you." He dismisses my worries without a thought.

"Of course." I laugh at his arrogance.

While Lowell drives us, he asks me about my talk with Lev. Knowing transparency is going to be key, I give him a rundown of my conversation, even telling him about the misunderstanding with Courtney and Lev dating. Lowell's silent, listening intently, until I get to the part about Courtney. With a frown, he shakes his head and reiterates what Lev told me.

"It sounds like you might still have some concerns?" he questions me.

I lift a single uncertain shoulder. "I'm trying to let things work out, but I'm worried it might cause conflict between you."

"What if you could see all of us together?" he suggests.

"What do you mean?"

"Well, I know Lev has been wanting to invite you out to the ranch for a while. We have Sunday dinner together before we visit Thayer. Why don't you come out around noon on Sunday? You can meet Shaw, spend time with both me and Lev, and see the ranch. It's beautiful out there."

Maybe it would help to be around them both, and honestly, it would give me a chance to see how this impacts their entire family. I haven't even thought about Shaw. What if he hates the idea of us three together? Besides, I want to see where they live and how they all live together.

I give him a firm nod. "I think it will help to be around you both at the same time. Plus, I've been dying to see this ranch. Even Sarah talks about the parties they had out there in high school."

He raises my hand to his mouth and places a kiss on it. "Good, I want you to have no doubts about either of us."

Ten minutes later, we pull up to a swanky wood and stone lodge. The place is enormous. Smoke is coming out of several chimneys, and I can't even see the sides of the building from where I'm standing. As we walk in, I gaze around in awe at the large fireplaces, log timber beams in the ceiling, and dance floor that spans the entire back of the ballroom. Everyone is eating dinner while a band plays something soft and sensual in the background. Lowell gives the hostess our name, and after finding the reservation, we're seated immediately.

Walking through the restaurant, I see beautiful and sexy women dressed similarly to me. Dresses with slits, high-low dresses, asymmetrical hems, and more. They're all designed to entice their partners and flow when dancing. I'm so glad Lowell sent me the dress. Nothing I had would have been appropriate.

The server comes to take our order pretty quickly. Knowing we're going to dance later, I order a light meal of grilled fish and a salad. Lowell chooses the filet mignon and a salad. He also adds a bottle of red wine.

"Last time, we focused on me. I'd love to hear more about you," Lowell murmurs. "Why did you become a doctor?"

My stomach clenches at the thought of discussing me, but his first question is easy to answer. "Well, I was a serious nerd growing up. I loved school, learning anything and everything, but I really gravitated toward the STEM subjects. My grandpa was a scientist, and we would spend a lot of time talking about the various sciences, the body, latest medical research, illnesses, and cures. When I was fifteen, he got sick. Colon cancer, and while he fought it for a long time, he could never beat it. Going through the diagnosis and treatments with him opened my eyes to the viciousness of this disease." Stopping, I take a drink of water to ease the knot in my throat. Thinking about my grandpa always brings tears to my eyes, along with a tinge of guilt. Sometimes I feel like he would be disappointed to see me now.

Swallowing, I continue. "When he died my senior year of high school, it really put this fire into me to go to school and become a doctor. My grades earned me a place in the Stanford premed program. I finished all the prerequisites in three years, then went to Stanford Medical University to get my M.D., and the rest is history."

He reaches out and pulls my hand into his. Rubbing his thumb over the top of my hand to soothe me, he tilts his head as he thinks about what I said. "Cancer is a devastating disease, and I'm sorry to hear about your grandpa. It sounds like he was a wonderful man and a tremendous influence in your life. I love the fact that he encouraged you to be a nerd too." His white smile flashes.

After a pause, he muses, "I'm surprised you didn't become an oncologist though."

Looking down, I take a deep breath to steady the anxiety bubbling inside of me. My eyes trace our clasped hands. Not surprisingly, Lowell's hand is large, but his fingers are long and tapered, almost elegant. I can't help but envision them stroking my body, stroking me, as if he was playing the piano or conducting a symphony. The silence starts to drag a bit too long, and I know my time is up.

"I did become an oncologist, but I haven't practiced oncology for several years." Lowell waits for me to explain, but I just shake my head. "It's not really a suitable conversation for a first date. Can we continue this discussion another time?"

Reading my face, he comprehends that this is something too serious for such a beautiful night and readily agrees. "I can wait until you're ready to trust me."

Grateful, I squeeze his hand.

Our dinner arrives, and we keep the rest of the conversation light, discussing books, movies, art, and other topics. Culturally, Lowell and I have a lot in common, and none of these topics are the same ones I discuss with Lev, not because he isn't interested but because Lev sees life differently. It's very clear that while they might be close, they're unique in personality and interests. Amazingly, they both fit with different pieces of me.

The restaurant announces the tango lessons will start in fifteen minutes. Finishing our wine, I excuse myself to the restroom for a minute. After using the facilities, I wash my hands and reapply my red lipstick just as a tall redhead comes up beside me.

"I believe I saw with you Lowell tonight, didn't I?" She glances at me as she swipes some gloss on her lips.

"Yes, I'm here with Lowell Monroe." Wary, I turn to her. "Do you know Lowell?"

Laughing huskily, she stares at me with envy in her eyes. "Let's just say Lowell and I are very well-acquainted. I'd give anything to be in your shoes tonight. The man knows everything about control and pleasure, and he's a superb dancer." She drops the gloss in her purse and strolls out the door.

My eyebrows rise in surprise. That was illuminating. As I walk to our table, I notice the redhead leaning over Lowell, whispering in his ear.

When I get closer, I hear Lowell clearly state, "Vivienne, we're over. Please leave the table before my date returns."

I sit down, and raise one eyebrow, silently demanding Lowell take care of this situation before it ruins our first date. His mouth quirks at my audacity, but he quickly stands up, forcing Vivienne to take a step back. Without taking his eyes off me, he comes around the table and holds out his hand.

"Please excuse us, Vivienne. I'm about to dance with the most intriguing woman I've ever met," he informs her, letting his voice carry to nearby tables.

With a laugh, I put my hand in his and let him lead me to the dance floor. Vivienne stares at us for a second, her mouth open, before she turns on her heels and stalks away.

"Smooth, Mr. Monroe, and I particularly like the part about being the most intriguing woman you have ever met."

"I'm very sorry Vivienne interrupted our date, but I didn't lie. You *are* the most intriguing woman I've ever met," he says seriously. His right hand reaches around to my back, then he holds up his left hand for me to clasp.

My hand slides into his and I rest the other lightly on top of his shoulder. As I get into position, I hear the instructor call out the steps and we walk through them. Silently, I snicker. I never told Lowell I could dance the tango, but in his arrogance, he assured me his ability to lead would be enough. Let's see if that's true.

With a mock frown, I attempt the eight basic steps but "accidentally" step on his toes several times. I then purposely step forward when I should step back, causing him to pivot sharply. Looking down at my feet, instead of up at him, I slide my thigh between his.

"I think I saw this part in a movie," I explain, barely able to stop myself from watching his reaction.

I'm breathless from holding in my laughter as I rub my leg up the inside of Lowell's. With lowered lids, I flick a glance up to watch him. His lips firm and he swallows hard. I lean in and kick up my heel before sliding my leg back toward my own body.

Lowell frowns when he realizes I can't dance. Stopping, he instructs me to follow four of the eight beginner steps first. With my lip between my teeth, I follow his cue and we smoothly but slowly step to the same four steps.

"Look at me," he murmurs when I continue to avoid his gaze.

But I don't think I can without giving away the game.

His hand reaches out and takes my chin, pulling it up to peer into my eyes.

I can't maintain the ruse and burst out laughing.

Understanding dawns and he glares at me. He leads me into the eight basic beginner steps at a far faster pace, but quickly realizes I can easily match his moves.

Wanting to challenge his rigid control, I step away from him, forcing him to follow my lead. He pulls me back into his arms. I kick up my heel and twirl, he spins me faster, then tightens his hold until I'm back in his arms. No matter what steps I take to get away, he makes sure I return to him.

His lips curve in a confident smile. He pivots, taking the lead from me, and sets a furious pace. I surrender, handing him control, and my willing submission releases something wild inside him. Our moves become precise, intricate, and lightning fast. He's dominant in his lead. With just the slightest pressure, he moves me in the direction he wants me, my body completely pliant to his guidance. His leg slides between mine, then he pivots. He forces me to move to the outside, to the inside, twirling, stepping, and pushing me to my limits. Our bodies align, then pull apart, and where we touch, fire erupts.

My heart pounds in my chest. Sensuality coats every move we make until suddenly the music peaks signaling the end is near. He steps between my legs, making the slit in my dress slide to the side until my entire leg is bare to his gaze. His strong, lean hand reaches down and grips my thigh, pulling it to his waist. Once it comes off the ground, his hand glides down to my ankle, circles it with his fingers, then pulls it around his hips. He leans forward until I'm forced to rely on him to hold me up. The lines of his body are taut as they hold us in position, my body intimately joined to his, then the music ends.

Breathing rapidly, our eyes are glued to each other. My heart is pounding with exhilaration and my body tingling with desire. His intense grey eyes drift to my mouth as if he wants to devour it. The crowd applauds and the moment is lost to those around us.

He pulls me up, letting my leg drop, and twirls me out to curtsy to the crowd. I sweep a hand toward him in acknowledgement. The entire time my body is buzzing with electricity and passion.

Smiling, we make our way over to the table, where he leans over and drops a quick kiss on my bare shoulder before excusing himself to the restroom. As I take a long drink of water, I notice Vivienne glaring at me from across the room. I toast her with my water, then ignore her.

Lowell comes back, still flushed, and drinks some water. He asks if I would like to stay and dance some more or head home. Looking down at my beautiful dress and back up at this intriguing man, I tell him I want to dance all night. A corner of his mouth lifts and he reaches for my hand.

Later that evening, as Lowell drives me home, my body hums with sexual tension. When leading, he demands my complete focus. Although, I couldn't help but challenge him at every turn. It was the most exhilarating evening I've ever had.

When we get to my apartment, he walks me up and comes inside. Without saying anything, he holds up his hands. Curious, I step into his arms and let him lead me into the dance. After a few steps, he pulls the same final move he did in our first dance, but as my leg wraps around his hips, he leans in and kisses me. His kiss mimics the dance, deeply sensual and tightly controlled. His passion is icy and searing, burning me up while forcing me to submit to the boundaries of the kiss. I cannot move one inch of my body without falling, leaving me completely at his mercy in every way, and by the time the kiss ends, the leg I'm standing on is quivering.

Releasing the pose, he holds me caged in his arms. "That is how I wanted to end the first dance," he says huskily. "Thank you for the date."

My voice is light as I breathlessly thank him in return, and after he walks out the door, I twirl around and around, thinking about the night. That was the most sensual and intense date ever. I can still feel the imprint of his fingers on my ankle and his hard lips on mine.

I'm kind of in a daze because I didn't expect the date to be this intense or magical. This easy. There were no awkward pauses or friction between us, and not once did I think of Lev, which I didn't think would be possible. I know it's only one date, but I can't help but think this could actually work between the three of us.

Chapter Fourteen

KATE

Lev said comfortable and casual, so I throw on dark jeans, a white tank top, and the softest, heather grey cardigan. Short black boots complete the outfit. Leaving my hair down, I spritz on some perfume and head to the living room.

Damp palms have me rubbing my hands down my jeans while I wait for Lev to pick me up. I'm not sure why I'm so nervous. Lev assures me Shaw will be fine with me dating him and Lowell, but my stomach clenches at the thought of sitting down to dinner with all three men. I sigh. If I'm being honest, my main issue is how to act around the two men I'm dating. Do I hold hands with both of them? Kiss them both? Or do I refrain from showing any affection when I'm around the two of them? This feels like it's going to be weird and I'm starting to second-guess going to their house. Exhaling loudly, I run my hands through my hair. It would be rude to back out now.

Lev arrives five minutes later, wearing worn faded jeans and a black Henley. *Damn, this man makes my knees weak.*

Smiling, he steps into the apartment and wraps his huge body around mine and holds me for a few minutes. Warmth sinks into me. He's my sun. Taking my face into his hands, he leans down to give me a lingering kiss.

"Hello, sweetheart. Ready to go?"

Licking my lips to savor his kiss, I give him a nod and grab my coat and purse. The air outside is crisp and barely resembles spring. With a shiver, I settle into the passenger seat of his truck for the twenty minute ride. Although it only feels like seconds later when we pull into a driveway with a sign that says Eagle's Nest above it.

"Is that the name of the ranch?"

"Yes, it used to be Walker's Ranch, but Shaw changed it when we all moved here. Our unit's call sign was Eagle, and he wanted the name to represent all of us, not just his original family. We each have a stake in the ranch, although Shaw runs the operation."

We're probably two or three miles from the entrance before I see anything else. A barn comes into view, a fenced pasture with horses, a corral, and finally, a massive but gorgeous, timber mansion that fits perfectly against the backdrop of the valley and mountains behind it like it's straight out of a movie.

"Wow, that's beautiful! And huge! How big is this house anyway?"

"Around fifteen thousand square feet. Shaw's dad built most of it, but we added to it when we took over. Most of the rooms are now suites with attached bathrooms. We expanded the patio area in the back to include a full outdoor entertaining area. Do you like it?" His voice is gruff as he asks the question.

"I'm sure it's perfect for you all. Plenty of room. Honestly, it's tough for me to imagine living here. I've been living out of a suitcase for the last three years." My mouth turns down. Seeing this house makes me feel like I have no roots. No home. My nomadic existence has suited me for the last few years, but this house reminds me of how much I've lost.

A slight frown crosses Lev's face, but he says nothing. After parking, he comes around the SUV to help me out, his big hand clasping mine and tugging me toward the house. Massive wood pillars frame tall double doors in black wrought iron. When we walk in, Lev takes my coat and purse and hangs them on a hook just inside the door. We head down the hall into an impressive living room with floor-to-ceiling windows that perfectly frame the mountains standing tall in the background. The living room includes a large sectional and several leather club chairs, and an enormous fireplace takes center stage, the rough hewn mantle holding a variety of pictures. It might look like something from the movies on the outside, but it feels like a home on the inside.

Walking up to the fireplace, I scan the pictures. The four men traveled the world together while stationed in the Army, and several photos depict them in exotic places, from Dubai to Singapore to Iceland. Earlier pictures show baby faces staring at the camera with devil-may-care grins and older pictures display harder faces and more reserved smiles. Their arms are slung around each other in each one, showing the closeness of their group.

I turn around to ask Lev about their travels and see a man standing off to the side. He has wide shoulders, a lean waist, and is about 6'4", if I had to guess. Tall like Lowell and almost as muscular as Lev, but surprisingly, he's more handsome than both with a strong, chiseled jaw, and dark brown tousled hair and eyes. No wonder everyone loved coming out here in high school.

Smiling, I walk up to him and hold out my hand. "Hi, I'm Kate Michaels."

His large hand reaches out and engulfs mine. "Shaw Walker. It's nice to meet you, Dr. Michaels."

He deliberately inserts my doctor title into the return greeting. I'm not sure if this is just a sign of formal manners or if he's trying to say something.

I address it head-on and leave it up to him to find a way forward. "Kate, please." Why does my voice sound so breathless? "Your photos are incredible. Travel is a passion of mine. Every year, I take a few weeks off and go somewhere new. My next trip will be to Southeast Asia, so if you have any tips for visiting there, I'd love to hear them."

Scrutinizing me, he asks, "Who do you usually travel with each year?"

My head tilts to the side while I consider his question. It's not his business, but I don't have anything to hide, so I answer, "Solo traveler, mostly. My mom sometimes joins me on my trips to Europe or to the countries where getting around is easier for her. Why?"

Frowning, he and Lev exchange scowls. "It's dangerous out there for a single woman traveler. You should really find a travel companion or group."

Shaking my head, I adamantly disagree. "I take every precaution when I travel. Life is short, and I refuse to let fear dictate my choices." I won't ever live in fear again for any reason. My hand creeps up, subtly touching the place on my shoulder where the first bullet hit me. My past and my determination to live beyond it shines clearly on my face.

Turning to Lev, who has been quiet throughout this exchange, I ask him for a glass of water. The whole time I can feel Shaw staring at me, but I ignore it. I'm not sure what to think of him yet. Maybe we just need to get to know each other better, but I have a feeling still waters run deep with this man.

"Please have a seat." Shaw gestures to the couch and waits until I'm sitting before choosing a chair opposite me.

Unwilling to sit here in silence, I focus on the enigmatic man in front of me. "Lev told me this is a working ranch. What does that mean exactly?"

He taps his thigh while he answers. "We run multiple operations here. Besides farming, we raise and sell beef and pig, and offer foals from our breeding program. I'd be happy to give you a tour."

The offer feels more polite than sincere, but I reply, "I'd like a tour, thank you. I don't think I've ever seen a farm, much less a big ranching operation like this one."

We talk more about the ranch, with only clipped answers coming from Shaw. Thankfully, Lev comes back with my water and takes a seat beside me on the couch. He picks up my hand and threads his fingers through mine. I reach over and give him a soft kiss to thank him for the water. When I turn back to Shaw, I catch his dark eyes staring at my lips before he frowns and looks away. Lev's eyes bounce between us, and a second later, he stands and pulls me up.

"I'm going to give Kate a tour of the house," he announces.

Shaw dips his chin in acknowledgement but says nothing. He doesn't even turn his head to watch us leave.

Grasping my arm, Lev pulls me toward a sliding door on the right.

Although I'm dying to ask what's going on, I rein in my curiosity and take my cue from Lev. My attention is quickly captured by the scene in front of me. The backyard is insane, an entertainer's dream. It has a large outdoor seating area with several couches, another fireplace, a TV, a dining table, and a full-size kitchen with a barbecue area. Giant boulders frame an organically shaped pool while a waterfall cascades down from the top, and a jacuzzi and sauna sit off to the right.

With a smile, I nod at Lev. "I could live out here. This is fantastic."

He wraps his big arms around me from behind, and I lift my face up to him for a kiss. I've gotten addicted to his kisses, or maybe I'm just plain addicted to him. Leaning down, he takes my lips in a slow kiss that goes on forever. Turning in his arms, I pull him closer and deepen the kiss, feeling strong hands roam down and cup my backside. We haven't seen each other in a few days, and I've missed him. A lot. I think he's missed me too. Exhaling, I lean back, breaking our kiss, to give us a few minutes to breathe.

"Sweetheart, as much as I'd like to stand here and kiss you, I think we should continue with the tour. Lowell will be down soon, and I know he'll want to spend some time with you too." Taking my hand, he leads me back inside and to the right, where I find a state-of-the-art kitchen with an enormous island.

"This must be your dream kitchen." I run my hands over the sleek countertops.

Lev flashes me an excited grin, and points out all his gadgets and little luxuries, like the pot filler on the stove. The stove itself is a state-of-the-art Viking Range, with six burners and a grilling area. I can't help but laugh at his excitement.

With a mock scowl, he quickly drags me through the rest of the house. I see a gym, indoor lap pool, bowling alley, and theater. There's also a ton of bedrooms. This place is magnificent. We're in the west area of the house when Lev pulls me into a bedroom and shuts the door.

Right away, I can tell this is his room. Not only does it smell like him but it exudes a masculine feel with its black furniture and grey accents. A large king bed with a soft grey down comforter sits against one wall, but it's not a sterile bachelor pad. Several pictures are displayed on his dresser, and I'm just starting to snoop when he picks me up and carries me over to the couch to sit down with me in his lap.

"So, where were we a second ago?" he asks, nibbling on my lips.

"I thought you were concerned about Lowell?" I tease him, my head falling to the side to allow his lips better access to my neck.

Pouty lips trail down to the spot where my neck and shoulder join, and I can't help but arch my back when he hits a particularly sensitive spot. With his incredible strength, he repositions us until we're lying next to each other.

My hands automatically move to his thick hair, burying my fingers in its softness.

With barely a pause, he continues his sensual assault, using his tongue to flick the spot again. Moaning, I arch up into him once more. His knee slides in between my legs and pushes them apart so he can lie between them. When he settles, his cock is nestled against me.

Need makes me wrap my legs around him, and the weight of

his big body on mine feels deliciously good. He's all hard muscles and heat, which makes me feel tiny, feminine, and protected. I pull his mouth to mine, kissing him hard and deep, with a razor-sharp edge of desire that demands more.

Then I strip off his shirt, needing to see and touch him. My hands trail down his warm body, stopping to flick his nipple and lightly score my nails across his lower abdomen.

Groaning, he yanks me up and whips off my sweater, tank, and bra in two seconds flat. When he goes to push me back down on the couch, I refuse, telling him I want to sit up, so he repositions himself on the couch while I straddle him.

"This is one of my favorite positions."

Grinning, he reaches out and flicks my nipple with his tongue. "Mmm, I can see the appeal." His large hands move up to cup my breasts, lightly stroking my nipples with his thumbs.

With a small gasp, I dig my hands into his hair and pull his head back to taste him. Touch him. My hands and mouth move all over his body, nibbling on his neck and stroking the hard muscles of his chest.

His hips grind up when I hit sensitive spots, and he moans. Seeing his response to me is exhilarating. The last time Collin and I were intimate, he ridiculed my attempts to please him, and I hadn't realized until this moment how much I needed this reassurance from Lev.

"I want to touch you," I murmur, stroking my hand over his zipper.

With a quick move, he lifts me up, unbuttons his jeans, and pulls his cock out of his briefs. Setting me back down, he positions me further back on his knees with his cock standing at attention in front of me. The strength he just showed blows my mind, but the thought quickly fades.

My hand reaches out and I wrap my fingers around him. Lightly skimming down its length, I tighten my grip at the base, and slide back up, adding a slight roll at the top. A rumbling noise comes from his chest, and I look up to see him, eyes dark and cheeks flush with need, staring down at where we're joined. My hand continues to move up and down, but my gaze doesn't leave him. I want to see his reaction.

Biting his bottom lip, he holds in his moans, but I reach out with my other hand to pull his lip free.

"Please don't. I need to hear what you want, what you like, how it feels. More than I can even tell you." Grasping him tighter, I stroke him again.

His breath leaves his body in a rush. "Fuck, that feels good, sweetheart. I've wanted your fucking hands on me since I met you. The only thing better would be those sweet lips of yours." As he talks, his hips thrust upwards when I stroke down.

Picking up the pace, I alternate between watching his face and watching his cock. Cum drips out of the top, and using my finger, I swipe it up and taste him.

"Fuck me," explodes out of his mouth as he watches me lick my finger. "Taste my fucking cum, sweetheart. It's all for you. Nobody else."

My nipples harden at the words falling from his lips and my panties become drenched. Rolling up my hand, I catch another drop, but this time I use it to lube his cock so I can go faster.

Dark green eyes flick to mine and he groans again. Faster and faster he meets my strokes. Panting, his body strains to reach the top.

"Fuck, sweetheart, that's it. Grip my cock tight. Just a little faster. Almost there." He suddenly grabs my hand, holding it tight to his cock and gives three hard thrusts before coming. His cum squirts on my breasts, his chest, and our hands. He sits there for a minute, eyes closed, as he tries to recover his breath.

Finally, he opens his eyes. "Thank you, sweetheart. I don't know what I did to deserve this surprise, but I'm a lucky bastard." After dropping a kiss on my lips, he leans forward and nuzzles my neck. "You're so fucking incredible."

He opens his mouth to say something else but his phone buzzes. With a curse, he glances at the clock on the wall and shakes his head. Scooping me up, he ignores it and carries me to the bathroom. Setting me on the counter, he grabs a washcloth, turns on the warm water, and cleans us both. Still an aching mass of need, the cloth is torturous, and as it swipes across my breasts, a moan escapes my lips. Lev tosses it on the counter and pulls me into his arms, but a knock on the door makes him pause.

"Damn it. That will be Lowell," he explains, throwing the cloth into the sink. "Right now, more than anything, I want to carry you over to that bed and bury myself inside you." He stares into my eyes and sighs. "But if you don't go with him, I won't have time to fix dinner for all of us."

Part of me wants to say "screw eating," but I know this is part of their Sunday ritual. I'm just visiting, and the last thing I want to do is change things, especially since Shaw didn't seem very welcoming earlier.

Chuckling, I hop down from the counter and walk over to pick up my clothes from the floor. Bending over, I hear an exaggerated groan from behind me and turn to catch Lev staring at me. Shaking with laughter, I turn toward him as I get dressed, making sure to cup my breasts fully to put them in my bra.

Lev growls, but the impatient knocking starts again. He rolls his eyes and angles his head in question.

I motion for him to open it and he raises an eyebrow while grinning.

Lowell strides in and stops abruptly when he sees me standing there in just my bra. Pulling my tank top on, I take an inordinate amount of time to smooth out the wrinkles. From under my eyelashes, I peak at Lowell and find him leaning nonchalantly against the doorframe watching me. It stirs the barely restrained passion inside me, and I clench my legs together. Snatching up my cardigan, I decide I'm too hot to put it on right now and fold it over my arm.

"Hello, Lowell. Lev says you're going to *finish* my tour?" Emphasizing the word finish, I silently laugh at his expression.

He seems to realize I'm teasing him and a glint sparks in his eye. "You didn't help her finish?" He turns to Lev with a frown.

Shit. That isn't what I meant. I mean, I did, but not to embarrass Lev… good grief.

Lev glares at Lowell. "A persistent bastard interrupted us."

"Hmm… shameful neglect." Lowell reaches out and pulls me to him. With a hand on my back, he guides me out of Lev's room. "How long until dinner?"

"About an hour," Lev tells him. "Don't be late."

Laughing, Lowell waves him off. "It might be worth it."

I glance over my shoulder and blow Lev a kiss as I walk away, hoping he's not mad, and he gives me a big wink in return. I guess not.

"So, where are we going?" Glancing up at Lowell, I see a smirk on his face.

"To finish your tour. So tell me, where haven't you been?"

Not sure whether to take him seriously, I rattle off a list of the places Lev showed me.

He informs me that I've seen nearly all of the house except for Shaw and Thayer's quarters, and of course, his rooms. With a firm hand on my back, he guides me to the stairs. Nerves start attacking me at the thought of being in his bedroom, but sparks of anticipation quickly replaces them. The only thing Lowell and I have done is kiss, but with the way this man dances, I can't help but feel anything between us will be intense.

At the top of the stairs, he motions to the left and tells me those are Thayer's rooms. Turning right, he strides to the first door and opens it. It's an office, filled with windows and shelves full of books, with more books and papers covering the large desk by the window. The clutter shocks me because this room doesn't even feel like Lowell.

"I know, it's a mess. For some reason, I can't work when everything is orderly. It's like I need a messy environment to see all the different threads to a story." His cheeks are red as he quickly pulls the door shut.

Intrigued by this new facet, I can't help but be flattered. "I'm surprised you let me in on your dirty little secret."

"I'm full of surprises."

My eyebrows rise, wondering what else is coming.

We walk to the next door and he opens it to a bedroom. All the furnishings are in shades of dark blue with black accents. This room feels like Lowell. It's super orderly, with a recliner that has a book lying on it and a formal-looking couch. The four-poster bed is unexpected and intriguing though.

On closer inspection, I notice strange black loops hanging from the posts. Walking over, I lay my cardigan on the bed and reach out to grab the loops, realizing that they're made of a soft black cord.

Lowell comes to stand close to me, and I ask, "What in the world?"

He reaches out and shows me how the loops slide up and down and lengthen and shorten. Putting my hand in one loop, he also shows me how they tighten. Slowly, I begin to comprehend the purpose of the loops. Flushing, I turn to face him, my one hand in the loop and my other at my side, waiting for him to tell me more.

Watching my face, he reads the desire to know more and reaches out to grasp my other hand. "Sometimes, it's better to show than tell."

Turning me around, he reaches for my looped hand and pulls it up to the top of the post. Once my arm is stretched out above me, he lifts my other hand over my head and pulls it through a loop beside the first one, then tightens it too. When he turns me back around to face him, the loops hold my hands above my head, tied to the post, and just like that, the fire Lev started earlier comes roaring back to life.

Trailing his hands down my body, Lowell leans in and gives me one of his trademark-controlled kisses. Then he brushes my hair back from my face before suddenly gripping it tightly in his hand and pulling my head back to deepen the kiss. He's so tall I have to stretch up on my toes to meet his mouth, which brings my stomach into contact with his cock. Moaning, I shift my hips, trying to press up against him some more, but he pulls his body back until I subside, then he lightly presses back into me. Rubbing his cock against me, I can feel how hard he is beneath his clothes. I move my body to get closer, and he presses me back against the bedpost.

"Stay there, and don't move unless I tell you. If anything gets to be too much, just say Tango."

He waits until I give him my agreement, and simultaneously, my willingness to let him do whatever he wants. Sighing, as if a huge weight is off his shoulders, he goes back to kissing me, using his grip on my hair to maneuver my mouth the way he wants it. Sometimes he pulls it back to deepen the kiss or to the side so he can skim his lips down my neck. I shiver when he runs across the hot spot on my neck, and he pulls back to watch me as he lightly strokes the spot with his finger. My body pulls away from the post in an involuntary arch, and in response, he bites down on my shoulder as punishment for disobeying his orders, just hard enough that an arrow of desire shoots straight down to my core.

Fuck me! How did I not know biting turns me on?

Soothing the bite with his tongue, he grips my hips and pushes my body back against the post once more, then reaches up to grasp my tank top and slip it over my head. He can't take it off fully due to the ropes, but he leaves it as another restraint on my body. Lean fingers skim over the bullet wounds, but unlike Lev, he doesn't place soft kisses on them. Instead, Lowell bites softly around each scar, turning them from something to hide into pinpoints of desire and need.

Unclasping my bra, his fingers map my breasts, getting to know their shape before cupping them to feel their weight in his hands. Pinching the nipples, he watches my body move restlessly. I don't make a sound though. He takes a firmer grip, twisting and pinching until a moan slips past my lips.

"Harder, please," I beg him breathlessly. He twists harder, but it's not enough. "Harder, Lowell." My pleas are demanding now.

Lowell steps away for a second. When he returns, he holds up his fingers, showing me the gold clamps in his hand.

I stare up at him, wondering what he's doing.

"These go around your nippes," he explains as he slides them on. "I'll tighten them, and you tell me when it's enough, okay?" His hands hover above my nipples, the clamps open and ready.

Oh, shit. Am I ready for this? I don't know, but I need it.

"Yes," I whisper, knowing he needs to hear my words.

He clamps them on my nipples, pinching them tighter and tighter in the ring. There's just a tinge of pain, but some of my need eases until it's finally enough. His hands reach out to move my breasts from side to side, and the clamps contract tighter, then release. Pain and pleasure.

Fuck, yes.

I inhale sharply. Aching, I can't help but beg Lowell to help me. "Please. I need to come."

He leans down and licks my ear. "Do you want me to use my fingers or my tongue?"

I'm almost lost at the question. Honestly, I want to say I don't care, but ever since I first saw his hands, I've been thinking about those long fingers inside me.

"Fingers."

"Really?" He's surprised by my choice. "Why?" Standing above me and staring down, he waits for me to answer him.

Embarrassed, I try to look away, but he reaches out and grabs my chin until my eyes find his "Your fingers are so long. I've been wondering how they would feel curled up inside of me." My face burns at the truth spilling from my lips.

His hand coils in my hair, and he reaches down to kiss me hard, a little less controlled than usual, as if admitting my need took him closer to the edge.

Unbuttoning and unzipping my jeans, he pulls them off. I'm almost entirely naked in front of Lowell now. Kneeling down, he presses his face against me, inhaling deeply before taking off my underwear.

Thank God I've had a wax recently.

I'm riveted, waiting to see what he'll do next.

His hands clench on my thighs while he lightly blows on the heart of me.

My hips thrust toward him, wanting more.

Instead, he takes a deep breath, stands up, and trails his fingers down. Then he groans as he slides them through the slit.

"You're already so wet from earlier. Mmm. What I wouldn't give to taste you. Next time, I won't ask." His fingers explore every bit of me, circling and stroking until I'm nearly weeping with need, but then he stops. "Tell me."

Tell him what? Why the hell is he stopping?

"Tell me what you need, and I'll give it to you," he coaxes me.

Control. While I need the words and sounds for reassurance, he needs the authority over me. Taking a deep breath, I lose the anger. We both need to hear the words, even if his reason is different from mine.

If it was Lev, I'd ask him to make me come, but Lowell needs *clear* words. Explicit. Honest. "Fuck me with your fingers, Lowell. Stroke me, slide them inside, curl them up, and fuck me. In and out and fast until my body explodes around them. Please." Holding my breath, I wait for him to move, my body trembling with the need to come.

Time slows. After a heartbeat or three hundred, he gives me a wicked smile and plunges his fingers into me. His other hand grips my hair, forcing my head back, until all I can see is him. He wants to watch me come. His grey eyes burn as he listens to the needy sounds slipping from my throat.

My hands grip the ropes above me tightly. Panting, I tell him, "I'm so close... Now, Lowell... please."

His thumb circles my clit while his other fingers curl up inside me and stroke me.

"Yes!"

I come hard, jerking up against him, my body clenching his fingers tight. Waves cascade out, my legs weaken, and Lowell's arm circles around to hold me up. As my tremors subside, he pulls out his fingers, and I shudder at the loss.

Breathing heavily, I lean against him, and shockingly realize I'm spent and almost entirely naked, but this elegant man is still hard as a rock and fully dressed. He stands me up against the post again, brushes the hair out of my eyes, then leans down to give me a hard, almost punishing kiss in its intensity. I can feel his cock against my stomach, and anticipation curls at what comes next.

Of course, the phone buzzes, interrupting the moment.

"Fuck," Lowell quietly swears. "I don't want our first time to be quick." Breathing heavily, he adjusts his cock, then reaches up to loosen the loops and pull my hands out. He takes the time to briskly rub my wrists and hands to get the blood flowing freely again.

Lowell slides the nipple clamps off, and I can't help gasping when the blood returns to each spot. My nipples redden. Then, my entire body turns red as I think about the clamps and how the pain turned me on. It didn't seem to faze Lowell though, as if he knew exactly what I needed.

He drops to his knees to pull up my clothes, but before he does, he grips my thighs and pulls them apart to see my swollen, wet lips. Stroking lightly across them, his eyes never leave mine as he brings his finger up to his mouth.

"Oh so delicious, Kate."

This man…

Shaking my head, I can't even finish the thought, I'm so turned on by him. I make myself busy by hooking my bra. My tank top is still above my neck, and I reach up to pull it back down. Shit, it's full of wrinkles now. Even though I'm hot, I reach for the cardigan and pull it on too. I'm sure my hair is a mess, and I need some cool water for my face. Flustered, I glance around for the bathroom. Spotting a door in the corner, I move toward it, but his hand reaches out and grabs my wrist. Startled, I look up into Lowell's face.

"I need to go to the bathroom."

He releases me and runs his hand through his hair. "Did I push you too hard?" Silence fills the air between us while he waits for me to answer.

Swallowing, I close my eyes for a second. "It's not… that. It's a… lot of things. I'm embarrassed because we haven't known each other long, and yet I let you do things to me I've never let someone else do. I'm dating two men, and I let both of you touch me today. I've gone several years without feeling, and now I feel too much." I stop to reassure him. "I like you. A lot. You're dominant and exciting, but everything is too much, it's overwhelming."

I shrug and step into the bathroom. Washing my face and rinsing off a bit, I comb my fingers through my hair desperately trying to find mold it into order. My green eyes are wide with a maelstrom of emotions in their depths, but they're also sparkling with life. Taking a deep breath, I open the door. Lowell is leaning against the wall in front of me.

"I like you a lot too," he tells me quietly. Tucking my hair behind my ear, he strokes along my jaw. "Regarding the dominance, we'll take it slow and figure out what you like and don't like. You have complete control and the ability to decide how we move forward. I'll push you beyond your current limits to find what you really need, but if you ever want to stop, it only takes one word." Leaning down, he gives me a soft kiss. "Now, let's go eat."

Lev frowns when he sees the lines on my wrist but says nothing. He simply raises an eyebrow at Lowell who nods. I guess they'll work it out later.

Dinner is delicious. Ravenous, Lev's famous spaghetti hits the spot.

Shaw's eyes never stop moving between the three of us,

capturing every little expression or word that slips. He remains silent until the end of the meal when the talk turns to the horses that are ready for breeding.

"Your horses are beautiful. How many do you have here?" I ask.

Shaw answers quietly, "We have thirty horses altogether, but most of them are working horses for the ranch. For the breeding program, we have nine horses. Two studs and seven mares. Do you ride?"

Wistfully, I shake my head. "I never had the time or opportunity when I was younger. Most of my time was filled with science and medicine."

He sits quietly for a moment. "If you would like to come out on Sundays, I'd be happy to give you lessons."

Unlike earlier, some of his animosity has dissipated, and the offer seems sincere. "I'd love to learn how to ride. Thank you." I smile at him then turn to Lev, who's staring at Shaw with narrowed eyes.

Standing, Shaw tells me he will see me next Sunday, then excuses himself.

Since Lev picked me up, Lowell decides to take me home. He gives me one deep kiss, then leaves me alone with my thoughts. Whatever I expected during my visit to the ranch, it wasn't this gamut of emotions. I feel like I've fallen into the deep end of the pool. My feelings are intense and real. I'm not sure I'm ready, but I refuse to run away.

Chapter Fifteen

SHAW

"WHAT THE HELL WAS THAT ABOUT?" LEV STRIDES ANGRILY INTO the room. "First you're an ass to her, then you offer to give her riding lessons?"

I thrust my hand through my hair in frustration. "I'm worried. You and Lowell just met her and yet it feels serious. I don't want this to turn into another situation that blows up in our faces. We have enough to handle right now with Thayer out. She's managing his practice and doing well. If something happens, we have to start all over with finding another doctor."

"Bullshit. This isn't about the clinic. You're scared. Nessa left us three years ago. She has another life. The destruction she left behind took a piece of each of us. To escape the pain, we threw ourselves into work and it paid off. We're all doing great, but I need more than work in my life. Lowell does too." He stands, arms crossed, scowling at me.

"You know she's leaving after this assignment, right? What then?" Turning my back on him, I glare out the window. "I understand you need more, but I think her temporary status is exactly the reason we… you… should find someone else. I can't stand the thought of another woman hurting our family."

Lev shakes his head in denial. "She's worth it. There's something about her I can't ignore."

"I agree," Lowell adds, striding into the room and into the conversation. "She brings something I've been missing into my life. Before her, I felt like I was living in a vacuum, but when I'm around her, I feel everything."

Turning back around, I closely assess their determination. Their fierce expressions tell me they're not interested in hearing my opinion. Throwing my hands up in the air, I give in.

"You throw a stranger into our lives and expect me to welcome her with open arms. I don't know if I can do that though. She's a nomad and I need things to be more permanent. But I agreed to give her riding lessons so I could get to know her better," I state with exasperation. "Why don't we start with friendship and see what happens? It's all I'm willing to offer."

Lev agrees and walks out to clean the kitchen, and Lowell dips his chin and strolls out as well.

Kate's a surprise, and Lev's right, there is something about her that draws you in and makes you want to stand in her space for a while. It's been so long since I felt even a spark for anyone. While Lowell and Lev often date, Thayer and I avoid women like the plague. Neither of us is interested in feeling that pain again.

Over the last three years, I've spent so many mornings getting up before the sun just so I wouldn't lie in bed and think about Nessa and what could have been. Do I want someone in my life? Sure. Sharing one woman though? It almost killed us when Nessa left. Is it worth the risk to our family? No.

Vanessa—or Nessa, as we called her—was in the Army with us. Although not a part of our elite unit, she managed intelligence for our branch of covert operations, which meant we were often together. One thing led to another and we each fell for her. The five of us shared everything. Work, home, and each other. When we decided to get out of the Army a few years ago, she took a job in Washington, D.C. instead of coming to Montana with us. We offered to follow her to D.C., but she refused, said she wanted to find one man to marry and have kids. Cynically, I knew it would be more acceptable to her career and future promotions if she had a single husband, not four lovers.

We knew she was ambitious, but until then we didn't realize we were only a temporary situation for her. Given the circumstances, we moved to Montana and she moved to D.C. We heard last year that she had married and had a baby, and while we were happy she found what she needed, it was like sticking a knife in an already festering wound. While most of us were content with a punishing work schedule, Thayer started pushing his physical limits more and more with adrenaline-fueled activities, which is how he landed in the hospital. No. Falling for someone who's only here temporarily will kill our family.

Chapter Sixteen

KATE

THE NEXT WEEK FLIES BY. PATIENTS AND TEXTING FILL MY DAYS AND calls fill my nights. We talk about everything except the past. And it's not just me either. The only thing they bring up from the past is the occasional childhood story or life in the Army, and it's almost the same for me. I'm afraid to reveal too much without opening a door I'm not sure I can close.

Saturday night, Sarah drags me out to a country line dance bar for a girls' night. Firmly against dating cowboys, she flirts with a few handsome tourists, but no one else. Her main focus is teaching me to line dance, insisting I need to learn if I'm going to live in Montana. When I remind her it's only temporary, she rolls her eyes and openly scoffs.

"I should make a bet that you'll end up staying, but I won't," she says with a teasing smile. "Although, if this town doesn't get any decent men in it, I may need to move myself."

A good-looking man in a Stetson and boots comes up to ask her to dance, but she shakes her head. "Girls night." With those words, she pulls me back to the dance floor.

The rest of the night is a blur of dance steps and laughter. If I hadn't danced so well with Lowell on our date, I'd seriously question whether I had two left feet. I barely remember getting home last night.

Groaning, I tap the phone to turn off the alarm and stumble into the shower to find my humanity. The hot spray soaks into my dehydrated skin until I'm feeling less like a dried husk and more like a person, but the pounding in my head won't stop. I blearily contemplate calling off the riding lessons, but I won't give Shaw the satisfaction. I doubt he would offer a second time. Nope. I'll just suck it up and get my shit together. My head presses against the cool tile.

Okay, maybe I need ten more minutes.

Twenty minutes later, I finally make it out of the bathroom. My hair's still damp and I'm running really late, but I think I'm decent enough for riding. I have no idea what to wear though. Aren't horses dirty? I grab an older, worn pair of blue jeans, a long-sleeve T-shirt, and my motorcycle boots. Even if they're not the proper attire, I figure they can at least get me through the muck.

Hurriedly grabbing a piece of toast and some coffee to go, I run out to my vehicle and push the speed limit the entire way.

I'm fifteen minutes late. The vehicle's barely in park before Lev has my door open and is pulling me into his arms for one of his bear hugs. Wrapped up in him, the tension of the week melts away. He smells rugged and divine and I inhale deeply. When I see his dark green eyes smiling at me, I pull him down for a long, long kiss. *Mmm, I've missed him.*

Minutes later, someone nearby clears their throat. Dragging my lips from Lev's, I find Shaw waiting for me. Heat burns my cheeks, even though I haven't done anything wrong. Well, except be late. I wince when I see the time on my watch. I realize I spent way too much time greeting Lev, and I'm now officially twenty minutes late for my lesson with Shaw. Oops.

With a groan, I ease out of Lev's arms. "I'm so sorry, Shaw. I should have texted Lev to tell you I was running late." I stroll over. "I wasn't sure what to wear. I hope this will do."

Shaw's eyes slowly make their way down every inch of me and back up, and my body blatantly responds to the approval in his eyes, even as my mind rebels. Something about this man makes me want to do something rash. Keeping my thoughts to myself, I wait until he nods.

With a glance at Lev, I ask, "Will I see you after my lesson?"

He winks. "I'll be here. Just come find me in the kitchen when you finish." With one last hard stare at Shaw, he walks off.

Shaw strides to the barn, and I follow him to a stall where a black horse with a white marking on its forehead stands. He informs me the dainty horse is a mare with a calm disposition, then explains how to approach her.

"What's her name?"

"Sugar."

"Well, hello, Sugar." I hold my hand out flat for her to sniff me, not wanting her to nip my fingers. I'm a little scared when her teeth graze my hand, but she only nuzzles me with her velvety soft nose. In awe, I stroke her face and neck. "She's super sweet. I can see why you call her Sugar."

Apparantly before I can ride, I need to learn how to manage and care for a horse. He patiently teaches me how to put tack on a horse, how to lead them on a rope, and how to start and stop the horse on the ground. Sounds silly, but this is huge for me. Shaw might call her dainty, but to me, she's big.

He assures me that once I've mastered the care, he'll teach me how to mount and ride the horse. Until then, he makes me repeat the steps several times. The saddle is heavy and cumbersome, and putting it on over and over makes my arms shake like jello. I get better each time I do it, but my completion time starts to slow considerably.

"Great job," Shaw's gravelly voice tells me. "Are you ready to try sitting on her?"

I nod enthusiastically. Finally, my reward. I search around for a stool, but he stops me. Instead of a stool, he cups his hands and describes how he wants me to step into them so he can lift me onto the horse. The first time I do it, I step into his hands and lean too far forward. One arm quickly grips my ankle while the other wraps tightly around my back.

"Sorry," I say a little breathlessly. Only an inch separates my lips from his firm ones.

He clear his throat and sets me down. Before we try again, he shows me how to stretch up and grab the horn of the saddle to steady myself.

Nervous now, my next attempt is too tentative, and I don't even get off the ground. After trying it a couple more times, I finally get it right, and he lifts me with ease to sit on top of the horse. Smiling widely, I reach forward and run my hands over Sugar's mane.

"Next time, I'll teach you how to mount a horse with a stool, but I prefer you have better shoes fitted for stirrups and riding. Speaking of which, I have something for you when we get done."

Without waiting for my reply, he picks up Sugar's rope and leads me outside the barn to the ring. He walks around the outer circle a few times to help me get used to her gait.

It doesn't matter that he's still holding the reins, I'm officially riding a horse. I can't stop smiling. "This is amazing. Thank you."

Shaw dips his head but says nothing. Finally, he slows Sugar to a stop, and patiently walks through instructions on how to dismount.

I try to follow the steps he gives me, but the ground is farther away than I anticipate, and I end up dangling on the side of the horse.

Strong hands grip my hips as he orders me to let go of the horn. Once I'm sure he has me, I release it, and he immediately eases me to the ground but continues to stand behind me. I turn toward him but my balance is a little wonky, and I have to grab on to him to help steady myself.

I scan his face, trying to figure out what he's thinking, but it's like looking at a brick wall… except for the little tick in his jaw. Something is bubbling under his stoic surface.

He abruptly steps back.

"Is everything okay?" I inquire.

"Yep, it's fine," he drawls. "Let's put Sugar in her stall."

Determined to show him I took his lessons to heart, I remove everything from Sugar, brush her down, and walk her back into her stall.

Smiling, I turn to him. "Thank you so much for today. She's beautiful and I'm can't wait to ride her again."

He searches my face, as if to check my sincerity. "You did well. I'm sure Lev has supper about ready."

Shocked, I look at my phone. I've been out here with Shaw for three hours! I didn't even notice the time flying by.

When we enter the house, Lowell swings by and kisses me. "I'd give you a hug, but…" He holds his nose and waves his hand.

"How dare you tell me I stink!" Laughing, I get a whiff of myself and have to agree. "How soon is supper? I have some gym clothes in my car, so if there's time, I'd like to grab a quick shower and change?"

He texts Lev, who replies that dinner will be ready in twenty minutes, which is plenty of time to shower.

As I leave to go to my car, Shaw hands me several bags and a box. Curious, I stop and open them, finding a helmet, tan pants, a long-sleeve black shirt, and the most beautiful, black riding boots.

Stunned, I shake my head. "This is way too much, Shaw. I can't accept it. Since you're giving me free lessons, I'd like to pay you for these items."

Folding his arms, he scowls at the offer. "You need proper boots and a helmet. I can trade the riding boots for cowboy boots, but they don't really seem like your style."

Flustered, my hand runs down the soft leather of the boots. Knowing he's not going to give in, I graciously accept. "These are definitely more to my taste. Thank you. Once I have a shower, I'll try everything on to make sure it fits."

I give him a thank you hug, then walk out to grab my gym bag. Coming back in, I pause, unable to remember where Lev's room is in this enormous house. Spotting the stairs, I make a beeline toward Lowell's room instead because it's easier.

After a quick shower, I slip into the riding clothes and boots. Swiveling in front of the mirror, I notice the pants are very, very formfitting, completely exposing every line of my body. Literally, every inch. If I ate a donut, I'm sure it would show in these pants. I'm not sure about keeping them.

The polo shirt and boots fit perfectly though. Heading downstairs with the helmet, I walk into the living room to show Shaw.

When I enter the room, the talking halts, and all three of them just blink at me. "Um, the shirt and boots fit perfectly, but I don't know about the pants. They seem… tight. Also, I wasn't sure how to put the helmet on?" I hold it out to him.

Shaw clears his throat, then clears it again. Stepping forward, he shows me how to find the symbol on the front. He then lifts my chin, takes the helmet, and carefully eases it onto my head. Bending over to search for the straps puts his face within millimeters of mine, and I find myself licking my lips while I stare at his hard jaw, beautiful lips, and long eyelashes. He finishes buckling the straps and his eyes lock with mine. He sways toward me, and for a second, I think he's going to kiss me. My eyes widen, but he jerks his head up and away from me.

His hand waves in my direction. "Everything fits. Perfectly." He walks over to stare out the window.

I glance over at Lev, and his eyes are shining with heat and laughter, but I'm not sure why. "Are the pants really supposed to be this tight?"

I turn around to show him the back, and a strangled sound comes from behind me. In a strained voice, he tells me they should fit tight, but also stretchy. I do a few squats, and I'm surprised with how much they stretch. Kind of like yoga pants, I guess. Okay, but I wish someone would have told me what to expect.

As I head back upstairs, I hear laughter roaring from the living room.

"You're really into torturing yourself, aren't you?"

"Fuck me," Shaw's ragged voice replies.

Changing into my leggings and a crop T-shirt, I put everything back in its bag or box, then carry it out to my car since I'll be leaving once supper is over.

Entering the kitchen, I ask Lev if he needs any help. He turns, takes one look at me, and starts yelling for Lowell. When Lowell comes strolling into the kitchen, he points to me and gestures toward the door. Grabbing my hand, Lowell pulls me out of the kitchen and into his lap in the living room.

"What's wrong?"

He points to my legs. "After the jodhpurs, he couldn't take the leggings. You're too fucking sexy. He's afraid he'll burn our meal. You'll just have to stay here in my lap until supper is ready, or it's likely we won't even get any."

Laughing, I loop my arms around Lowell. "Good, I haven't kissed you in a week. Did you miss me?"

Gripping my chin, he gives me one of his smoldering looks, then kisses me in that demanding, controlled way that's uniquely his. With a long-suffering sigh, Shaw heads toward the kitchen.

After supper, all three men walk me to my car. I give Lev and Lowell a kiss, and Shaw a hug goodbye. It's weird. I almost feel like I'm dating all three men, even though Shaw doesn't seem to like me.

Chapter Seventeen

KATE

I can't believe it's May, and I've been here two-and-a-half months. Time's flying by. The practice keeps me incredibly busy, but I manage to see Lev or Lowell at least once a week. On Sundays, I go out to the ranch and have a riding lesson with Shaw and supper with all three.

My friendship with Shaw is slowly coming around, but my attraction for the quietly enigmatic man is getting stronger too. I haven't told anyone because I don't want to destroy what I have with Lev and Lowell, but I can't stop thinking about him. Shaw, on the other hand, seems perfectly content to keep me in the friend zone, which is for the best.

I sent him a bourbon of the month gift to thank him for the lessons and riding gear. This seemed to be the opening he needed to feel comfortable texting me. While he doesn't say much, he makes me text him whenever I go out with Sarah to let him know where we're going, then again when I get home. He's completely overprotective, but I think he's like that with everyone.

Rolling my shoulders, I let out a sigh of relief. Thankfully, we only had a few patients today, so everyone was able to leave at five o'clock, giving me plenty of time to get ready before Lowell gets here.

After a quick shower, I pull on silky lounge pants and a button-down silk shirt. My nipples pebble as they slide against the smooth fabric. It's a bold move to go completely commando. Since the shirt is silk, Lowell will figure out pretty quickly I'm not wearing a bra. He'll then start to wonder if I'm wearing underwear. Until he knows for sure, it will drive him crazy. I grin. I love to test his control.

About fifteen minutes later, Lowell walks in with that long, easy gait of his. I'm in the kitchen, pouring a glass of wine when he comes up behind me, his long arms reaching around for my glass.

"Hello, Kate. Mmm... thanks, I needed this drink."

Without replying, I let my body rub against his as I stretch up to get another glass. Hmmm, which one? This one. I pick up the bottle to pour me a glass. Wait. No, I think I need the stemless. Reaching up again, I exchange the stemmed glass for a stemless one. Hard to decide between stemless or stem, right?

Hearing him inhale sharply behind me, I laugh silently. The thin silk of my outfit makes it feel like I'm rubbing up against him naked. I finally stop playing and pour myself a glass.

He lowers his wine to the counter and brings his mouth to my ear. "Put your hands on the upper cabinet, and don't move them."

Excitement skates up my spine and my body responds to his command with a flood of desire. I immediately place my palms flat on the panel door above me.

Once my hands are situated, he pulls my head back to search my eyes. I silently snort. As if I'd be that careless. My face is as blank as a new canvas. Leaning down, he gives me one of his sharp, controlled kisses.

I love and hate his kisses. I love that they represent him so uniquely, but I hate the low simmer of desire that leaves me balanced on a knife's edge. Never spiking, never raging.

As he draws back, I smile and force a yawn in response. "Hello, Lowell. Please excuse me, it's been a long day."

Narrowing his eyes, he studies me for a second before smiling darkly. His hands slide around my body to unbutton my shirt. Finding my bare breasts, he laughs huskily. "Somebody wants to play, huh?" His fingers lightly skim my nipples, rubbing circles around their peaks.

Sharply inhaling, I arch my back, pushing my breasts further into his hands. My body follows his when he pulls away, leaving his hands the only point of contact. They're barely a whisper, torturing me with their soft caresses.

"Please," slips out of my mouth along with a contented sigh.

"Tell me," he commands.

Pressing my lips shut, I wait, shivering in anticipation of his next move.

When he gets no further response, he turns me around to face him, then lifts me onto the counter. Taking each of my hands, he cups them under my breasts, as if I'm offering them to him.

"Mmm... a snack? Don't mind if I do."

Firm lips latch onto my nipple, licking and sucking hard until it's swollen and stiff. My fingers twitch with the need to break the pose and clasp his head tighter to me, but I don't dare. I want more, and I'll only get it if I follow his commands.

He switches to my other nipple, and I'm surprised to feel something cold slide onto the first one. Glancing down, I see a glint of gold.

Fuck me, he brought the nipple clamps. Guess he wants to play too.

I haven't seen those since my first visit to the ranch.

Once his lips leave my body, his hand reaches up and clamps the second nipple too. This time, a small gold chain links one clamp to the other, essentially attaching the two. He removes my hands from my breasts, and they swing lightly into place. The clamps pull tight with each tiny movement, and I hiss at the sting they leave behind.

My breasts sway, and the clamps pull and release, shooting

desire straight down to my clit, as if another invisible chain is tying my breasts and clit together. With a low groan, I begin to appreciate the addition of the chain. I flood with wetness each time. My hand unconsciously moves to bring myself some relief, but it's captured by Lowell.

"I didn't give you permission to touch yourself, or to come." Lifting me off the counter, he helps me stand. "Leave your shirt open."

His cheeks flush and his grey eyes glitter with dark lights every time he looks at me. For several minutes, he just stands and stares, until I can see his own passion catching up with him. Reaching out, he pulls on the chain swinging between my breasts to bring me flush up against him.

Gasping at the slight pain caused by the action, my hands reach out and grab his shirt, fisting it tight. My pain becomes the key to releasing him from his control. His mouth crashes down and consumes me. He's relentless, forcing me to take what he gives and return it with equal measure. This is what I want. Not controlled kisses, but passion and dominance. One goal of mutual pleasure and destruction.

Picking me up, he carries me over to the island and lays me down on top of the cold marble. The silk shirt provides little protection and I arch my back to escape it. Lowell's eyes immediately fall to my breasts, like I'm a feast laid out just for him, and he lowers his mouth and licks each one.

His dark grey eyes find mine, waiting and watching, as he releases a clamp. When the bite of pain makes me moan, he instantly soothes the nipple with his tongue. He wields it effortlessly, stroking and flattening his tongue against the tip, until there is only pleasure. I move to clutch the back of his head, but he gently grabs my wrist and places it by my side.

His gaze snares mine, a command in its depths, and I huskily agree to leave my hands where he wants them. For my reward, he returns his attention back to my nipple. He plays with it for another minute before sucking it into a stiff peak and placing the clamp back on. I whimper, then moan. The brief respite from the clamp only seemed to make it more sensitive, and a fresh wave of pain and pleasure rolls through me. Moving to my other breast, he repeats it all again. When he gets done, I'm writhing in a sea of pleasure edged with pain.

His eyes are dark grey obsidian. At my submissiveness, at my pain, at my pleasure, all of it. It fuels the fire in him. Knowing I make him burn is gasoline to the fire raging within me.

"Tell me what you want," he orders me.

"I want you, Lowell," I beg.

He lifts me up and removes my pants. Pulling my feet up, he lays each one flat on the cold counter, then spreads my legs apart. Cool air caresses the most intimate part of me, and he stands up straight to take in the full view. I'm completely at his mercy.

"God, you're beautiful and so very responsive," he says in a voice tight with need. "And tonight, you're mine."

Leaning over, one hand caresses my breasts while the other strokes my core. Gasping, I writhe on the cold marble, awash in pleasure, and breathless for his next move. Will he choose pleasure or pain this time?

"Breathe," he commands me.

I exhale, and the second the breath leaves my body, one hand pulls on the chain while the other strokes the heart of me. Pleasure and pain. The string of desire tying them together becomes a living flame.

Gasping, my quivering legs widen. "More."

"Tell me who you belong to," his voice is demanding, but I see the need to hear my words burning in his eyes.

"I'm yours. My body is yours," I cry, surrendering all control to him.

At my words of submission, his mouth replaces his fingers and I become utterly incoherent. His wicked tongue takes me to the edge, over and over, but he refuses to let me fall. Sucking and flicking, he wrings every drop of pleasure from my body. This is my reward. I push up on my elbows wanting to see him between my legs.

His grey eyes flash to mine, and he thrusts his fingers into my body. Pleasure rolls through me and my head falls back. When my hips try to lift to meet the thrust of his fingers, he uses his mouth to hold me in place.

Shaking with the need to come, I'm incoherently begging him for my release. "Please, Lowell, please."

In response to hearing his name, his fingers thrust faster and his tongue follows the same rhythm.

Feeling the edge of my orgasm, I cry out, desperate to come. "Lowell, I can't stop it."

He lifts his head, and the world pauses for a second. With a dark smile of utter satisfaction, he curls his fingers up inside me to stroke my most sensitive spot. His other hand releases the chain, and the sensations of the two prove to be too much. My body slides off the cliff into oblivion.

Muscles clench tightly on his fingers, milking them as if they were his cock inside of me, while darkness wraps around my peripheral vision. The waves of pleasure are intense, rolling through me, leaving me boneless and unable to move. Lowell plants light kisses on my inner thighs while he waits for me to recover.

After a few minutes, the tremors stop, and while I should probably be embarrassed, I lay there spread before him, staring at this incredible man. He brings out a side of me I never knew existed. A side I need, where I don't have to maintain the rigid control necessary to keep my secrets in the dark. I allow him to see all of that in my face.

"Beautiful. Simply beautiful," he remarks in a raspy voice.

His hands clench the edge of the counter, telling me his control hangs by a thread. He doesn't ask for more, but I know he wants it.

Pulling him down on top of me, my kiss tells him about the

passion still coursing through me. This time, I devour him, stroking the need pounding below his placid surface. Breathing heavily, I whisper, "Thank you for giving me what I need. Let me do the same."

I motion for him to rise and ask for his help in getting off the island. Once I'm up, I slide onto the barstool to bring my mouth in alignment with his cock. With nimble fingers, I undo his belt, but his hands grip mine to hold them still. Knowing he needs the words, I feed them to him.

"I need to taste you, lick you, and suck you. And when you're on the edge, I want you to lose that famous control of yours."

Swallowing, he releases my hands to finish undressing him. Shoving his pants and briefs down, his long, hard cock waits for my grip. My tongue reaches out and licks from the base to the tip, savoring the taste and manly smell before opening wide to take him into my mouth. Going down as far as I can, I swallow before pulling his cock back out to the tip, sucking along the way. I swirl my tongue around the rim of his head, then repeat it all again.

"You're stunning with your mouth wrapped around my cock. That pink tongue licking and swirling. That's it." He makes little sound, but his hand grips my hair tightly.

My other hand lightly caresses his balls before moving to explore the base of his cock. His breath hisses out when my fingers find the silky patch between his legs, and he thrusts into my mouth hard. Continuing to linger in this spot, I time the stroke of my finger with my mouth going down on his shaft. Faster and faster. My other hand pulls down as my mouth goes back to the tip. *Fuck, he's so hard.*

His harsh breathing tells me his control is wavering on a razor thin edge.

Lowell pulls my head back to watch me for a second, then he guides my head forward, slowly taking over. He withdraws his cock all the way, then slides it back into my mouth, taking it further each time.

"Just another inch. That's it," he half demands and half begs, his voice so low I almost can't hear it.

He repeats the maneuver, making me take one more inch. Gagging a little, he stills, letting me breathe. When I settle, he strokes in and out, exactly to that point each time. Sounds of approval drop from his lips while his hips piston back and forth faster and faster. Not once does he let go.

"That's it, take my cock, all the way. Fuck." A finger lightly traces the hollows in my cheeks. "Your sweet, wet mouth was made for me. Seeing your plump lips stretched across my cock, sucking every inch, makes me impossibly hard."

A couple more thrusts, and with a loud gasp, he comes, filling my mouth. I swallow, and he moans at the sensation. Breathing heavily, he releases my hair and pulls out of my mouth, then leans down and kisses me. It's not one of his controlled kisses, but a proper, hard, messy fucking kiss showing a serious lack of control.

I love making him lose control.

"My Kate," he states cooly, but the expression on his face tells me the words mean something to him.

We dress and decide to just get food delivered from Lev's bar. While I clean up the counter, island, and barstool, he calls in our order. When it arrives, he unpacks the food, and I grab the wine. When I place it down in front of him, I can't help but smirk.

Raising an eyebrow at my taunt, he takes a slow sip. "Pushing my buttons because I stole your wine?"

Looking away, I think about it. "No, pushing your buttons to make you lose some of your infamous control. I need to know I'm not just a plaything for you to wind up and direct. I enjoy submitting to you and discovering this side of me, but I worry it's just physical. Between us." Sweating, I'm nervous now that I've blurted out my real thoughts. *Fuck.* I should have just let things progress naturally. My hand trembles slightly when I pick up the fork to take a bite. Silence reigns until I finally find the courage to meet his stare.

Grey eyes smolder with unreadable emotion. "I didn't know you felt that way."

My heart plummets. I don't know why I thought this was a good idea. Shit. Needing to get away, I stand, but he reaches over and grabs my wrist, stilling me.

"Let me finish. I absolutely want more. I haven't been able to read you to understand whether this was a casual, physical relationship or if you were open to something more. You never share much of yourself with either of us, but especially with me. Every bit of information we glean is by accident. We've been content to let you set the pace, but if you want this to go further, we're going to need you to open up."

My body sinks back on the chair, partially in relief, but surprise too. And the ever present fear, of course. "You're right and wrong. I feel like I've shared so much with both of you. The parts of me that very few others know. They might be simple likes and dislikes, but for the last few years, I've had no one. Having someone on the other end of a phone is priceless to me."

I pause and take a sip of wine. "You're right. There's more. A hell of a lot more, but it's ugly. A few years ago, something terrible happened that had so many repercussions I felt like I was repeatedly drowning. Once it stopped, I was so thankful to be on dry land, so to speak, that I could only concentrate on living one day at a time. In order to function, I had to lock it all away."

Lowell is completely still, taking in every word I say, his intense eyes assessing me carefully.

Thinking about what he already knows, I figure this might be the easiest part of my story. Pushing back my plate, I clench my hands together. "Over four years ago, I was a practicing oncologist at Carton Hospital in San Francisco. Most of my patients were older, but I treated a few kids too. One of those kids was a twelve-year-old boy named David who had leukemia. During one of his visits, I discovered he met the eligibility requirements for a new clinical trial. We prepped him for a month to get his weight up and his blood counts stable. When it was time for the trial, his panel came back with something that knocked him out of eligibility. The cause was a medication I prescribed to manage his nausea. I didn't know it would impact his potassium levels. Stopping the medication improved his blood results immediately, but they couldn't let him into the trial. A few weeks later, David got pneumonia and died."

Lowell puts down his fork and reaches for my hand.

Feeling my eyes burn, I squeeze it and take a couple more drinks. After a deep breath, I continue. "Two weeks later, his father came to the hospital. When he reached the oncology ward, he cornered a group of doctors and nurses and held them at gunpoint. I was down the hall when I heard him screaming my name, demanding to see me. When I showed up, he shot me. It wasn't enough though. In his rage and grief, he shot seventeen other people, including my husband, Collin, before committing suicide. Besides David's father, thirteen of my friends and colleagues died. The remaining five of us recovered, but none of us came out of it the same."

My voice is hoarse as the tears start to flow. Guilt burns through me. All those lives shattered by my careless decision and his grief.

Lowell stands and picks me up, then he carries me over to the couch and sits with me in his lap. Rocking back and forth, he holds me while I cry until the tears dry up again. He hands me a tissue.

"Some days, I can't cope with the guilt. So I bottle it up and hide it where I can't feel it or see it. On the days I can't hide, all I see are their faces and the faces of their kids, spouses, parents. I see Ellie's new baby without a mother, Jordan's wife raising four kids by herself, Carl's husband, and so many more. Every day, I fought cancer with these people. They were my friends." Looking down at my hands, I shudder and give him more. "You once asked me why I moved from oncology to general practice. The truth is... Hospitals wouldn't hire me after the incident. I was too much of a liability. While they never directly discriminated to my face, I couldn't get another oncology job anywhere."

Devastation creeps into my voice. My heart still breaks at the loss even though it's stupid. I can still be a doctor, just a different doctor than I dreamed of for so long. And mourning a career when I get to continue living feels wrong.

Clearing my throat of the emotion, I continue. "A few other things happened in the two years following the event that caused me to leave San Francisco. Unfortunately, the medical community is small and the memories long. I stopped using my first name of Elizabeth and started using an abbreviated version of my middle name, Kathryn. As Kate, I became a traveling doctor, and here I am."

His hands smooth down my back as he gathers me tightly to him. He's quiet for a minute, carefully choosing the words he cherishes so much. "I'm so sorry you've gone through this horrible ordeal. It will get easier, but it will never go away. While it doesn't help, I do understand, and I think you'll find Lev and Shaw will too. In the Army, you make decisions based on intelligence, gut instinct, and training. I know I did, and when I was wrong, people died. Am I still responsible? Yes. Is it all my fault? No. You have to decide how much blame to hold on to. You didn't give David cancer or give his dad a gun and force him to pull the trigger. You made a decision based on your training, and unfortunately, given your inexperience, it was the wrong one. The only thing you can do is learn from it. I know that doesn't help, but we're here if you want to talk about it."

Thinking it over, I realize I've been accepting the blame for the entire thing, including what happened afterward. It's not surprising. Everyone blamed me. Not my mom, of course, but the rest of the world. And when you hear it often enough, you begin to believe it. David's father took the easy way out, and with him dead, all the harsh judgment fell onto me.

Exhausted, my brain refuses to think about it anymore tonight. I scan his eyes, then stroke my hand down his face. "Thank you. You've shined light into my dark tunnel. It means more to me than I can say."

Firm lips meet mine, then he shrugs. "You should speak to Shaw. As our unit leader, he had to make tougher decisions than most, and not all of them worked out for the best. His nightmares likely rival yours. You could help each other."

"I'll think about it."

He plays with my hair for a second before asking, "If you don't mind me asking, what happened to your husband?"

Telling pieces is always risky for this reason. Each piece is an emotional minefield waiting to blow up.

"Physically, he recovered. Emotionally and mentally, it changed him forever. He committed suicide almost two years later."

Tears flow again. I know I need to explain, but I'm hitting a wall. I've never shared this much before and it's bringing all the buried emotions to the surface.

Lowell smooths a hand down my back. "No more tonight."

Chapter Eighteen

LOWELL

WAKING UP THE NEXT MORNING, I SAVOR THE WARM FEELING OF Kate in my arms. In the past, I never would have spent the night, but with her it's different. I want to be with her. Besides, there was no way in hell I was leaving her alone after telling me about the past.

Her sweet pink lips beg to be kissed and I lean down to capture them with my own. She stiffens, and her eyes fly open. I chuckle. I guess she isn't used to sleeping with anyone either. That little reaction gives me immense satisfaction. Her tension eases when she recognizes me, her smile a bit wobbly, but it's there.

"Good morning, Lowell."

I lean back to assess her face. "Mmm. I love waking up with you in my arms. How are you feeling?" Her eyes are full of guarded determination. I'm not surprised. She's been incredibly strong and stubborn in dealing with the past on her own. It's going to take time for her to open up fully and share those burdens.

She makes a face and responds quietly, "I'm not sure yet. Better now that I know you didn't run away. Desperately in need of coffee, but ready to get to work."

"I'll get a pot going for you. Unfortunately, I have a conference call with my editor in about an hour. Are you okay with me sharing your past with Lev and Shaw?"

I watch her face close down. Her first instinct is to tell me no, but I know how she feels about Lev, and of her budding attraction for Shaw, so I'm hoping she changes her mind.

She takes a deep breath and gives me a nod. "I guess so."

Brushing my lips against hers, I whisper, "Thank you. I don't like to keep secrets from them, and I don't want you to have to keep reliving the story."

Giving her another quick kiss, I get out of bed and stretch. Her eyes track down my body, taking in every inch, including my morning wood which only hardens further with her eyes on it.

Groaning, I reprimand her. "Stop. I won't be able to concentrate because I'll be thinking about you staring at my cock all day."

Her eyes fly up to meet mine, but a small smile appears.

That's better. "I'll text you later." Dragging on my clothes, I head out the door, leaving her to get ready for the day.

Driving to the ranch, my thoughts are buzzing. I sent a text to Lev and Shaw before I left, so they'll be waiting when I get home. Lev will want to become her knight in shining armor, but I'm not sure what Shaw will do or say. Given his past, he'll probably empathize with her story more than most, which means he'll try to help her.

Reaching the house, I run upstairs to grab one of my laptops, the one that allows me access to classified information. Things like police reports. Walking into the living room, I notice both Lev and Shaw are sitting on the edge of their seats, waiting to hear about our Kate. Setting down the laptop, I strike a few keys to start a search on Kate's story while I tell them what I know. When the search results ping, I twirl the laptop around so we can read the details.

After skimming the report and confirming the shooter is

dead, I explain how she lost her friends and colleagues, almost lost her life and her husband's life, and finally her career, because of a grieving father with a gun.

Shaw pales. When he digests the information, his head drops into his hands.

Lev's eyes close briefly before he jumps up and starts pacing. "Wait, she's married?"

"Her husband committed suicide a couple of years later. So essentially, she lost her husband too," the gravity of my tone breaks through to him.

Lev stops pacing and stares at me. "Fuck!" he roars. "I knew it was bad when she kept avoiding any personal discussions, but damn, I didn't know it was this bad. Is she okay? Should I go over there and stay with her?"

"She said she was fine this morning and ready to start the day." Running my hands through my hair, I turn to Shaw. "I just don't buy it though. Shaw, what do you think? You're probably the only person who has gone through anything remotely close to this situation."

Shaw looks up, his face drawn as his own past reflects in his eyes. "She's been dealing with it by herself for a long time. Too much hovering could make her retreat. Too little and she could feel like we don't understand. Let's keep in contact with her today, and tomorrow night Lev can stay with her for a while. When's she ready to talk, I'll be here for her. How did you get her to talk in the first place?"

"She told me she wanted more than just a physical relationship with me, with us actually." My gaze finds Lev, then returns to Shaw. "I want a serious relationship with her, and I told her I thought Lev did too." Lev gives me a curt nod of agreement. "But because she never shared anything serious with us, we weren't sure of her. I don't think she even realized how much she was holding back. And I have a feeling there's more, but I think this is all she could tell us right now."

Looking up, I see Lev and Shaw thinking along the same lines.

"Fuck." Lev immediately starts pacing again.

Chapter Nineteen

KATE

ALL THREE MEN TEXT ME THROUGHOUT THE DAY, CHECKING ON ME, making sure I don't need anything from them. I'm relieved they know and don't hate me or want me to stop seeing patients. There have been times over the years when employees at a hospital or practice found out about the shooting and decided it would be better if they were assigned a different doctor.

But it also makes me want to crawl into a hole and hide. I feel so exposed and vulnerable right now, like I've been flayed open. My first instinct is to run, but it would devastate me to leave them, so I shove it all down deep inside.

My phone buzzes with another text. It's Lev asking me to go away to the winery this weekend, and the nervous worry I've been carrying around all morning, dissipates. Instead, a giddy feeling invades my body. Every place I've gone the last few years was either alone or with my mom. A weekend away with Lev sounds incredible. Plus, I haven't been away from the practice since I arrived, and a change of scenery will help clear my mind. I send him a quick yes and let him know we'll close at four p.m. today.

Smiling, I round the corner and barely avoid running into Sarah.

Her eyes narrow. "Hmmm. Someone is doing better. That's good. After the way you looked this morning, I thought I'd have to knock some heads together."

After my discussion with Lowell last night, I realized Sarah should also know the truth. She's the first true friend I've made in a while, and I don't want her to find out from someone else.

"Hey, do you have a minute?"

Frowning at the expression on my face, she follows me back to the office and closes the door. Sitting in the two chairs in front of the desk, I walk through what I told Lowell last night. Stunned, she sits there for a minute, then reaches out to pull me into a hug. I start crying at this immediate gesture from her big heart.

She lets me sob for a few minutes before pulling back and blurting out, "Did I ever tell you about the time I dropped a baby?"

I stop crying and wipe my face.

When she sees my incredulous expression, a look of chagrin flashes across her face. "I don't even have an excuse. I had been a nurse for five years, and as I was trying to weigh him, he bowed up and slid right out of my hands. Thankfully, it was only the counter, and he landed just right, but it could have been devastating."

Thinking back, she shakes her head. "For a long time, I couldn't even hold a baby without freaking out. Finally, I decided avoidance wasn't an option. As a nurse, I have to handle children, including babies. Determined to get over my fear, I started holding them for a brief time until I could work up to weighing one again."

"That was an accident! You're a wonderful nurse," I laughingly protest.

"Well, I'm sure you didn't give David a nausea medication to get him kicked out of the trial, did you? Before him, did you ever have a patient qualify for a study?" She waits for my answer.

"Well, no."

"Point proven. Best practice would have been to discuss it with a doctor who had experience with trials, but honestly, doctors make decisions all the time and correct them later. You didn't get that chance," she tells me. "The whole thing was a terrible, tragic accident. It won't affect our friendship in the slightest. We're BFFs for life now, girl. You can't get rid of me so easily." With tears in her eyes, she hugs me again. "I'm so sorry though, for everything you've been through."

Relieved to hear her words, I feel so grateful I ended up here in Montana. It feels like a fresh start, something I didn't think would ever happen again.

Chapter Twenty

KATE

OPENING THE DOOR LATER THAT EVENING, LEV STRIDES IN AND encases me in a massive hug, and the rest of the lingering tension releases from my body. This man knows how to give good hugs. It's like all the warmth from him seeps into the cold tundra inside of me, and melts it piece by piece.

"Hey there, stranger." I'd missed seeing him earlier in the week because he'd been busy opening a restaurant in Bozeman, his first in that location.

"Hello, sweetheart." Raising his head, he studies my face intently. "It changes nothing for me. I've been all in from the beginning. I'm devastated for you, and anything I can do to help, let me know and I'll do it. I'll be here to help you with your past, but know this, I want your future. That's where I want to go with you."

My breath catches and I stare at him, stunned to see the serious expression on his usually easygoing face. My eyes tear up thinking about it, because I want a future with him too, but he still doesn't know it all. Until he does, I don't want to make any declarations to him.

Smiling to let him know I heard him, my response is simple.

"Thank you, that means a lot to me. The last few years have been hard. People have judged me harshly without even knowing all the facts. I started asking for shorter assignments so I could move on before they could find out or recognize me. It's made my life incredibly lonely to be cut off from the most basic of friendships, but it meant I could continue to work and help people." I can't help but place a kiss on those pouty lips of his. "The acceptance from Lowell, Sarah, and you has meant the world to me."

Raising my hand to his heart, he lets me feel its strong and steady beat. "Sweetheart, we're the lucky ones." Leaning down, he gives me a long, deep, passionate kiss full of everything he doesn't say, and I thoroughly bask in the sensation of warmth and emotion this man gives me so freely. Groaning, he breaks away and sighs. "As much as I'd like to stand here and kiss you, we have to get going so we can get to the winery before dark. Are you ready?"

Grabbing my bag and jacket, I step over and punch in the code to set the alarm. Minutes later, my bag is in the back and we're on the road, my hand firmly held in his.

A little over two hours later, we pull into a driveway surrounded by vines on each side. Row after row of green lines producing yummy goodness. It's been a while since I've been to a winery.

Chuckling, he tells me, "If I'd have known you would be this excited, we'd have come sooner."

"I thought about it every day since our first date. At the time, I wasn't ready to go away with you for the weekend, but now I am." A blush spreads across my cheeks with my less than subtle hint. I want him, but I'm nervous because it's a big step for us.

Inhaling sharply, he squeezes my hand. The valet is waiting when we pull up front, and Lev hands him the keys before grabbing our bags from the back. Entering the lobby, I slowly spin around to admire the sophisticated boutique hotel. The style is more French country than Montana, with its huge whitewashed fireplace. Besides the cozy spots all over the lobby, there's a restaurant and bar where people can gather and socialize.

After checking in, Lev hands me a key to the room. On the fourth floor, we walk into a room made for romance with its airy, white linens and view of the vines. It feels like a grand room in someone's house, not a hotel. There's even a small gas fireplace set into the wall.

"Very romantic," I tease Lev as he drops our bags onto the luggage rack.

"Well, I figured it couldn't hurt." Grinning, he gathers me in his arms and peppers small kisses down my neck. "Dinner is in a half hour, if you want to change and freshen up. Or we could just stay here for the rest of the evening."

Laughing, I push him away. "I'm starving." His raises his eyebrows suggestively, causing me to groan and push him away. "For food. Feed me."

After an exaggerated sigh, he flops down onto the bed to stare up at me. "Why don't you go first, as it won't take me long to get ready?"

Chuckling, I head to the bathroom, grab a quick shower, brush my teeth, and put on some make-up. Then I pad back out in my towel to find some clothes for dinner.

His eyes trail across my smooth, damp skin, and jumps up from the bed. With only a few strides, he reaches me. "Are you sure you want to go to dinner? I can order us room service to eat here. Just the two of us. Naked." His hand caresses my shoulders, slipping down to hook his finger in my cleavage and tug lightly on the towel.

"Stop. Food first."

His finger slides to the side to caress my nipple, and heat pools lower on my body.

I let the towel slip a bit. "Feed me, and I'll reward you later."

"Hmmm, reward?" He leans down and licks his way up my

neck. "You're all the reward I need, but I guess we need to eat." His stomach growls, and he gives a loud laugh. "Fine, fine. I'll get a shower." With raised hands, he backs away.

Rifling through the suitcase, I pull out a black silky tank top, royal blue pleated skirt, and black fuzzy cropped cardigan. Strappy black heels complete the picture. Getting dressed quickly, I'm arranging my hair when Lev steps out of the bathroom with a towel wrapped around his hips.

It's my turn to drool. His body is thick, muscular, and perfect. My hands clench as I hold them at my sides instead of touching him like I want.

"Breathe, sweetheart." With a wicked smile on his face, he moves closer.

"Stop. Nope. Seriously. I need you. I mean, I need food. Then you. Don't come any closer." Swinging my head from side to side, I reinforce the words coming out of my mouth. It would be more effective if I could give him some privacy, but I can't. My eyes refuse to peel themselves away from the sexiest man I've ever seen.

With a wry smile, he grabs some clothes, but instead of turning away to dress, he deliberately drops the towel to stand in front of me for a minute.

Deep breath. Wow. Another deep breath. His body is magnificent. I know I'm staring, but I can't stop. I've seen him without his shirt, but the entire package is overwhelming. Lev's built, with sheer muscles that seemingly stack symmetrically on top of each other to create a magnificent package. Speaking of package... Sweet baby. I'm hot and achy now. Mission accomplished.

He smirks and slides one leg into a pair of boxer briefs, then the other. He looks so good. Too damn good. I'm really trying to talk myself into turning away, but it's impossible. When he finishes buttoning the green button-down that clearly matches his eyes and grabs a grey sport coat, I'm finally able to turn away.

Fanning myself, I turn to the mirror to finish getting ready. I almost don't recognize the flushed face and sparkling eyes staring at me. I haven't seen myself turned on in a long time. Spritzing a bit of perfume and adding a dainty gold necklace, I turn to face him. "I'm ready."

He picks up my hand to place a kiss in the center. "Beautiful." Tingles radiate in my palm. "I'm the luckiest man."

Entering the restaurant, I see beautiful tables set with candlelight, a fireplace burning low in the background, and soft lighting, creating the perfect romantic ambiance. As we sit down, the owner comes over personally to deliver our wine menu and talk to Lev. He's a slightly older man, maybe mid-forties, with an old-school fake tan and sparkling white teeth. The kind of man you might see in California, not Montana.

"Lev, glad to see you. How do you like your room?" Reaching out, he shakes Lev's hand, but his eyes dart over to me.

Smoothly, Lev stands to return the handshake. "Howard, how are you? Everything is superb, thank you. Our room is beautiful, and we're looking forward to dinner. Tomorrow, we'll explore the grounds and get the full wine tasting experience."

"That's great. Sounds like you have everything you need." He moves over to my side of the table, picks up one of my hands, and brushes a moist kiss on the back of it. I think. Surely he didn't lick my hand. I try to tug it from his, but he tightens his grip. "And who might you be?"

Lev's eyes are locked on him as the man continues to hold my hand. "My girlfriend, Kate Michaels. Kate, this is Howard Gentry, the owner of the winery and hotel."

"Nice to meet you, Howard. Your winery and hotel are incredible." Pulling my hand from his, I slide it under the table.

"Thank you, but the beauty outside does not compare to the beauty before me." He has the audacity to rest his hand on my bare shoulder and lightly rub back and forth. I wish I'd thought to put on the cardigan.

My eyes flick to Lev with a silent demand.

A hard expression comes over Lev's face when he sees Howard touching me, and he gives me a nod to let me know he'll take care of it. In one smooth move, he pulls me up from the chair and into his side. His hand firmly sweeps across the same shoulder, erasing Howard's slimy touch.

"We apprcciate your hospitality. Please, don't let us keep you from enjoying your other important guests. I believe I saw the Mayor of Helena walk by a second ago?"

Howard's eyes drift from my head to my toes, as if to memorize every inch of me. Returning his eyes to Lev, a jolt goes through him, and he nervously swallows at his dangerous expression. "You're right. I must see to the other guests, thank you for the reminder. Please have a wonderful dinner and excuse me. It was nice meeting you, Kate Michaels."

Lev remains standing for another minute, his eyes narrowed on Howard.

I tug him back down. "It's fine."

He shakes his head once. "No, it isn't. In the past, I've always dealt with his rep, not him. After meeting him, I'll have to rethink any future orders."

While I agree, I don't want to sit here and dwell on that creep the rest of the evening. "You handled it perfectly. Thank you. Let's just enjoy our dinner." I reach up and smooth the frown lines on his forehead.

Capturing my hand, he links his fingers with mine and picks up the wine menu. "You're right. This is our weekend."

After ordering, Lev leans forward with a serious look on his face and murmurs, "When Lowell told us your story, he mentioned you wanted more than just a physical relationship with him, with me. Is that true?"

"Yes." I'm not sure where this is going. He seems restless, almost like he's nervous. "Lowell is…" I don't know how much to reveal about my relationship with Lowell.

"Lowell is? Sweetheart, I want you to talk to me." His hand raises my chin so I can see he's sincere.

Reaching out for my wine, I take a sip, then continue, "Lowell is very dominant physically, but he can be detached emotionally. I couldn't tell if he was interested in only the physical, or if he could see more for us."

Lev searches my eyes for something. "It's good that you push him for more. He needs to know he can't remain detached if he wants a relationship. How are you feeling about dating us both? Or being in a relationship with us both?"

"It's been easier and harder than I thought. I don't know where the lines are drawn. It's easy to care about you both, and each of you connect with different sides of me. But I have to be honest, it's hard to think about the future. Why do you think this can work? What do I do if I start to have feelings for someone else?"

Lev stiffens when he hears the last question. "Is there someone else?"

Shifting restlessly in my chair, I pause, then quietly tell him about my growing feelings for Shaw. "I don't know what to do. Please don't get me wrong, he has never shown me anything but friendship, but I have these feelings and I feel like you should know. I'm trying to be more transparent with you and Lowell."

Relief crosses his face. "Sweetheart, if you have feelings for Shaw, you need to speak to him about those feelings. From my perspective, and Lowell's, we love our brothers, and if one of them makes you happy, then that makes us happy."

Confused, I tilt my head. "How can you be so sure this won't blow up in our faces?"

Silently, Lev reaches out and takes a drink of wine. This is the first true sign of nervousness he has displayed tonight. "I don't know that it won't. In fact, it's one of my biggest concerns." He pauses. "You should know that we fell for a woman in the past. All four of us. She worked in intelligence with Lowell and helped Shaw lead our operations from the control center. It was very serious."

"All four of you dated someone else? Had a relationship with her?"

His eyes become distant with memories. "Her name was Vanessa. Shaw and Thayer called her Nessa. She was closest to those two, but she brought something to all four of our lives. We didn't set out to date one woman, but given the secrecy demanded for our operations, it was hard to have a relationship outside of the Army at all. Sharing everything, including our love, felt right."

Jealousy punches me in the stomach as I listen to his story. "What happened?"

"She wanted a political career. Being in a relationship with four men would have hindered that ambition. Vanessa broke it off, moved to D.C., climbed the ladder, got married, and had a baby. She got what she needed. After our last tour, we resigned from the Army, moved to Montana, and dealt with the fallout the best we could."

When his gaze turns to me, his green eyes are dark with remembered hurt. "Shaw burned the candle at both ends to expand the ranch until it was five times the size of the original operation. I jumped into helping Shaw, then started my restaurant business. Lowell escaped into writing. Thayer…"

He pauses for a second. "In the beginning, he threw himself into every adrenaline-fueled activity he could find, with little regard for his safety. Thankfully, he stopped pushing himself. Until he heard about the baby at Christmas. Even though it had been three years since we last saw Vanessa, the baby triggered him. He started pushing his physical boundaries again, and his accident happened not long after."

All four of these men have been through their own kind of hell. I'm not sure if it helped them to know the others were hurting too or if it made it worse. "I'm so sorry, Lev, sorry that you all lost someone you loved." I squeeze his hand. "I can only imagine how hard it was for her to make that decision and lose all of you."

Lev rears back, a bleak expression on his face, as if my last words hit hard. "What?"

"The world can be very cruel. Standing against the norm, whether or not it's by choice, is an incredibly tough thing to do. Sometimes it's just a slash of the knife from the words thrown at you, sometimes events occur that bring you to your knees and rip your world apart. I'm not sure a relationship with four men is an easy thing to choose."

"It's not that I don't understand." He takes a deep breath and blows it out. Silence reigns for a few seconds, then his eyes dart from me to stare out at the night. "I was hoping for a miracle, I think."

I study his face, trying to understand what he's thinking. Going through the conversation, I realize he thinks I'll make the same decision as Vanessa and leave them when the job is finished.

"Lev, I'm not Vanessa." Laying my hand on one of his clenched hands, I wait until his eyes meet mine again. "While I can completely sympathize with her choices, my life is in a completely different place than hers. My normal was ripped from my hands and shredded beyond repair. My normal is having people think I'm at fault for the murder of thirteen innocent people. Fourteen, if you count David's father. Since I've been here and met all three of you, I've realized my normal means I need to grab on to happiness with both hands."

I bite my lip, wanting to be honest with him. "I don't know what the future holds for all of us. I'm worried this will fall apart, and that's with just you and Lowell. What happens with me and Shaw? What if Thayer comes home and hates me? This could end very badly for me too. All these unknowns would have scared me away before because I wasn't strong enough to take any more hits and still survive. Now I have you both, and I don't feel so alone anymore. I'm growing stronger every day. All

I can do is tell you I want to be in a relationship with you and Lowell."

He's still, digesting my words, and I can't help but cup his strong jaw. "I'm officially putting my heart on the line. It's the scariest thing I've done in a long time, but I can't hold back what I feel. All I can do is hope you feel the same."

A shudder racks Lev's body, and he takes a deep breath. "I'm sorry. The old hurt kind of took me by surprise. For a second, I was back in the past and not here with you. I feel the same. I want to be your future, not your past. We'll take it one day at a time."

Relieved, my tension eases. We order dessert and a wine tasting to finish the meal. While we wait for it to arrive, I silently wonder about Vanessa. What was she like? Another woman who fit with these incredible men. Jealousy would normally be punching me in the stomach, but knowing she walked away, I only feel sadness. For me, these men are the sun, shining into a dark sky after a storm, creating a double rainbow in their wake. Bright, beautiful, and a sign of things to come.

I'm not sure what to do about Shaw yet. Should I talk to him about my feelings? Although Lev suggested I bring it up, I don't think I will. Given what Lev just told me, Shaw is struggling with the past and Vanessa.

AFTER HAVING SUCH A SERIOUS DISCUSSION, ALL WE WANTED TO DO was hold each other all night. We were worn out from the long day of travel, and last night's topic wiped us out emotionally. Wrapped up tightly in his arms, it only took me seconds to fall asleep.

Lev's dark lashes caress his high cheekbones. For several minutes, I lay in the morning sun and watch him sleep. It's the first time and I want to savor this moment. When he rolls over onto his back, I get up and grab some coffee. The view of the vineyards and nearby mountains calls to me, and I end up on the balcony. Dew shimmers on the grass in the early morning light. It's peaceful here.

A sudden noise comes from behind me, and I turn to see a half-naked Lev strolling toward me with a cup of coffee in his large hand. He reaches down to give me a soft kiss on the lips.

"Hmmm, good morning, sweetheart. I could get used to this view every day," he states, although he doesn't seem in the least bit interested in the vineyards. Rather, his attention is focused on me.

"Good morning. Totally agree. The views are incredible. Both of them." I wink at him. "I'm looking forward to the tour and wine tasting today. Aren't you?" Stretching, I raise my legs to the balcony. The robe slips a bit, getting close to flashing him, but I don't reach to close it. He stares at the edges of my robe as if he's willing it to part more. "What time is the tour?" I ask him intently, setting my coffee cup down.

"Good idea," he replies doing the same. He plucks me from the chair into his arms only to drop me on the bed. For a second, he stops, waiting for my consent, and when it leaves my lips, he immediately strips off his sweatpants.

Laughing, I untie my robe in response and slip it off.

He sucks in a harsh breath when he sees me lying there in a tiny navy blue thong and nothing else. "How the hell did I miss that thong last night?"

"Probably because I was wearing a long T-shirt over it."

His hands reach out and trail from my neck to my breasts, circling them a few times before carrying on toward the top of my thong. His fingers trace back and forth without entering.

"What happened to the shirt?"

Exhaling softly, I shiver when his fingers dip slightly below the top of my underwear. "I must have removed it during the night. Sleeping with you is like cuddling with the sun."

Lowering his head, his mouth replaces his fingers as he places small kisses along the same line. "So, you're saying I'm hot?" I feel his lips form a smile before a long slow lick sweeps across my lower stomach.

Whimpering at the light touches, my legs fall open in anticipation, and his attention moves to my legs. Pulling up my right leg, he puts it over his shoulder and leans down to suck lightly on the inside of my thigh. His nose is so close to my center, I shiver from the breaths I can feel blowing across my damp panties.

He doesn't stay there for long though. His lips lay kisses on my leg all the way up to my knee. Turning my leg slightly, he reaches out and licks behind it. My breath catches in my throat. Watching my face, he hones in on a spot and sucks.

My hips rise restlessly when tingles race back down my leg to my clit. How did I not know about I was sensitive there? Panting, I wait for him to continue, but he's staring down at my thong. The air caresses me, and I realize it must have shifted when he turned my leg, and I'm now almost completely exposed to him.

With a deep groan, he reaches out with his index finger to shift the thong to the side, completely baring me to his gaze. Lightly tracing my slit, he looks up at me before dipping his finger into it. I moan at the feeling of his large finger exploring my body. Pulling out, he brings his finger up to his mouth to taste me. Reaching back down, he dips in one finger again, then spreads my wetness all over. Again and again, he does this. Never increasing the pressure or the number of fingers.

Shifting, my breathing is heavy, and I can only lift my hips and silently plead for him to go deeper. The light touch is driving me crazy.

As if in a trance, he lowers my leg, grabs on to my thong, and pulls it off me. Pushing apart my legs, he shifts his body further down until his mouth can take over from his fingers. Unlike his light touches, his mouth devours me, licking up every bit of the wetness before delving into me. His tongue is a spear, and my hips move in time with the thrusts from his tongue, but it's not enough.

"Lev, please. I want you inside me."

Shaking his head, he gives me a long lick. Shuddering, my head falls back, leaving him to continue. He lifts my body so I'm slightly elevated and continues his assault. Except now, he's shifted his focus to my clit. Panting, I groan as he tongues the hard nub before pulling it into his mouth and sucking on it. My head rolls from side to side as the pressure builds. I'm so close. My fingers dig into the sheets and fist them. A few seconds more and I come hard; the pleasure intense. I hear my cries, but it's like they're in the distance as waves roll from my core outward until I'm completely spent. Lying there, watching him watch me, his green eyes glittering with satisfaction and heat, is everything I thought it would be, but now I want more.

Pulling him up and over my body, I kiss him deeply, showing him both my gratitude and need for more. I want him inside me, thick and pulsing, his body moving with mine.

"Sweetheart, you're irresistible." His lips skim my neck to his favorite spot and he gives it a long suck.

Arching my neck, I grip his head and wrap my legs tightly around him, wanting to feel every inch of him against my slickness.

Shuddering, he releases my neck and rasps, "I need you, Kate. More than anything, I want to be inside you."

When I whisper yes, he jumps off the bed and strolls over to his bag. Condom on, he returns and lays his big body over mine. For a second, I worry he won't fit.

"I… haven't… in over three years." I bite my lip.

With a serious nod, he eases into me, and it takes a minute for my body to adjust to the sheer thickness of him. About halfway, he stops. When I whimper and move restlessly, he flashes a wicked smile and slides in the rest of the way.

Widening my legs to ease the feel of him inside me, I breathe in and out for a second, then flex against him.

He groans. "I love the feel of you wrapped tightly around me." His hips pull back until he's halfway out, then he slides back in again.

Darts of pleasure slide up my spine and I clench him tightly. "God, I've forgotten how good this feels."

With those words, he captures my lips with his and begins to thrust in and out in a slow, controlled rhythm.

My entire body flushes with desire. Everything starts building up inside me again until I'm nearly incoherent with the need to come. It's not enough. I meet his thrusts harder, trying to urge him to go faster.

The most devilish grin crosses his face. "Want to switch places?"

His words have me nodding immediately. "Yes, now."

He scoots off the bed with us still joined, then eases down into a sitting position on the edge of the bed.

With my legs on either side of him, he goes even deeper than before and we both groan at the feel.

"Ever since that time on my couch, all I could think about was you riding my cock, and since this is your favorite position…" his voice trails off.

I reach out and trace his flushed cheeks with my fingers. His dark green eyes are almost black with need, yet he waits for me to take control. My hands explore the hard muscles in his chest and his smooth, tanned skin. Soft and hard. Light and dark. Fascinated by the contrast, I take time to explore every inch of him. He twitches inside me and thrusts upward to remind me he's waiting.

So I grip his shoulders and push him backward on the bed. When he's down, I place one hand on his shoulder and move my hips.

His lips flatten and his hands find my hips to grind me down onto him harder and closer.

My eyes find his and I lean slightly forward until he slides partially out of me. Clenching tightly, I slide back down, and when the breath whistles out of him, I know he's on the edge like me.

"How does that feel?" Without waiting for his reply, I stroke down almost to the bottom and clench even tighter when I pull back up. Hovering at the top, I pulse on his tip and his fingers flex tightly on my hips, almost as if he wants to yank me back down.

"Sweetheart, you feel so fucking good. You're so tight and wet. I'm so hard and you're squeezing my cock…" He thrusts up into me.

Hearing the desire in his strained voice and seeing the flush on his cheeks, my eyes close and savor his words. I needed to know how much he wanted me, that he wasn't pretending. In response, my hips move faster and faster. Pleasure rolls over me, and I hear his harsh breathing interlacing with my own.

"Mm… you feel so good inside me, Lev. It's been so long," I reply with a whimper of need. "I'm so close."

Lifting my body, he drives into me faster. Angling his hips, his cock hits just the right spot. Moaning loudly, I hold on tightly as we fuck harder.

In a strained voice, he tells me, "Touch yourself. I want to feel you come on my cock."

My hand slides down and my fingers part my fold so I can rub myself. I look up to find Lev watching my hand. I clench around him when a tremor hits me, and he speeds up.

"That's it, sweetheart. Come for me," he urges, his voice harsh with need.

His cock swells and it pushes me over the edge. My orgasm roars through me.

Lev gives a loud grunt and grips me hard, holding me down on his cock as he follows me, thrusting twice more before he stops completely. Panting heavily, his hands fall slack and his chest heaves while he works to catch his breath.

I fall forward onto his chest.

"Damn, sweetheart. I love how you feel sitting on my cock,

but that position is hard work." Laughing, he shakes out his hands and arms, then wraps them around me in a tight hug. "You're so beautiful when you come. Thank you."

He strokes my back as we sit there for a few minutes. Tapping my shoulder so I'll raise up, he lifts me off him and gets up to take care of the condom. Coming back to bed, he kisses me before carrying me into the shower. After carefully washing my sensitive body, we dry off and go back to bed.

He raises up on his elbow and studies me. "Every moan, whimper, and word you whisper goes straight to my cock every time. It makes me hard as a rock to hear your pleasure." After a slight hesitation, he continues. "But I get the feeling the words mean something more to you?"

He waits as I stare wordlessly at him.

Plucking at the sheet, I drop my eyes, so I don't have to see his face when I answer. "After he was shot, Collin didn't want me near him. Even the few times he let me touch him, I couldn't tell whether it felt good or not. He would just give me this blank stare. Even when I went down on him, he wouldn't tell me to stop, and while he physically got off, I don't know if he enjoyed any of it because he was so silent. I thought at first it was his condition, and I was okay with that reason, but he laughed when I suggested it. Instead, he coldly explained that my touch disgusted him, but he needed to get off. I stopped trying." Pausing, I find his eyes. "I can't stand silence."

Gathering me tightly to him, his voice is gruff when he replies, "I'm a loud, noisy fucker, and the only reason I held back was because I didn't want to scare you. Now I know I can be me."

The tension eases, but a wave of irrational fear comes over me. With every right answer, I fall deeper, and it terrifies me. I don't think I can survive anything else. Instead of responding, I burrow into his strong arms and take refuge for the next half hour until it's time to get ready.

The tour and rest of our stay is incredible. Part of me feels stronger after this trip. This weekend gave me back something I lost four years ago. Actually, a piece I threw away, because Collin had convinced me of my failure to excite him or anyone really. Never again.

We're leaving in a few minutes to go to the ranch so I can have my riding lesson and spend my usual Sunday with all three of them. It feels like going home.

Chapter Twenty-One

SHAW

Watching Kate step out of Lev's SUV, her face lit up with laughter makes me ache something fierce, and that pisses me off to no end. My inability to get off the fucking fence is driving me crazy. Watching her with them, seeing them fall deeply for her, also pisses me off.

Kate takes one look at my face and walks right past me into the barn. *Shit!* She probably thinks I'm pissed at her now. Although honestly, I am. It's totally irrational, but she's disrupting our lives. Just when things were finally normal, she waltzes into our lives.

Well, except for Thayer, but the only reason he went on that dangerous ski run was because of Nessa's baby announcement. It's been three years. He's over her, but seeing proof of how far she's moved on took Thayer to a very dark place. At least Nessa is in D.C. I can't help but think what would happen if Kate left. Montana is our home. We have nowhere else to go. She's already imprinting herself on everything around here, including us.

As my eyes adjust to the darker light, I hear her speaking sweetly to Sugar. "Hello, Sugar, sweetheart. I missed you. We're going to spend some time together and ignore the cranky man, okay?" Waiting for the horse to nuzzle her, she continues. "Us girls have to stick together, right? I had a wonderful trip with Lev, and I refuse to allow grumpy to ruin it. If we could only give him some sugar to sweeten him up." The horse snickers, and with a low chuckle, Kate holds out a piece of sugar for her.

While she talks and feeds the horse, I stand behind her, gritting my teeth, even as I admire the picture in front of me. Those jodhpurs cup her tight little ass so sweetly, my hands clench with the effort it takes to hold back. Without realizing it, my feet carry me closer to temptation. A fresh scent of raspberries and honey drifts up. Inhaling deeply, I savor the smell that is uniquely her, and my cock twitches. As I exhale, she turns and scowls at me.

"What is your problem today? I'm here on time. And stop sniffing me. I showered." She waits with her hands on her hips for my reply.

Frustrated and tired of holding back, I pull her in tight so she can feel my hard cock. "Why don't you give me a little sugar and sweeten me up today?"

My lips find hers before she can respond with a smart reply. I don't want to hear it, and I sure as hell don't want to kiss her. This is her fault. The need to punish myself and dominate the situation rides me hard, until she does the one thing I least expect—she kisses me back.

The tension between us explodes and the kiss changes to something wild and uninhibited. Her passion is a match to my control, burning my boundaries and making me feel for the first time in three years. Backing her up against the stable, our kiss becomes my entire focus and the only thing I need in that moment. It's air to breathe and a fan to the fire consuming me.

Her face wrenches to the side, and she pushes on my shoulders to step back. "Stop. We can't."

A growl of denial escapes me. "Why the hell not?"

Exhaling, she takes a few deep breaths, then slumps against the stable door. "Before Lev and Lowell, I would have taken you up on your offer. Now? Now, I... want more." Her cheeks flush with ribbons of pink. "I want a relationship, and I don't want to settle for less. You haven't even come to terms with wanting me physically, much less just wanting to know ME. If you had, you wouldn't be this angry. Am I wrong? Do you know what you want?"

Fuck, no. That's why I'm so pissed.

Her direct approach fires up the anger inside me. Two can play this game. "Aren't you temporary? Once your assignment is over, you'll leave for the next town. Why not have some fun with me too?"

She scoffs. "Are you looking for a guarantee? There are no guarantees. Not for you, and sure as hell not for me. I can't predict the future. I've agreed to give these relationships a chance. It's a hell of a risk for me. If I had known prior to coming here I'd end up in one relationship, much less two, I'd have run far away."

Hugging herself, she blows out a breath. "Something happened when I met them. Lev and Lowell fit different sides of me, and I need them both. It's been a long time since I've needed anyone, but I need them. A job is a job. I can work anywhere. I understand Lev and Lowell have a life here with you and Thayer and their work. I have no intention of asking them to leave here." The sincerity shining in her eyes conveys the truth of her words.

Her passion lingers on my lips. "You kissed me back like the world was on fire and I was the water that would save you." Frustrated and hard, I taunt her.

Fuck, what am I doing? When did I turn into this cruel bastard?

Her eyes narrow as she spits out, "It was temporary insanity that made me want you, even for just a second." She steps around to leave, and without thinking, I reach out and grab her arm. I don't want her here, but I don't want her to leave either.

Her face whitens. "Let me go. Now."

I immediately let her go.

Her green eyes are fierce in their anger. "I made a promise to myself long ago I would never live with another man who didn't treat me how I deserve. You need to get over your anger and think about what you want. I won't pretend the kiss didn't happen, but I can make sure it never happens again." She stalks off toward the house.

"Wait," I protest. "What about our lesson? My time is valuable, and I set aside this time for you. Is this how you treat all your responsibilities?" Wow, it's like my asshole just grew another asshole. Anger is filling me up inside, and I can't see past the red cloud engulfing me, wanting to lash out at someone. No, not someone, just her. When the thought hits me, I take a deep breath to try and bring myself back under control.

The second my words hit her, her pale face flushes with anger. "No, this is how I treat assholes. When you offered to teach me, you should have been clear this was going to be a burden. I agreed because I thought it was an opportunity to get to know you. I'm sure the stable in town has an experienced teacher on staff. I'd rather pay them for lessons than spend one more second around you."

My eyes narrow at the thought of her getting lessons from some idiot who will spend most of his time hitting on her. "Don't be silly. They don't know what they're doing."

She throws her hands up. "Argh! I'm a grown woman, and I sure as hell don't need your permission."

Lev comes running up to Kate and slides his arm around her. "What the fuck is going on out here? Shaw?"

"Apparently, I'm not good enough for a fuck or a lesson," I snap.

Her head jerks back as if I'd slapped her. "Lev, would you mind taking me home? I won't be staying for lunch today." Spinning around, she marches toward Lev's vehicle.

Lev's face is livid when he turns back to me. "What the fuck, man? Why are you being such an asshole? This isn't first grade. You don't piss off the girl you like. If you don't want to be with her, that's fine, but regardless, you *will* fucking treat her with respect. Do you understand? She's important to me, and for that alone, you need to get your shit together. Are you hearing me?" Jaw tight, I give him a curt nod. "We'll talk about this later."

Shit. It's rare to see Lev pissed off. I don't say a word as he turns around and stalks over to the vehicle to take Kate home.

Scowling, I turn around, only to find Lowell standing behind me, his fists held tightly to his sides. I brace myself.

"If I didn't know you cared for her, I would lay you out right now, but you need to cease this bullshit and take a stand. Either you want to build something with her and us, or you don't. Straddling the fence because you're scared will lose you more than just her," he spits out before striding away.

"Fuck!" I need to get out of here so I can think.

Chapter Twenty-Two

KATE

Once home, I curl up on the end of the couch and prop my head on my hands. Every detail plays on repeat in my head. I don't even know how things got so out of hand between Shaw and me, but it escalated fast.

His dark brown eyes were snapping with anger the second I got out of the truck, but I wasn't late for the lesson. Did something else piss him off and he just took it out on me? Or is he pissed because he wants me? We've been dancing around each other for weeks.

My lips are still tingling from the memory of his kiss. I knew the chemistry was good between us, but damn, I didn't know how hot we could burn. His anger lit a fire, but feeling his hard body pressed against mine for the first time set me ablaze. Every ounce of me came alive just for him, and I couldn't resist showing him how I felt. For a moment, I lost myself to the desire, but he couldn't hide the tinge of anger in his hard lips. Memories from the past ripped through me and I knew I had to pull away. What had spewed out of his mouth a moment later justified my concerns, even if it was utter bullshit.

When he grabbed my arm, I had a flashback to Collin, but thankfully Shaw released it. I didn't feel threatened by him, but tolerating his manhandling is a different matter. I'll never let another man treat me like Collin, no matter the circumstance.

Exhaustion hits me and I can barely keep my eyes open. I slide deeper into the cushions and pull the throw over me. With the TV on for noise, I let myself drift. My phone pings and I reluctantly lift it up to view the message.

> Lowell: How are you doing?

> Kate: I'm shocked and pissed off. Plus, I'm tired. Need a nap.

> Lowell: Thayer woke up. We're on our way to the hospital. We'll talk later about Shaw. Sleep well, love. Let us know if you need anything.

Thayer's awake. Blond hair and a bright smile flashes in my mind, the only impression I can recall from the pictures on the mantle. I try to bring up details, but it's impossible. In most of the pictures, he wore a hat and glasses as if he didn't want to be recognized. Unease skates down my spine.

Chapter Twenty-Three

KATE

"WHAT ARE YOU DOING THIS WEEKEND?" I ASK SARAH.

She turns and grins. "I've got a date, and not with a rancher or a cowboy. No boots. No hat. We're going to the Montana Club. Sophistication city."

"Oooh, that's a wonderful place. Lowell took me dancing there, and it is definitely swanky. What are you wearing? How did you two meet?"

"A dark blue strapless midi with a slit to here. It screams sexy sophistication." She holds a hand at the very top of her thighs. "A friend introduced us. He's an actor on hiatus for the summer."

"An actor. Wow. Show me a pic."

Sarah brings up a pic on her phone, showing a blond man with movie star good looks and a serious number of tattoos. "He's playing in this new mini-series on one of the premium channels. I haven't seen it yet, but I'm binging it this weekend."

"Oof, he's hot. Lucky man meeting you. I can't wait to hear all about this date." Grinning, I waggle my eyebrows at her.

"Fingers crossed. Seriously, he better not be a dud." She frowns slightly before shrugging it off. "How's Thayer? Have you gotten any more news from the guys?"

"They've been up there all week. Thayer drifted in and out the first few days, but they said he's fully awake and alert now. They're running tests to see how much feeling he has in his extremities and if he's experiencing any nerve damage. That's about all I know right now."

"Are you doing anything this weekend? We could hang out Saturday night?" Sarah loops her stethoscope around her neck.

"Tonight, I'm going to Helena to see a movie. By myself. But let's definitely get together on Saturday. Just text me. If plans change because of your new Romeo, let me know."

"It's a date." She hurries to grab her things. "Got to go. I need every minute to get to the level of sexy I want to achieve tonight. Text you tomorrow. Have fun tonight."

"You too!"

I grab my phone and search for a list of movie times. If I leave in the next thirty minutes, I can grab a bite at Lev's restaurant in Helena before the show starts. Rushing upstairs, I get ready, and I'm out the door with only a couple minutes to spare.

Even the short distance to Helena gives me too much time to think. While I've gotten a few texts from Lowell and Lev this week, Shaw has been silent. My mouth turns down. I thought I'd at least get an apology, but it's been crickets. Maybe all his focus is on Thayer or maybe he's avoiding me.

Unfortunately, Lowell left last night to go to New York to see his editor, and Lev left this morning for a wine auction in Las Vegas. It's the first weekend I've been entirely alone in over a month. They've changed my life so much with their presence that it feels like I'm missing a limb.

Dinner is delicious, of course. After eating, I head to the movie. It's dark in the theatre but I can easily see I'm the only person sitting alone. For the last three years, I've gone to plenty of movies by myself. This is what my life was like before them. How did I not realize how isolated I had let myself become? I think I tolerated it because I felt safe. There wasn't anyone to berate or judge me. Shaking my head, I reach into the popcorn and let myself get caught up in the movie.

On the way home, I hear my phone ping with a message, but I refuse to look while I'm driving. A few minutes later, I'm incredibly glad I didn't check, as a massive deer runs out of the brush, slamming into my vehicle. The SUV spins around, then hurtles into the guardrail. Instead of stopping, it proceeds to flip over the barrier and tumble down a hill into a ravine. Upside down when it stops, I'm left hanging by my seat belt.

Shit.

My shaky hands press against the pounding in my chest, and I take a few minutes to calm myself. The accident happened so fast. My lights shine into the dark night like a beacon.

I wonder if the deer made it?

Stupid, I know, but I can't help hoping it did. I'm alive, and I want it to be too. Although, it's likely injured.

Pain streaks across my shoulder when I raise my hand to check for injuries. My head hurts. I reach up and run my fingers along my forehead and encounter a laceration along my hairline. I probe the edges and a sticky wetness coats my fingers, which means it's bleeding. The blood isn't flowing so I leave it and move on to map the rest of my head. There are no other bumps, cuts, or depressions.

Both arms are sore but functional. I can wiggle my toes. Breathing is almost steady with no raspiness. A head injury seems to be the worst of it, I think. Although, I'm stuck in the vehicle. Thankfully, I have an in-vehicle service that detects when I've been involved in an accident, and a voice informs me that emergency services are on their way.

It's the last thing I remember until I wake up in the emergency room. After shining a light in my eyes and probing the tender area on my head, they get my personal information, then wheel me off to x-ray. When I return two hours later, Shaw is sitting in a chair beside the bed. Frowning, I peer around for Lev and Lowell, then remember they're still out of town.

"What are you doing here?"

At the sound of my voice, he jumps up. "When Lev heard about the accident, he asked me to come get you. He can't get a flight out until late tomorrow. I haven't gotten a hold of Lowell yet." His eyes are dark and intent as they rake over all my cuts and bruises. Lingering on the bandage on my head, he says nothing for a minute, then continues. "If you don't mind, I want to stay and help."

Relief pours over me. I'm thankful he's here and seems to have put aside his anger for now. "Thank you. I'm feeling pretty battered right now." Shaw steps out while the nurse helps me back in bed, but the second it's done, he reclaims his chair beside me.

The doctor returns fifteen minutes later. "You're a very lucky lady. Besides the usual cuts and bruises, you came out of this with a concussion. It could have been a lot worse." Pausing, he shows me the x-rays because he knows I'll want to see them myself. "As a doctor, I'm sure you know the drill. You need someone to stay with you for the next forty-eight hours and periodically wake you up."

I bite my bottom lip and dart a glance at Shaw.

He's staring intently at the doctor. "Do I need to give her any medicine or an ice pack?"

"I'll prescribe painkillers for the next couple of days." Looking back at me, he continues. "Besides the head, you'll be extremely sore. Ice as needed. Take it easy for a few days. If you notice any unusual symptoms, contact me." He hands Shaw my prescription. Then turning to me, he props his hands on his hips and narrows his eyes. "Absolutely no driving. I mean it. Take it easy. I hate treating doctors. You make the worst damn patients."

I thank him for his excellent care, and he waves as he spins out the door to his next patient. The nurse walks in with a wheelchair and raises an eyebrow at Shaw.

Shaw's face turns red and he dips his chin. "There's a pair of

Lowell's sweatpants and sweatshirt for you by the bed. I'll fill your prescription, then pull my truck around to the entrance."

My lips twitch. Everyone worries about doctors, but it's the nurses that hold the real power, and they know it. Once dressed, she wheels me out the front door where Shaw is waiting by a large green truck with the passenger door open. Damn, it's too massive for me to get in by myself.

Shaw comes forward and gently scoops me up as if I'm a child. He carefully sets me down in the front seat and pulls my seat belt around me. A blanket appears out of nowhere, which he tucks around my legs.

"I hope you don't mind, but I'm taking you back to the ranch. It will be easier for me to watch over you there; plus, Lowell and Lev will want to see you the second they return."

Without replying, I lean my head back and close my eyes. Waking slightly when we get to the ranch, I'm vaguely aware of Shaw picking me up to carry me into the house. I lay my head on his shoulder and let him take me wherever he wants.

He smells incredible, I think drowsily. Outdoorsy, with a subtle hint of musk.

Setting me gently down on a bed, he pulls out a T-shirt from one of the drawers. Once I've exchanged the sweatshirt for the soft, cotton shirt, he eases me down on the bed and strips off the sweatpants. I'm asleep before he finishes.

Per the doctor's orders, he continues to wake me periodically throughout the night. Once I answer all his questions, he lets me drift off again.

In the early morning hours, I wake to find him sleeping beside me, his big, warm body loosely wrapped around mine. The long night shows on his haggard face. Shifting, I try to move farther away, but his arm comes down to hold me in place, and I wince.

"Shaw, let me up. I need to go to the bathroom."

Waking immediately, he stands beside the bed and rubs his hand across his face. I feel myself blush when I see his morning wood. Without saying a word, he reaches down and lifts me into his arms.

I loop my arm around his thick neck. "Whoa, I can walk."

He completely ignores my protest. In the bathroom, he points out the extra toothbrush lying beside the sink and the washcloths stacked in a drawer in case I want to freshen up. He informs me he'll be waiting outside the door when I'm ready.

I want to roll my eyes, but even my eyeballs hurt. The reflection in the mirror is pretty grim too. Besides the bandage on my head, bruises are forming in several places. I'm going to have at least one black eye. Shadows along my jaw and down my neck indicate more bruising. My shoulder throbs and I slip the T-shirt down to assess the damage. A deep red stripe almost two inches wide appears. The seat belt left a wicked impression behind.

Pain everywhere. I need some painkillers. Hurrying, I finish up, open the door, and find Shaw leaning against the wall. Wide shoulders, a tapered lean waist, and thick thighs is all I see.. And, of course, those snug boxer briefs showcasing everything he has to offer.

He straightens, picks me up, and carries me back to bed. After giving me a couple of painkillers, he slips into bed and pulls me close. Stiffening, I lay there for a few minutes. His hard body and acres of warm skin remind me of just how close to naked he is right now. Feeling my tension, his hands lightly rub up and down my back in a soothing manner. I wonder how he feels about the two of us in bed together, but I'm too exhausted to ask. Instead, I surrender to sleep.

Chapter Twenty-Four

KATE

THE SUN IS SHINING BRIGHTLY WHEN I WAKE AGAIN, BUT SHAW IS gone. I ease into a sitting position and take a few moments to study my surroundings. I've never been in this room, but it's undoubtedly Shaw's room.

Masculine tones of black and maroon should make the room dark, but the huge wall of windows on my right keeps it from feeling gloomy. They also showcase the mountain view perfectly. There's not much in the space, but that's not surprising. Shaw seems like a man who cares little for clutter or unimportant things. Two ginormous chairs and an ottoman are sitting in front of an imposing fireplace. I bet that's a cozy reading spot in the winter. A glass of wine, or in Shaw's case—bourbon—and it would be a haven from the world.

He enters, and when he sees I'm awake, his long legs eat up the distance between us. I'm both relieved and disappointed to see he's dressed, not that I can do much in my condition even if he did want me.

Dark eyes are full of concern. "How are you feeling? Would you like to use the restroom? What about something to eat? I can scramble some eggs for you."

Knowing I can't leave yet, I agree to both. After carrying me to the restroom, he waits until I finish and takes me back to bed. Twenty minutes later, he returns with scrambled eggs, toast, bacon, and fresh orange juice.

I immediately grab the juice and swallow half of it down. My throat is completely dry. "Wow. You didn't have to go to all this trouble. A piece of toast would have been plenty." This man knows how to take care of someone. It must be ingrained in his DNA.

"Those painkillers are pretty powerful. You need more food than your usual." He runs his hands through his hair. Sitting on the side of the bed, he gives me the bad news. "Lev and Lowell are stuck. They've grounded flights in both cities due to storms. So it's you and me today."

I blink at his news and wonder if he's upset about this latest update. To reassure him, I offer a way out. "I can call Sarah. She's qualified to look after me. Then you can go back to whatever you had planned for this weekend."

Instead of relief, he frowns heavily. "If that's what you want."

I don't but it might be for the best. Picking up my phone, I call Sarah. She doesn't answer, so I leave a message. "Hey, Sarah, it's Kate. I had a minor accident last night. I'm okay, but I have a slight concussion and need someone to stay with me. If you're free tonight, give me call. Thanks!"

Shaw waits as I finish breakfast. "Do you want to watch TV or read a book?"

Drowsy after the long night of constant check-ins and the hearty breakfast, I'm surprisingly still tired. I shake my head and slide deeper into the bed. "I think I'll rest some more."

Something's beeping. I wake. Tubes and machines are scattered around me, giving essential fluids and readings. Groggy, I stare at where they're attached to my body. Why am I in the hospital?

Gunshots reverberate in my head. A cold hospital floor. My blood pouring out of me at an alarming rate. The images slow. Gasping, I skim my chest. Bandages across my torso. "I'm alive." Crying in relief, gratitude fills me for just a second before I remember... "Collin."

Repeatedly hitting the call button for the nurse, I can't help but be thankful for the placement of the shots. An inch here or there and I would have died. Finally, a nurse arrives, and I grab her hand. "Did my husband survive?"

She pats my hand and assures me Collin is alive. A fresh flood of tears is the only reaction I can give. I smile up at her, but her expression makes me pause. Poker face. She's hiding something. Worried, I beg her to tell me, but she only reaches up and adjusts the drip. My thoughts become foggy again as the sedative works its magic.

"Collin!" Tears stream down my face.

A deep voice enters the darkness surrounding me, imploring me to wake up. "Kate, angel, wake up. It's okay. I've got you."

Slowly, I surface from the dream. Except it's not a dream. It's a memory. A memory of the exact moment I realized I survived the shooting. Tears stream down my face. It's been a long time since I thought of that moment. It must have been the hospital visit that triggered it.

Shaw's large hands continue their path along my body. Soothing. I lean into his strength and pull some into myself. My eyes meet his dark brown ones. I should probably apologize for interrupting his sleep for the second night in a row, but I don't want to break the silence between us.

Shaw grabs a tissue from the nightstand and gently wipes my face, collecting my tears until there are no more.

"You were crying in your sleep, yelling for someone called Collin?"

My fingers twist the hem of his shirt, then smooth it out. "Hospital triggered my memories of the past. It's the first time I've been in one since the shooting." Exhaling, I run shaking hands over his chest as I gather my courage to tell him. "Collin was my husband."

"I'm so sorry for your loss."

"Thank you," I murmur, feeling his heart beat under my palm. "I'm sorry I woke you up."

He gathers me gently in his arms. "The past never lets me sleep long. I've learned to grab a nap when I can. But you don't have to worry. I'm here, and I'm not leaving." He continues to murmur softly to me until I fall asleep.

The sun is setting in the sky when I wake, the windows showcasing the vibrant pinks and oranges streaking across the horizon.

Shaw walks in and his eyes assess me closely. "Good, you're awake. Would you like some dinner? Lev stores extras in the freezer, or I can grill a steak for you."

My stomach rumbles loudly, clearly answering for me. Blushing, I nod. "Steak sounds delicious." I scoot to the side of the bed, but he stops and picks me up.

"Hold on." Secure in his arms, he stares down at me.

I slide him an exasperated look. "Shaw, I can walk, and I'm feeling much better."

His soft expression hardens into a glare.

Making a sour face, I loop my arms around his neck and let him carry me all the way to the patio.

He gently deposits me on a chaise and walks over to start the grill. Without his heat or the sun to warm me, the night air is chilly.

Shaw notices my shiver and grabs a blanket off a nearby couch. Brown eyes linger on my legs for a brief second until they're completely covered.

"Thanks," I say, snuggling into it. "It's so beautiful out here. I've never seen stars shine so brightly."

He glances up at the sky and nods. "I've been to many places —the jungle, deserts across the world, and almost every major city, and yet nothing compares with the night sky here in

Montana. It was all I could think about the entire time I was in the service." There's a note of sadness in his voice when he talks about the past.

He turns off the grill and plates the steaks. "Let me grab the salad from the fridge and some drinks. Do you want me to carry you over to the table?" He jerks his head at the one on the patio.

Rolling my eyes, I give him a mock glare. He laughs in return, and I stare at him in stunned silence. I've never seen him laugh. His whole face lights up, the semi-permanent scowl disappears, and he looks relaxed and happy.

Noticing my staring, he quickly stops laughing. "What is it? Are you feeling okay?" He strides over.

Putting my hands up in the air, I stop him. "I'm fine. I've never seen you laugh, and I was enjoying it. Especially since I was the one who made you laugh."

Clearing his throat, it's his turn to roll his eyes at me before he heads to the kitchen, but in the window's reflection, I see him smile.

Chapter Twenty-Five

SHAW

HER BATTERED BODY LOOKS EVEN WORSE TONIGHT. BRUISES COVER her delicate skin, growing darker with every second that passes, a stark contrast to her pale body. An air of fragileness clings to her. Even with all the damage to her body, she's so gorgeous and warm she makes me throb with need. I turn away so she can't see the desire in my eyes. That's the last thing she needs especially after our fight.

Thank goodness she thought to give the hospital Lev's name when she got there. He didn't even have to ask me to go. As soon as I heard him say, "Kate's been in an accident," I was grabbing my keys. Unsure of what I would find when I got there, my heart beat a mile a minute the entire trip. Her room was empty when I arrived and for a second, I assumed the worst. And it hit me in a way I didn't expect.

A passing nurse told me Kate was getting some x-rays and would return in a bit. Her words eased some of my fears, but it wasn't until I saw Kate for myself that I truly felt relieved.

Her elegant hand sweeps a long lock of blond hair over her shoulder to keep it from falling into her food. After taking a bite, she glances across the table with a contemplative expression in her green eyes and I tense, wondering what is going through her mind. Hopefully, not the fight we had a couple days ago, the one I still haven't apologized for starting.

She clears her throat. "Thank you for taking care of me. I'm sorry I interrupted your life and sleep, but I truly appreciate it."

I shift uncomfortably. "Lev and Lowell would never forgive me if I left you to fend for yourself after a terrible accident." It's the truth and a damn good answer, but her face floods with disappointment. She quickly tries to mask it with a smile, and I grind my teeth at the sight of it. Her hurt kills me. "To be honest, I couldn't get to the hospital fast enough. I don't know what that means, except I care what happens to you." Her smile solidifies into something more genuine. I shrug. "The rest doesn't matter. Like I said, I don't sleep much."

Green eyes narrow in speculation. "Is it the past? Your life in the military, I mean." When I don't say anything, she continues. "Lowell said I should talk to you because you would understand what I've been through."

"I do," I admit reluctantly. "It's a heavy burden to hold someone else's life in your hands. Soldier or doctor, our decisions carry severe consequences." My throat dries up. I hate talking about the past, but if I can help her, I will. "Their ghosts live with me, the men who died under my command. Every day I think about them. Regret, guilt, anger, sadness. I feel it all. As their leader, they were my responsibility. Sometimes the call came from above, and other times, I made the decision, but in the end, only their death matters. It's something I accepted when I became an officer, but nothing prepares you for it. People make mistakes every day, but with you and I, those mistakes cost people their lives."

She blows out the breath she's been holding and nods. "Specializing in oncology… I knew I would lose patients. Cancer is a brutal enemy, but I swore I would do everything in my power to give them the best chance at life, and when I couldn't save them,

I used their deaths to fuel my determination to try and save the next one."

Her voice drops until I can barely hear her, as if she's afraid to speak about the past. "The attack ripped into our lives like an F5 tornado, and when it was gone, the aftermath was devastating. And it was my fault. I never thought I'd be directly responsible for the loss of friends and colleagues. The guilt eats at me. I try to keep it locked up tight." She gives a derisive laugh. "Funny enough, it hits hardest when I'm happy. It likes me miserable. Alone. I've been fighting it more lately."

Because she's happy with Lev and Lowell. It hits me hard when I think of how I jeopardized her happiness with my anger. She shifts in her chair, and I shove the thought aside.

"How do you cope?" she asks, biting her lip.

I grimace. "Not very well. Some days are better than others. The nights are the worst. There's not enough to do to occupy my mind, and it dwells on the past. But it's different for me. My biggest fear is forgetting their faces. I owe it to them to remember. To honor their sacrifice." I watch her for a second. "The hard part is finding a way to forgive yourself. It's not easy, but I don't want it to be. They were good men, and they deserve to be remembered, even if it costs me a piece of my soul."

I lean back in my chair. "You deserve happiness, Kate. You didn't choose who lived or died that day, a higher power chose the paths of everyone in that hospital. Remember the fallen, honor them, but don't let the past destroy your chance at a future."

"I'm fighting to stay… for me and them," she assures me. "It's hard to believe how empty my life was just a few months ago. Now, it's full of little moments that mean everything to me."

A stab of regret and jealousy hit me simultaneously, but I don't know what to say.

She opens her mouth, then closes it.

"Tell me," I demand, my body tense.

"I don't want to come between all of you," she hesitantly begins. "I... care about you, Shaw. But things are strained between us and it affects Lev and Lowell, although they rarely say anything about it. A couple of days ago, I thought it was an impossible situation, but yesterday and today has shown me we can get along. We just need to try harder. What do you think?"

I can't. If I let go of my anger, you'll slip right through my defenses.

Her green eyes plead with me to answer.

"You're right," I admit reluctantly. "I'm sorry for the other day. I was angry and took it out on you. I'll do better." I open my mouth to explain, but Lev comes rushing onto the back patio.

"Kate, sweetheart." He leans down and gently gathers her in his arms for a tender hug. "You scared the hell out of me." He places little kisses on her lips. "How the hell did it happen?"

She smooths a hand over his face to soothe him. "A deer hit me, but I'm lucky. Just a slight concussion."

I stand and pick up our plates to take them to the kitchen.

Kate's hand on my arms stops me. "Thanks again, Shaw. You've been wonderful. And thanks for the talk. I need to find a way to move forward, and it helps to hear your view."

I stare into her green eyes. "I'm here for you. Whatever you need."

Leaving Kate in Lev's capable hands is tough. I liked taking care of her, knowing she needed me. I watch while Lev settles on the patio with her in his lap. Unable to watch anymore, I load the dishwasher and clean up.

When I enter my room, I pause for a second. Lost and unsettled, I stand there for several minutes thinking about the last two days.

Buzzing on my phone brings me out of my introspection. It's the city letting me know Kate's vehicle is in impound. It's the perfect excuse to escape.

I text Lev to let him know I'm going out for a while, and to give Kate her painkillers in another half hour. He replies that he's good to take over her care. Lev was frantic while he waited for a flight, calling and texting every hour. Seeing his face when he arrived, I know he's in deep with her. I scoff. Hell, he's already in love with her. I've never seen him with anyone else like he is with Kate. Not even Nessa.

Not that Lowell has been much better, but he's good at hiding his emotions. The fact that he got angry with me showed me more of his feelings than any words could have said. Lowell only feels deeply for those in his inner circle, those he considers his family. He's been blowing up my phone the entire time too. The only reason it's quiet now is because he's in the air.

If I can take care of Kate's vehicle, it will show her I'm trying to do better. Lev and Lowell too. Actions over words.

Hearing her story tonight, it's the least I can do. The things Kate went through and all she lost from that one incident is heartbreaking. She's a remarkable woman with a steel spine under that beautiful exterior, standing strong despite the crippling guilt.

It takes little time to get to impound. I ask the officer on duty for the location of Kate's vehicle and he gives me the keys before pointing toward the back corner. As I walk toward it, my knees tremble and almost give out. It's a complete wreck. There's not a place on the vehicle that isn't damaged. The front is crumpled, the ceiling and sides caved inward, and the windshield shattered.

Moving closer, I glance into the driver's seat and notice the blood and twisted seat. Thankfully, the vehicle has front and side airbags. I'm not sure she would have survived without them. Tears come to my eyes when I think about what could have happened. My hand reaches up to rub the ache inside my chest, and the urge to get back and pull her into my arms is almost overwhelming. Before I leave, I take a few pictures of the vehicle so I can show them it is totaled, then gather the rest of her personal belongings.

Lowell is getting out of his SUV when I arrive back home. He waits as I get out and grab Kate's stuff.

"What are you doing? Where's Kate?" he demands.

"With Lev. I left to check on her vehicle." My voice is tight as I relay the state of her vehicle to him. "She's damn lucky to be alive." Pulling out my phone, I show him the pictures.

His body sways when he sees the damage. "I need to see her." He rushes off toward the house. "Hurry!"

Walking in, Lowell walks right over and carefully plucks Kate out of Lev's arms. Then he carries her over to a chair and sits down. His hands skim every inch of her, needing to reassure himself she's alive with only mild injuries. His face is intense. Kate reaches up, clasps his head in her hands, and gives him a deep kiss. Stopping, he pulls back and stares at her. Blinking rapidly, he cups her cheek and kisses her like the oxygen she is to him. There is nothing controlled in his response, only pure emotion.

Watching them makes me ache, and not physically either. Sensing someone's eyes on me, I turn and see Lev watching me with his eyebrows raised high. Sending him the pictures of her smashed SUV via text, I wait for him to view the wreckage.

His phone buzzes, and he pulls up the text. Harshly exhaling, his face whitens, and he hunches over, fists clenched around the phone, staring down at the images. With a shake of his head, he looks at me, his eyes full of fierce emotion before letting his gaze slide to Kate. He moves to the chair next to Lowell so he can reach out and touch her.

The moment is emotional and intimate. Feeling left out and a little bit lost now that I'm not needed, I call out good night to them all and move toward the hall.

Slipping into bed, all I can think about is the last twenty-four hours and her wrecked vehicle. In the Army, I knew how brief life could be, but I'd forgotten that fact in safe Montana. My indecisiveness and anger stemmed from a deep fear of losing someone else, but I realize now I could have lost her without ever even knowing or loving her. Not anymore. My decision is clear.

Kate's scent is all over the pillow next to me, a reminder of the last two nights. My arms and bed feel empty without her. I yank the pillow closer and let the last two sleepless nights pull me into the dark.

Chapter Twenty-Six

KATE

Lowell and Lev's bodies are wrapped tightly around me when I wake late the next morning. After seeing the wreckage, none of us felt like being alone, so we all piled into Lev's bed. Given how exhausted we all were, it's no surprise we slept in this morning.

All the numbness has worn off and the pain is even worse today. Stretching hurts. Blinking hurts. I force myself to stop complaining. I'm alive and here with them. Sliding down to the end of the bed, I make my way to the bathroom. After I use the restroom, I brush my teeth and turn on the shower just as a knock sounds on the bathroom door.

"Sweetheart, do you need help?" Lev murmurs.

Opening it, I pull him into the bathroom. "I need help showering. It hurts to lift my arms and I need to wash my hair."

"Mmm, a shower with you? I'm in." Grinning, he pushes me back into the bedroom so he can use the restroom first, then opens it and crooks his fingers for me to enter.

"Lift your arms." He quickly peels off my shirt. Inhaling sharply, his fingers lightly trace over the bruises standing out all over my body. He shudders and gently pulls me in for a hug. His voice is barely a whisper when he says, "Fuck, I'm so glad you're okay. I can't imagine my world without you in it."

His words give me everything. I wrap him in my arms and hold him.

After a minute, he kneels down to help me take off my underwear, strips off his boxer briefs, then helps me into the shower. Hot water cascades down my sore body, easing the tightness in my muscles.

Behind me, slippery hands full of soap glide lightly over my body. Lev is careful, especially around the cuts and bruises caused by the accident. He turns me around to wash my front, and as his large hands skim my breasts, a moan slips out.

"Does it hurt or feel good?"

"Good. Don't stop."

With slitted eyes, I watch him soap each breast and nipple carefully, but I can't contain the whimper of need when his hands slide down to wash between my legs. Heat rises within me, but I know I'm too sore right now.

Finally finished with my body, he moves me again to start on my hair. I tried to rinse out the blood yesterday, but clearly, I missed some spots. The water turns pink the first time he washes it, but by the second time, it finally feels clean. Smiling, I turn and give him a hug.

"Damn, you feel good, sweetheart. Too good, especially right now." Turning me back around, he pushes me out of the shower, lightly swatting my ass as I leave.

"Thank you for the help."

Instead of closing the shower door, he stands, water streaming, while he watches my every move.

He's making sure I'm steady on my feet, but I can't resist teasing him a bit. With only a small portion of the towel, I take the time to dry every inch of my body. His cock, already hard from washing me, is now almost purple. Licking my lips, I watch him fist it.

Starting out with slow strokes that go from base to tip, he gathers up some soap to make it slick. "I want to see you. Drop the towel." His demand is husky as his hands move faster.

I drop the towel. Spreading my legs wide, I lean back and thrust my hips out so he can see more of me.

"That's it, sweetheart. You make me want to drop to my knees and taste your sweetness." His hands are stroking his cock fast and tight now. "All I could think about when I was in Las Vegas was how you felt the last time we were together, dripping all over my cock as you sat in my lap and rode me hard. Your breasts bouncing up and down, nipples hard and tempting. Tell me, are you wet?"

Trailing my fingers down, I slide them inside, stroke a few times, and pull them back out, wet and glistening. Showing them to him, I slip my fingers into my mouth to lick them clean.

"Damn. I want you so fucking bad."

With a low groan, he strokes his cock a couple more times and comes hard a second later. Panting, he leans against the shower wall for a second while his body recovers.

I blow him a kiss and wrap the discarded towel around me. As I enter the bedroom, Lowell's propped up against the headboard. His face is stern as he glimpses the bruises showing above the towel.

"What the hell is he thinking…"

Holding up a hand, I explain to him it was a solo performance. "Although I wish I could, my body is way too sore for any extracurricular activities. I did watch."

Dropping the towel, my hands slowly pull on the leggings and a soft shirt recovered from the gym bag in my car. Combing my hair, I leave it to air dry. Once I'm finished, I walk over to Lowell and give him a kiss.

"I'd like to watch you sometime too. Would you like that?"

His eyes narrow, pretending to think about it, but the heat riding his face makes it a mockery. "Maybe I'll let you. Not today. I'm going to shower alone and get dressed. Ask Lev to make us some breakfast."

Pushing back the covers, he stands, and the first thing I notice is his cock tenting his very loose boxers. I guess hearing me with Lev turned him on. Wrenching my gaze up, I catch his smirk before he stalks off.

Chapter Twenty-Seven

KATE

Shaw's lounging comfortably on a large chair in the living room, his feet propped up on the ottoman. A baseball game plays on the TV in front of him, but he's not even watching it. He startles when I sit down on the couch across from him.

He leans toward me. "Can I get you something to drink or eat?" Without waiting for an answer, he stands and turns in a circle, then pulls the throw from the back of his chair and covers me with it.

There's a tenseness about him that I can't quite put my finger on. "I'm good. Lev's going to cook some breakfast." I glance at the clock on the wall. "Or maybe lunch. I'm not sure."

He nods, then walks away. A minute later, he returns and sets a glass of ice water on the table beside me. "Do you want the remote? I wasn't really watching the game anyway."

It hits me that it's Sunday. A week ago, we were fighting in the barn… and kissing. My eyes drop to his lips. "I forgot it was Sunday. When are you guys going to visit Thayer? I feel bad that you've been taking care of me all weekend and he's been left alone."

Shaw sits down in his chair. "I went and saw him early this

morning. We can all take turns today. You shouldn't be alone yet."

I raise an eyebrow. "The watch period for my concussion is over. I'm sore, but I need to go home this afternoon. We've got a busy week ahead, and I need to review patient charts."

Shaw gives a fierce shake of his head. "Have them reschedule. You need time to heal."

"I didn't realize you were also a doctor," I say drily. "I'm not canceling my patients. Stop worrying. My work isn't strenuous. Sarah will be there to help if I need it." The stubborn tilt to Shaw's chin tells me he's not happy with my decision, but it's not up to him. I decide to change the subject. "How's Thayer doing?" I ask.

Shaw narrows his eyes at my tactic, but thankfully, follows my lead. "The doctors have been running tests all week. We find out his prognosis today. He can move his toes, which is a good sign. Once we know what's next, he'll be able to leave the hospital."

"That's great news," I remark with relief. I know how much they all care for each other. "Let me know if there's anything I can do to help."

Lowell comes striding in and sits down on the couch next to me, pulling my feet into his lap. "Everything okay here?" His gaze swings from me to Shaw.

Shaw dips his chin. "We're good."

The two of them have a silent conversation for a second, then Lowell turns back to me. "Lev is fixing his famous pulled pork for lunch. Should be ready soon. Do you need a pillow?"

"No, but I could use some ibuprofen," I reply with a grimace. "No more painkillers. I don't like to take them because they make me groggy, and I have work to do this evening."

Lowell studies my face, then nods. "I can work from your place."

Surprised, I tilt my head. "You told me you only like to write in your office. Something about the clutter in the space helping you to be more creative."

Shaw laughs.

Lev comes out of the kitchen with a couple of plates and Shaw jumps up to help him finish setting the table.

I place a hand on Lowell's arm. "I'll be fine. I promise. Let's eat lunch." Standing, I place the throw on the couch and take a seat at the table.

Once all of us are seated, Lev looks across the table at me. "We have to go to the hospital this afternoon to visit Thayer. We'll drop you off at your place, but I'll return an hour later and stay the night. I work at The Black and Gold Monday, so it makes the most sense for me." He passes me a plate with a bbq pork sandwich and fries on it.

Noticing the satisfaction on all of their faces, I realize they aren't going to let this go. I really want to be irritated, but I can't. It feels good to have someone taking care of me when I'm hurt. "On one condition."

Lev winks at me. "Maybe. Tell me your condition first."

"You bring dinner," I tell him. "I usually do my shopping on Saturday mornings, and since I missed it yesterday, there isn't much food in the house."

The tension eases from their shoulders.

"Deal," Lev answers with a smirk.

With a shake of my head, I take a bite of the sandwich. It's really good. "Why is this considered famous?"

Shaw chuckles. "When Lev was first starting out, he called his foster mom, Clara, for some tips. She sent him her best recipes. The pulled pork was one of them, and it was the first item he put on the menu at The Black and Gold. It quickly became the most requested one too. Proud of him, she asked him to send her a copy of the menu, so he did. When she got it, she called and gave him an earful."

Lev's face turns pink. "I named it Sarge's Pulled Pork sandwich because I knew it was his favorite. She was so mad and wouldn't speak to me for weeks. I thought she'd get over it, but the woman was stubborn. I finally changed the name to Clara's Famous Pulled Pork and sent her a copy of the new menu. Happy as a lark, she immediately called to tell me I made the right decision."

"She sounds amazing," I say with a laugh. "Are there any other things on the menu that came from her? What about the spaghetti?"

Lev scowls. "That one is all mine." He stops and thinks for a minute. "The menu has changed over the years. I'll never stop serving the pulled pork, but most of the menu rotates seasonally. The banana pudding pie is her recipe. Every bite brings back a childhood memory. Even Lowell will stop in and get some."

Lowell flashes a wistful smile. "There wasn't much she couldn't cure with her banana pudding pie or her chocolate chip cookies."

Even Shaw nods. "She adopted me and Thayer along the way. Used to send us care packages too. Amazing woman."

I smile at the thought of all these grown men receiving sweet care packages full of chocolate chip cookies. "What about your parents, Shaw?"

He lifts a shoulder. "My mom passed when I was young, but my dad was a good man. Hardworking. A lot like their Sarge. Gruff, but a good heart."

Lowell's alarm on his phone goes off. "Let me help you clean up, then we need to get going. Thayer's going to be bouncing off the walls today."

Chapter Twenty-Eight

THAYER

FEAR MAKES MY HEART POUND WHILE I WAIT FOR THE GUYS TO arrive. I asked the doctor to give me my test results once my brothers got here so they could hear them directly. I feel some sensation in my legs, but I know I'll need therapy to strengthen my muscles.

It was so stupid to let that baby announcement get to me. It's not like I even miss Nessa anymore, but I thought I'd have a family by now. Instead, she has everything I so badly want in my life.

Forcing myself to take a deep breath, I drop my head and close my eyes for a few minutes. Hearing the door open, I watch Shaw, Lev, and Lowell enter the room.

"Hey, guys. Damn, you look rough. What's up? You didn't get any news from the doctor, did you?" I tense, worried he might have told them before me so they could help lessen any impact.

Shaw puts a steady hand on my shoulder. "It's nothing to do with your prognosis. We'll explain after the doctor leaves. He's on his way now."

Lowell looks at Lev and they have a silent conversation. Lev's brows furrow in disagreement. My frustration builds.

Usually, I'm involved in our conversations, but I'm out of the loop tonight.

The doctor enters the room and explains the diagnosis. "Hello, everyone. Let's get to the point, shall we? Thayer, your spinal cord is bruised in your lower lumbar region. Thankfully, the medication we gave you helped the swelling go down and we have a clear idea of the damage. You're damn lucky. It's moderate, which means it will go away with time and rehabilitation. But don't take this lightly, it's a serious injury. Rehab is nonnegotiable. No extreme sports or other physical exertion for a while. We'll schedule you for a follow-up in a month. Do you have any questions?"

After our questions are answered, the doctor leaves. I swallow hard as I take in the information. I'm not known for my patience, but I know I can't shortcut my recovery. It also means a wheelchair for a while. I break out in a cold sweat.

Shaw's expression tells me he's already in planning mode.

"We'll get the house ready and have ramps installed at all the entrances and exits. In addition, I'll switch rooms with you so you can have the ground floor. If you want, we can set up a room for your therapy too," he tells me, squeezing my shoulder.

"Shaw, damn it. Give me a second to breathe," I demand, my voice strained. "What if I never get back to my old self?" I need to push myself physically. It keeps me sane.

"Then we'll deal with it. We count our victories and plan our next moves." Arms crossed, he stands steadfast, staring me in the eyes.

Frustrated, I stare at him. "What victories?"

All three of them glare at me like I'm stupid. Shaw spits out, "Until you woke up from the coma last week, we thought we would have to plan your funeral. The fact that you're alive is our biggest victory. With time, you'll walk again. Those are the victories we'll celebrate. We can only take this one step at a time. So fucking wallow in your pity for a day or two, but then we've got work to do. Do you hear me?"

It's his military, take-no-prisoners tone. Fall in or fall out. My gaze travels from Shaw to the other two, and I can tell I'm outnumbered. I grit my teeth, but nod in agreement. Shaw has never steered me wrong in the past, and he's not about to abandon me now.

Deciding to change the subject, I assess each one of them in return, noting their exhaustion and anxiety. "What's going on with you three? Am I really causing this much trouble?"

Lev takes point as the spokesperson, which surprises me. Usually, Shaw or Lowell will lead the serious discussions. "While you've been in the hospital, we employed a doctor to take over your practice. Dr. Kate Michaels."

"Is it not working out? What's wrong?"

"Damn, give me a second," he snaps, making my eyes widen. "She's a fantastic doctor. The practice is doing fine." Relief pours through me. "It's… Lowell and I have started dating her."

Now I'm confused. "That's unusual for you and Lowell to be interested in the same person. How long has this been going on?"

"I started dating her first, then Lowell. She fits us both." Looking at Lowell, he continues. "Two nights ago, she was in a serious car accident. Thankfully, she came out of it with minor injuries, but we've all been taking care of her the last few days."

Relief makes me smile. "So, she's dating you and Lowell? Well, I'm happy you guys found someone to date who likes you both, but I'm warning you, I will want my practice back someday so don't get too attached."

"It's not just a fling. Lowell and I are serious about her," Lev states firmly. "Also, she might only be dating the two of us right now, but she has feelings for Shaw too. They haven't moved on them yet" Lev stares at Shaw, silently asking him to say something.

Stunned, I try to digest the meaning of the three of them interested in the same woman. It's Nessa all over again. "Wait, all of you? Shaw, you too?"

Shaw squares his shoulders. "You should know, all of you, the accident changed things for me." His eyes move to mine. "I fought my feelings for her because I didn't want another Nessa in our lives, especially one who could leave us again, and I didn't want to make life decisions with you in the hospital. But when I saw her mashed-up vehicle, the fight drained out of me. She's an incredible woman, and if she feels the same, I want more." His eyes are apologetic.

Angry, I realize they're serious. "No, this cannot be happening. We don't need another Nessa tearing up our lives. It almost killed us last time. And look at me. In the hospital because I couldn't deal with a baby announcement." Sneering, I ask, "Am I supposed to just fall in line and fuck her too?"

Lowell steps forward. "Watch your mouth, Thayer. We know this comes as a shock, and right now, we're all figuring things out. Regardless, Lev and I are in it for the long haul. If Shaw and Kate work things out, that's up to them. We're brothers no matter what, and we'll always be here for you, but things have changed."

Dread pools in my stomach. While I was in a coma, life threw some big fucking curveballs. I know these guys though, and if I try to fight them on this, they'll get pissed and dig a trench. This is the motivation I need to get better and get home. I'm suddenly very eager to meet Dr. Kate Michaels.

"Like you said, let's just take things one week at a time. First, let's get me home. I'll need room to maneuver in a wheelchair." The words are like ash in my mouth. Swallowing my anger and resentment, I ignore the Kate conversation for now and focus only on the next step.

They engage in the usual wordless conversation when I ask them to leave, but I don't care. I'm tired and need time to process. They each squeeze my shoulder and head out, leaving me to the thoughts swirling around in my brain.

Chapter Twenty-Nine

KATE

Sarah is a tremendous help the next week. She easily handles most of the patients, allowing me to take breaks to sit down and rest. My bruises are still black or deep purple, but the soreness is easing. Either Lev or Lowell has stayed with me each night at the apartment. Having them around to take care of me has made me think of what it would actually be like to live with them permanently.

Groaning, I stretch my body to ease the stiffness in my muscles.

"How are you doing today?" Sarah asks, rounding the corner.

"Good. The soreness is disappearing. What's the patient roster like today?"

"It's quiet. If you don't mind, I might go out for lunch?"

Staring at her, I watch her blush. "Lunch, hmm. Is that what you're calling it?" Laughing, I watch the pink turn to red. "Is it the actor?"

"His name is Remington Foster, and yes, we're having lunch." She pauses and a bewildered expression crosses her face. "I can't believe it myself, but we haven't had sex yet. What's even more weird is how much I'm enjoying this merry-go-round of continuous foreplay."

"Remington is a sexy name. Go have fun and a great lunch." The board lists three patients this afternoon. "In fact, just take the rest of the day off. I can handle this afternoon."

"Seriously?" She thinks about it for a second. "Thanks, I'm taking you up on that offer." Pointing down the hall, she tells me Mr. Dorser is ready for me in Room 3.

Later that day, I finish up the last patient. The office is pretty quiet for four in the afternoon. Walking to the front, I let Paula and Brittany go early too.

The phone rings. "Hello, Lockeland Valley Medical Practice, how may I help you?"

"Where's Paula or Brittany?" a demanding male voice asks.

"They are not available right now. I'm Dr. Kate Michaels. Can I help you?"

Silence reigns on the other end. "This is Dr. Thayer Bradford. Is Sarah around?"

Thayer?

"Hello, Thayer. Sarah isn't here either. I'm Kate Michaels, and I hear you're going home soon. I know the guys have been really worried about you. How are you doing?"

"Dr. Bradford, please. While you might be dating my brothers, we don't know each other well enough to be informal." His voice is full of animosity. "Don't worry about me, Dr. Michaels. I'll be back to take over my practice soon, and you had better be taking excellent care of my patients. Tell Sarah to call me when she gets in tomorrow. Goodbye."

I set it down once I hear the dial tone. Thayer sounds like a stuffed-up prick. The guys have told me a little about him. Apparently, he comes from old money. Based on our first conversation, I can only wonder why they never taught him any manners.

Handing Shaw a glass of red wine, I move to the end of the couch and curl up. Lev had an emergency at one of his restaurants in Helena and couldn't stay the night. I insisted I didn't need someone with me, but Shaw showed up an hour later with a duffel bag and informed me he was sleeping on my couch.

Taking a sip of my wine, I fiddle with the glass and stare at him, wondering what's going on. He texted me several times this week to check on me. It was nice. Our promise to treat each other better is working, but tonight he seems kind of nervous, and the dark circles under his eyes tells me he isn't sleeping.

"How was your day?" I ask tentatively.

Taking a long drink of wine, he sets the glass down on the coffee table. "Kate, I need to apologize to you for my behavior at the barn that day."

Wincing, I try to deflect. I'm not sure we're ready to discuss our argument.

"You're tired. Why don't we just relax and watch TV? No need to go into anything else right now."

He shakes his head. "I'm sorry for how I acted. When I saw you get out of Lev's vehicle that day, I could see you two had stepped up your relationship. You were glowing. Lev was smiling. It had been a long time since I had seen him so happy. I couldn't stand it. Part of me was angry that you were dating both him and Lowell. I'd rather they each found someone than have it be the same person."

Confused, I wait for him to explain. "Why? I care deeply about each of them. Honestly, I doubt I could choose between them."

"Because I want you."

"I don't understand." I knew he wanted me, physically at least, but I don't understand why he didn't want me to care for Lev and Lowell.

"It was like Nessa all over again. We each fell for her, and look what happened. Although it was the opposite last time. Nessa fell for Thayer and me first." Rubbing his hand through his hair, his eyes are distant as he remembers the past, and a frustrated sigh leaves his lips. "I didn't want to enter another relationship where my family is at risk for getting hurt again. If one of us is dating a woman and it doesn't work out, it doesn't impact the entire group. Then, along comes you. Your position is temporary. I couldn't see a scenario that wouldn't end with our destruction."

My throat tightens and tears glaze my eyes. "Lev told me about your relationship with Vanessa. I get it, but it has nothing to do with me. I refuse to give them up. Every day I spend with them, I fall deeper. Hearing you tell me they're happy gives me hope for the future, and I haven't felt hope in a long time." I scrub at the tears running down my face. "For the past few years, I didn't feel like I deserved to have a life. The guilt of being alive constantly ate at me. Many of my friends and colleagues would never have the chance for happiness. Why should I? But Lev and Lowell have changed everything for me."

Shaw moves to his knees in front of me, and I automatically set my glass on the end table. He picks up my hands and brings them to his mouth for a sweet kiss. "Don't cry, angel, please. That's just it. I don't want you to give them up. It was fear for them, for me, and for the life we've established here. I knew I had feelings for you, but I didn't want things to change. The only way I could be around you was to shove those feelings, and you, away."

Where is he going with all this? Is he telling me he cares about me?

"Your accident changed things for me. I kept swinging between bone-deep relief that you were going to be okay and terror at what could have been. I was glad both Lev and Lowell were gone because it meant I could take care of you, and I desperately needed to be by your side. Hell, I barely slept that first night for fear you wouldn't wake up." Wiping away my tears, he waits for me to say something.

"Are you saying you care for me? It's not just physical?"

Squaring his jaw, he dips his chin. "Yes. I care about you, Kate. I want to be with you. I want you to give me a second chance. Or hell, a first chance."

Staring down at our linked hands, I see my pale fingers intertwined with his tanned, blunt fingers. I do have feelings for him, but do I see him in my life? Thinking about the night of the accident, I realize when I saw him in the emergency room, I knew everything was going to be all right because he would take care of me. And he did. Can I trust him with my heart though? I don't know.

"You were an asshole." His mouth turns down at my words. "I was beginning to have feelings for you before the fight. They haven't gone away, but I won't engage in a roller coaster with you. If you're not sure, let's just be friends."

"I want to be your friend," he says firmly, his fingers reaching up to trace the line of my jaw. "But I want a hell of a lot more too."

I study his face, noting the sincerity in his dark brown eyes. "This is your only chance. Don't screw it up."

He laughs. "Don't worry. If I do, Lev and Lowell will bury me."

Damn. That laugh gets me every time.

Leaning forward, he tilts up my chin to give me a long, deep kiss that is every bit the inferno it was that day at the barn.

Chapter Thirty

SHAW

Pulling the truck into the garage, I turn off the ignition and think about my discussion with Kate last night. Thank the fuck she's willing to give me, or us, a chance. I'm not sure what I would have done if she had said no. It took me a while to come around, but life has a way of making things crystal clear. When I saw her mangled vehicle, I wanted to lock her safely in my house forever.

She told Lowell and Lev this morning about our plan to go on a date this weekend. I didn't get a chance to speak to them, so I know they'll be waiting for me inside. We're overdue for a conversation anyway, about this and other things. Picking up my duffle, I head inside.

Lev has breakfast waiting on the table, and Lowell strides into the room and sits down without getting anything to eat. Lev holds off too. My eyes drift to my eggs with longing, but I put down my fork.

"I fucked up. I know." Not a twitch from either of them. "I apologized to her, and I apologize to both of you too. I'm sorry." I meet their gaze head on, letting them see my sincerity. "Every time I saw her with the two of you, a cloud of rage and fear would descend on me. My mind kept picturing Nessa walking out of our lives. I didn't want to go through that again. It took us a long time to get over her, but when Kate had her accident, things cleared up real fast for me. There are no guarantees. You take the happiness you're offered and hope for the best or be alone the rest of your life." Falling silent, I wait for them either to forgive or punch me.

"Don't fucking do it again," Lev growls, standing up to get a plate of food. "I mean it. She won't give you a second chance. Even if things don't work out, she deserves your respect. Do you hear me?"

Gritting my teeth, I hate the thought of it not working between us, but he's right. "I understand and agree."

Turning my head to Lowell, I observe the icy, expressionless look in his eyes. When he blocks me out, I know I've fucked up. "I care about her." He knows that single statement tells me everything I need to know about his feelings.

"I know she loves both of you. I see it in her eyes. You give her laughter and hope, and so much more," I assure them.

Tension eases out of Lev, and he sits back down. "I love her, man." He stares steadily at me. "I love her more than Vanessa. She makes me feel on top of the world when I'm with her."

Lowell shocks me when he says, "I didn't love Vanessa like the rest of you, but I cared about her a lot. Kate though… I could fall in love with her." A small smile plays on his lips, like a secret he doesn't want to share yet.

We sit in silence for a few minutes, thinking about the past and Kate before I bring up the subject of Thayer. "I've got men coming tomorrow to build the ramps for the front and back doors. I'll need your help to move my furniture upstairs so Thayer can have the downstairs bedroom."

Lev jumps in. "Wait, let's move my stuff upstairs. Then you can keep the main master."

Shoveling a few bites into my mouth, I take a few minutes to eat. "Okay. I'd like to stay near Thayer anyway, so that works. One last thing, Thayer's going to be an issue. He called the practice yesterday and was incredibly rude to Kate. He'll feel vulnerable in the wheelchair, which will make him lash out even more. We need to figure out how to handle it before he gets home at the end of the week. I want Kate to feel comfortable when she comes to visit, but I don't want Thayer to feel like we abandoned him either."

Lev runs a large hand down his face. "Once he's home, we should give him a couple of weeks to settle. Then, we'll invite her out for Sunday dinner. That will limit the time they're together, but it will show him we're serious about her."

We all share a look. This isn't going to be easy.

Chapter Thirty-One

KATE

WHEN I PULL UP TO THEIR HOUSE, SHAW IS WAITING FOR ME. FOR our first date, he's taking me fly-fishing. The idea of fishing in a river kind of freaks me out. Won't it be cold? What about snakes? Worse, I could suck.

Like a gentleman, he opens the door of my rental car. "I promise I'm not that bad at dating. I'll even feed you." His eyes are scanning my face.

Laughing, I slide out into his arms. "It's not the date or the man, but I'm not sure how I feel about fishing. I've never been."

Shocked, he just stares at me. "Are you serious? You've never gone fishing?"

"Nope," I exclaim loudly, popping the P. "And I'm nervous, which is rare for me."

"You're in expert hands. I've been fishing since I could walk and hold a pole at the same time. My dad taught me to fish in the same river where I'm taking you. You'll do fine."

Waving my hand, I motion for him to lead on. "I'm all yours."

Stopping, he pulls me in close for a sweet kiss. "Well, not all mine, but definitely mine for the day." Sliding my hand into his, he squeezes it. "Hop in the truck."

Soon he's driving around the back of the house onto a dirt road. His pride in the farm is apparent as he shows me the various buildings and operations they run. I've been to the stables, but that's about it. I didn't realize there were so many other buildings out here. Noticing a new building going up, I ask him what he intends to do with that one.

"That's for Lev to make wine. He wants us to put in a small vineyard on that hill." He points out the hill behind the structure, currently covered in lush field grass.

Their lives are all so intertwined. Sometimes I worry about my place in it. Is there room for me? What happens if it doesn't work out with Shaw? My stomach clenches with anxiety, but I push it down deep. Today's about Shaw and me.

"That's wonderful! He's got such an excellent palate that every wine he picks turns out to be so good. In fact, I've drunk most of the wine he left at the apartment. I can't help myself," I admit with a grin.

"You should check out the wine cellar in our basement. He's proud of his stash. I'm not much of a wine drinker, but you're right, he's got good taste."

Shaw pulls up to a wide, flat river, and backs in so we can get the stuff out of the bed of the truck. The bed of the pickup is in the shade of a huge leafy green tree. Warmer today, it will be the perfect spot for our picnic later.

Waiting for him to help me out, I survey the land surrounding us. We're in a valley filled with grass and wildflowers. On the edge of the valley is the mountain I saw from Shaw's bedroom. It must be the source of the stream. Bubbling water greets me when I get out of the truck. The river is rushing out of the mountain to get to the lake sitting placidly below the valley. The air smells like summer and sunshine, and it makes me think of Shaw.

"It's beautiful." I glance over at Shaw, and find him watching me intently. "A perfect piece of serenity."

Face brightening at my response, he pulls open the tailgate and hands me two poles. "Would you mind carrying these?"

Reaching out, I grab them and watch as he pulls out some rubber pants, a net, and a tackle box. Leaving the picnic basket, cooler, and blanket in the truck, he leads me to a spot on the bank.

"Let's set everything here."

He hands me a pair of rubber pants. When I hold them up, I notice they have built-in boots. Kind of like a kid's onesie but made of rubber.

"Do I take off my shoes?"

"Yes. Take off your shoes. These might be a little big but use the suspenders to tighten them." He slips off his boots and tugs on his pair. With deft movements, he shows me how to make it fit better. Motioning me over, he flips open the lid of the tackle box and shows me which slot holds the flies.

Gross. I peer inside. "They aren't real flies. What are they?"

"Essentially, it's a concoction of materials designed to look like a fly or other type of bug. The fish don't know the difference until they bite. Once they bite, you reel them in pretty quickly," he explains.

"I'm really glad you don't use real bugs." My mouth twists and I scrunch up my nose as I reach down and pick up a small black one. "Where do you get them?"

"Some I made when I was younger. Some I've bought."

Shrugging, he walks through the various pieces of the pole, from the reel to the tippet, then shows me how to put the bait on the end. Reaching out, he tucks a few more flies into the pockets of our waders, and we head out toward the water.

Sticking his pole into a rock to hold it, he steps in behind me. He shows me how to hold the pole, then gripping my hips, he moves me into a good standing position. Sliding his hands along my body, he positions my arm up and back to show the starting point. By this point, I can barely pay attention to what he's saying. The friction between our bodies is setting off little sparks, and he smells so good, like sunshine, man, and an undertone of musk from his cologne. Suddenly, he throws my arm forward and brings his body in tight to mine as he leans over me. Inhaling, I hold my breath until I can regain some focus back.

"Okay, those are the basics. We'll practice the overhead cast a few times, then you'll be ready to go."

Swinging my arm up and back, he throws it forward again. Struggling to pay attention, I grasp the gist of it and nod. My body is tingling as he steps away, taking the heat and smell of musk with him. He motions for me to cast.

Shit.

Okay, holding the fly line in one hand, I grip the rod, rotate my arm backward, then fling my arm forward to the ten o'clock position. The fly line flows out into the water. When it stops, the fly floats gently on top of the water. Gasping, I smile and turn to Shaw.

"I did it! I'm fishing."

His head tilts back as he laughs. Damn, that laugh gets to me every time, turning his usually serious face into a younger, lighter version.

"Okay, I'm moving upriver to cast my line. I don't want us to get tangled."

Watching as he uses some weird sidearm throw, he casts out the line. "Why did I go overhead when you cast from the side?" I ask, puzzled.

"Experience. Beginners start with the overhead cast because it's the easiest." He talks about the various types of casts. I'm not really paying attention, but I love to hear him talk. His passion for fishing is exciting. Standing there with my feet in the water, listening to the river and him, I can see why he likes it so much. It's peaceful, and here in the middle of Montana, the world is light-years away.

He shows me the spot on the other side of the river where his dad first taught him to fish. We talk about his father and their relationship. His mom died when he was a baby, so it was always him and his dad. He was a great dad, but a ranch this large took up a lot of his time, which meant he didn't have much time to spare. Still, he taught him everything he knew, from fishing to ranching.

"When did he pass?"

"A little over three years ago." He frowns. "We had a falling out over my decision to join the Army instead of going away to play ball. About ten years passed before we spoke again."

"I'm guessing he wanted you to play ball. I heard from Sarah you were All-American and had a scholarship to an SEC school, and supposedly, you left a high school sweetheart in the dust?" I grin when I repeat the gossip.

A slight blush tinges his cheeks. "This town is way too small." Pulling at his cap, he runs a hand through his hair before settling it back on his head. "She's right and wrong. When I went into the Army instead of taking the scholarship, the high school sweetheart left me in the dust. Seems she was quite taken with having a big shot footballer for a boyfriend, but not an Army grunt."

True love. "And the scholarship?"

"Football came easy to me, but I never loved it. As I started my senior year, I realized college would be a lot like high school." Rolling his shoulders, his eyes are distant. "I wanted to feel like I was making a difference in the world. The Army was more of a calling than a career choice to me."

"I understand completely." His eyes swing to mine, and I tell him about my grandpa, his cancer, and his influence on my decision to be a doctor. "Becoming an oncologist felt like a calling to me. A chance to help people like my grandpa, who had no control over the outcome of this horrific disease and how it affected his life."

Frowning, he asks, "Did you grow up with your grandpa? What about your parents?"

I explain how my dad was never in the picture, but I didn't really miss him because I had my grandpa. And my mom, who is absolutely incredible and tough. "She supported my dreams, but she was also determined that science would not be my only accomplishment."

I shake my head when think of all the things she made me do. "She was always enrolling me in extracurricular classes like art, gymnastics, computer coding camps, and of course, dance. She was determined that I would be more than just the science nerd my grandpa wanted me to be."

"It definitely paid off. Lowell raves about your ability to tango," he reveals.

We've been talking nonstop for at least two hours, only pausing when he caught a fish. Right now, he's telling me a story about Lev's first time fishing. When he pulls his sixth fish out of the water, I roll my eyes. Unbelievable. I haven't caught a thing, not one tiny little fish yet. Shaw's a fishing ninja.

When he sees the expression on my face, his lips twitch, and he releases the fish back into the water.

My stomach growls. Done with fishing, I reel in my line and wade out of the water. "I'm hungry. What's in the picnic basket?"

"Are you giving up so quickly?"

"Maybe? Or maybe I need food," I reply with a scowl.

"Ouch, someone is grumpy." He takes my pole from me.

We walk back to the bank, trade our waders for shoes, and head over to the truck. He hops up into the bed, lays down some cushions and a blanket, and pulls out the picnic basket. Hopping back down, he grips me around the waist and lifts me into the truck. I scramble back toward the cushion and plop down with a heartfelt sigh.

The sun's been beating down on us all morning. I take off my hat and smooth a hand over my ponytail while Shaw hands me a glass of ice water. As I drink up, he pulls out several containers and plates. Opening them, I notice we have sandwiches, fruit, cheese, crackers, and some kind of dip. Plus, a bottle of wine.

"Yum! Lev knows how to pack a picnic."

"Excuse me?" Glaring at me, he motions to himself. "I'll have you know I put this together, not Lev."

"Oops, sorry," I tell him, leaning over to kiss him softly on the lips. When I pull back, he's sitting there with his eyes closed and a small smile on his face. Seconds later, his eyes open, his brown eyes molten as they run over me.

"That's the first kiss you've ever given me," he points out.

"I've given you several kisses."

"Not one I didn't initiate first. It feels damn good." He pours wine into a glass and holds it up for me to take before grabbing his own. "Cheers. To our first date and to new fishing adventures." Clinking glasses, he takes a drink, then leans over to pop a strawberry into my mouth.

Leaning back on the cushions, we eat and laugh and talk for a while. Once the picnic is cleared, Shaw moves the basket and pulls me into his arms.

Sweeping the hair back from my face, his chocolate brown eyes stare down at me, searching for my secrets. Languidly, he lowers his head and captures my lips with his own. Fire instantly erupts between us, but he reins it in, keeping the kiss from raging out of control. His lips slip from mine slowly, taking a second to suck on my lower lip before swiping his tongue over it.

"So, how was your first day of fishing?" he asks huskily. His lips trail down the vee of my T-shirt while his hand slips up my bare leg to the bottom hem of my shorts.

"Right. Fishing," I reply, my voice strained with need. My body jerks slightly whenever he touches a sensitive spot. "It's peaceful out here and soothes my soul. I'm not sure about the fishing. It would be nice if I actually caught a fish instead of just standing there watching you catch them." My fingers run through his silky brown hair.

"It's your first day. It'll happen." His hand skims inside the hem of my shorts, causing me to inhale sharply. He smiles at my reaction. "And the date? Good or bad?" With his hand caressing my thigh and his soft lips scattering kisses on my cleavage, the teasing is driving me crazy.

"I'll tell you when it's over. So far, it's been torturous," I jokingly say. Wiggling, I try to move closer to him, but he holds me in place to tease me further. "Please."

Stopping, he gazes up at me before closing the distance between us and aligning his body tightly with mine. Wrapping my arms around him, I settle in close. Like Lev, he's definitely got some muscle, and he's tall like Lowell, but his body fits mine perfectly.

Shaw moves his hand further into my shorts to grip me from behind. His fingers spread wide, mapping every inch of that cheek. "I've been wanting to get my hands on your ass for months, ever since you first tried on those jodhpurs. Never has a pair of clothing turned me on so badly until you walked out in those tight tan pants and presented me with your backside." His fingers continue to caress and squeeze before he grips it hard. "I'm only going to say this once. This is mine. I claim it. One day, I'm going to lick it, bite it, spank it, and hopefully, fuck it. Do you hear me?"

Damn, that turns me on. "So, you're thinking long-term now, huh?"

He growls. "Yes, damn it. I'm in this for the long haul. Now say it."

My breath hitches when I think about all he is claiming. With a deep breath, I take the biggest leap of faith and surrender to this thing between us. "I'm yours. My ass is yours. To lick, to bite, to spank, and to fuck."

With those words, his tight control vanishes. He captures my lips, delving deep while his hands roam over my body. Wherever he touches, fires spring up and burn. Where Lev's like the sun, all warmth and laughter, Shaw is an inferno. Soon, my entire body is blazing with need. Gasping, I wrench back my head for some desperately needed air.

"Are you okay?"

Biting my lip, I tell him, "Yes, I want to feel you." His body is tantalizingly hard, chiseled from his years in the Army and being a rancher.

Trailing my hands down his shirt, I motion for him to remove it. Sitting up, he strips off his shirt and lays back down. I nestle in close and breathe in the musky scent of his cologne. Something about the smell makes me ravenous. Licking his neck up to his ear, I hear him groan.

He rolls us over until I'm on top and places my hands on his chest. Smiling, I softly brush my hands over each muscle from his shoulders down to his abs. Shaw grips my ass and holds me down tight to his cock. Whenever I touch a sensitive spot, he squeezes my cheeks and thrusts up.

"This isn't fair, is it?" Mischievously, I grab the hem of my shirt. Slowly lifting it, I glance down at him. "But it is our first date." I drop the hem and he growls with frustration. "Just kidding." I whip off my shirt.

His hands move to cup my breasts.

I'm wearing a red, lacy bra with very little coverage.

"Red is my favorite color."

Cupping and pushing my breasts together, he leans up and kisses between them. Licking each mound, one hand tweaks my nipple while his other hand reaches around to undo the clasp in the back. As he falls back down, he pulls off my bra.

Air hits my breasts and I put an arm in front to shield them. "Hello. We're outside."

He grabs my hands and holds them out to the sides. "Nobody's out here for miles, angel, and I want to burn this memory into my brain so I can pull it up whenever I want."

His brown eyes catalog every inch of my breasts. Brown eyes harden when they see the bullet wounds. With a twist of his body, he leans in close to kiss each one. "You've had too many close calls."

My fingers smooth out the frown lines on his face, and I

smile, waiting for his eyes to meet mine once more. "I'm here, with you."

Freeing my hands, I use my nails to glide over his nipples. He inhales sharply as I lightly flick them until they are as hard and stiff as mine. "Dirty, angel."

Scooting back a little, I lower my head to lick and suck on them before trailing down to the taut skin right above the waistband of his jeans. Sucking hard, I hear his harsh breathing as his body twitches beneath me. I place my hand on his jeans, right over his cock, so as he bucks, he surges right into my palm.

Raising my head, I see his hands coming toward me before he hauls us into a sitting position and gives me a hard kiss. Using my hair, he pulls my head backward until my breasts are offered up to him. His tongue swipes over every miniscule inch of my breasts. Moaning and whimpering, I stand on the edge in a blaze of desire.

Tugging at his hair, I wait until he lifts his head before capturing him in another fierce kiss. Tongue sweeping and sucking, I show him how turned on I am by him. I rock back and forth before pushing him back down on the bed of the truck. Placing my hands on his chest, my breasts sway faster as I pick up the pace.

"Damn, angel. You look magnificent riding me. Let me help you."

He yanks off my shorts and underwear, then his own. I find my spot and grind down on top of him, wanting to feel his cock between my legs as he rocks us back and forth, gradually speeding up. The breeze caresses my breasts like the lightest of touches, and I whimper.

"I want you," I gasp. This might be our first date, but I've wanted him for weeks. Tired of playing games, I lean down. "Tell me you have a condom."

He searches my eyes. "Are you sure?"

A light sheen of sweat covers his body, making it glisten in the afternoon light. I trail my fingers over the slick surface of his muscles. "I feel like we've had weeks of foreplay. I want you. Inside me." I hold my breath, waiting for him to decide.

He grabs his jeans and pulls out a condom from his wallet. Ripping off the corner with his teeth, he rolls it on. His hands move to my hips, and he lifts me up to slide inside, inch by inch.

Both of us groan at the sensation.

"Shaw," I murmur, shifting my hips back and forth.

"I wasted so much time resisting you," he tells me. Large hands hold me tightly, and he rolls us over until he's on top. "I need to go deeper." He picks up my leg and puts it on his shoulder. With a swivel of his hips, he sinks into me, going deeper and deeper.

My body clenches down on the length of him. "Again."

He thrusts again and again, steady and deep, like the man himself. My body quivers and I feel my orgasm gathering with every stroke.

Panting, I beg him. "Faster. Don't stop."

With those orders, he immediately sets up a fast pace, in and out, taking us both to the edge and over. Breathing heavily, we fall into each other.

Little tremors run across my body, but I refuse to move. "I could stay here forever."

His dark brown eyes light up. "Seriously?"

"Yes," I reply huskily.

"That can be arranged," he informs me before reaching down to grab the condom. He slides out, making me whimper.

"I've changed my mind," I tell him. "We can go fishing any day."

As I intended, he laughs, then helps me dress. Once the gear is loaded back in the truck, he leans over to kiss me. "Who knew fishing could be so stimulating? It was a fantastic first date, and I look forward to the next one."

"Me too," I say with a wicked smile. "Maybe I'll even catch a fish." I reach up and kiss him. It seems only right our first time would be in the outdoors on the ranch.

We meet Lev as I'm leaving. "How was the fishing, sweetheart?"

"Well, I didn't catch any fish, but dessert was delicious." Winking, I throw a grin at them both.

Lev roars. "I'll have to tell you all about my first time fishing with Shaw sometime." Not knowing Shaw has already told me this story, I smile. He turns to Shaw and informs him, "I've moved upstairs. Thayer's stuff is now in my room. I'm going to his rehab session but wanted to let you know. The doctor confirmed he can come home in a few days."

Shaw asks him a few more questions, but I've tuned them out. My gut churns with anxiety wondering how Thayer's presence will impact our relationship.

Chapter Thirty-Two

KATE

ANXIETY STAYS WITH ME ALL WEEK. MY GUT INSTINCT, RAZOR-SHARP from the last few years, is warning me things are about to change. The past has a way of rearing its ugly head the second it sees how happy I am. This time, I can't tell exactly what is coming, but I don't like the feeling. I'm happy and I see a future here. It would break me to lose them.

It hasn't been quiet. Not a day goes by that I don't get texts and calls from all three men, but I haven't seen them once, and with Sarah on vacation in Los Angeles, visiting her new leading man, it's been a lonely reminder of the past three years.

With summer here, we have fewer patients. Brittany left early today to run errands for her wedding, Paula's manning the front desk, and I'm "working" in my office. I snort. More like moping.

My phone rings, and I look down to see who's calling. Smiling, my voice is husky when I pick up. "Hello, Lowell."

Silent for a second, I can feel his focus shift to the phone at my greeting. "Hello, Kate. I heard you had a delightful trip to the winery with Lev, and a rousing fishing trip with Shaw." He pauses for a second. "No, I don't know any details, but knowing those two, I can guess. And I'm jealous. Which brings me to the reason I'm calling you. The Montana Club is having their salsa night. Would you accompany me?" He pauses. "And I'd love for you to stay here with me tonight. In my bed. You know, the one with the loops?"

My body clenches just thinking about his room, my hands captive in those loops of his. Clearing my throat, my body shifts in anticipation as I answer with a rasp, "I'd love to go dancing and stay with you tonight, Lowell. What time should I be ready?"

"Six o'clock. See you soon."

About an hour later, I close up the practice and head upstairs to get ready. Salsa is dramatic and it requires something sexy. Padding into the bedroom, I choose the sexy dress I bought specifically for dancing with Lowell. It's a black, halter neck dress, skimming tight to the body until just past my rear, where it flares into a sheer flirty miniskirt. The back is nonexistent. It's perfect and will drive him crazy. Sitting down, I rub scented lotion on my body and pull on strappy gold sandals.

Lowell knocks on the door at exactly six o'clock. Opening it, I smile as I skim my eyes down his long, lean body. Mmm... smart and sexy tonight. No blazer. Just a black button-down and black pants. Returning my gaze to his face, I notice he's slightly pale with dark circles shadowing his eyes.

They darken to slate grey after scanning me. "Hmmm. You're delectable. Are you ready?" The question seems to be asking for more than one answer.

In response, I hand him my overnight bag. "I'm ready."

Montana Club is packed tonight. I see a few familiar faces from our last visit, including my favorite person, Vivienne. Lowell sees me staring at her and reaches down to grasp my hand. Squeezing it, he places it in the crook of his arm before leading me to our table.

After ordering a light meal, I sit back and take a sip of my wine. "Lowell, darling, are you sure you want to salsa tonight? You look exhausted. We can have dinner, then go to your house and just relax this evening?"

Encircling my wrist with his fingers, he turns my hand over

and brings it to his mouth. Placing a kiss in the center of my palm, he responds quietly, "It's been a busy week preparing the house for Thayer and finishing the first draft of my book. Tonight is my reward. Salsa and you in that dress. Us in my bed." His grey eyes smolder and my stomach dips.

I breathe deeply in and out to ease the ache from his words. "Tell me about your latest book."

A knowing smile crosses his lips. "It's a new series I'm working on, where the main character is a woman spy, but her allegiance is unknown."

He tells me the premise for the first book while we eat. Once dinner is cleared, they start the lesson portion of the night for those individuals who don't know how to salsa.

"I'd like to join the lesson, if you don't mind. It's been a while since I danced the salsa." Remembering how our last lesson went, I'm looking forward to teasing Lowell. Or is it challenging him?

Stepping onto the dance floor, the instructor begins with the basic front to back eight count. Of course, I exaggerate the swivel of my hips. Lowell's eyes follow my hips down to the skirt flaring scandalously high at the top of my thighs, just in time to get a brief glimpse of my scarlet thong.

Inhaling sharply, he leans down to murmur in my ear, "Are you ready for tonight's lesson?"

"I'm all yours." My intent and submission are inherent in the small statement.

On our first date, Lowell's personality seemed to reflect the tenets of the tango. A perfect mirror. Precise and controlled. Pleasure where he placed or denied it. I wouldn't have thought the salsa would fit his personality at all. The moves are too fluid and relaxed, and the dance itself is full of passion. A strong outward display of emotions is something Lowell usually avoids, but the confidence in his eyes suggests I'm in for a surprise tonight.

We dance the basic steps for the first few minutes. Forward, back, side to side. Hips swiveling in tune with each other. The lesson portion ends, and the moment the dancing begins, he flings me out to the side. Swirling, I come back, and he bends me over his arm, bringing our hips close, rolling with me from the side, back to the front. My lower body presses against his as I swing around, feeling the force of his desire. The fluidity and power in this first move assures me his command of the dance, and me, is absolute.

Throwing back my head, I laugh with sheer excitement before whipping up and catching one of his hands. Twirling, I step to his side and swivel before twirling back toward him to catch the other hand he is holding out. The fast pace of the music drums a sensual beat into my blood, every step designed to entice and capture Lowell. My hips roll and I move into his body, the motion a mimic of what's coming later.

Unexpectedly, his passion and emotions pour out in a blur, raw and real, resulting in moves designed to inspire lust and need. Tonight, he's someone else, someone with the blood born to move like this, his body alive with his own need instead of just demanding mine.

We shift and move rapidly. Owning the dance, the floor, and each other. Our hands fly as fast as our feet, and our bodies curve toward each other and flow back out. As the music nears the end, we slow, coming in tight together, my front flush to his, as if we're one body stepping forward and back instead of two. The music gets softer and softer until it ends. We stop. Still in each other's arms, our chests heave as we stare at each other, communicating all our feelings silently to one another. The sound of clapping pops the bubble encasing us.

Wrapping my hand around his neck, I stretch up and whisper in his ear, "I need you."

Lowell doesn't disappoint. He has a brief conversation with the waiter to put the charges on his member account, and we're out the door and in the vehicle five minutes later.

I shiver, but not from the cold. Anticipation, need, and nerves rack me. Tonight, Lowell's control is only a thin veneer instead of his usual iron mask. Suddenly, he's a tiger, released from the zoo into the wild, boredom and apathy replaced with purpose and hunger.

One minute we're in his vehicle, and the next, his room. Dropping the duffle, he backs me into the door and gives me a scorching kiss. Where cool and controlled existed before, raw, unhindered passion now replaces it. My desire rips out of me, and my need to be consumed by this man explodes. I kiss him back with all the feelings I have for him and all he is. Tasting him, sucking on his tongue, I show him I want it all.

Groaning, Lowell breaks away and trails a finger over my puffy lips, down my neck to the vee in the halter, until it stops at the hem of my flirty skirt. His finger slides up and into my underwear to stroke me. Time halts, emotions flit across his face while he watches me respond to him, but he abruptly stops and swivels away from me.

Confused, I watch him. He strides over to the chair in the corner and carries it to the other wall where he carefully places it sideways in front of a full-length mirror. Motioning me over to the chair, he turns my body until it's facing the seat.

I press my legs together in anticipation.

In a raspy voice strained with need, he directs me into position. "Put your knees on the seat and face the back of the chair."

Turning my back to him, I follow his command.

His hands settle on my bare shoulders. Long fingers caress my neck, circling it for a second, and this small movement makes me pant with anticipation.

He's breathing heavily, his control thin. Sliding his hands down to mine, he picks them up. "Bend over."

Placing them on the back of the chair, he waits until my hands settle. For a brief second, I can feel how hard he is, and my body quivers.

Movement on the right makes me turn, and I'm caught by the images of us in the mirror.

Lowell pushes my dress to my waist and folds to his knees

behind me. If I pushed back an inch, I could rub against him, but I don't because he hasn't given me the command to move.

Running his hands up the sides of my legs, he tugs off my red lace thong and places it in his pocket. "Spread your legs wider." His breath is a whisper. "That's it." Firm hands grip the back of my thighs. "The taste of you has been on my mind and tongue for weeks. I crave you like an addict. Images of you on the island transpose into images of you on my bed, on my desk, on the hood of my SUV, floating in the pool. Finally, I can indulge myself again."

This man kills me with his words, sending desire trickling down my legs.

In the mirror, I watch his head dip down, but the feel of his tongue is a stark reminder that I'm watching myself. It's a warped feeling. In my head, I'm watching a sexy blond in a scrap of a black dress, and a tall, devilishly dark man pleasuring her on his knees. It's voyeuristic and captivating. The man's head is moving, his hands gripping her thighs, causing the woman to arch her back and spread her legs to allow deeper access.

The combination of sight and touch overloads my senses, and intense pleasure spears through me. A moan escapes, my hands tighten on the back of the chair, and my eyes drift shut.

He stops.

I gasp. My body is so close.

"Open your eyes and watch me take you over the edge," he orders.

My eyes open and meet his in the mirror. Satisfaction gleams when he sees the glaze of passion on my face, but he returns his focus, and his tongue, to my body. This time, his strokes are quick and firm, and soon, I'm racing toward the edge.

The woman in the mirror peaks. My senses explode, along with my body. "Lowell!" I cry out, heat rippling out from the center as the orgasm rolls through my body.

Unable to move, I stay in position, heart pounding, and work to catch my breath for the next round. While the orgasm was powerful, my greedy body wants to feel him inside me. I shift my focus from our bodies to his face, which is flushed with tightly held passion. Need shines darkly on his face. Fists clenched tightly, he waits for my words.

"Lowell, I need you inside me. I want to watch the two of us together while your long cock fills me up inch by inch. Slow, then hard and fast, until we're both burning with the need to come."

His eyes are transfixed by the image of me, of us, in the mirror. But his hands are busy now, unbuttoning and unzipping his pants, my words a trigger. Taking his cock in hand, he strokes it a few times before rolling on a condom.

The tip brushes against me, and I watch it slide in inch by inch. Panting, I groan; it's so slow I want to scream. But in the mirror, it's too quick. I want to press rewind and see it again.

Finally, he's seated to the hilt. Smiling darkly, he grips my hips and rotates his, letting me feel every inch of him inside me. Moaning low at the sensation, I push back onto him, but he smiles darkly and pulls out, and I almost whimper at the loss. Driving back into me inch by inch, it's torture and satisfaction simultaneously as he repeats this maneuver again. And again.

The pace picks up and everything becomes a blur in the mirror. All I see is his body moving back and forth like a piston. All I feel is his powerful cock fucking me hard and fast. It's the last thing I remember seeing. My orgasm is close. Squeezing him tightly, I hear his harsh groan in response.

"Lowell, please." The need in my voice tips him over the edge, and he sets a furious pace, driven to send us both into an explosion.

He thrusts deeply, and we both come, drowning in the sensation of each other and the moment. I can feel him pulsing inside me. Squeezing him again, I hold tightly, knowing he can feel the tremors in my body.

Moments later, my head falls to my hands, and his drops to

my back. We stay like that for a few moments, his hands skimming my body in a calming motion until my breathing eases.

He leaves and I hear the shower turn on. Standing on shaky legs, I slide out of my dress and walk over to the bathroom. It dawns on me that he's almost fully dressed. After removing his clothes, he stands in the shower, waiting for me to join him, but I'm caught by the picture in front of me. Lowell is tall and lean, but muscular. Similar to a basketball player's physique.

My eyes meet his. Without his no-nonsense black-framed glasses, he looks younger, happier, and very relaxed, based on the smile he gives me.

"I know I can be closed off, but I want you to have no doubts about my feelings. These last few months have been the happiest of my life because of you. Beyond intriguing, you inspire me with your mind and your generous heart." His hand traces my face.

My breath stalls. "I…"

His thumb stops on my lips. "I'm falling in love with you, Kate. You mean the world to me."

"Oh, Lowell. I'm already in love with you, and I see you. All of you, not just what you choose to show me." Standing on my tiptoes, I bring his head down to meet mine. There, under the spray, I kiss him with every ounce of feeling in my body. I want this man to know, to have no doubts, that I love him. Drawing back, I watch a smile crawl across his face.

Our shower is languorous and full of soft touches, but when we walk out of the bathroom, I'm not quite sure what to do. I reach in my bag to grab the sexy nightgown I packed when he stops me.

"I have something I'd like you to wear tonight," he says, his voice husky.

He prowls over to the bed, where I see something gold glinting on it. Picking it up, it appears to be a series of chains linked together. Is it a necklace? I stand still while he puts it on me.

Lowell clasps one link around my neck. Attaching a second chain, he lets that one drop straight down my body. A third chain with nipple clamps similar to the ones he used on me at my house hooks onto the second chain and loops over to each nipple. Reaching down, he sucks each nipple to a peak before lightly clamping them. He doesn't tighten them, so there's no sting of pain; just a tugging sensation.

Continuing along the center chain, he hooks on an additional chain that wraps around my waist. From this chain, he hangs a final long chain with two gold balls attached.

"What are those?" I question him, my voice a mere whisper as I stare nervously at the golden balls gleaming in the soft light.

"Ben Wa balls. I'm going to insert them into you, okay?"

I bite my lip but agree. He strokes me a few times to make sure I'm still wet, then carefully inserts them. Their coldness startles me, but it quickly goes away. Then I feel nothing. They don't vibrate. I'm not sure what they're supposed to do.

Wanting to see the chains on my body, I stroll over to the mirror. Midway, I halt and take in a sharp breath. With every step, the balls knock together inside me, causing tiny vibrations. Standing still, they filled me, but not much else. However, walking and moving is a different story. My arousal goes from a low, satisfied hum of one to a ten in a matter of seconds.

This should be fun. With a deep breath, I continue toward the mirror. Gold glints across my body. Chains. Is this a stamp of ownership? A knowing smile plays on the lips of the woman in the mirror. Maybe she owns the man in the standing behind her in the mirror. Her body dressed in gold, each asset highlighted, powerful, and desired. That's her. Me.

Feeling a featherlight touch against my butt, I turn my back to the mirror and notice a small chain hanging down from the one around my waist, swinging against my cheeks.

Lowell's hand reaches down and pulls the chain between my legs. Running his fingers lightly down the chain, he caresses each cheek. "We can add a plug to this in the future." He watches my eyes widen at his words.

Apparently, this is a gift that keeps on giving.

Taking my shoulders, he leans my back against his front, facing the mirror. His right hand reaches up and wraps around the chain on my neck in a clear mark of dominance. His left hand plays with the chains, pulling and tugging on them, causing sensations to break out all over my body.

His eyes are glittering but very little emotion is showing anywhere else, a direct contrast to what he'd exposed earlier. This is the Lowell I know so well, emotions contained. He's retreated into his zone. Or so he thinks. I raise my eyebrow at him.

Grasping the chain at my back, I wrap it around his cock. "Hmmm, maybe we should get you a little jewelry. A cock ring made of gold perhaps? Or a chain with a plug?"

His cock twitches, and he throws his head back, laughing loudly. Pulling up my chin, he kisses me softly but thoroughly before wrapping me up in a robe. I turn to watch him pull on a T-shirt and black boxers.

"I thought the plan was to keep me naked and wrapped in chains and loops all night?" I tease him.

"Wrapped in chains, yes. Naked, up to you. I thought we'd go downstairs and get a piece of Lev's sinfully delicious chocolate cake and a glass of wine. You don't have to wear the robe. Neither Lev nor Shaw would mind." His voice is smug and so is his smirk.

The image of me in the middle of them all plays in my head. I've never experimented with multiple partners in bed. Then again, I've never dated multiple people at once either. Who would I want though? Mixing Lowell and Lev doesn't feel right. Lev is passion, sunshine, and exuberance. Shaw? Two dominating men, directing my every move? Yes, please.

With a wink, I loosely belt the robe, leaving enough space to show off the fine gold jewelry wrapped around my body, then walk out the door. Lowell follows with a chuckle, his hand caressing the small of my back through the silk.

By the time we make it downstairs, I can barely focus on anything Lowell is saying. Those damn Ben Wa balls are knocking together, and it's all I can do to put one foot in front of the other. After an interminably long time, we make it to the kitchen.

Chapter Thirty-Three

KATE

Shaw and Lev are standing around the island when we walk into the kitchen. Eyebrows go up at the sight of me in a short silk robe and gold body chains.

Shaw greets me before exchanging silent words with Lowell. "Hello, Kate. I've missed you this week."

"I've missed you too, Shaw," I reply in a husky voice, thinking about the last time I saw him.

Lev finally tears his eyes away from the chains and clears his throat. "Hello, sweetheart. You two are home early. How did the salsa dancing go?"

Smirking, Lowell responds, "I'd say it went very well. Vigorous and very stimulating. Right, love?"

Both Lev and Shaw groan.

I can't help the smile of satisfaction that crosses my lips. "I'm starving. Lev, I hear you've been holding out on me?"

Lev darts a glance at Lowell.

"I told her about your chocolate cake. We came down to get a piece, and a glass of wine," Lowell explains.

Lev jumps up and brings over a cake platter. Inside is a beautiful, dark, three-tier chocolate cake smothered in rich, chocolate icing with strawberries on top. It's beautiful. Almost as beautiful as the three men surrounding me. Slicing a piece, he hands us the cake and two forks, then grabs the bottle behind him and pours us each a glass of wine.

Taking a bite, I moan. This is the best chocolate cake I've ever eaten, and since it's one of my top three favorite desserts, I've got plenty to compare it with.

"This is so damn good. If I didn't love you before, I do now. Want to move in with me?" I laugh but I can't help but wonder how he'll react to my declaration.

He stares at me with something that looks like love in his eyes, then he laughs and jokingly responds, "When you can love me for me, and not my food, then we'll talk about moving in together." His green eyes move from me to Shaw and Lowell, as if to gauge their reaction.

Conscious of the hidden meaning, I'm serious when I reply, "The time to have that discussion is coming soon, I believe."

He gives me a serious nod in return.

Straightening up, I fold my arms across my chest. "Now, for the serious question of the night, do you have any ice cream to go with this masterpiece?"

He winks and walks over to the freezer.

I glance up and catch Lowell in deep thought.

When I silently question him, he shakes his head and leans down to captures my lips in a passionate and utterly delicious kiss. The flavors from the rich, dark chocolate of the cake and robust wine heightening the sensual experience.

Breaking the kiss, I stare up at him with a question in my eyes. He only strokes a finger down my face before picking up his fork.

Shaw, ever the observer, notices my flinch when I move back into my seat after the kiss. "What's wrong? Are you hurt?"

Blushing, I reassure him, "I'm very good. Not hurt."

Lowell, for some reason, feels the need to explain. "She's aroused. There are two Ben Wa balls inside her and she's feeling their effects." He takes a sip of wine.

I give him an incredulous look.

Stunned silence follows at Lowell's announcement.

"Fuck, I can't take anymore. I'm out of here. Going to take a shower." Lev walks around the island and peeks into my robe, then gives me a sweet kiss good night. "A long very cold shower." He glares at Lowell.

Lowell chuckles softly.

Raising my head, I meet Shaw's burning gaze. My face feels like it's on fire. Embarrassed, I turn back to Lowell and catch him having another silent conversation with Shaw. "What would you say to having Shaw join us tonight?"

Shocked, I stare at him. "What? Together? But it's your night."

Lowell notices I didn't immediately say no. "Is that your only concern? If so, I've already had an incredible night with you. I plan to have many, many more nights with you. As long as you're happy, why would I mind?"

Well… damn. A warm feeling crosses my chest. Many, many nights. I sigh. Lowell wanting to share me with Shaw never crossed my mind. Images of them both flow through my mind, making my nipples tighten and body shift restlessly. I suck in a deep breath.

Shaw steps forward, a frown on his face. "If this makes you uncomfortable, we can wait. Like Lowell said, we'll have plenty of nights."

Coming to a decision, I decide to go for it. "If Lowell doesn't mind…" I look up at Lowell and see his smile. "I want you both."

A smile blooms across Shaw's face. "If you'll excuse me, I'm going to take a quick shower while you two finish your cake and wine. I'll meet you in Lowell's room." Striding over, he grabs my head in his hands and crushes me with a deep kiss until I'm clutching his broad shoulders.

Yes, I want this man.

He breaks off the kiss and walks out of the room.

When I turn back to Lowell, he's holding up one of the strawberries. "Yes, please." Juice squirts out, running down my chin and dripping onto my left breast. I lift my hand to wipe it off, but Lowell grabs my wrist, stopping me.

He slowly leans down and licks it off. "So sweet, love. It reminds me of another sweet from earlier this evening." Chuckling, he helps me stand. "I'd pick you up and carry you, but I believe we should walk off this cake, don't you?"

I narrow my eyes at the devious glint in his eyes. I'd forgotten about the Ben Wa balls. After taking a few steps, I gasp. The sensation is even stronger now. I glare back at Lowell, who's laughing behind me. I don't mind them, but combined with the sensitivity from our first round, it's a bit of a torture fest.

Chapter Thirty-Four

KATE

By the time we're back upstairs, my nipples are hard and stiff, and I'm throbbing with need. Lowell takes my robe off and leads me over to the bed. Standing by the side, I wait for his instructions. His natural, controlling nature is coming out to play and he needs me submissive to his demands.

Pleased with my actions, he murmurs, "You deserve a reward." Laying me down on the bed, he spreads my legs and inserts a finger into me to remove the Ben Wa balls. Once they're gone, he begins to stroke in and out. "Mmm, you're so wet already, let's go straight to three." He inserts two more fingers. My hips rise to meet the thrusts of his long fingers. "That's it. Fuck my fingers," he murmurs.

His hard body covers mine and he sucks hard on my aching nipple. I arch up against him, but he pushes me back down, then tightens the clamps.

Whimpering, my head rolls from side to side, pleasure and pain swirling inside me.

"Fuck," Shaw's deep voice fills the room.

He's standing to the side, watching us.

I return my gaze to Lowell's implacable face. My body is already close to the edge. "Please, Lowell. Help me come."

Tilting his head, he smiles darkly and removes his fingers.

I lay there, waiting for him to decide our next course of action, knowing he's not ready for me to come yet.

He sucks his fingers clean, then reaches down to part my folds. "You're so deliciously wet. Shaw's cock is going to feel so good sliding into you. Look at her, Shaw."

Groaning, Shaw slides a finger into me, then brings it to his mouth and sucks it. "Damn, you're so fucking sweet."

"Let's get you into another position."

Lowell helps me sit up, gives me a kiss, then shows me where he wants me next. On my knees, facing the end of the bed.

Once I'm in position, he pulls a loop out of the corner rail before motioning for Shaw to do the same on the other side. They each pull one of my hands through a loop until I'm strung up between the two posts at the end of the bed. My body is on display, ready for their next command.

They undress quickly and my breath hitches as I glance from one to the other. Possessiveness and desire roar through me. They are mine. Mine tonight and mine tomorrow.

Lowell moves to stand at the end of the bed, facing me, and Shaw gets on the bed behind me. I should be nervous at this moment, but I'm not. Instead, it's intoxicating. Powerful.

I can feel Shaw's hard body pressing up against mine before he sits back on his heels. His hands drop to my ass and he rubs my cheeks reverently. "Gorgeous." Grabbing some oil from the nightstand, he rubs it onto every inch.

The sensual strokes have me pressing back against him, brushing his cock, and he slides it along the inside of my cheeks. I can't help but moan at the thought of him there. This time, he grabs my hips and holds me to him. It feels so big against my tiny hole. He slides it up and down, as if to mimic the act. My mind explodes and I widen my legs in anticipation.

"Patience, angel. We have to get this beautiful hole ready first." He exhales sharply. "Lowell, do you have any plugs?" His hands continue to massage the oil while he waits for Lowell to hand him a plug and some lubricant. "Have you ever had a plug, angel?"

"It's been a while. I experimented a bit in college." Anticipation rolls down my back. "I loved it."

A harsh breath escapes him and he reaches down to squeeze his cock. "You're killing me. Tonight, the plug."

Agreeing, I turn my attention back to Lowell. He's been quiet, watching me and Shaw, until now. He snags the chain tethering my clamped nipples together and tugs me forward to kiss me hard. As his hands loosen the clamps for a few minutes, tingles rush in, causing me to cry out. His tongue instantly soothes each nipple, licking and lightly sucking until the pleasure chases away the pain. I smile. I swear, this man loves my breasts more than the rest of me.

With Lowell sucking my nipples, I'm lost in a haze until I feel Shaw's finger probing my back hole. Rimming it, he spreads lube, then slips inside. I gasp at the thickness of it.

Shaw adds a second finger and a raw sound escapes me. He strokes them in and out. He's right. I'm so tight down there. Breathing heavily, I hold my breath.

Lowell leans over my shoulder to watch Shaw. "Hmm, you love Shaw finger fucking your ass, don't you, love?"

"Yes," I admit with a whimper.

Shaw withdraws his fingers. "When I tell you, I want you to bear down just a little bit. Do you understand?" When I nod, he pushes my shoulders and head further toward Lowell so he can have better access. "Now."

As I bear down, he slides the plug all the way inside. He gives it a few strokes, causing me to moan loudly before he pushes it snug to my ass. Pulling me to sit up, I inhale sharply when it moves inside me.

"Are you okay? How does it feel?" Shaw asks, his hand rubbing me.

"Full. Good. I forgot how good this feels," I admit, my voice barely a whisper.

Shaw pulls my head around for a long, deep kiss. "Lowell needs you."

Lowell is stroking his cock, waiting for me, and I open my mouth. He firmly grips my head and pulls back to get a better angle.

My hand moves to hold him, but something pulls tight, and I realize my wrists are still tied. Lowell will be controlling me entirely. Pace, thrust, depth. I groan. With this position, I must take whatever he gives me. My only power will be the skills my mouth deploys to incite his pleasure.

He slowly enters my mouth and strokes in and out while I suck and lick his cock. His eyes glitter as he looks at Shaw behind me and gives him a signal. "That's it, love. Take my cock while Shaw fills that sweet pussy of yours."

A second later, I feel Shaw's cock at the opening. Lifting me up a bit, he brings me down entirely on his cock in one thrust.

They're both in control of me now. My hands grip the cords on each side.

They work together to keep their rhythms in sync. Lowell slides in deep, almost pushing me down onto Shaw's cock before Shaw uses his strength to lift me up again.

Lost in a sea of sensation, raw sounds spill incoherently from my lips, the pleasure overriding any ability to think or speak.

Lowell breaks out in a sweat as he struggles to keep a slow pace. Finally, Shaw starts speeding up, and Lowell takes his cue. My lips stretch to take his hard, deep strokes.

"That's it. Take every inch of my cock with your plump, pink lips and your sweet tongue," he groans.

His pace is furious and jerky before he suddenly slows and comes. He grips his cock while I lick up every drop, and after a second or two, he pulls out. My head falls forward, resting on his stomach for a moment. Breathing heavily, he strokes my hair where he had clenched it.

"That was incredible. I love you."

"I love you too, Lowell," I reply.

His eyes light up at my words. Love flows between us. Silent, but powerful. After minutes, which feels like days, the kiss draws to a temporary conclusion.

Sweeping my hair out of my face, he buries his face in my neck and breathes me in.

"Lowell," Shaw bites out, his control at its limits.

Lowell raises his head and gives me a brief kiss, then nods.

I push back into Shaw and he resumes his stroking.

The loops on my hands prevent me from touching him in return. Dropping them down, I arch back into his thrust, working to find a way to get him deeper inside of me.

"I know. I need to be deeper too," he says gruffly. Rising up on his knees, he pushes my face down into the mattress in front of me, before sliding in deep.

My body quivers. "Shaw, that's it. All the way." This is exactly what I need. "Faster."

Shaw's hips pull back once, then he begins to stroke in and out, hard and fast. "That's it. You're so tight and wet around my cock. With that plug in your ass, it's like having two cocks in you at once. One day, Lowell and I will fill you up like this, and you'll be wrapped around us so tight."

With each stroke, the plug moves with his cock, and it feels like two different cocks are fucking me at once. All I can do is whimper at the thought of the two of them. "So close. Now." I hover at the precipice.

Reaching down, Shaw strokes and pinches my clit and my body explodes like a firework. Heat rushes out from the center, making my toes curl. "Shaw!"

My body clenches his cock and the plug, but it doesn't stop with one wave. Lowell releases the nipple clamps, and my body trembles as another wave hits.

With my release, Shaw thrusts one more time, then I feel him pulse within me as he comes. Hands grip my hips, keeping us fused together.

"It gets better and better." He leans heavily on me while he tries to catch his breath. "Thank you."

"Mm. You're incredible," I murmur.

My body shivers when he pulls out both himself and the plug, and I can't help but groan at how empty I am now. Emotionally, though, I'm full. I shift my body to sit up and Lowell immediately removes my hands from the loops, massaging each wrist to make sure they both have circulation.

Yawning, I run a hand through my hair. I'm exhausted.

After cleaning up, I fall into the center of the bed, Lowell and Shaw on either side of me. All three of us together. I'm not alone anymore.

Chapter Thirty-Five

KATE

THE NEXT MORNING, I DRAG MYSELF AWAY FROM LOWELL AND SHAW and head back to my apartment. Thayer is coming home today, and I feel like they could all use some alone time to get him settled. Plus, after his first call to the office, I'm nervous about meeting him. Here I am, a complete stranger, in a relationship with three of his brothers. I'm sure he'll wonder how this happened so quickly.

I keep busy by running errands. Initially, they were going to wait to introduce us, but things have progressed so much they think waiting will give Thayer the wrong impression. I'm going to the ranch for lunch tomorrow for the official introduction.

Even though Lev's got the food covered, I want to contribute something. Lev's chocolate cake is delicious, but it's rich, so I decide to make an angel's food cake with a strawberry whip cream frosting.

The rest of the evening, I alternate between worrying about Thayer and thinking about Lowell and Shaw. While being with both of them at the same time should have felt awkward, it didn't. Everything flowed so easily between me and them. I blush when my mind conjures an image of the three of us. It's a new side to me I never expected, but their dominant needs give me the freedom to let loose. I think less about what I should be doing or if they're enjoying it. Instead, it's all about our needs.

In every other part of my life, my type A personality rarely lets me be a follower. My brain is too busy thinking about everything to spend more than a second on one single area. With Lowell and Shaw, letting go felt amazing. Giving that control to someone else and knowing they will only give or take what I need is liberating.

In my twenties, my mind was consumed with school, my residency, my marriage, and my first real job as a doctor. When my life fell apart, survival consumed my thoughts, and life narrowed down to a pinpoint. Every step I took was carefully plotted to make sure it wouldn't backfire.

Now, my horizon is broadening again. Strength and self-awareness have given me the freedom to be the woman I was meant to be. Loving all three of them exemplifies this newfound confidence. But our relationship is fragile, and I'm not sure how it will hold up against Thayer.

I stretch and groan at the soreness, especially those muscles that haven't been used in a while. Grinning, I head to the bedroom, flop down on the bed, and I'm out.

Sifting through my closet the next morning, I decide to wear a strappy red sundress and cork wedges. With my hair down in its natural state, it says pretty and summery without trying too hard. I think. My nerves are getting worse. Taking a deep breath, I stare at myself in the mirror and stick out my tongue. The mirror returns the gesture, and I laugh.

I carefully prop the cake stand in the passenger seat of my rental and start the drive over to their place.

That's another thing I need to sort out. Getting a new vehicle. I need to decide which SUV I want to purchase next. While I love Lowell's, I'm not sure I want to spend that much. I consider asking one of them to go shopping with me, but I kind of love the thrill of beating the salesperson in negotiations, which would be hard to do with a man beside me. Maybe I'll go next week.

Parking in front of the house, I see Shaw striding from the barn. We meet on the passenger side of my car. His hands slide around me and he swoops down for a passionate kiss.

"Angel, I know it's only been a day, but after our night together, I can't think of anything else. I miss you. Maybe we should all talk about you coming over on the weekends and staying with us? I know you're busy during the week, but I feel like we don't get enough time together. Not just the two of us, but all of us together. What do you think?" His brown eyes search mine for answers.

I frown. "Let's wait and see how things go. Thayer's only been home for a second, and I don't want to barge into his life. Especially right now when he's feeling unsettled. I'd love to be with all of you, but I want it to be right too."

Running a hand through his hair, he blows out a breath. "I understand your point, but let's not push back the decision too far."

I agree and reach down to grab the cake out of the vehicle. Entering the kitchen, I hand it to Lev.

"What?! You didn't have to bring anything but your delicious self, especially not food."

"I can cook, you know. You're not the only one. By the way, that needs to go into the refrigerator until we're ready to serve it." I rise up on my tiptoes and give his pouty lower lip a nibble. "It's an angel food cake, with strawberry whipped cream frosting."

He gives a soft groan and reaches down to deepen the kiss. We're kissing for a few minutes when I hear something I haven't heard in a while. A soft whirring sound that stops behind me. Dread fills my stomach and a light sweat breaks out on my forehead. That sound. I whirl around.

A man with blond tousled hair and icy blue eyes is staring at me from a wheelchair. Gasping, I back up into Lev.

What the fuck? Collin?

My panic becomes full-blown. Collin is sitting in front of me.

Terror rises, the image blurs, and my head shakes from side to side in denial.

"You're dead. You're dead," I whimper hysterically.

Tremors shake my body, and I scramble to stand behind Lev. When he tries to turn and face me, I grip his shirt and lock him into place between me and Collin.

Lev yells for Shaw, who comes running into the kitchen. While he doesn't understand the reason, he quickly grasps my terror, comes around Lev, and picks me up. The whirring sounds again, and I whimper.

Men are yelling as he takes me from the kitchen to his room. Sitting in a leather chair, he holds me close in his lap. Away from the noise, my logical brain tries to understand what happened, but the other part of me just clings to Shaw.

Collin is dead. He can't be here in Montana. He can't.

I try to breathe, but I can't. Chest heaving, I grip Shaw's shirt to get his attention. Panic starts to take over.

"Easy, angel. Breathe in with me. One. Two. Three. And out. One. Two. Three. That's it. Again." Shaw studies my face as he carefully counts breaths with me and smooths his hand down my shoulders.

After a couple minutes, my breathing subsides back to normal. "Who is that man in the wheelchair?"

"That was Thayer." Reaching over to the side table, he plucks up a frame with all four guys in it and hands it to me.

It's the first photo I've seen Thayer in without a hat and sunglasses. He bears a strong resemblance to Collin. In this picture, his hair is cut short, not the tousled length I saw in the kitchen. Their faces have a similar shape, the man in this picture has a strong jawline and cleft chin while Collin's was rounder and fuller. The light blue eyes though…. they're almost identical in color. They pierce through me like a knife, making me bleed.

I reluctantly hand the picture back to Shaw. "He looks like my husband, Collin."

Shaw tenses as he takes the frame. "How much like him?"

"The same tousled blond hair and the exact color blue of his eyes. Thayer's face is shaped differently, squarer than Collin's, but he could definitely be his brother." I pull up the photo of Collin from the beach on my phone and hand it to Shaw.

He inhales sharply as he stares down at it.

I wave my hand. "Plus, you add in the wheelchair and it's as if Collin came back from the dead. I couldn't see Thayer, only Collin. He was paraplegic after getting shot." I flinch at the memory. "My mind tells me he's dead, but my eyes feel like it's a lie when I look at Thayer."

"Kate—" His phone buzzes, cutting him off. Reading the messages, he sends back a quick reply. Then his hands wrap around my head and he stares at me, his brown eyes reassuring pools of chocolate. "That's definitely NOT Collin down there. Do you hear me? I promise you, it's Thayer. I've known him for years. He's my friend and brother." He gaze is steady, letting me absorb his words. "Do you mind texting me that photo of Collin? I'd like to share it with everyone. It'll help explain what's going on."

After Shaw shares the photo and explanation, several pings come back. Lowering the phone, he shares the messages with me. Lev and Lowell have a couple of ideas that could help the immediate situation.

"Thayer actually wears his hair more like the photo in this picture, not the tousled mess it is now. He hasn't had a chance to get it cut, but knowing his OCD behavior, I'm sure he's already got an appointment scheduled for next week. In the meantime, what if we put a hat on him and ask him to sit on the couch in the living room instead of in the wheelchair? Would you try to meet him again?"

My voice is silently screaming *NO!* as I sit there, but eventually, I nod. This means a lot to our relationships. But to go down there willingly and stare into Collin's eyes again? I don't know if I can do it. Just yesterday I was patting myself on the back for my strength, but today it feels like it's crumbling to dust. I squeeze my hands tightly together, knowing I have to do this and hating it.

"I'll try. I'm sorry, but that's all I can do," I reply with a whisper.

"That's all we're asking. We'll be right there with you, holding your hand the whole time, I swear."

He stands up and my feet drop to the ground. The crushing hug he gives me helps. I don't know if he's trying to lend me his strength or if he knows how much I just need to be held, but it steadies me. Clasping his hand, I follow him back to the living room.

Lev and Lowell are standing in the center of the room. Lev's hands are clenched and his eyes dark green with worry. Tightness around Lowell's eyes and mouth are the only indication of the current underneath his calm surface. Having stalled long enough, my eyes slide to the man sitting on the couch.

Panic swarms me, but I search for the differences I know are there. Having his hair up in the hat helps remove the immediate visual impression of Collin. Thayer has a strong, square jaw and cleft chin. He's broader in the shoulders. His hands are blunt, not long and fine like Collin's. With him sitting down, I can't tell how tall he is, but he seems taller than Collin's 5'11". The more I scrutinize him, the more I can almost see Thayer instead of Collin. Until I look into his cold, ice-blue eyes.

Collin... Shaking my head, I correct myself. *Thayer. That's Thayer Bradford. Dr. Thayer Bradford.*

It's hard to get past them. Collin's eyes were sparkling, blue bursts of light before the shooting, but afterward, they resembled the same coldness reflected back at me right now.

Thayer frowns the longer I stare at him without saying anything. His eyes assess me, trying to read my mood, but he doesn't know me well enough. Shaw squeezes my hand, and Thayer's eyes immediately narrow on our joined hands. When his eyes move away, I exhale for the first time since I entered the room. Without his eyes locked on mine, I finish sweeping the rest of his features and body, finding little resemblance to Collin. I ease my grip on Shaw's hand and sigh.

My sigh brings all eyes back to me though, including Thayer's. My mind is still reconciling the fact that this is Thayer, but I can't meet his eyes without feeling the need to flinch, scream, or run. I might be able to hold a conversation if I stare at his chin.

My voice is tight and raspy as I greet him. "Thayer, I'm very sorry for my reaction, and I hope you can forgive me for ruining your homecoming. I'm Kate." I know I should say I'm happy to meet him, but I just can't bring the words to my mouth.

"It's fine. I understood once I saw the picture of your husband." His voice is deep and clipped when he responds. Thankfully, his voice is nothing like Collin's smooth, cultured voice, and it helps ease a bit more tension from my shoulders.

His blue eyes capture mine, and I shiver. I think that's about all I can handle. "I'm going to go home now. I hope we can talk more next time." His chin dips down in acknowledgement, but he doesn't encourage me to stay.

Shaw, Lowell, and Lev protest, but I insist. I need time to consider this new angle. I didn't even get into the bigger issue of the wheelchair. Giving each of them a hug and a fake smile to Thayer, I pick up my purse and head out, leaving them to their private homecoming and me to the despair rolling over me.

Chapter Thirty-Six

LEV

I'M MINDLESSLY WIPING DOWN THE BAR WHEN SHAW AND LOWELL walk in and plop themselves on a barstool. They both look as shitty as I feel. None of us are sleeping. I'm lost in the dark without my sunshine.

Lowell's writing at all hours of the day and night. At this rate, he'll have three books ready to publish in a month.

Shaw's breaking his back, getting up before dawn, driving the ranch hands crazy with his demands.

Kate texted us a few times during the week, but the messages were short and noncommittal. When I pushed to see her, she would only reply with a request for time. None of my jokes or memes got a reply, even though I know she read them. My heart aches for her pain, but I'm worried she'll use this as an excuse to run.

"You look like hell, Lev." Shaw's voice snaps me out of my thoughts.

"Pot, meet kettle, Shaw. You too, Lowell." I throw down the towel and pour us all a beer. "What are you two doing here? Who's with Thayer?"

"He's at rehab right now," Shaw says, picking up his beer

and taking a long drink. "It's hard to discuss Kate around him. He's relieved she isn't at the house."

I give him a hard stare. "We seem to have two issues, but it might be easier to tackle Thayer instead of Kate's ghost." Seeing their agreement, I continue. "How can we help him come to terms with Kate? I don't even know what the fuck's wrong with him. He's never been the type to dismiss someone without getting to know them. Something else is going on, and we need to dig into it and help him. The first thing we should do is have a house meeting and tell him Kate's background. If he understands her background, he'll give her a chance. What do you think?"

"It might help. Thayer's floundering right now. He went skiing and woke up several months later to find his life changed beyond recognition. It's going to take time. Time for him to heal and find his footing," Shaw says slowly, his face pensive.

Our phones buzz, and Lowell picks up his first. "It's Kate. She's going to take a week off and visit her mother. Sarah will manage the patients next week, and she's asked one of the doctors at the hospital to come into the office for a few days. Sarah said it's the same one Thayer used in the past, so she feels they're suitable." Lowell's fingers tap a rhythm on the bar. "Is she running?"

I heave a sigh. "God, I hope not, but I don't know. Let's give her some space while she's gone. In the meantime, we can work on Thayer."

Be careful. I'll miss you, sweetheart. Hitting send, I hover over the phone to text her my love but end up putting it down. I don't want to pressure her.

That evening, Thayer, Lowell, and Shaw are sitting in the living room when I get home. Grabbing a beer, I join them. Shaw and Lowell have been telling Thayer about Kate's past, but I'm not sure it's going well. His face is impassive as he listens, asking few questions.

Once they stop, Thayer pulls out a report and hands it to Shaw. "Her story's sad, but that doesn't rule out her being a gold digger. Her husband came from old money and had a substantial trust fund. She inherited everything when he died. Over thirty million dollars. A year later, she barely had five million in the bank." Frowning, Shaw skims through the report, then hands it to me and Lowell.

Shaw gives a growl of frustration. "I don't care what she did with the money. If she gave it away or went on a shopping spree. It says she hasn't spent any of it since then. Why is this important?"

"I've spent my whole life avoiding gold diggers. I go into the hospital for six months, and all of you fall for this stranger. Did you even complete a background check on her?" Thayer asks, his face twisted in frustration.

Lowell's normally placid nature erupts in anger. "I completed an employment background only. We thought about conducting a more thorough investigation, but we decided it wasn't necessary for her employment. Later, when we became involved personally, we decided to wait for her to tell us. It's obvious her past is painful. We needed time to build our trust, and hers."

Lowell starts pacing around the room, as if to control his overflowing emotions. "In one day, she lost almost everything that mattered to her. Guilt weighs on her like a boulder. She's rootless because people who discover her past automatically judge her guilty, making it difficult for her to stay in one place. Two years after the shooting, her husband killed himself. And maybe she's hiding something else. I can't imagine what it is, but if she hasn't told us yet, you can bet your ass it's bad. But you know what? I don't fucking care. She can tell me when she's damn good and ready." He throws his hands up in the air.

"I would have thought you of all people would see the logic in digging deeper. You've let someone filled with secrets into our home. She comes here for a temporary assignment, and within five months she's ingrained in the lives of three wealthy men? Come on. That's a bit fast, don't you think?"

"Why would I care? I know she's not after my money. Once you get to know her, you'll understand she isn't remotely interested in it. But the bottom line? For me? I love her. I love the fact that she sees me. Not the author, not the robot. She sees the person I thought I'd left behind a long time ago. So no, I don't care what information you think you have on her. I know her." Lowell breathes heavily, full of anger.

Thayer's jaw, wide open from watching Lowell combust, closes with a snap. "You're not even acting like the old Lowell! Neither is Lev. He's just sitting there quietly instead of blowing up at me. The only person here acting normal is Shaw. This is what I mean. She's turned this house, and all of you, upside down."

Taking a drink, I decide to correct his impression. "She's not turning it upside down. She's making it right. For so long, Lowell shut himself away. Shut his emotions behind a fucking brick wall for years. Kate refuses to accept the façade. He's able to show her how much he cares." I take another long drink. "For me, Kate's sunshine and laughter. She eases the intense emotions that rage within me. I don't feel like I need to be a workaholic to exhaust myself or blow up at someone. For the first time, I'm truly happy." Blowing out a deep breath, I glance at Shaw.

"When she came here, I pushed her away and held her at arm's length for months even though I knew she was meant for me. I didn't want another Vanessa coming in to destroy us when she left. Kate's honesty and willingness to risk everything for us is intoxicating. Vanessa never risked anything; she was a taker. Kate makes me see more is possible, a real future." Shaw stops, letting Thayer digest his words.

"You called her Vanessa," Thayer murmurs quietly, his eyes downcast as he realizes Shaw has moved on completely. "I'm sorry. I don't trust her. She wouldn't even look me in the eyes. I know she told us it was because of her husband, but was it? There's something else there, I can feel it. You know my gut is usually right. She's jumpy, and I want to know why." He leans forward. "Invite her over when she gets back. Let's see if I'm right. If I'm wrong, I'll back off." Using the controls, he leaves the room, the wheelchair whirring a quiet backdrop after the shouting.

Rubbing a hand over his scruff, Shaw blows out a deep breath. "He's not wrong, you know. Something about the whole episode was off the other night." Holding up his hand to stop Lowell from speaking, he says wearily, "I'm not saying I don't trust Kate, or that I think Thayer's right about the gold-digging. Looking at the picture of her husband, I know she was freaked out about how closely Thayer resembled Collin, but there was something else under the surface. And whatever it is, we need to resolve it. For her sake. Not for Thayer's. But I also don't want to push her too hard. When she gets back, let's invite her over for Sunday dinner." Standing, he strides out of the room.

Lowell shakes his head at the turn of events. "I would rather just be honest and straightforward instead of inviting her over for dinner and hoping it comes to light." Taking off his black frames, he rubs his eyes, then puts them back on. "I'm going to bed." He follows Shaw's path out of the room.

Sitting there, gazing out at the starry night, I sip my beer and think about my sunshine. I understand both sides, but my biggest fear is that if we keep pushing her, she'll run away. For good.

Chapter Thirty-Seven

KATE

SHORTLY AFTER GETTING BACK TO TOWN, I GET A TEXT FROM SHAW, inviting me over for dinner. Biting the inside of my cheek, a million thoughts swirl in my brain. What if I can't handle being around Thayer? What if they choose him without giving me a chance? This could blow up in so many ways.

I drop onto the couch with exhaustion. Spending a week with my mom gave me some distance from the situation, but it didn't resolve anything. Time is ticking away with Thayer's return, and I've gone from absolute bliss to a pool of fear.

My phone buzzes again as Shaw adds a few details and asks for a confirmation. I take a deep breath and slowly exhale. I need to see them so badly. My heart physically aches without them near.

Kate: I'll be there tomorrow. I've missed you.

When I get to the ranch the next afternoon, my body tenses when I hear the whirring of the wheelchair. Opening the door, Thayer scans me from head to toe before backing up to let me into the house. Shoulders thrown back, I step in and move to the side to allow him to close the door.

Glancing at him, I notice he's cut his hair since I've been gone, and it helps. My first thought isn't of Collin anymore, thank goodness.

"Hello, Thayer. Where is everybody?" I ask with a slight tremble in my voice.

Thayer flings his hand toward the living room. I wait for him to lead the way, but he's too much of a gentleman and motions for me to go first. Sweat breaks out on my upper lip and panic rises. My mind scrambles for an escape.

"Are you going to stand there all day?" he sneers.

Taking a few steps forward, I hear the wheelchair roll behind me. The soft whirring sound is universal. My hands shake as I wipe off the sweat on my upper lip. Thankfully, my back is to Thayer, so he can't see what I'm doing, or I'm sure he'd find a reason to be hateful. I stride off toward the living room quickly, hoping to outrun the sound, but the more steps I take, the louder the whirring gets until I'm almost panicking.

Stopping, I take several deep breaths.

Thayer rolls up beside me. "What's wrong with you? Are you sick?"

Shaking my head from side to side, I notice a bathroom tucked under the stairs. "Excuse me, please. I need to use the restroom."

Skirting around Thayer, I practically run into the room and close the door, sagging in relief. I don't know if I can do this; am I strong enough? I splash cold water on my face and wrists, trying to regain my composure. The mirror reflects the fear inside me. Closing my eyes, I work on breathing for a few seconds before opening them. The fear is still there, but hopefully I appear calmer on the outside.

When I step out, Thayer is waiting for me.

Damn it. Why couldn't he leave me to find my own way? I've been here several times. "Oh, you didn't need to wait. I know the way," I tell him, hoping he will take the hint and go.

Smiling widely, he gestures to the living room. "After you."

Steeling my spine, I walk toward the living room. The only sound I hear is the chair following close behind me. Too close. Panic creeps up again. Breathing shallowly, I work to catch my breath. Turning my head slightly, I see the chair in the corner of my eye and walk into the doorway to the living room.

"Ouch. Damn it." My face smarts from the impact with the doorframe and tears fill my eyes. The chair stops next to me.

"What the hell? Are you drunk?" Thayer peers at me, trying to figure out what's going on.

"No, I'm not drunk. It's the afternoon," I snap at him. Angry now, I glare at him, hoping he'll move away, but he doesn't. My fear spikes, and I grip the doorframe behind me. "I simply ran into the door. Do you mind?" Gesturing for him to move the chair, I wait.

His eyes narrow in speculation. Grasping the controller, he moves the chair in my direction, and I back into the wall. His face lights up with anger. "Are you afraid of the wheelchair? You're a doctor, for fuck's sake. How can you be afraid of it?"

Lev, Lowell, and Shaw stand and cross over to us when they hear Thayer's loud voice questioning me.

"What the hell's going on?" Shaw growls, his voice tight as he eyes swivel from Thayer to me. Given that Thayer has me practically backed into the corner, I can see how this might look.

"It's nothing. I wasn't paying attention and walked into the doorway," I interject.

"You walked into it because you're afraid of the wheelchair." Thayer's anger spills over as he gleefully explains the situation. "She's a fucking doctor, and she's scared of a man in a wheelchair. Wow, what compassion."

When Shaw turns his gaze toward me, I close my eyes. I can't hide from this. Straightening, I pull back my shoulders and open my eyes to face the music. "He's right. But he's also wrong. Can we all sit down?"

Thayer wheels himself toward the living room, and I indicate someone else to follow his lead and put some distance between us. Lev follows Thayer. Lowell reaches down and grasps my hand to pull me toward the living room, leaving Shaw to bring up the rear.

Lowell guides me to the couch, Lev and Shaw sit in the chairs beside us. They all turn toward me, but Lowell's grip on my chin commands all my attention. "You don't have to tell us anything. It's none of our business. I love you, and I stand by whatever decision you make here. We all have nasty, rotten skeletons in our closets. Yours belong to you."

"No, I need to hear this story," Thayer demands, his anger spilling over once more. "Not only is she a gold digger, she's obviously a piss poor doctor too."

"I don't give a fuck what you want," Lowell states quietly in return, a muscle ticking in his jaw. "She doesn't have to tell this story. She owes you nothing."

Taking a deep breath, I exhale in a steady stream. My throat tightens, and my eyes burn.

I clear my throat a few times. "You want the truth? Fine. Then, you can fuck off." Swallowing, I jump into the beginning. "The gunman shot Collin once, but his aim was perfect. It impacted Collin's vertebrae and spinal cord. For the first few months, both Collin and I were in recovery. Our only focus was living. Once we were out of the hospital, I went home. Collin went into a rehabilitation center to learn basic functions as his nervous system had been greatly impacted."

I request a glass of water. My eyes track over to Shaw, whose hands are clenched. I don't know if he's angry or what, but given that he won't meet my eyes, I'm not sure. Lowell's thumb caresses my hand. Thankful for that small gesture, I glance at his grey eyes and give him a weak smile.

Lev comes back with the water and takes a seat beside me. After taking a few sips, I set it down and continue.

"Even after months of rehab, Collin never regained sensation in his lower body." Thayer's face whitens. "He was diagnosed as paraplegic, and not only did this impact his life, he let it take everything from him." Thayer's eyes bore into me intently. "Collin was a neurosurgeon. After the shooting, his muscle control was weak and inconsistent, and he had a permanent tremor in his hands. Neurosurgery is extremely precise and requires dexterity, and the ability to operate for hours without stopping. Even after months of rehab, he wouldn't be able to perform at that level."

Picking up the water, I use the coolness to ease the tension in my throat. I'd never told anyone this part of the story. While my mother guessed some of it, she never knew the full picture.

"When he finally came home, he was so cold to me. I hoped with time he would realize he was alive, and while changed, his life could still have meaning. He could be a doctor, even perform general surgery, just not neurosurgery. Or if he wanted to do something else, I would help him find a new path. I tried to get him to go to group therapy, but he refused. The only time he left the house was to go to rehab. He spent the rest of his time researching spinal cord injuries, trying to find a cure. We visited every doctor in the world who specialized in spinal injuries, but none could give him back his dream."

Knowing the toughest parts are coming, I take a few minutes to just breathe.

"Each disappointing visit ate at his hope until not an ounce was left. For a month, I think he was just empty. There was little response to anything. He stopped going to rehab. Stopped talking. It was as if he was frozen, waiting for death. When death didn't save him, he filled himself with rage and bitterness. All of it directed toward me. I was the reason this had happened, after all."

My lips twist in remembrance. Lev puts his arm around me and squeezes me tight, and Lowell sweeps my hair back from my face. I turn to each of them and smile.

"His hate was brutal, a living thing that grew daily. It was as if a creature entered our home and took over. He allowed it free reign to spew constant hate and abuse. At first, I fought it. I tried everything possible to get him to counseling or get through to him. Nothing worked. I gave up, and my brain stopped thinking and started listening and believing. If it wasn't my fault, then who's fault was it? A grieving father's? It was a deliberate act of violence in response to my decision. I didn't pull the trigger, but I was at fault."

My hands shake when I reach out for the glass of water, but I manage to take a drink. Not trusting myself to set it down, I hand it to Lev.

"Once I accepted it was my fault, the verbal abuse stopped having the same impact. It didn't stop. No, he had too much fun spewing hate at me. It had new life, after all. It could see I believed him. But it wasn't enough for Collin. He needed me to hurt. That's when the physical abuse began." Shaw jumps up and starts pacing. "At first, he would squeeze my arm or pull my hair when I was helping him in and out of the chair. It was so subtle; I didn't even realize it was going on. He would berate me for picking him up the wrong way or for not putting my hair up, telling me it got caught in his arms, and I believed him. The thought of him deliberately hurting me was ridiculous. He was in a wheelchair and needed my help. Until the night when the creature lost control and the wheelchair became a weapon."

The anger drains from Thayer's face. "The last few months of our marriage were hell. Every day. I only got a reprieve at night because I slept in the guest bedroom. During the day though, he used it to hurt me. He would constantly run into me until my body was black and blue from the waist down. When I avoided him, he used his need for assistance to draw me closer."

Staring at Thayer, I acknowledge his earlier statement. "You're right. I'm afraid of wheelchairs, but I can control it at work. I can't control it around someone who looks like my husband and is full of anger. Those are too many triggers for me."

"Why didn't you leave him?" Thayer's voice is rough as he

asks. For the first time since I met him, his ice-blue eyes burn like blue flames.

Laughing hysterically, I reply, "Yes, let's examine why I didn't leave my husband. Before the shooting, he was the man of my dreams. He thought the world of me. We were the golden couple. Both specialists in our field, young and ready to take on the world. After the shooting, there was so much anger and hate from friends and colleagues, from the press, and from the public… I felt I deserved it. All those people couldn't be wrong. It must be my fault. So when my own husband started punishing me for it, it didn't feel wrong. Why would I leave? I was lucky to have him. He was one of the only two people left in the world who loved me."

Lev squeezes me tighter. My voice is soft as I finish explaining. "Thankfully, my mom came to visit, and when she saw what was happening, she made me come home with her for a month. While I was there, she painstakingly wiped the abuse away. She made me realize that even if it was my fault—which she could not convince me it wasn't—that it didn't give him the right to abuse me. Nobody had the right to abuse me, especially not my husband. She gave me my self-worth and strength back. I knew I couldn't live like that anymore, so I went home to tell Collin I was leaving."

Rolling my shoulders and neck, I try to ease my tension. Shaw comes over to rub my shoulders, but I pull away.

"When I got home, Collin was worse. It was as if my physical ability to leave triggered something fanatic in him. I told him I was divorcing him. He spewed abuse for hours before going to bed." My eyes drift to the past, thinking about that night. "Later that night, I woke up to find Collin sitting by my bed with a gun in his hand."

Lev drops his head into his hands. "He didn't say anything. I didn't say anything either. We sat there for hours, staring at each other. At first, I was terrified, but then anger came to my rescue. In the morning, I told him I was going out to get breakfast and if he was going to shoot me, he should do it before I left. He shook his head. I left to get breakfast. While I was gone, he committed suicide."

Sadness chokes me when I think about that day. Shaking it off, I glare at Thayer, anger shining brightly in my eyes. "So now you know the worst of my story. This was fun. Next time, let's flay you open and pull out your guts, okay?" I watch his face flush with embarrassment and shame.

Standing up, I smile sadly at Lowell, Lev, and Shaw. I don't know what to think about today. One part of me understands they needed to hear the story, but the other part wishes they had just stood up to Thayer and told him to fuck off. I know it's unreasonable. After all, I insisted on telling the story, but I don't delve into their wounds from the Army or make them tell me how it felt to have Vanessa leave them and marry another.

It's my story. Having to share my history to defend my fear makes it worse, and it pisses me off. I'm tired of defending myself. At least Lowell spoke up and asked if I wanted him to tell Thayer to fuck off.

Tugging Lowell off the couch, I walk out, holding his hand. When we get to my car, I give him a deep kiss to thank him for offering a way out.

"I'll text you later," I tell him as I get in the car.

Driving back to the apartment, sobs rack my body so badly I have to pull off the road.

Fucking asshole, Thayer. Fuck you!

My hand holds my stomach, as if to keep my insides from spilling out further. It takes me an hour to regain my control and drive home.

Chapter Thirty-Eight

THAYER

Staring out at the mountains nearby, my mind replays Kate's story over and over, as if the self-flagellation can abolish my guilt. I pushed her into telling the worst part of her history, and for what? To prove to my brothers she wasn't who they needed or loved? Why? I've relied on their sound judgement and gut instinct for years. Hell, in the Army, they saved my life more than once. Yet I doubted their feelings for the one woman they've known intimately for months, and I've known only for days. I know they don't love easily, but I refused to take that into account.

Her story was devastating and remarkable. As a doctor, I empathize with her simple mistake. Medications impact individuals differently, and to have one decision result in the unintended deaths of so many was devastating. As doctors, we enter the field to save lives, not destroy them.

As a previous soldier, I admire her tenacity in surviving and rebuilding her life with the pieces that were left to her. She literally went through a war and came out the other side weary and wounded but with a renewed determination to survive.

As a man though, I cannot reconcile her capacity to love and trust my brothers after all she endured at the hands of her husband. How? And not just one, but three men. After the cruelty and abuse her husband heaped on her, I cannot fathom her ability to take another chance with them. The guts of it all.

I need to cultivate some of that gutsiness for myself. Instead of moving on from Vanessa, I let her life decisions shape mine, my anger and bitterness driving me from one adrenaline-fueled stunt to the next, until it led to my downfall.

Air displaces behind me, and I know Shaw is standing there. Turning around, I brace myself for his anger. Instead, I find a mix of emotions swirling in his eyes. Anger, fear, sadness, and even understanding.

Raising my hands, I stare at him in misery. "I don't even know what to say. I knew she was hiding something, but I never expected she hid such hate and abuse. And I didn't trust you to know your own damn minds. To know whatever she was keeping from you wasn't because of you, but because she couldn't speak of it." He says nothing, all his words muted. "Fuck, I wish you would just punch me." Raising my jaw, I move closer to him. His hand clenches with anger, as if the need is there, but he doesn't move.

"I'm not going to fucking punch you, Thayer. Although, I did think about it. This whole situation is so unlike you, I don't even know where to begin digging. Given your background, you know skeletons are real," Shaw says wearily.

Nodding, I think about my shit childhood. While I didn't lack for anything money could buy, I lived in a house full of secrets not fit for the outside world. Thinking about how they would appear to an outsider, I shudder. I would hate the person who shined a light on those skeletons.

"All I can think about is her story. All of it. Not just the part about her husband. To go through all of it and come out the other side? It's a miracle she loves and trusts you bastards at all." Rolling back over to the windows, I wince when I hear the whirring sound of the chair. After hearing Kate's story, it haunts me. "You're lucky to have found each other."

"What is driving all this, Thayer? Help me understand, man."

I shrug. "I don't know. I was in the hospital, scared I wouldn't walk again, and suddenly you're speaking about finding one woman to share again. This inescapable feeling of fear, anger, and despair rose up in me," I say gruffly, barely able to get the words out.

Shaw's quiet as he thinks about it from my angle. "It's a hell of a lot to take in when you haven't been around for the last six months."

"It's not that I haven't been around for six months. The passage of time is different for me. One day I'm skiing recklessly downhill, trying to outrun my demons, and the next day I'm hearing I've been in a coma for six months and may not be able to walk again. For me, it's as if two days passed, not six months. And my brothers found someone to love without me," I explain helplessly.

"I'm sorry, Thayer. I know it doesn't help, but I truly mean it." Standing beside me, he drops a hand on my shoulder and squeezes. "But this can't continue. We need her. I need her. I'm here to help you in whatever capacity, but you need to figure out your shit. If by some miracle she doesn't run, she will be a part of our lives."

"Where should I start? I feel like I've got three strikes against me. I look like her husband, I'm in a wheelchair, the instrument of her torture and abuse, and I've only shown her my asshole side. It feels hopeless." My fingers pick at the controller on the chair as I wait for his answer.

"Mm. I've been giving it some thought, but I wanted to be sure you were open to hearing it first," Shaw says reluctantly. Motioning for him to continue, I turn the wheelchair around to face him. "We need her to see the man underneath." Shaw's voice is distant as he reasons out the strategy for moving forward. "When I first met you, I thought you were an entitled prick. Your arrogance when speaking to others was outrageous. Hell, I didn't like you at all."

Grimacing, I give a half-hearted laugh. I never knew he didn't like me. "What made you change your mind?"

"After that first big skirmish we were in together. When those wounded men were brought to you, you were relentless. Your determination to save their lives was astounding. Nothing could hold you back. Not the sheer number of hours you worked, the conditions, or the type of wound. It didn't matter. If there was a possibility a soldier would live, you were there to drag them from death's door. Over and over. I knew then I wanted you at my back and as my friend."

My face heats at his words. I never knew why we became such close friends. Shaw's picky about who he lets into his inner circle. At the time, I just felt lucky he'd picked me.

"Umm, thanks. So, what are you suggesting?"

Shaw crosses his arms and stares down at me. "You need to get her to see beyond your physical appearance and the wheel-chair. If you spend time at work every day, you'll show her your best self. Not the asshole she met today. What do you think? Are you up to going into the practice?"

Looking down at the wheelchair, I realize this is another battle. One I have to face head-on. If I want all of them to forgive me and us to move forward, I need to figure this out.

"I'm up for it," I state firmly. "Would you mind letting Lev and Lowell in on the plan? I have a feeling they really don't want to talk to me."

"I'll tell them. Now, I've got to go figure out how to grovel myself," Shaw says gruffly.

Lost in ideas on how to tackle the situation, I wave him off.

The eyes are the worst, I think.

Grabbing the tablet, I start searching for a few items.

Chapter Thirty-Nine

KATE

Nightmares plague the rest of my weekend. Grim scenes from the past. Cutting words and bruises dominate my thoughts. And, as always, the night we stared at each other while he held a gun in his lap. There are so many mixed feelings about that night. Fear and anger, of course, but primarily, relief. Relief that I didn't have to face him again. That he took matters into his own hands. Which is always followed by guilt. Why couldn't we have found a way to move forward? Even if it was not together?

In one way, I was relieved Lev, Lowell, and Shaw knew about this last skeleton. When I called my therapist on Sunday, she said that telling my truth was the final step toward peace and recovery. Holding it in gave it too much power. She cautioned me against letting my anger drive a wedge between me and my happiness. Let my victories define my future, not the fucked-up past.

My mind is filled with conflicting emotions of anger and relief when I get a text from Shaw, asking to come over. Staring down at the words for a few minutes, I finally stop debating and send him a reply to come over around six tonight, which is about two hours from now.

After a shower and brief trip to the grocery store, I'm fixing dinner when I hear him knock. I open the door and gesture for him to come inside. His intense brown eyes search my face, trying to see beneath the surface.

"I'm making dinner. Would you like to eat with me?"

Exhaling, he tucks his hands into his back pockets. "I'd love to. Is there anything I can do to help?"

I nod. "You can set the island while I finish the beans and rice. We're having chicken enchiladas, if that's okay with you?"

He grins and starts setting down plates and silverware. "What would you like to drink?"

"Water, or I've got Mexican beer in the fridge. The bar is over there if you want something different," I say with a wave of my hand.

"This is good." He finishes and grabs our drinks.

Pulling the chicken enchiladas from the oven, I set them on the stove with the rice and beans. "Please bring your plate over and serve yourself."

I motion to the food, then walk over to the island and place sour cream and tortilla chips on it. Walking back to the stove with my own plate, I fill it up and sit down next to Shaw.

"I'm not sure I deserve this dinner," Shaw murmurs as he takes his first bite. Groaning, he takes another. "I know I don't deserve it now. It's damn good."

"You don't deserve it. This is one of my comfort foods, and after everything that happened this weekend, I needed it." Taking a bite, I close my eyes and savor the taste. "You're just lucky I invited you over."

"I *am* lucky. I'm sorry I didn't stand up and tell Thayer to fuck off." His hand runs through his hair. "To be honest though, I'm not sure I would. For years I was our unit's leader, and I relied on their expertise to help guide our missions. Even when they disagreed with each other, I always listened to each of them when they felt it was critical."

Tilting my head, I listen to his explanation. "A relationship is not a unit or a democracy. It's built on trust and support.

You didn't exhibit either in my case. I felt backed into a corner."

"I get it. I do. I'm sorry. My fears overrode my natural instinct to protect. I let Thayer corner you because I wanted to know what you were hiding." Frowning, he looks down at his plate. "When Vanessa left, she told us our unique relationship had never been in her plans for the future. It was always a temporary situation for her. It was devastating. She never gave us any clue she felt that way." A lingering expression of disbelief covers his face. "When I confronted her, she said, 'You never asked me.' A simple fact in her eyes that ruined us. We didn't realize until that moment we had never asked about the future. We didn't know her past. We didn't share our hopes and dreams. So, when we could all see you were hiding something, it ate at our insecurities. It's no excuse, I know."

Rolling my shoulders, I take a sip of my beer as I think about what he just said. "The past has a way of influencing the present. I understand. It's something I fight against all the time. Unfortunately, the past won the other day for both of us. I couldn't control my reaction to the wheelchair, and Thayer pounced. You couldn't support me in the way I needed because of your past with Vanessa."

"I wish that wasn't true. Hearing what you went through broke me. It broke all of us, including Thayer. He knows what he did was wrong." Shaw goes on to explain the type of person Thayer is when he's not being an asshole. "If it's any consolation, your story is salt in an old wound. His mother was abused by his own father, and if there's one thing in this world Thayer can't stand, it's the abuse of a woman or child."

"I'm sorry to hear about his mother, but I have to say, I'm glad he's suffering." My voice cracks with hurt and anger. I finish eating and put down my fork.

Shaw stands and leads me over to the couch. Sitting down, he takes my hand and pulls me into his lap. "Thayer is like a brother to me. Just like Lev and Lowell. We wouldn't be so close if he had different values than we do. I hope you can give him another chance to redeem himself. He could use someone like you in his life."

Playing with his fingers, my own tremble a bit. "I'm not sure. Between his hatefulness, the wheelchair, and the similarity to Collin, it's tough."

"I understand. Maybe it will help to focus on the professional instead of the personal relationship. Thayer needs to start taking over his practice. He feels he could start with a few hours a day for the next few weeks. While he has a lot of rehab and recovery, this will give him something to work toward until he can fully take it over again. Why don't you treat him like a colleague and focus solely on the day-to-day needs of the practice?"

I gasp. I'm angry at the thought of having him near me for a couple hours every day. How much hate and bullshit will he vomit?

Breathing deeply, I wrangle my thoughts to something less emotional. At some point, I need to figure out my future with these men, and I can't do that until Thayer and I have either resolved our differences or agreed to ignore each other.

"Fine. If he even looks at me wrong, I'm done," I warn him.

Kissing my fingers, he murmurs his agreement. "Agreed. Enough about Thayer. Can you forgive me? I'm so sorry, Kate. I let my own past cloud my judgment. If it's any consolation, your story crushed me. I can't get your words out of my head."

Staring into his dark brown eyes, my voice is serious when I tell him, "I prefer honesty and transparency, and I want our relationship to include those traits. I forgive you, all of you, but I need men who will stand up for me, not let others influence them. Don't do it again."

His lips swoop down and capture mine in relief. Slow but thorough, his kiss shows me his love. It burns through me, incinerating my anger and hurt, leaving only love behind. My arms wrap around him, pulling him in tight. I kiss him back deeply, showing him how much I need him and his love. His mouth devours me as his need rises to meet mine.

My fingers find the buttons on his shirt and work to unbutton them. Tearing my mouth from his, I pull his shirt off him. Tanned skin and hard muscles made from life on the ranch meets my gaze. I glide my hands from his broad shoulders down his chest, stopping only to trace the scars on his soldier's body. Kissing a few of the most serious ones, I close my eyes with gratitude that he made it out alive. I caress every delicious inch of him before grasping his head in mine to kiss him again.

Feeling his hands at the hem of my shirt, I raise my arms so he can pull it off. I'm not wearing a bra, so I hear his sharp intake as my breasts come into view, bouncing slightly after being freed from the confines of the shirt. One hand settles in the middle of my back, and with a slight push, he bends me backward and finds my nipple with his lips.

I tunnel my fingers into his thick, brown hair, tugging it from one breast to the other. "This one is more sensitive." His mouth latches onto the second, licking and tonguing it, and my hands grip his hair to hold him to me. "Shaw!" Pulling up his head, I lean over and capture his lips with mine again. My tongue slips in and out, playing with his, mimicking the dance to come.

His hands grip my waist as he guides me down to the couch. Not a second later, he's hooking his fingers into the waistband of my shorts to pull them off, leaving me in nothing but a lacy thong. Throwing the shorts over his shoulder, he slides down between my legs and stares up at me.

"The things I want to do to you are going to take a lifetime. Tonight, I want to taste you. Burn you into my soul until you can't escape me," he rasps, his brown eyes molten with emotion.

His hand reaches out and pulls my underwear up tight. Groaning, his lips glide over the lace, leaving feathery kisses over every inch.

I raise my hips, trying to get more pressure, but he resists.

His mouth moves to the inside of my thighs, along my hips, trailing up to my stomach.

"It's too light," I complain breathlessly.

He continues with his featherlight touch, except his tongue now joins the journey. His mouth travels all over my body, delving into crevasses, hollows, sometimes tickling, other times striking gold when he hits a sensitive spot.

Rising, he pulls off my thong, then pushes my legs apart. He reaches out and strokes a finger through the wetness between my thighs.

"You're so wet for me," he says, a note of satisfaction in his voice.

He pulls back and takes off his jeans and briefs. His cock, released from its confines, stands at attention, hard and veiny.

Licking my lips, I plead, "I want to taste you."

Grunting, he grabs his cock and squeezes the base. "Angel, I don't think I can let you this time. I'm wound tight. All I can think about is tasting you."

Pulling a condom out of his jeans, he lays it on the coffee table before settling between my legs again. His head drops and his tongue follows the path his finger just took, swiping me from top to bottom.

"Damn, that's sweet," he says, licking his lips.

His mouth finds the center and he sucks hard. My hips come off the couch, and using his shoulders, he spreads me wider while his hand flattens on my stomach to hold me in place.

"That's better. Do you want me to do that again?" he asks, a wicked grin on his face.

I stare down at him. "Yes." Holding my breath, I watch his tongue sweep out and stroke me. His dark brown eyes, almost black with desire, watch my face as he continues tormenting me. Spearing me, his tongue hits the nerves at the rim of my core.

He stops. "Angel, do you like me tasting you?"

"Fuck, Shaw. Yes. Don't stop. Please." My hand grips his hair and pulls him back down. "Please."

Giving a dark chuckle, he devours me. Licking, sucking, and feasting with his tongue.

It doesn't take long for me to come. "Shaw!" My orgasm rolls over me, but he doesn't stop until I beg. "Please, I need you inside me. Not your mouth. I need you."

Up on his knees, he rolls on the condom before settling between my legs again. This time, his cock is flush against me. My hips roll, relishing in the feel of him at the entrance. Large hands reach up and hold my head.

"I fucking need you. Please don't leave me," he asks, his voice hoarse with emotion.

With that statement, he drives his cock into me slow but hard. Thrusting again and again, he makes sure I feel every inch of him inside me.

One arm grabs my leg and holds it out to the side so he can thrust deeper. "I'm not going anywhere." My hand sweeps behind his head to pull him down for a kiss. Tasting myself on him, I mimic his thrusts as I kiss him roughly. "Damn, that feels so good. Harder."

His eyes watch me intently, and the emotion they display washes over me. "I love you, Kate. Angel. I love your mind, your generous heart, your laughter, and your incredible body," he groans. "And I don't care about the passage of time or lack of it. I love you." His pace picks up, and he starts moving deep and fast. "I love the taste of you on my tongue. I love the feel of you wrapped tightly around me." He moans low. "I love your sweet ass."

"Faster. Please."

His hand slips between us and takes me over the edge. Tremors shoot through me as I tighten on his cock. "You're so fucking close. That's it. Come for me. Please." He presses down tight on my clit, and I come. The second I cry out, he follows me over the edge. "Kate!"

Breathing heavily, he lowers my leg and cages me in his arms, holding me tight while he places small kisses on my lips.

"I meant what I said, Kate. I love you." His lips tease mine back and forth.

"I love you too, Shaw." Brown eyes shoot up to mine. "I love your honor and sense of duty. I don't love your stubbornness. I love your dedication to your family. I love your pride in your work and in the ranch." Grinning, I finish with, "I love your cock too."

Leaning down, he kisses me thoroughly. "I could go for round two." Picking me up in his arms, he takes me back to my bedroom. "I think I remember you stating you wanted to taste me?"

Laughing, I wrap my arms around his neck. "I definitely want to taste you."

Chapter Forty

KATE

I smile at them, pretending a level of excitement I certainly don't feel. "I've got some wonderful news for you. Dr. Bradford will be coming in to work for a few hours every day, starting today. I'm not sure what time he'll be here, but I need your help. As you may know, he's currently in a wheelchair while he heals, so we need to prepare the practice. Paula and Brittany, if you could clear the areas around the patient lounge and front desk, that would be great. Sarah, if you could help me clear this back hallway and the patient rooms, I would appreciate it. Any questions?"

Smiles break out as everyone gets excited about Thayer's return. My own smile feels fake, but I slip on my professional mask to go with it.

"So, you've met Thayer, huh? What did you think?" Sarah's bouncing around, clearing the office so he can get his chair back here.

Looking around, I realize this is the only office and I'll have to share it with him.

Freaking A. It just gets worse, doesn't it?

Rolling my shoulders, I head out the door toward the patient rooms to move a few things around and give him space to maneuver. Sarah comes up to me as I'm finishing the last one.

"That good, huh?"

"What? I didn't say anything." I bite the inside of my cheek, not wanting to tell her I loathe her boss.

"Thayer's a great boss and friend, but you're my friend now too. What is it?" she demands, moving a plant from one of the rooms to a corner of the hallway.

Debating, I realize she's going to feel the tension. Plus, I may need her help to avoid him. Grabbing her hand, I drag her back to the office and shut the door. The entire story spills out, from the fact that Thayer looks like Collin to the storytelling debacle. Tears come to her eyes when I tell her about my past.

"Stop. I can't handle tears. It's over. I survived. It's all good." I pass her a tissue and flash her a weak smile.

"Damn it, Kate. You've gone through hell. I don't understand how you can still be so strong and independent. It's like you're superwoman," Sarah says, swiping away her tears. "I can cry for my friend. Both of my friends. That doesn't even sound like Thayer."

"That's what Shaw said too. I didn't know if I should believe him, but I'm glad to hear it from you. I wasn't sure if I should tell you. Not just because I don't like talking about the past, but because it shows Thayer in a bad light. Although, he was an ass." I look at her. "But you're bound to notice if I freak out or there's tension between us. I wanted you to hear my story from me."

Sarah slings an arm around me. "I've got your back."

"Thanks, that means a lot. Now let's get this day started." Smiling, I give her a quick hug. I haven't had a friend like Sarah in a long time. It's amazing I found her now. "We need to get dinner soon. I'm dying to know how your trip to L.A. went."

When she blushes bright red, I raise an eyebrow. Sarah doesn't embarrass easily. Maybe she's really falling for this guy. "So much to tell you. Dinner and drinks soon, I promise."

Around ten in the morning, we hear a commotion in the lounge. As I walk to the front, I see a group of people standing in a circle around Thayer. Everyone is smiling and laughing, greeting him with pats on the back or quick hugs. His face is lit up and he's joking around with them. It's like he's a different person. Charming, witty, caring.

Sarah walks over and leans down to give him a hug. Her face is stern though as she whispers in his ear. Frowning, he tilts his head and opens his mouth to say something back to her, but stops when he notices me standing in the doorway.

I step closer to him and notice something odd. Yep, it wasn't just a trick of the light. His eyes are dark blue now, not the icy blue that previously matched Collin's. Puzzled, I stare at him for a second. Contacts. Looking at the whole picture, I realize with his most recent haircut and dark blue contacts, the resemblance to Collin is like a faded photograph. Faint with blurred lines, as if they're only distant relatives. Relief fills me. Thankful, I give him a nod.

He dips his chin in return. Turning back to his fans, he addresses the crowd. "I can't tell you all how happy I am to see you. It was very nice of you to send me all the great cards and plants. I appreciate all the get well wishes. You might have noticed my sleek piece of metal here." He taps the wheelchair. "The wheelchair is going to be a part of my future until I regain my strength and heal completely. Please forgive me if I bump into you or get in your way. I apologize in advance for my poor driving skills."

The crowd laughs. "I'm sure Dr. Kate has been taking very good care of you, and she'll continue to do so. I'll slowly return to the practice, but you can expect both of us to be here for a long time. Now, let's get today's show on the road."

Rubbing his hands, he backs out of the crowd and maneuvers over to me. "Hello, Kate." He watches my reaction to the wheelchair for a second. "We need to talk, but I want to be sure we have time to do so. Why don't we see a few patients this morning, then we can chat at lunch?" His eyes plead with me to agree.

Why do I get the feeling he'll be here most of the day instead of a few hours? "Okay. I appreciate the effort with the contacts. It helps," I reluctantly admit. "Why don't you take Sarah with you today? I've already discussed my prep with her." Motioning to Sarah, I give him a steady look, then call my first patient.

The morning flies by and I finish a bit early. Pulling up a medical journal on my phone, I start reading the article as I walk back to the office. Rounding the desk, I drop into my chair.

WTH?

Scrambling up, I look down and note Thayer's red face.

OMG! I just sat in his lap.

"So... sorry," I stutter, scrambling to the front of the desk. "I forgot you were here. I've been using this office while you were out, and I was engrossed in this article, and I just didn't think. Did I hurt you? Do I need to call your rehab center?" Looking around for the phone, I realize I have mine in my hand. I start searching for the rehab center's number.

"Kate, stop. Take a deep breath," Thayer says in a firm voice.

His eyes are filled with laughter.

"You're laughing at me?"

"Laughing *with* you, I hope. It's fine. It didn't hurt. In fact, it felt damn good to have a woman in my lap again." His eyes trace over my curves, as if he's just now noticing them. Holding up his hands, he solemnly says, "I promise. It's all good."

My hand reaches out to grab the arm of the chair behind me, and I sink down into it. Looking across the desk, I realize it feels weird to be on this side. I like this office, but now it feels like I'm intruding.

"Okay, let's talk." Waving my hand at him, I indicate he should begin.

Smirking, he tilts back his head and says, "Right. I apologize for my behavior toward you. Not only should I have trusted my brothers' judgment, but I also don't know you, and I never should have taken my anger out on you. I'm sorry. It won't happen again."

I stare him down, trying to understand if he is sincere or not. Shaw said he felt remorseful, but the apology was clipped, the words forced out of him.

"Are you sorry?"

"I just said I was, didn't I?" he asks angrily.

"What you did was beyond cruel. What if I'd had a PTSD episode? You accused me of having a lack of compassion, then cornered me into giving you a piece of my past. I don't feel you're really ready to apologize. I think you're only doing this because of my relationship with Lev, Lowell, and Shaw. If that's the case, you can keep your apology. I don't need it. I can treat you with professionalism, and we can stay out of each other's way."

"You're impossible," he snaps, running a hand through his hair. "But you're also wrong. I'm incredibly sorry. You don't know the depths of my remorse. My mother was abused, and the thought of someone making her relive one moment of her torture fills me with murderous thoughts. And the fact that I did that to you… I can't even tell you how sorry I am. And I hurt my relationship with my brothers." He shakes his head from side to side, almost as if he's shocked by his own behavior. "Give me time to make it up to you. Please. I promise I'm not a bad guy. Just an ass. Sometimes. And stupid."

Releasing my anger, my voice is soft when I reply, "I accept your apology. Hell, my therapist thinks it could be good for me. I haven't spoken about the abuse to anyone but my mother and her. Now I've told you, your brothers, and even Sarah this morning. It's like I'm an open book."

"Thank you," he replies. Pulling his chair forward, he pulls up the files from this morning. "Let's talk about the patients."

Chapter Forty-One

THAYER

Rolling out to the back patio, I pull up to the table to dig into the pork chops and gravy Lev just set down on the table. I'd starve if it wasn't for him.

Shaw hands me the platter and kicks off the conversation. "Thayer, how are things going in the office?" His simple question is an obvious smoke screen for what he really wants to know.

"It's good to be back. Patients are happy, and there are no complaints about Kate. She's a really great doctor. Smart, compassionate but professional. We've collaborated on several cases, and we're doing well. She and Sarah are thick as thieves."

He narrows his eyes to let me know he wants the personal information, not the glossy version I just gave him. Lowell and Lev have also paused their eating to hear what I have to say.

The truth spills out in a tidal wave of confusion. "She only converses with me as a doctor. We haven't had one personal conversation, not even small talk about the weekend or my rehab. Nothing. She completely avoids me unless it has to do with the clinic. I don't know how to break the ice yet, but I'll keep trying." Stirring the food on my plate, I stare down at it, unable to meet their eyes.

Lev snorts. "You were an ass to her. It's going to take more than a month of working together to get her to open up." He scratches his chin for a second. "Should we invite her back out here? I want to see her in our house, not just at her apartment, spending time with everyone."

Lowell and Shaw nod in agreement.

"I can help with getting her back here," I murmur, quietly thinking about what I can say to get her to change her mind.

"If you can get her to come back out here to visit, that will go a long way to getting off my shit list," Lowell states in a matter-of-fact tone before taking a bite.

I hate that I disappointed my brothers by being such an ass. We haven't really hung out together since the day I forced Kate to tell us her story. But I don't blame them. If I had a wonderful woman like Kate and my brothers hurt her, the silent treatment would be the least of their concerns.

We all finish dinner in silence. As they leave, I stay out on the patio, gazing at the stars and thinking about Kate.

THE NEXT AFTERNOON, KATE AND I ARE IN MY OFFICE, FINISHING our daily recap with each other. Every day, we meet and share updates on patients' health and confer with each other on any potential treatments. Sarah often joins us, but she left early for her date.

Rolling over to the bar cart, I pour myself a glass of whiskey. "Want one?"

Kate hesitates before agreeing. "That sounds really good. Today was a beast."

I pour a second glass and hand it to her. Taking mine, I roll over to my desk. Having the desk between us, hiding the chair, seems to help Kate with her wheelchair fears. Staring into the amber-colored drink, I contemplate how to broach the subject with her.

"Just spit it out," she says with an irritated sigh.

I look up to see her fixed stare. "I notice you haven't been out to the house lately. They miss you and want you with them, and I know it's because of me, but I don't know how to fix it."

Rolling her shoulders, she leans her head back on the chair and takes a sip. "I love the ranch, but I'm not sure whether it's a good idea for me to visit. At first, I was avoiding it because I didn't want to see you any more than necessary." I flinch at her candidness. "Spending the last month in the office with you has helped me put you into a more professional category. Now, I tend to see you as Dr. Bradford instead of Collin. I guess I'm afraid seeing you in a personal setting again will remind me of him."

"I understand." My mind scrambles to think of a solution that will resolve her fears. "What if we start with something small? You're going out on a date with Lev tonight, right?"

"Yes, he's picking me up in… Oh shit, any minute now." She tosses back her drink and stands to go.

"Wait, what if I went to dinner with you two? It could help you to see me in a personal setting without the feeling of being trapped at the house. What do you think?"

Her forehead wrinkles as she thinks about it. "I—"

Lev strides in and sweeps her into his arms. "Hello, sweetheart." He leans down and gives her a deep kiss.

Watching them stirs something deep inside—a longing for something meaningful. The same one I felt when I saw Nessa's baby announcement.

"Ahem," I cough lightly.

"Fuck off," Lev growls, still nibbling on her lips.

Laughing, she arches away from Lev's kiss and looks at me. "Okay, let's do this."

Lev's gaze slides between the two of us. "Do what?"

Kate jumps in before I can answer. "Thayer's going to dinner with us this evening."

"What?" Lev snaps, his eyes narrowing on me. "Why?"

Kate smacks him on the arm. "Stop. It's a good thing. If I'm going to start coming to the house again, I need to get used to him outside of the office and his doctor role."

"It's not a role. I'm a certified doctor," I drily remind her.

"Yes, I know. Top of your class, war hero, rich background, blah, blah, blah. But that's not what counts," she says, dismissing my entire life with one statement.

"Hey, that's important stuff. It matters." Grimacing, I expound, "Maybe not the money, but the other stuff matters."

Her hand twirls in the air. "What matters is if you can be a good friend. Can you be on your best behavior?"

I give her my haughtiest stare. "I'm excellent company, and I'll show you the well-mannered man my mother raised me to be." When she nods reluctantly, I clap my hands together and turn to Lev. "You haven't taken me to dinner in a long time. Where are we going?"

Lev rolls his eyes at my pitiful remark. "The only reason you eat is because of me." His gaze swings to Kate and he searches her expression. He must find what he's looking for because he gives in. "We're going to the Thai place up the road. Nothing fancy. I'll drive, but you're buying your own."

"What kind of date is that?"

"Kate's my date. You're crashing it."

"That's no way to treat a man in a wheelchair."

"It is when the man is as rich as you, and when you're trying to make up for being an ass." He winks at Kate. "In fact, you should buy us dinner."

I snort. "Not going to happen."

As we get to his SUV, Lev picks me up and helps me into the back seat, then stores the wheelchair. My face burns. I would give anything to be able to walk over and just get in the vehicle. *Soon*, I promise myself.

"Have you eaten here?" Kate asks me as Lev starts the vehicle.

"Ever since they opened. My favorite is their Pad Kee Mao."

She nods enthusiastically. "Mine too! I eat here way too much, but I can't resist." Kate flashes me a radiant smile.

My breath catches. I think that's the first real smile she's given me. One without reservation. She's breathtaking. She catches me staring at her and her smile fades. I give her one of my most smoldering smiles, and she laughs. Seriously. Laughs. She definitely doesn't see me in that light. Maybe it's not just her. What would any woman want with a broken man? And I'm not just referring to the wheelchair. Gritting my teeth, I tear my gaze away from hers and glare out the window.

At the restaurant, her good mood continues to lighten the atmosphere, making Lev and I laugh repeatedly. Many of her stories are about her solo travels and the comical situations she's found herself in. Frowning, my gaze slides to Lev. I don't like the idea of her traveling to all these foreign countries by herself. He silently agrees and tells me he's working on it. I sigh with relief.

"So, Thayer, what's your favorite place?"

"It would have to be France. From Paris to St. Tropez, I love it all. The history is amazing, the culture and food outstanding, and the scenery is stunning," I tell her. "But it's more than that. It's their elegantly casual approach to life and love that draws me there."

"I've never been to Paris." Kate's voice is wistful when she replies. "I should put that on my list, but it always seems like it's meant for lovers, not a single traveler."

"Get one of my brothers to take you. I'm sure they would love to go. Lev loves France because of the food and wine." Her faces soften when she glances over at him. *Or I could take you*, I think to myself. Looking down at the wheelchair, my lips twist. *Maybe not.* I change the subject by asking about her favorite place.

The driver is waiting when they drop me off. I pick up Kate's hand and give it a squeeze. "Thank you for letting me crash your date. I hope to see you at the house soon."

Not wanting the night to end, I hold her hand a bit too long.

It feels both strong and delicate, and for the first time in a very long time, my body stirs. Surprised, I stare at her, thinking about the two of us together. Then I shake my head at the absurd thought and let it slip from my grip. Maybe I need to go on a date.

Kate wipes her palm down her jeans.

My eyes follow, but I turn before she can see how her rejection affects me. I leave them at the apartment and head home. My mind is filled with a million different thoughts. Most of them about her. Smiling, laughing, attentive, the feel of her hand in mine at the end. I realize I've been a fool.

Chapter Forty-Two

KATE

AFTER SEEING THAYER OFF, WE HEAD UP TO THE APARTMENT AND Lev squeezes me. "That wasn't so bad, was it?"

The worry in his voice makes me realize how tough it's been on them all. "He's definitely charming, and it was a good night. Spending the last few weeks at the office with him, I almost forgot he was your brother and not just another colleague. Knowing him professionally has given me a glimpse of his true personality. The staff respects him. Patients love him. He's a smart and dedicated doctor. He doesn't let anything, much less his injuries, slow him down."

Seeing the worry on his face, I smooth the fine lines between his brows with my fingertips. "I'm the reason we haven't made any progress. I've been hiding and avoiding. Hiding behind my professional mask. Avoiding any personal conversations. Avoiding the ranch to stay in my safe space. He's done every-thing to help us overcome our initial issues."

"He's always been super-focused. It's probably why he and Shaw get along so well. Sometimes to his detriment, as you know," Lev murmurs, his attention starting to wander. He pushes me against the door and his head drops to place little kisses down my neck to my shoulder.

Easing my head to the side, I encourage him to explore further. "Mmm, that feels good. Before we get distracted, he made a good point. I shouldn't be afraid to come out to the ranch. How about Sunday? I could come out for linner?" I ask, arching into his lips.

"Linner?" His head pops up, confusion in his eyes.

I shrug. "You know. We usually eat at three in the afternoon, so it's kind of like lunch and dinner. Linner."

"It's supper, but I don't care what you call it as long as you're coming over." His grin tells me how happy he is that I'm going back to the ranch. "Now, where was I? Oh, right, that spot on your neck that I love so much."

Reaching out with his tongue, he swipes over it and I gasp, angling my head for more. It's as if he lights a fire with a single match. Heat races through me, incinerating any desire to go slow. My need to touch him is immediate. "Stop for a second."

As soon as he raises his head, I grab the hem of his shirt and pull it up until he can grab the neck and tug it off.

Warm brown skin covers acres of muscles, tempting me to run my hands down his pecs to the ridges of his hard abs. I score my nails lightly across each one, and they jump beneath my touch. My hands coast over his body, mapping every area, as if I'm searching for something new.

He groans and grabs my head in his hands, pulling back my hair to see my face. "You're killing me, sweetheart." Falling to his knees before me, he yanks off my blouse and bra and tosses them to the side. His mouth is everywhere, sucking, kissing and licking until I'm writhing beneath him.

Fingers jerk at the button on my pants. Pulling them down, along with my thong, he bares my body and I hear him groan. Without missing a beat, his mouth skims along the crease of my thigh, then his tongue gives me a long lick up the center.

I whimper with need. Not tonight. My hands grab onto his head and shoulders to stop him. "Lev, I need you," I rasp, my voice barely coherent.

He stands and strips off the rest of his clothes. "I know, sweetheart. Me too." Backing me up against the door, he picks up my leg and thrusts into me. Dark green eyes close to savor the feeling before he thrusts deep and hard again.

"Deeper," I demand.

Pulling both legs up and around his waist, my body comes flush against his, and I throw my arms around his neck to hold on. There isn't an inch of space between us. I groan. We begin and end together.

"Is that better? Deeper?" He groans and thrusts again without waiting for my answer.

"Mm, yes." I can feel every inch of him, all the way. "That's it. Faster. Harder." My body is completely open to every thrust. Squeezing inside, I grip him tightly.

"Ahh, yes, sweetheart. Do that again."

I do, and he grunts and thrusts harder, making my body slam against the door. That's it. I want to feel him pounding into me, showing me how much he wants me. Sweat covers our bodies, making it hard to hold on, but I refuse to let go. Sensation coils inside me, until it suddenly explodes and I fall apart. His hand slaps against the door, and a couple strokes later, he comes too. I drop my head against him and lick his shoulder.

Without letting me go, he carries us into the bedroom and places me on the bed. Then he drops down beside me.

Still breathing heavily, I shove my hair out of my eyes. "I love you, Lev."

Taking my head in his hands, he stares into my eyes, making sure I can see how much he means it. "I love you, sweetheart. I fucking love you so much." He pulls me into his arms and holds me tightly.

ON SUNDAY, I DRIVE OUT TO THE RANCH IN MY NEW SUV. IN THE end, I decided just to get a newer version of the one I wrecked. It starts raining hard on the way. Now, I'm really glad I went by the dealership this morning to pick it up because it handles really well in bad weather.

When I get there, Shaw rushes out in the rain with an umbrella and quickly helps me from the vehicle into the house. The foyer is chilly because of the air conditioner, and I rub my hands down my arms to warm them. A sweater is thrust at me, and as I pull it on, the notes of citrus and vanilla clinging to its folds tells me it doesn't belong to one of my men. I turn around and see Thayer sitting in his wheelchair.

"Thank you." I'm at a loss for a second. "Won't you get cold?"

"If I do, I'll grab another," he assures me. Dark blue eyes watch me closely.

Relieved to see him wearing his contacts, I return his look with a smile. "Your cologne smells good." Smiling, I turn toward the rest of them. They're all silently holding a conversation. I'm guessing it's because of Thayer's gesture.

"We're becoming… friends, I guess," I explain a little nervously. The last visit here was brutal, but I want to reassure them that things are changing for the better.

Lowell steps forward and gives me one of his cool, controlled kisses. In return, I glare at him. He knows those kisses drive me crazy and make me want to push his buttons. His answering smirk tells me he's looking forward to our next round.

"I've missed you. Come spend the night with me next weekend, okay?" Although his invitation is delivered indifferently, his eyes reveal how much he wants this. His hand tucks my hair behind my ear while he waits for an answer.

"Yes, I will," I agree huskily.

Lev punches him on the arm. "Hey, you bastard. You snuck that in there."

"You just spent the night with her," Lowell snaps back.

"Alright. That's enough. She's not a toy," Shaw says, inserting himself between the two of them. "Since Lev has to finish cooking supper and Lowell has you next week, I guess that means I get you today." Sprinting forward, he picks me up and throws me over his shoulder.

"Hey! Don't you think you should ask me?" My voice is breathless as I hang upside down.

"No. See you later." He waves at the three men and strides toward the east side of the house.

Smacking him on the butt, I demand to be let up. "I can't breathe, Shaw!"

Stopping, he pulls me off his shoulder and into his arms bridal style. "Is that better?"

I loop my arms around his strong neck. "Yes. Where are we going?"

"My room," he informs me.

I wink at him. "So you can have your way with me?"

"I have plans for your sweet ass. I've been dreaming of it lately. So lush and curvy, waiting for my hand to make it strawberry red, and my cock to be buried deep inside." Need flares in his dark brown eyes.

Swallowing hard, I cup his jaw. "I'm all yours."

His eyes close briefly at those words. "You won't regret it."

Entering his bedroom, he lets my feet drop beside the bed and his lips lock onto mine. His kiss is reminiscent of the day in the barn, demanding and restless with a sharp edge of desire. It's as if seeing me back in his house, in his bedroom, is dry kindling to the fire raging in him.

Turning my head to catch my breath, I step out of his arms and push him backward to sit on the bed. With a few tantalizing moves, I strip down to a green see-through bra and thong I put on just for him today.

Groaning, he growls softly, "Angel, you're so fucking beautiful. And mine. All mine." His hands reach out to pull me against him, but I step back.

Sliding down one bra strap, then the other, I slowly release the clasp and let it fall. Cupping my breasts in my hands, I tease my nipples into hard points, then lift them up toward him. I play with them while he watches. It's intoxicating to be the focus of his attention.

His hand reaches down and unbuttons his jeans. Pulling out his cock, he strokes it while he watches me. "Turn around." His voice is raspy as he commands me.

I turn very slowly until my back is to him. Hooking my thumbs into my panties, I bend over completely and slowly slide them down, pausing when I reach my feet so he can get the full view.

He groans and curses. "Bring that sweet ass over here."

I stand and shake my head, looking down at myself, then him. "Clothes off." He strips down in three seconds flat. Laughing hard, I remind him, "I'm not going anywhere. I'm all yours, remember?"

Yanking me between his legs, he licks up the side of my breast and latches onto my nipple. Sucking hard, he waits until they form hard peaks before biting down. Moaning, I clench my thighs together as I feel the tug below. Switching sides, he does the same to the other one.

While his mouth plays with my breasts, his hands caress my butt. At first, he's light with his touches, barely skimming the surface. Whenever I moan with desire, he massages roughly, as if he can barely contain the need simmering within him.

"Pick out a plug from the top dresser drawer," he orders me. Walking over, I open the drawer, and my eyes widen with surprise. All kinds of toys are in here, beads and vibrators, plus items for spanking, like a leather flogger. Unsure, I grab one of the plugs, and walk back over to him.

His brown eyes are watching me closely. "See anything else you like in there?"

I shrug. "I've never used most of them, so I don't know their purpose. I like the flogger though." At the thought of him spanking me with it, I can't help but clench my legs together.

His eyes darken and his breath catches, then firm lips meet

mine in a hard kiss, silently telling me how he feels about my reply. When he pulls away, he guides me down and over his lap. At first, I feel silly and vulnerable with my head hanging down the other side. I squirm and brace myself for his hand, but it never comes. Instead, fingers glide silently up the inside of my thighs to my core. Stroking, he spreads my wetness to the most sensitive part of me, and his clever fingers play and stroke until I'm quivering in his arms.

Unexpectedly, his hand lands firm on my butt, and I squeak. A second later, fire rushes through me and I can't hold back my gasp. It feels so good. I hear his dark chuckle just before he lands another. Without thinking, I arch up, wanting more.

"So sweet and pink," he murmurs, his hand sliding over my cheeks. "But stop holding back. I want to know what drives you crazy. Do you hear me?"

I nod, and his hand comes down hard, making me gasp from the pleasure.

"That's it."

His fingers return to stroking my clit, and I release the breathless little moans filling my throat. "More."

He stops to open the bottle of lube. Then his hand slips between my legs, spreading liquid all over my back hole. Two fingers plunge into my dripping wet pussy, stroking me languidly, then a thumb slips into my other hole. Sweet mother, that feels amazing. I moan and push up into his hand.

He groans and works my body until it's on the edge. Soon, the plug is at my entrance. "Push," he orders me, sliding it fully inside when I do as he commands.

I'm so fucking turned on right now. "I want you inside me."

He helps me stand. "Bend over the bed."

I turn and do as he says. His hand smooths across my cheeks, then he spanks me hard several times. Inhaling, it takes my body a second to catch up, then it ignites in a firestorm of pain and pleasure.

Shaw murmurs sweet encouragement as he continues to

spank and soothe. The only time he stops is to stroke the plug in and out. This rhythm continues over and over until I'm consumed with the need to be fucked. Hard.

"Shaw, oh, God. Fuck me already. Please," I beg him.

"I am, angel. Hold on." He maneuvers me until my knees are on the edge of the bed and my ass is in the air. "Put your head on your hands. Raise up a bit more. That's it." His hand caresses each cheek. Smack. Caress. Moaning. I feel him remove the plug and place the tip of his cock at the entrance. "Now, I want you to bear down when I push forward. Got it?" His voice is tight as he instructs me.

"Yes, fuck, yes. Shaw, please."

The head of his cock inches forward, stretching the tight hole, until I feel like I can't bear it, and then it's in. The pressure eases and he slides the rest of his cock inside. Breathing slowly, I absorb the feeling of him filling me up. Smack. My ass clenches and he groans. Stroking slowly, he alternates between rubbing my ass and spanking it. I'm delirious as I wait for each one. He picks up speed.

"Touch yourself. Now. Stroke your clit," he demands. "I want to hear you." I moan. "That's it. You're so fucking beautiful. Your ass wrapped around my cock. Are you close?" His breathing is harsh and his voice strained.

"Yes," I sob. "I'm right there." Heat gathers, blood rushes, and my heart pounds. I race toward the edge, but need one more push. "Spank me. Now."

His hand smacks down, twice. It's the push I need. I give a long moan as I come, clenching around his cock. Waves of heat and pleasure roll through me. He jerks twice, and I feel the pulse of warmth he releases inside me. For several seconds, he lightly caresses my back, until the both of us catch our breath.

"I'm going to slide out now, okay?"

I merely nod. Speaking is too much effort.

As he slides out, wetness trickles down my leg. I don't move. A minute later, a warm washcloth takes care of me. Flopping down to my side, I stare up at Shaw. His eyes are almost black with emotion.

"I love you. Now. Tomorrow. For all time." He sweeps my hair back so he can see my eyes clearly.

I pull him toward me. "I love you, Shaw." Giving him a brief kiss, I flop back down. "Can we stay here for a while? I'm exhausted."

Laughing, he slides down onto the bed and pulls me close to him. "Let's take a little nap before supper, okay?" Kissing my forehead, he wraps his big body around mine and pulls a blanket over us.

Chapter Forty-Three

KATE

WE SETTLE INTO A STEADY PATTERN OVER THE NEXT FEW WEEKS. I spend Saturdays and Sundays at the ranch. Shaw and I usually go horseback riding or fishing. Lev and I cook together and plan out his new winery. Lowell and I read, play chess, and talk about books. It's incredible.

Thayer and I have even become friends, sharing medical journals and watching movies together. Thankfully, I don't see Collin anymore. Although, Thayer hasn't removed the contacts around me yet. We both know his eyes will take some time.

Thayer's been back at the office for two months, and in that time, we've gotten to know each other's medical expertise. We often bounce treatment plans off each other, and honestly, it's a relief to have someone of his experience backing me up. Between his intelligence and military field training, he's light-years ahead of me in general medicine and injuries.

It's Friday, and we're walking through a final recap of our patients for the week. "Mr. Carlisle doesn't have any past history of blood pressure issues, does he?"

Rubbing his chin, Thayer responds, "No, he's healthy as a damn horse. I don't know how because his diet sucks. He rarely exercises, and he drinks like a fish. Why?"

"He asked me for a prescription of Viagra."

Spitting out his drink, Thayer roars with laughter. "That sly dog. I wonder who he's dating?"

"I could have sworn he said Paula? Anyway, I'm guessing it's fine for me to write him a prescription." I jot down a note.

"Paula? Our office manager Paula?" His face is shocked as he questions me.

"No, you think?" Trying to picture those two together, my mouth twists, trying to hold back my laughter.

"She's the only Paula in town. Unless it's someone in Helena. Good for her!" Laughing, he takes a drink.

"Well, we want our staff taken care of, don't we?"

"*Our* staff?" he repeats.

I stiffen. "Sorry, I meant your staff."

"Hey, no, it's okay. I like the sound of 'our staff.'" He rolls around to my side. Taking my hand in his, he waits until my gaze finds his. "I mean it. It caught me by surprise, but I like the idea of working with you on a permanent basis."

I bite the inside of my cheek while I think about it. Permanent. I haven't had a permanent situation in a long time. Even though I told them all I was staying, I hadn't thought about what that means for me. "Thank you. I like working with you too." It was really sweet of Thayer to offer reassurance. I reach over and give him a peck on the cheek. "I appreciate the sentiment, but I can always work at the hospital or one of the other practices."

"It's not a sentiment. I mean it. Just think about it?" His fingers play with my hand. "Can I ask you something?"

I nod, although I have no intention of really thinking about it. We're already around each other too much. Here and at the ranch. We're friends now and I don't want to ruin it. "Absolutely."

He shifts closer. "Do you ever see me as a man?"

I rear back and stare at him. He's serious. I glance down at my hands to give myself a second to think. "I've sort of ignored that part of you." I bring my head up and face him. He deserves an honest answer. "You're an incredibly handsome man. Smart, funny, sophisticated. Sexy." I can't help the last part, although I know it will only feed his ego.

"Sexy? You think I'm sexy? And you're ignoring all this? Damn, I've totally lost my touch!" His wide grin tells me he's not offended by my comments. "I'm hurt. I think you're incredibly sexy too. Smart, partially funny, caring, generous, compassionate, sexy. Wait, did I say sexy twice?"

Blushing, I smack his arm. "Stop."

"Would you kiss me?" His voice is husky as he asks.

I search his face to see if he's serious. "I don't think it's a good idea, Thayer. Besides, you're being greedy. I just gave you a kiss."

"That light brush against my cheek? That was a kiss? I don't think my brothers have been kissing you properly if you think that was a kiss. I mean a deep, passionate, fuck me kiss. One that steals your breath and heart at the same time. That's the kind of kiss I want from you," he states firmly. "Not a peck."

Inhaling sharply, I stand, pull my hand from his, and walk out. I refuse to answer him. We're colleagues. Friends. I'm dating his brothers. Yes, we get along good now, but that's it. Yet the tone of his voice tells me he's serious. He wants a kiss. I shake my head. How did I miss the signs?

Chapter Forty-Four

THAYER

ENTERING THE LIVING ROOM, I HEAD STRAIGHT TO THE BAR CART IN the corner and pour myself a bourbon. Rolling over to the windows, I drink and stare at the mountains behind the house.

My pride hurts, but it goes deeper than that. She doesn't even see me as a man. I would say it brought to my knees, but you know. My fist pounds on the arm of the chair. Fuck this stupid piece of metal. Fuck it all. Watching her be in love with my brothers and seeing her respond to them is fucking torture. Every day I'm around her it gets worse. It took time for me to see past my fears, but lately, all I see is her. And she doesn't see me… at all.

I'm staring down into my glass when I sense someone in the room. Looking up, my eyes meet Shaw's. It would be him. Quiet fucking bastard. Toasting him with my glass, I return to staring outside.

"What's wrong?" he asks sharply.

I grimace, knowing this is going to piss him off. "I asked Kate to kiss me." A derisive laugh escapes me. "Shocked her. She doesn't even think of me that way, or so she says. A colleague and friend." Giving a harsh laugh, I take another drink.

"What the fuck?" His voice is hard as he questions my sanity.

"Nothing happened. Although not for lack of want on my part." I take a sip of the bourbon and feel its burn. "How the hell am I going to get her to see me as a man? I'm half a man right now. This fucking wheelchair. I'm not the man I used to be, and I don't know how to be the man I am right now." My voice drops as I confess my fears. What the hell am I even thinking? What do I have to offer her?

"Okay, let's slow down for a second. Why do you want Kate to kiss you? I thought you were fine with being her friend. What's changed?"

"Being around her all day. Every day. She's incredible. I watch her when she's here with you, Lev, and Lowell, and it's intoxicating to see her love for you. And then, I can't help noticing all these little things about her. The movies she likes, her favorite foods, the smell of her hair, the frown she gets when she's thinking about a patient, her excitement over horseback riding… I can go on and on. Is this what you see?" Need pounds inside me. Need for her attention. Her love.

Growling, Shaw rubs his face with his hands. "You never do things the easy way, do you? You're falling for her, and she isn't even aware of you. I guess we did a great job in getting her to see you as a doctor and friend." He chuckles. "Seeing you as a man is going to be tough, and something you'll have to handle on your own. But if she shows any inclination to be with you, then you must sit down and talk to us about it. Full transparency. She's ours. She can also be yours, but only if it's what she wants. Until then, tread lightly."

"I don't know how to get her to see me as a man. If I wasn't in this fucking wheelchair, I'd wine and dine her, but I'm not the old me. I'm… whatever the fuck this is, and with her past, why would she want a man in a wheelchair who also resembles her ex? I'm delusional." My hands grip the glass, tempted to throw it against the wall.

Shaw reaches out and takes it from me. "You underestimate her. Don't. If you want her to see you as a man, act like one. A wheelchair isn't going to make a damn bit of difference." With a hard stare, he sets the glass on the table and walks out of the room.

Could he be right? Should I just ask her on a date? I asked her for a kiss and she said no. I don't want to fuck this up.

Chapter Forty-Five

KATE

THINGS HAVE BEEN STRAINED BETWEEN ME AND THAYER THE LAST three weeks. Ever since he asked me for a kiss, it's all I can think about, but I'm not sure I want to see him in that light. Weak moments catch me off guard though. In the middle of the day when I'm standing next to him, smelling his tantalizing cologne, or when he's passionately discussing a patient's treatment, my gaze drops to his lips and I imagine what it would be like to kiss him..

They all kiss so differently. Lowell's kisses swing between cool and restrained and wild and deep. Lev's kisses reflect his passionate personality but often change to suit his mood. Shaw's kisses are demanding and fiery, as if he needs my lips to quench his thirst for me. It's hard to tell how Thayer would kiss since he runs both hot and cold with me.

Entering the office, I see Thayer trying to stand. "What the hell?!" I shout.

It startles him, and he wobbles.

I step up to catch him.

He grips my arms to hold himself up. "Rehab went well this morning. I stood on my own. I thought I'd try it again."

"Were you wearing a support belt this morning?" I give him a hard stare to let him know I'm not stupid.

"Yes. I didn't think it helped that much. I was wrong." His eyes are twinkling with amusement.

I scowl at him. "This isn't funny."

"It's not, but it feels damn good. To stand here like a man with you in my arms." His eyes travel down between us to where I'm plastered up against him. His voice is husky as he murmurs, "I guess I can delete that worry off my list. Fuck. I'm hard as a rock at just the feel of you. Throbbing, in fact. Want to feel?"

I choke on air. "No, I don't want to feel." He smells really good. I inhale and lean forward. My body softens, liking the feel of him against me. "Let's get you back in the chair."

His hands reach back to grab the arms, and I slowly lower him into the seat. "If we must."

I look down and notice his tented pants. My cheeks burn and I hurriedly glance up. Unfortunately, my eyes meet his dark blue, contact-covered eyes, and that's all it takes. I drop my gaze to his lips and lick my own.

Seizing the moment, he leans forward and snatches my lips in a kiss, and suddenly, it's as if I'm drowning. A deluge of desire washes over me until I barely know my name. All I know is this kiss. This moment. I meet every thrust of his tongue with mine, but nothing exists outside of it, nothing but the feel of his lips and stroke of his tongue. The phone rings, jerking me out of the kiss, and I stand quickly.

"Kate," he murmurs, his voice strained with lust. "I…"

I place a finger on his lips. "No. Please, don't. I can't believe that happened. We should just forget about it." What the hell? I didn't even like Thayer. I mean, I like him, but do I *like* him, like him? That kiss sure as hell felt real. Confused, I shake my head at him.

"No, I'm not fucking forgetting that kiss. Ever." He reaches out to grab my hand, but I hold out my palm. "Kate, damn it. Let's talk about this."

Shaking my head, I walk back toward the door. "We'll talk later, Thayer." Or never. "I've got patients to see." I close the door behind me and walk out.

"Fuck!" I hear him roar.

I manage to avoid him the rest of the day.

Chapter Forty-Six

KATE

A DAY TURNS INTO A WEEK. I RARELY ALLOW MYSELF TO BE ALONE with him, but no matter what actions I take, I can't block that kiss from my thoughts. Not only is it on constant replay, but it's a switch. Now, I can't stop noticing him—his smile when he greets patients, the way he jokes with the staff, the look of wonder on his face when he holds a newborn, and so much more. Hell, even his damn forearms are sexy, with light blond hair and roped muscles. Rehab is rebuilding his body stronger than ever. I sigh. He's too damn sexy.

Rolling my eyes at my incessant monologue, I duck my head into the office. Thankfully, Sarah is still there, so I have a buffer.

"I'm heading upstairs to get ready. I'll order us a car and pick you up at seven." Sarah and I are having a girls' night out.

"Sounds good. Wear something sexy, okay? I'm in the mood to dance," she orders me, shimmying back and forth to emphasize her point.

"Where are you going?" Thayer interjects, his voice tight.

"As if I'd tell you," Sarah says with a laugh. "You would pass it along to your brothers, and we'd have too much testosterone at our girls' party. Nope. Find your own fun."

Sarah drops the patient folders on the desk and waves

goodbye to Thayer. "I've got to go get ready. Sexy doesn't happen by snapping my fingers."

She squeezes my arm as she passes me, her eyes twinkling. I tilt my head, trying to figure out her angle. Our original plans were just to have dinner, but now we're suddenly going dancing?

"Two hours. Be ready," I remind her.

Waving to indicate she heard me, she leaves out the back door.

With my safety net gone, I chew my bottom lip while I awkwardly hug the doorway, refusing to get any closer to him.

"I can't get our kiss out of my head," Thayer tells me quietly. "Why won't you talk to me about it?" Mute, my eyes drop to the carpet. I don't know what to say. Lifting my eyes to his, I silently plead with him to let me have more time. "Damn it, Kate. Just go." His voice is hard when he gives in to my plea.

Thankful for the reprieve, I head upstairs to get ready. There are so many emotions clouding the air between us. Too many. From hate to fear to colleagues to friends to that kiss. It's all a whirlwind, and I need time to sort it out.

Pouring a glass of wine, I relax in the tub for a few minutes. Everything has been going so well the last few months. My relationships with Shaw, Lev, and Lowell are incredible. We're in love. The happiness I've found with them is full of possibilities.

I don't even know if Thayer wants anything serious, and I'm not looking for anything less. Maybe he's just reacting to the proximity of me in his life.

My phone pings, letting me know the ride share will be here in forty-five minutes. *Shit!* Pulling the stopper, I dive out of the tub. Lotion, makeup, a few curls in my hair, and I'm halfway there. Tousled hair will have to do tonight.

The clothes in my closet are incredibly boring. A red lace bodysuit catches my eye. Bold and a little see-through, it's perfect for a girls night out. Black jeans, stilettos, and a few gold accessories complete the outfit.

The driver sends me a text to let me know he's arrived. Grabbing my clutch and phone, I slip out the door. Twenty minutes later, we arrive at Sarah's. She sashays out the door in a black bodycon dress, looking fierce and way too overdressed up for a girl's night.

"Damn, girl. That dress is sexy. Are you going to tell me what's going on?"

"Thanks." She pushes up the girls and smooths down the dress. "You look hot. Love the bodysuit."

I narrow my eyes on her. "Uh-huh. Spill."

"Don't be mad," she pleads with me, her bottom lip jutting out in a pout. "I found out Remi is coming to town tonight, along with his friend. We're meeting them at the club."

Confused, I laugh. "What? You're not trying to set me up, are you? I've got to tell you, I don't need one more man right now. Seriously, I have more than my fair share."

"No, I want you to meet Remi and tell me what you think. The man is driving me crazy. One minute he's cold as ice, and the next he's plastered up against me. I can't tell what's going on. Will you help me?" she begs, batting her fake eyelashes.

"Stop. Of course, I'll help. That doesn't explain why you told Thayer our plans," I remark. Raising my eyebrow, I cross my arms and wait for her answer.

"Well, everyone knows Thayer can't keep a secret worth a damn. One or all of your men will show up before the night is through. Hopefully, we'll both have 'happy' endings tonight." Grinning mischievously, her fingers give air quotes to the word happy.

"Sneaky, my friend. Okay, you're forgiven. Maybe we should bet on which one will show up?" Knowing she can't resist a good bet, I wait for her to take the bait.

"You're on. If Thayer was his old self, I'd bet on him, but given the circumstance, I think it's a toss-up between Lev and Shaw." Tapping her finger on her lip, she thinks about it for a second. "I'm going with Shaw. He seems like he's more possessive than Lev. Who do you think will show up?"

"What are we betting?" I ask with a grin.

"How about drinks tonight? Whoever wins pays the bar tab."

High stakes. "Deal. I'm betting Lowell shows up."

"What? Lowell? Mr. Serious? No way."

I simply smile. "That's my bet. We'll see who's right."

Pouting a bit, she throws up her hands. "If only Thayer and you were dating. He'd be a sure bet."

I vehemently shake my head. "Thayer and I are not dating. We kissed. That's it."

Her mouth drops open. "What?! When did you kiss Thayer? And why am I just hearing about it?"

I walk through what happened between me and him the other day. "I don't know what to think. One minute he's an asshole, the next we're working together and becoming friends, then suddenly, he's attracted to me? I don't think he knows what he wants. He's all over the place." I throw my hands in the air.

"Thayer's a good man. Not only do I respect him as a physician and a boss, but he's also a really good guy. When I first started working for him, he was icy cool toward me. One day, I decided to have it out with him. Apparently, he was afraid I would fall in love with him or his money." She snorts at the memory. "I've never laughed so hard in my life. I told him I'm only interested in men who are covered in ink and have rock-hard bodies. He laughed at my answer, but I could see the relief in his eyes. He told me he'd always had to fend off gold diggers."

"Seriously? Money seems to be a weird issue for him. He was afraid all I wanted from my men was their money. As if I didn't make any of my own. I'm a doctor. What the hell is his deal?" I ask, still outraged about his comment that day.

"You don't know?" She waits until I shake my head. "He comes from old Boston money. His ancestors came over on the Mayflower. They built America. He had a huge rift with his parents when he took his medical degree and joined the Army, but in the end, he's their only heir, so they patched things up. When his father died, he inherited close to a billion dollars."

I almost choke. That's a hell of a lot of money. And here I thought Collin had been rich. I let out a low whistle. "Wow. I knew he came from money, but that's a whole other level of wealth. No wonder he's kind of screwed up. I'd be paranoid too." My eyes drift as I think about the substantial inheritance I received from Collin's estate when he died. That kind of money can do so much for others.

"We're here! How do I look?" she demands, plumping up the girls again.

"Well, if you push those girls up one more time, they're going to fall out of the top of that dress," I say with a snicker.

She beams. "Perfect. That's exactly the look I want. Let's go."

Well, this should be an interesting evening. Waving bye to the driver, I step out in front of the Montana Club. Walking in, I wonder if there's a dance theme tonight. Last time I'd been here, it was for salsa night with Lowell. My nipples peak, thinking about the way that night ended.

"Over there," she says, pointing to a VIP booth in the back.

Sarah grabs my hand and pulls me toward the two men waiting for us. She wasn't kidding when she said Thayer wasn't her type. These men are stacked, with heavy tattoos and hard bodies. One resembles the picture she showed me, blond hair and golden-brown eyes with movie star good looks right down to the cleft in his chin. The other has dark brown hair and eyes, a strong, chiseled jaw, and an equally hard expression. Both men wear buttoned-up shirts with the cuffs rolled up, showing off their remarkable tattoo sleeves.

Sarah goes up to the blond first. He bends down to her petite frame and gives her a firm kiss.

Turning her in his arms, he sets her back against his front. "Sarah, this is my... friend and agent, Brax Jardin. Brax, this is Sarah." His golden-brown eyes watch the other man intently.

But Sarah being Sarah doesn't wait. Holding out her hand, she cocks her head closer to Brax and murmurs, "Aren't you tall, dark, and handsome, emphasis on the dark? I get it now. You and Remi are together, aren't you? And I'm crashing the party?"

His eyes widen in surprise at her quick read of the situation. "Sarah." He greets her, engulfing her tiny hand in his larger one for several seconds while he studies her. He stiffens and lets go of her hand, wiping his palm on his jeans as if the feel of her hand bothers him.

Sarah raises an eyebrow but instead of calling him out, she introduces the two men to me. "Remi and Brax, this is my friend, Kate."

They both reach out and shake my hand. "Hello, it's nice to meet you both. I've heard a lot of good things about you, Remi." I feel like an unnecessary third wheel to the three of them, but I'm utterly fascinated by the way they're orbiting each other. Brax shifts in closer to Remi, who is hovering over Sarah. But it's Sarah move to include Brax in the circle that surprises me.

We all sit down and order drinks. Remi keeps the atmosphere lively with stories about his latest movie, but the undercurrent is intense. Remi and Brax are communicating silently back and forth, but Brax's eyes dart to Sarah more frequently than she realizes. He's intrigued.

"I'm going to dance," I inform them. Hopping off the stool, I shoot Sarah a quick glance, but she waves me off. I see a very "happy" threesome in her future if she can get Brax to give her a chance. Ha, as if it's his decision. My bet's on Sarah.

Smiling, I hit the dance floor to an upbeat song and abandon myself to the music. It's not often I get to let loose. A few bodies press up against mine, but I maneuver away before they can touch me.

A tall, lean body wraps around me, and I whip around, prepared to tell them off when I realize it's Lowell.

"You just won me free drinks," I tell him, looping my arms around his neck.

His hands glide down my sides to my hips and pull me tight against him. "As if I'd let you dance with anyone else."

For the next hour, we're lost to our own sensual world.

"Let's stop. I need water," I plead, pulling him back to the table.

Sarah's mouth drops open when she sees Lowell. "I can't believe Lowell is the one to come get you. How did you know?" Her mouth twists in disbelief.

I laugh at her expression. "We dance here all the time. Now, let me order a couple of drinks. On you, right?"

"On me," Brax interjects. "I'm picking up the tab tonight." His tone is firm.

After ordering, I pull her off to the bathroom. "Are you okay? What's happening between the three of you?"

"Apparently, Brax and Remi have been together for years. When he met me, he couldn't forget about me. He wants to invite me into their relationship," Sarah reveals with a shake of her head. "Brax is observing us. It's quite nerve-wracking."

"What do you think is going to happen?" I ask, knowing Sarah's already worked out a plan in her mind. She might appear to be a petite blond doll, but her mind is sharp and she's damn good at reading people.

"I'm going to give them time to work their shit out. Hopefully, we'll end the night together. If all goes well, I'm going to suggest I come to Los Angeles for an extended visit and spend some time getting to know them both. Men run the world, but for some reason, it takes time for them to figure out what I knew in the first minute." Rolling her eyes at their inability to see things clearly, she steps forward to wash her hands.

I chuckle. "They're not going to know what hit them when they both fall for you. I almost feel sorry for them."

She glides red lipstick across her lips and rubs them together. "I know, right?! Seriously though, did you see those tats? How the hell can one woman get so damn lucky?" Blowing out a breath, she gives her hair one last fluff.

We finish up and head back to the table. Brax is talking to Lowell about optioning the movie rights for his recently completed series. "Here's my agent. Send her the details. We'll talk." He texts the information to Brax.

For the next half hour, they talk about Lowell's books and who should play each role. Giving Sarah a wink, I stand. "Enough shoptalk. We're heading out. Sarah, I'll see you Monday. Remi and Brax, it was nice to meet you both, and thanks for the drinks." I can't help rubbing it in that I won the bet even if she lucked out when Brax decided to pick up the tab.

She glares at me.

After getting in his SUV, Lowell turns to me. "I can't believe you bet on me. Nobody in a million years would have bet I would be the one to show up. Why?"

Lifting one shoulder, I glance at him. "You're a very possessive man, and dancing is our thing. I knew you wouldn't be able to tolerate the thought of me dancing with another man."

He hesitates, then blurts out, "I watched you. To see if you would dance with someone else."

I smirk. "And?"

His hands clench on the wheel. "I'm glad you didn't. In fact, I'm so happy I'm going to give you a reward."

My body instantly responds to his words. "I deserve one, don't I?"

Arriving at the ranch, we barely get two feet into the foyer before the other three men find us. Their eyes widen as they take in every inch of my red bodysuit, black jeans, and heels.

Lev's eyes widen. "Damn, sweetheart. This is what you wear out with Sarah? It's a good thing we sent Lowell. I'm not sure Shaw or I would be able to control our asshole-ness. It would be a caveman throwdown." He pulls me into his arms. "Damn, you feel good. Whatever you're wearing, I want to buy you five more. I can feel every inch of you against me."

Shaw's scowl eases, and he pulls me from Lev's arms into his. "What the fuck? Those jeans are painted on. Personally, I think you should only wear those for me." Winking to show he is joking, his hands slide down to cup my butt. Giving me a quick kiss and squeeze, he lets me go.

Looking at Thayer, I smirk. "Sarah knew you wouldn't be able to keep a secret. We even bet to see who would show up. She bet on Shaw."

Thayer laughs loudly at that thought. "Shaw? Shaw wouldn't be caught dead on the dance floor. The man has zero ability to dance. And who did you bet on?"

Snuggling up against the man standing quietly behind me, I lace my fingers through his before replying, "Lowell, of course." Smiling up at Lowell, I pull him toward the stairs. "I'm thinking I want my reward sooner rather than later."

Behind me, I hear Thayer loudly question my choice. "Lowell?! Seriously?"

Lowell's quiet chuckle fills the air. "Damn straight." Kissing my hand, he pulls me into his bedroom and shuts the door.

Chapter Forty-Seven

KATE

I brush my lips over Lowell's, and when he doesn't stir, I decide not to wake him. Yawning, I glance at the clock and notice it's midnight. My stomach rumbles loudly, reminding me I didn't eat any dinner. I'm tired, but my stomach won't let me go back to sleep until I feed it.

Slipping from the bed, I put on my robe and head to the kitchen. Lev keeps the fridge packed with yummy things to eat. After pouring a glass of water, I open the fridge to search for a snack.

Mmm... pie.

Pulling out a caramel and dark chocolate cream cheese pie, I cut a slice and prop myself up on the barstool to eat. Silky smooth decadence explodes on my tongue. Damn, that man creates perfection. I savor each bite while a myriad of thoughts run through my head.

I wonder how Sarah's night went? If I know her, she's a well-satisfied woman. She might not be able to walk tomorrow, but meh, walking's overrated.

Can't say I'm doing too bad myself. I silently snicker, thinking about the last two hours with Lowell.

I slide the last piece of pie in my mouth, my tongue licking every bit from the fork.

"I've never envied a fork in my life until now," Thayer's smooth voice wraps around me.

Startled, I swing around to watch Thayer enter the room. I tilt my head and consider his wheelchair. I didn't hear any whirring.

He taps the arm. "Manual."

My stomach tenses. "Why did you switch?"

"Because you flinch every time you hear me coming. I don't think you even notice it, but I do, and I hate it," he reveals in a gruff voice. "If I could maneuver around in the office better, I would bring this one to work, but the halls are too tight."

That's one of the kindest things someone has ever done for me. I smile at him. "It's more work for you."

"My doctor felt it would be fine, given my recent results," he informs me. "I'm stronger. Rehab is going well. If I keep this up, I'll graduate to a walker." He makes a comical face, but I see the gleam of determination in his eyes.

He rolls further into the kitchen and I almost fall off the barstool. All I see is miles of golden skin. My heart stops before I realize he's actually wearing a pair of shorts. I indulge myself, allowing my eyes to travel over every inch of him, cataloging each detail. He's beautiful. His chest is broad, tapering down to lean but muscular abs. Although his legs are slimmer now, surprisingly, there is still quite a bit of muscle.

Muscular arms ripple and biceps bulge with effort as he maneuvers the wheelchair up to me. Given that he's also covered in a slight sheen, I'm guessing he's been working out.

"If you don't stop looking at me like that, I won't be responsible for the consequences," he rasps, shifting his body. "Especially with you wearing that very brief, very sexy robe that is doing a piss-poor job of covering you."

Registering his words, I look down to find he's right. Wiggling, I try to pull it down to cover me, but it ends up gaping open at the top and flashing Thayer. I hear him groan.

"Beautiful, stop wiggling, you're killing me," he says with a groan, waving his hand at his lap.

My eyes drift down and see his hard cock outlined in those brief shorts. Licking my suddenly dry lips, I wonder what he looks like. Is he long? Thick? While I'm contemplating his cock, his hand reaches into his shorts and pulls it out. Sucking in my bottom lip, I almost whimper at the sight.

He gives it a long stroke. "Do you like what you see?"

"Yes," I admit with complete honesty.

"Come here," he demands, crooking his finger.

I shake my head. "We can't. This isn't right. Do you even like me? More than physically, I mean."

His mouth drops and he tucks his cock back in his shorts. "Are you kidding me?" My face must tell him I'm not. "Every time I'm around you, I'm in awe. Not just because you're beautiful and smart. I admire the steel in your spine, your ability to see hope for the future, and your capacity to love. If you give me a chance, I promise, you won't regret it."

I stare into his icy blue eyes and realize it's the first time I've seen him without contacts since that horrible day... but they don't remind me of Collin anymore. I'm too aware of Thayer to see another man. "What are you asking?"

"For a date," Thayer responds promptly. "And another kiss if it goes well."

"One date?" I ask, tilting my head to study him.

Bright white teeth flash. "To start. I want it all, of course. I'm a greedy bastard, but right now, I just want a chance." The smile on his lips never wavers, but I see the slightest hint of worry in his eyes that I'll say no.

He wants it all.

His answer eases some of my uncertainty, but I'm not about to let him off the hook. I lean down and capture his lips in a kiss, stealing his breath and giving him mine in return. The kiss gives me my answer. Drawing back, I linger, staring into his icy blue eyes. "Yes, I'll give you, us, a chance."

"Thank you, beautiful. You won't regret it."

Chapter Forty-Eight

THAYER

Lev drops me and my new car at the practice. I bought it earlier today. It's not possible for me to drive yet, but I'm damn well going to get in and out of the vehicle using my own muscles. I've been practicing the maneuver, under Shaw's watchful eye, all morning.

Unable to climb the stairs, I text Kate to let her know I'm here. She comes down a second later, her blond hair in a ponytail, wearing a green maxi dress, delicate sandals, and a tremulous smile. "Hello, Thayer."

I wheel up to her. "You're gorgeous. Do you mind driving?"

She peers behind me at the vehicle parked in the small parking lot. "Thank you. You're pretty handsome yourself. More relaxed than usual, but I like it a lot. And I'd love to drive."

She follows me to the car, but when she bends down to help, I wave her away. "I've got this. If you wouldn't mind storing the chair in the trunk, that would be great." I open the door and use my upper body to get into the passenger seat. Once my legs are in, I nod at her to grab the chair and close the door. Exhilaration fills me. I did it with her watching, and it felt damn good.

She slides into the driver's seat.

I hear her inhale.

"Is this new?" she asks, taking another sniff.

"Bought it today," I inform her. "I'll be graduating to a walker soon. A car will give me more freedom. What do you think?" I rub the leather interior.

She gives me a wry smile. "What's not to like? It's a Maserati Quattroporte. The ultimate in luxury. You and Lowell shop at the same dealer?" Her fingers wrap around the steering wheel. "Where are we going?"

Impressed with her knowledge, I shake my head. "How did you know what it was?"

Her hands fall to her lap. "I went to the dealer to look at buying an SUV like Lowell's, but I like the simplicity of the Range Rovers. Plus, they get me through the toughest terrain. Why?"

"No reason," I say nonchalantly. "We're going to Pike Lake. Do you know how to get there?"

She folds her arms across her chest. "Is this a weird money thing? I don't know if anyone told you, but I'm a doctor. I make damn good money, and I like driving nice vehicles."

I flick an irritated glance at her. Why does she feel this need to call me out? "Let's just go. If we don't leave, we won't get a good spot before it gets dark." She doesn't say a word, simply raises one eyebrow. I wave a hand. "It's nothing. Really." Her head turns to stare out the window. I thrust a hand through my hair. "Fine. It's stupid. Some women look for men who drive expensive cars, especially ones that cost over a hundred thousand."

Her green eyes turn toward me in amusement. "Are you dating me for my vehicle? I hate to tell you, but I only bought the Range Rover Sport. It's a smidge less than your hundred thousand price tag, so I guess it doesn't qualify." She snaps her fingers. "Oh wait, I know. You're dating me because I can drive. Are you going to dump me when you get your driving privileges back?"

I stiffen. "I told you it was stupid, but it was also rude. I'm sorry." She says nothing, and I hold up three fingers. "I mean it. Old habits die hard. I haven't dated someone in a long time who was just interested in me." I chuckle. "The dig about driving was a good one though."

She rolls her eyes. "Were you even a Boy Scout?"

I lower my hand. "No. My father would never have allowed his son to congregate with the masses. I wanted to join though."

She leans forward and pushes the start button. "I've only agreed to one date, Thayer. Remember that the next time you open your mouth." With a quick maneuver, she reverses the car and exits the lot.

I open my mouth to ask her if she knows where she's going, but I see her glance at me from the corner of her eye and I shut it.

Ten minutes later, we reach the entrance to Pike Lake.

I point to a road on the left by the mountain. "Take that road."

She follows my directions until we reach the midpoint and parks. After getting my chair, she waits.

I get seated, then open the back door and pull out a blanket, the picnic basket, and a large white tube. With everything in my lap, I motion to the sidewalk beside the lot. "That way."

This is the tricky part. Once we get to the grassy area, I'll need her to help me push the chair to our spot.

When we arrive, my eyes follow the grass several feet to my favorite spot and a lump forms in my throat. Swallowing a few times, I shove aside the pride blocking my words. "Would you mind pushing me over to the spot left of that far tree?" I point in the direction I want to go.

She leans down and takes off her sandals before handing them to me, then grips the handles on the chair. "Ready?"

In the end, it takes both of us to get over to the spot. We're hysterical by the time we reach it.

"Arm workout—done," she says with a laugh. "You're heavier than you look by the way. Must be all those new muscles."

My embarrassment fades and I groan. "I had no idea thirty feet would feel like a mile. I won't blame you if this is our only date, but let me feed you first and show you my favorite view."

In response, Kate takes the blanket from me and spreads it on the ground. When I hand her shoes to her, she tosses them on one corner, then takes the tube and puts it on another. "There. That should hold down the blanket for us." She sits with a sigh. "You wouldn't happen to have something to drink in that basket, would you?"

With a slow smile at her lack of hovering, I set the basket down on a third corner and maneuver myself out of the chair and onto the blanket beside her. "Never fear, beautiful. Lev packed the basket." I reach inside and pull out a bottle of wine and a couple bottles of water.

Once we each have a glass, I hold mine up. "To a memorable first date full of bad remarks, strength training exercises, good food, and hopefully, redemption."

She snorts. "To barely tolerable company, a unique location, good wine, and a chance to redeem yourself." She clinks her glass against mine and takes a drink of the wine.

"I think I'm scoring more points for Lev tonight than myself," I say with a chuckle. Reaching into the basket, I take out the small charcuterie board Lev prepared for us and set it on the blanket.

"Fancy," she remarks, picking up a piece of toast with bruschetta on it. "Tell me. Do you take all your dates to your favorite spot?" Her green eyes are intent while she waits for my answer.

I hurriedly reassure her. "It's a favorite spot, but I've never taken a date here. I swear." When I raise my hand in the three-finger salute again, she shakes her head at my antics.

"Good save. Put your hand down. If you tell me something is true, I'll believe it. I don't need you to show me the pledge each time," she tells me in an exasperated tone. "You're one of the most honest people I know. To your detriment, sometimes, but I don't think you lie."

The pressure on my chest eases. "You're right. I don't lie. In fact, I abhor it. My entire childhood was filled with lies. My parent's perfect marriage. Our perfect lives. My father, pillar of the community, and dedicated family man. All lies."

She lifts a defensive shoulder. "Sometimes it's easier to lie than to let people see your life is falling apart or worse to expose yourself to their judgement." Her voice drops. "Even now. I don't like to lie, but I will if it allows me to continue living my life in peace."

I frown and take her hand. "I hope one day you won't feel like you have to lie to save yourself, but I need you to promise me you won't lie to me. It's the one thing I can't tolerate." My eyes search hers, trying to see past the wall she has between us.

She reluctantly nods. "I won't lie to you. Or to Lev, Shaw, and Lowell."

"Thank you," I tell her, exhaling in relief. The darkening sky has me glancing up. I reach over and grab the tube to set up the telescope. "The stars in Montana are amazing. They feel close enough to touch. When the world presses in on me, I come here and find the stars. And my balance. It puts things in perspective." I gesture to the eyepiece. "Take a look."

She peers into the telescope. "Is that the Milky Way?"

"It is!" I exclaim. "Away from the cities, the sky is darker here, especially in the winter. You can see stars, planets, meteor showers, the Northern Lights, and so much more. Different times of the year show different things. My favorite is to come up here in winter when the cold makes the skies crystal clear."

"How did you get into stargazing?" she asks softly.

"In the Army. Our unit went to some extremely isolated areas and the sky never appeared to be the same. It intrigued me how the same elements could look different if you changed your location," I explain, giving a self-conscious laugh. "Plus, there wasn't a hell of a lot to do in those places." Except prepare for battle.

She hears the words I don't say and reaches over to squeeze my hand. "This is amazing. Thank you for taking me to your spot." Her fingers snag a strawberry and brings it to my lips.

"I think I'm supposed to be feeding you," I huskily remind her, but I open my mouth and bite down on the juicy fruit.

She swivels her wrist and brings it to her mouth. "We can feed each other." After taking a sip of her wine, she points to the sky. "I never took astronomy. Tell me about the stars."

For the next hour, I move the telescope to my favorite constellations, point out each one, and tell their stories. She listens and looks, getting excited when she can see the points that make up the image and disappointed when she can't connect them.

"So, they're all named after figures from Ancient Greek mythology?"

I nod. "Those are the names I know, but different cultures created their own stories." I point to a constellation. "The Cherokees saw two bright stars in the Canis Major as two dogs guarding the path to the land of the souls."

When I turn my head, her lips are right beside mine.

"Kiss me, Thayer," she says breathlessly.

I spear my hand through her hair to cup the back of her neck and bring her to me. "I would love to." My lips descend on hers, and it's like a thousand stars exploding around us. One kiss doesn't even scratch the surface. I kiss her over and over, unable to stop, the need having built over the last few weeks until I could think of nothing else.

For her either. Her lips easily match the urgency of mine, as if she has also been holding back for ages.

Cool night air seeps into our secluded space, making her shiver, and I break away. "Why don't we leave and grab dinner?" My body throbs, but I shove the need down deep. We have a long way to go, and this is one thing I refuse to rush. After Nessa, I need Kate to be sure of what she wants.

It takes us a while to get it all back in the car. The strenuous effort makes me groan. "Sorry. Please don't hold this against me."

She winks. "Depends on what you feed me for dinner."

It's later than I thought. Most restaurants will be close to closing. "How about Thai?"

"You may get a second date after all," she replies with a husky laugh. "Our favorite place?" When I agree, she puts her foot down. "Good thing we have a fast car."

Chapter Forty-Nine

KATE

SUNDAY AT THE RANCH IS MY FAVORITE TIME OF THE WEEK. ALL OF us in one place. Sometimes I drift between the men and other times, we all lounge together in the living room. When I walk in today, I hear them laughing at the back of the house.

"Hello," I call out.

"Out on the patio," Lev shouts.

I hurry out and find them in the pool, enjoying the last of the warm September days, splashing each other, and calling out insults. When I see the basketball hoop at one end of the pool, I finally understand.

"Who's playing who?" I ask, dropping down onto a lounge chair to watch the game.

Lev winks. "Thayer and me against Shaw and Lowell. We're winning."

With Lev's attention on me, Shaw body checks Lev and scores. "Now we're winning."

The competition is fierce, but all my focus is on their smooth bodies moving fluidly through the water. Even Thayer is playing pretty hard, but he's been putting in a lot of hours in the pool during rehab. Looks like it's paid off. His chest is filled out and not once does he wince in pain.

Thayer sees me watching and blows me a kiss. Lev smacks water in his face. "Pay attention. Lowell's coming up on your left."

He wipes his face and swivels, arm outstretched to block, but he misses and the other team scores.

Lowell and Shaw's arms go up in victory.

"Don't forget the wheels," Lowell calls out with a laugh. "I want them shiny."

Lev throws him the finger and lifts himself straight out of the pool. Dark hair slicked back and tanned, hard body on display, I'm practically drooling. I watch him prowl over to me.

He leans over, abs crunching, to kiss me playfully on the lips and water drips onto my heated skin. "You're a little flushed. Want something to cool you off?"

My tongue flicks out to lick my bottom lip. "Mm, that would be nice." I trail my fingers up and down his muscular legs. Lev has the best legs out of all of them. Thick, ropy muscles and... "What are you doing?" I narrow my eyes at him.

He walks over to the pool and steps down into it. "Helping you cool off."

I shriek and level my best glare on him. "I don't want to go for a swim, Lev. I mean it."

His broad shoulders shrug and he pulls us down into the water. Once under, I slip out of his arms and head straight toward a pair of legs on the other side of the pool. Twisting to the side, I slide between them and come up out of the water.

Thayer turns around and grins. "Must be my lucky day. I caught a mermaid." Strong arms band around my middle and he pulls me to him. "A kiss for your freedom." Icy blue eyes stare down at me. He loves being in the pool because he can walk without assistance. I wrap my arms around his neck and lightly rub my body against his. It isn't often I get to feel every inch of him next to me. He grunts and shifts to adjust himself. "Definitely my lucky day." He taps his lips with his finger. "Right here."

Placing my lips on his, I bask in the sun and warmth of the day while I stand there kissing this man I'm beginning to care for more and more. We've been dating a few weeks now. We're taking our relationship slow and savoring every moment. The last thing we want to do is rush.

My nipples harden and I feel his fingers caress the back of my thigh. I want to lift my legs around him, but with a sigh, I release him and step back.

"This slow pace might kill me," he tells me, his voice strained with need. "Give me a minute."

I deliberately turn and brush him as I leave. "Take all the time you need. I'm not going anywhere."

With a throaty chuckle, I swim toward the stairs and step out. Lev is still in the pool, laughing and splashing with the other two. I bend over and squeeze the water out of my hair. Then, I strip down piece by piece until I'm in the red strappy bikini I just bought on sale. All the laughter stops immediately.

Shaw extends a hand and I grasp it to take the final steps out of the pool. "Thank you."

A large hand runs down my backside. "My pleasure. Nice suit. There's a drink waiting for you." He leads me over to the lounge chair I was sitting on earlier and hands me a fruit juice concoction that I love, then grabs the chair next to mine.

Tired from last night spent, I doze in the warmth of the sun for the next hour until supper is ready. With slow movements, I stretch and make my way to the outdoor kitchen where Lev's grilling hamburgers. I pinch his butt. "Need some help?"

"You know better," he remarks with a wink. "But I'll take a kiss. I didn't get the one I wanted earlier." He pouts.

"Didn't you get enough kisses last night?" I tease him, snatching a fry from the basket next to him.

"Never," he murmurs, dipping his head to find my lips with his own. "Mmm. Better. Here. Take those to the table. Try not to eat them all."

I lift a shoulder but grab the basket and set them by Lowell.

When I sit down on his right, I sneak another fry and pop it into my mouth. Then I look around. Lowell shakes his head but says nothing. Shaw's involved in conversation with Thayer, talking about stocks and investments. Apparently, Thayer is a mastermind with investments, always following the news and making adjustments to their portfolios.

I wonder if he'd help me?

Lev places the platter of burgers down and the next hour is full of food and talk of the upcoming week. Shaw's going to a horse auction, Lowell's finishing the draft of his new book, and Thayer and I will be at the practice.

I remind Thayer. "Don't forget, Sarah is gone to L.A. for the next three weeks. She's going on a test run with those yummy men of hers." All four of them raise their eyebrows. "What? I can appreciate a fine-looking man, or two… or four," I remark with an outrageous wink. My finger traces the ink on Lev's arms, thinking of the pics Sarah sent of her men at the pool with tattoos all over their bodies.

"Ahem," Lowell says with a raised eyebrow, his grey eyes glinting with a hint of jealousy behind his black rims.

"Don't worry," I tell him. "They can't dance." I look around the table. "Or ride a horse. Cook divine food. Or play doctor."

Thayer's lips twitch. "How many times do I have to tell you I'm a real doctor?"

I laugh. "You're a damn fine doctor too. If you'll excuse me, I'm going to grab a quick shower to get the chlorine off before I drive home." I leave them all behind while I freshen up a bit.

After the shower, I walk into Shaw's room and find him sitting on the bed, waiting for me. "I wish you didn't have to go. Sometimes it's tough to find time together. I'll miss you this week, but I know you'll be in good hands."

I stand between his outstretched legs and place my hands on his shoulders. "Maybe one day. We've only known each other seven months. There's no rush."

He heaves a sigh. "Take your time, because once you move in, we're never letting you go."

I kiss him several times. "I love you. Be careful driving. Text me. Call me. I want to know how your days are going."

He brightens. "I love you too. Let me walk you out."

"I have something to ask Thayer, but I'll come find you all in the living room when I'm done," I reply.

Walking down the hall and across the house, I knock on Lev's old bedroom.

"Come in," Thayer calls out.

The room has completely changed since the last time I was here. Instead of Lev's masculine black and grey room, it's cool luxury in blues, tans, and whites. I whistle. "Your room is like a magazine."

Thayer rolls forward, a blush on his face. "Some of us are more sophisticated than others."

I lift a shoulder. "It's gorgeous, but I didn't come here to chat about your decor. I wanted to ask if you would help me invest my money. It's been sitting in different banks for the last few years, but hearing you talk this afternoon, I realize I should probably do something with it."

He stares at me with a horrified expression on his face. "Tell me it's in CDs or money market funds or something."

"No, savings accounts. Banks only cover you up to a certain amount, so I had to split it all up," I say with a shrug. "I'm not sure what to do with it."

"How much is it?" he asks me softly, something uncomfortable on his face.

"Over five million," I tell him.

He grabs my hand and pulls me over to sit on the bench at the foot of his bed. "Don't get mad, but I have to tell you something." Thrusting his hand through his hair, he mutters something unintelligible, then starts talking. "Please don't get upset. When I first met you, I ran a thorough background check on you. I run one on everyone who is close to me, but with you it was personal. I wanted to prove you were a gold digger, so I went deep with my investigation."

He winces at the angry expression on my face. "I'm sorry. Obviously, I know you're not a gold digger now, but old habits die hard. Anyway, the report told me you inherited over thirty million dollars from your husband's death." Thayer stops there and stares at me.

Of course he ran a report. Knowing him now, I don't mind, but I'm glad he didn't tell me earlier. Still, I fold my arms across my chest and glare at him. "Not everyone cares about money."

"You'd be surprised," he murmurs, his face full of past memories. "I could only find five million. What happened to the rest of it?"

I wring my hands and shrug. "I gave it away."

He reaches forward and lifts my chin. "You gave away twenty-five million dollars? To who?" As soon as the words are out of his mouth, it's like a lightbulb goes off. "You gave it to the victim's families, didn't you?"

I just look at him. After the shooting, it felt wrong to inherit Collin's trust. Blood money. Even now, I refuse to spend any of it on me, but if I can increase it, it could be a huge help to others. I'm not sure who I would give it to, but I'll think of something.

He says nothing for several minutes, digesting the information. "I'll help you. Let me put together a couple of options, then you can decide which direction you want to go." Leaning forward, he kisses me softly. "You're one hell of a woman, Kate."

KATE

It's black with racing stripes and hand brakes, and everyone loves it, including Thayer. He's been so excited to get rid of the wheelchair, but I could see the dread in his eyes when he talked about graduating to a walker. He's desperate to stand and walk, but if he could skip this step and go straight to walking without an assistive device, he would. But it's important he work through all the stages of his treatment.

So, I spoke to the guys, and we decided to get him something to make the transition easier. This walker is cool. Kids and adult patients love it, and it totally eclipses Thayer's image of a grandpa using a grey walker to get around. The gratitude on his face is as brilliant as his smile.

Later, when the office is quiet, he pulls me against him, hands roaming while he murmurs little words of appreciation for his new walker. The relief I feel is immense. After Collin, I've tried to avoid interfering with Thayer's recovery, but his response reassures me and a little of my fear abates.

His mouth hits a sensitive spot beneath my ear, and I gasp. With Sarah gone, the office has become a sensuous torture zone. Near each other all day, I'm hyperaware of him—the timbre of his voice when he speaks, the subtle smell of his expensive cologne, and the way his entire face lights up when he laughs. Our hands wander whenever we're close. A brush of our fingers. The gravitational pull of our bodies whenever we're in a room together. Stolen kisses throughout the office. Secret smiles and inside jokes.

It's driving me crazy.

"Want to go on a date with me tonight?" I ask, a tantalizing idea coming to mind.

"I'd love to." He glances down at the black pants and button-down he wore to the office. "Do I need to go home and change first?"

"Nope. It's casual," I reply with a glance at my dressier pants. "I'm going to slip into something a bit more comfortable. Finish up. I'll be back down in fifteen minutes."

He glances up at the ceiling. "What I wouldn't give to follow you upstairs."

I lean over and whisper in his ear, "A bed is overrated." Sauntering to the door, I turn and wink at him. "Be right back."

He chuckles.

Fifteen minutes later, I walk into the office wearing a casual A-line flowy skirt, a cropped sweater, and a pair of tennis shoes. "Ready?"

Thayer grabs his walker and follows me out. "Where are we going?"

"You'll see," I tease him, motioning him to the car.

When I pull into the large lot twenty-five minutes later, he laughs. "A drive-in movie? I didn't think these things still existed."

Once I park, I bring up the menu on my phone. "Here's our options for dinner. Hot dogs, pizza, or nachos. I'm going for a hot dog. You?"

He grimaces. "Pizza."

I laugh at the expression on his face. "Be polite. This is a date. If you're lucky, we'll see a good movie and make out like teenagers."

His face lights up. "I'll be on my best behavior."

The food is surprisingly good. We finish and grab some popcorn just as the movie starts. It's an action flick, with lots of running, some espionage, bad guys dying and good guys winning, I think.

Halfway through, my mind is entirely focused on the man sitting next to me. We turn to each other and stare. We've been dating almost three months and have yet to move to second base. Kissing and touching everywhere but the areas we want it most.

I slide in closer to him. The windows have a slight tint, but not enough to disguise our actions if we go too far. I peer into his eyes as my hand moves lower, intent on touching him. Small buttons give way, and I slide my hand across his chest. "Rehab is doing remarkable things for your chest. All I could think of doing the other day was running my hand across it." I trail my fingers over his hard pecs and circle his nipples.

His hand slips under my crop top. "You obviously planned this date with one objective in mind." Shifting his body toward me, his lips find mine while our hands roam across each other. "Damn, I do feel like a teenager again. Dying to touch your breasts, feel their weight in my hands."

"I like going slow, but it's also driving me crazy. I thought a little relief would go a long way for us both," I say breathlessly. My hand drops to the buckle on his belt, and he inhales sharply. It takes moments to undo it and the button beneath before my fingers are sliding down his zipper. The moment my hand wraps around him, he groans.

His kisses get frantic the moment I start stroking him. "I have to warn you, it's been too damn long, and I'm already so fucking turned on, it won't take much."

Thick and smooth, I slide my hand up and down, feeling every inch of him in the dark. It's as if I'm blindfolded. I map the ridges and valleys, caress the rim, and picture him in my head.

He hardens further, his hips shifting up the slightest bit to push into my hand, and I realize he's close. I pick up speed.

His eyes dart between my eyes and hand, unable to choose just one. "I'm close," he warns me in a raspy voice. A second later, he explodes in my hand. Dropping his head back against the seat, he stares at me. "This movie date is brilliant, but next time, we bring better food and towels." Grabbing napkins, he cleans us both.

I laughingly protest. "The hot dog adds to the ambiance, but we're definitely doing this again."

The car nearest to us starts their engine, startling us into looking at the screen. Credits are rolling. "Oops, guess the movie's over."

On the drive back to the office, he holds my hand. I pull into the lot and lean over to give him a long kiss good night. "I'll see you tomorrow."

"Good night, beautiful. Thank you," he says gruffly. His mouth opens to say something else, but he stops and looks away. He gets out with his walker and slowly makes his way to the driver's side door to open my door.

He waits by the car until I'm inside and the door is closed. When I hear it start, I walk down the office hallway and turn the lights off.

There's a knock at the door, and my heart jumps with hope. I open it.

Thayer's standing there, eyes burning with need. He takes a careful step forward. "I need to touch you more than I need to fucking breathe right now, feel you come wrapped around my fingers first, then my cock. If this isn't what you want, tell me to go home."

When I say nothing, he pushes inside and backs me into the wall until our bodies are pressed together. "A half hour ago, I exploded in your hand, and yet I'm still hard as a rock." His hand slides beneath my skirt and between my legs. He shoves my panties aside and spreads my legs with his knee. Plunging one finger into me, he groans. "You're drenched for me, aren't you?"

In answer, I spread my legs further. "Yes. I've been wet for weeks. Every day it gets worse. I think about having sex with you in the office. On your desk. In your chair. Hell, even the closet is looking good."

He plunges another finger into me. "That's it. Ride my fingers. There isn't a surface in this office I haven't thought of bending you over. You wear that damn perfume and the tiniest whiff of it gets me hard, but the worst is when you're searching for a solution and the tip of your tongue slips out to touch your top lip. All I can see is you on your knees using that tongue on me."

I grip his shoulders and raise my leg to his hip. I've been on the edge of coming for the last hour. "Faster." His thumb flicks my clit, and that's all it takes. My body pulses and my orgasm hits. "I don't think that's going to be enough."

"I'm just getting started," he informs me, raising his hand to lick his fingers. "How do you feel about couches?" Thayer grabs his walker and motions with his head.

"Love them," I reply, stripping off my sweater and dropping it on the floor. Halfway there, I slip out of my skirt and toss it to the side.

He murmurs something intelligible but stops to yank off his shirt.

By the time we reach the office, items of clothing litter the hallway and we're both naked. We come together in a clash of bodies, lips, and hands, frantic with need. After stumbling to the sofa, he sits and I climb on top, wrap my fingers around his hard cock, and slide all the way down until I'm seated on him with nothing between us. I lean back, hands on his knees, and swivel my hips.

Cords stand out on his neck. "Fuck, why do you feel so good?" He thrusts up. Suddenly, his hands grip my hips. "Damn it. We forgot the condom."

I freeze. It didn't occur to me. I'd been with the others for months. "I'm on the pill, but if you want, I can grab one."

"Those lucky bastards," he murmurs, then shakes his head. "Good thing I came earlier or this would be disappointingly short. Having nothing between us is a fucking dream." With his hands on my hips, he lifts me up and pulls me down.

It's the last thing either of us says. I lean back again, letting him watch our bodies come together and slide apart, but slow isn't an option for us tonight. Too many days of foreplay have driven us mad. Our hips move frantically, needing to feel the other's body fall apart.

With a soft cry, I explode, and he immediately follows. I tumble forward, landing on his heaving chest, and he spears a hand through my hair to hold me tight in his arms, our bodies still joined.

A trickle of wetness slides down my thigh and with a wince, I ease up, then stand. "Be right back." Dashing to the bathroom attached to his office, I grab a washcloth. There's a well-satisfied woman in the mirror. Cheeks flush, eyes bright, lips swollen. I like her. A lot.

I stroll back into the office and hand him the washcloth. Then, I leave to search for our clothes. Once I've found them, I put on his button-down and toss him his briefs. He hands me the bourbon he grabbed while I was gone.

The image of the four of them in Army fatigues in the middle of nowhere catches my eye. "What made you decide to join the Army?" It's something I've always been curious to know. The other three have all had very different reasons for joining.

He takes a sip, then hands me back the glass. "People have practically prostrated themselves for my family and their money. The doctor track only made things worse. Most of the time, I focused on my residency and little else. It was exhilarating and challenging but it still felt like something was missing until I did my rotation in the ER. Everything clicked. I loved it—the urgency, the severity and variety of cases, and surprisingly, the lack of identity. They only care if you're the doctor who's going to help them."

His finger slides down my face. "When I finished medical school, I had this bone-deep need to do something important. Somewhere where they didn't care about my name. The Army offered it all. Experience I wouldn't get anywhere else, in a high-stakes environment with people who couldn't care less about my name, and to top it off, the longer I stayed, the better man I became. Then, I found them." He waves a hand at the picture. "And I refused to leave until they did."

After putting the glass down, I snuggle into his side, and he grabs the blanket off the back of the couch. "Stay with me. Just for a little while." I know he needs to get home and do his nighttime PT, but I don't want to give this up. Not yet.

Chapter Fifty-One

KATE

Lips nibble on the back of my neck. Thankfully, our last patient left a while ago.

"I love when you wear your hair up," his husky voice says from behind me.

I hold up my phone to show him the time. "Don't you have to be at rehab in forty-five minutes?" Helena's at least forty minutes away.

"Go with me," he pleads. "We can grab dinner at Lev's restaurant after. Maybe he can even join us."

"You know I love Lev's food and will do everything to avoid cooking dinner," I say with a mock sigh, easily giving in to his request. The possibility of having dinner with two of my men tonight is also tantalizing. "Fine, I'll go." Tossing the chart on the desk, I open the drawer and grab my purse.

We barely make it to his physical therapy on time.

His therapist eyes me and growls at Thayer. "Cutting it close. I almost left."

Smothering a laugh, I find a seat and watch the burly man put Thayer through his paces. He's good and thorough, constantly pushing Thayer to up his game. I like him.

Thayer's sweating when he finishes. "Let me grab a shower."

His arms go out to hug me, but with a laugh, I step back. "Oh, I have to stop by and see Paula's granddaughter while we're here. I promised her."

I frown. I've heard Paula mention her granddaughter, but I didn't know she was in the hospital. I'm kind of hurt nobody told me.

My phone pings. It's a text from Sarah.

> Sarah: I hope you don't mind, but I listed you as a reference today. It's for a private clinic here in L.A.

Sarah's three weeks turned into a permanent move. It's been over a month since she's been gone.

> Kate: Damn. This makes it real.
>
> Sarah: I know. I'm excited but nervous. Brax doesn't want me to work, but I can't sit home and twiddle my thumbs all day.
>
> Kate: You know I'll give you a glowing reference. You're a rock star nurse. Are you coming home for Christmas?
>
> Sarah: If I didn't, my grandmother would kill me. Besides, the entire family wants to meet Remi and Brax. I'll let you know more in a couple of weeks. Guess where we're going for Thanksgiving? Paris!!!
>
> Kate: Oooh, sounds sexy and romantic. Have fun! I can't wait to see you.

Thayer comes out and slides a glance at my phone.

"Sarah's applying for positions in L.A.," I inform him with a glum expression on my face. "It's permanent."

"It's not far," he says wryly. "We can visit."

"And Remi and Brax are taking her to Paris for Thanksgiving," I slip in, adding a dramatic sigh. "Lucky woman."

"Paris might have to wait until I'm healed, but we can go next year," he promises me. "Lev and I have already talked about it." He ushers me into the elevator.

I smile, knowing he's the one who suggested it. "To the most romantic city in the world with all four of you? Yes, please!"

"Paula's granddaughter is on the third floor," he says quietly, his ice-blue eyes studying me closely.

I flash him a puzzled look. "I can't believe I didn't know she was sick. Is it serious?"

"Very serious," he replies. "She's been here off and on for the last year."

My stomach clenches, and I suddenly know. I open my mouth to tell him I'll be in the lobby, but the elevator door opens and Paula's standing there with her son and daughter-in-law wearing a hopeful expression on her face.

"Thayer!" she exclaims. "Thank you for coming. We really appreciate you taking the time to stop by. A second opinion will make us feel so much better." She eyes me for a second. "Dr. Michaels, are you okay?"

She doesn't know. My mouth stretches into what I hope is a smile. "Paula, I'm so sorry to hear your granddaughter is sick." Everywhere I turn, I see bright, colorful drawings and stuffed animals. The children's ward. They do so much to make things look cheerful, but in the end, it's still a hospital and their child is sick.

"Leukemia," she whispers, as if afraid to say it out loud. "ALL."

My hand trembles and I stuff it into my pocket. "I'm so sorry."

"We'll review the chart, then come back to talk to you," Thayer tells them, taking my arm.

By this time, I'm shaking from head to toe and scrambling for an escape. "I can't believe you brought me here. What the hell were you thinking?" My voice is low, not wanting Paula and her family to hear us fighting, but I'm ready to scream at the top of my lungs.

"Please help them. Just take a look at the chart with me. This isn't my area of expertise, but I couldn't refuse," he pleads with me to understand, but I can't believe he's cornered me like this.

I turn around and catch Paula's worried expression. "Fine. Give it to me," I tell him. My eyes scan the labs and treatment plan. Even after four years away, the chart is as familiar to me as the day I left. "It's good news. She's in remission."

A sob of relief escapes before I can hold it back, and I shove the folder into his stomach. "They still have a long road ahead of them. Once she gets through this phase, she'll have to undergo maintenance to monitor her cells for regrowth or a relapse, but she has a fighting chance."

"Thank you. Let me tell Paula and her family. I'll be right back," he states quietly, a worried expression in his eyes.

I walk out. I don't know where I'm going, but I refuse to stay here and wait for him. My breath catches and tears stream down my face as I stumble out of the hospital. Painful memories jab their barbs in deep, but it's the pain of Thayer's betrayal that hurts the most. The cold November wind cuts through my coat, but I barely feel it. I look around and realize I don't have a car to get home. I start walking until a diner catches my eye and I fall into its cozy arms.

"Coffee, please," I tell the waitress. She takes one look at me and hands me a box of tissues from under the counter. "He isn't worth it, honey."

"Thanks," I murmur. My phone buzzes. It's Thayer. I pick it up. "Why?"

"Because somebody we care about needed us," he replies in a quiet voice. "I couldn't say no. I know I should have told you, but the words wouldn't come."

I hang up. When the phone rings again, I turn it off. Completely. For hours, I sit there and think about the past. Not just the bad times, but the good ones too. Before the shooting. I don't know if time has given me perspective or the strength I've found with them, maybe both, but this time, the dark doesn't pull me under.

Weary, I slide into a cab and take it back to the practice where the lights are blazing like a beacon welcoming me back. All four of their vehicles are in the parking lot. For a second, I'm tempted to run, but I can't. Not anymore. This is my home. Sometime between the third and fourth cup of coffee, I realized I couldn't hide from the past anymore. Not if I want to move forward. With them. What I've found here is worth the fight.

I enter the office and see Thayer sitting behind the desk with his head in his hands. He stands when he sees me, a relieved expression on his face, and moves toward me.

The look on mine stops him. "What you did was wrong. You should have told me about Paula and asked for my help. We could have figured out a way for me to read the file without having to physically be there, but typical Thayer, you bulldoze your way through, and I'm left raw and bleeding on the side of the road."

He pales even further as if he didn't think of it that way. "Please don't leave me," his voice cracks. "You're right. I fucked up. I completely misjudged everything. I'm so sorry, Kate. Please forgive me." He walks over and takes my hands in his.

"Go home, Thayer," I tell him, unable to deal with this tonight. "I think it's best if we don't see each other for a few days."

He jerks back and folds his arms. "No, I'm staying."

"Maybe you should give her a few days," Shaw says from the doorway.

"Did she come back?" I hear Lev shout from the front.

"She's here!" He shouts back.

"Thank the fuck," Lowell's quiet voice reaches me.

Lev and Lowell join Shaw in the doorway with worried expressions on their faces. It hits me hard. Damn it, I should have called.

Thayer moves until he's in front of me. "I'm not leaving. This isn't the first time I've fucked up, and it sure as hell won't be the last." He spreads his arms wide. "I see it in your face everyday. I know you want more. I see the longing when you sneak in an article on cancer during your lunch break. It's your calling. Stop letting the past take the thing that you love."

His words echo in my mind over and over. What I wouldn't give to go back, but I can't. "What parent in their right mind would allow me to be their child's doctor?" Defensive, I wrap my arms around my stomach to hold myself together. "Worse, what if it happens again and another child dies because of a decision I make. I can't go through that again. I've accepted it. Why can't you?"

"Because you were born to do it, and I hate to see talent wasted," he utters with conviction. He stares at me for a second, then heaves a sigh. "The way I went about it was wrong, and I can't promise to leave this alone, but I'll back off for now."

"You ask too much of me," I murmur, tears slipping down my face.

"I love you," he remarks softly. "You've seen me at my worst and my most vulnerable. And you're still here. I'm still here. We're in this together. No matter what. All of us."

I stare at him suddenly understanding everything. This man will fight to the ends of the earth for me. They all will. I know this with every fiber of my being, but they don't. I realize they're scared I'll leave them. It breaks my heart to know I haven't given them the words they need to hear. "I'm beyond angry with you Thayer, but god, I love you too. So much." I turn until I'm facing them all. "I love all of you. We belong together, and no matter what happens, I'm not going anywhere. I promise you. My home is here with you."

Chapter Fifty-Two

KATE

December came roaring in with a nasty blizzard earlier this week. Being from a milder climate, it was awe-inspiring to see Mother Nature wipe the land clean in a matter of hours. Montana has been my home for ten months now, and I can't imagine living anywhere else.

Thayer and I are still taking things slow, but even with our rocky beginning, I'm equally in love with him as I am with my other three men. He's still arrogant and pushy, but I understand now how far he'll go for those he loves, including me.

Tonight, we're going to the Cattleman's Christmas Ball in Helena. It's our first event together, and I'm incredibly nervous. According to Shaw, all the ranchers in the state will be going, so that means literally everyone will be there. It's been a long time since I've been in a huge crowd of people and I'm incredibly nervous someone's going to recognize me and ruin the evening.

Shaw and Lev went up early to talk to the other ranchers about the vineyard, Lowell's in his room getting ready, and Thayer's writing an article on his condition for a medical journal. He felt his experiences as a patient could help other doctors determine the best course of treatment. In seven months, he's made remarkable progress, but he knows it can be better. Always pushing. Glad it's not just me.

Buckling the straps on my shoes, I step up to the mirror and study my reflection. I smile with satisfaction. They're not going to know what hit them. The dress is two pieces designed to look like one. The top is a strapless, black lace bustier. The bottom is a full, green satin skirt that hangs to the floor with a slit on one side to the top of the thigh. Formal, but sexy. Black strappy high heels complete the picture.

Stepping out from Shaw's bedroom, I head toward the living room to wait for Lowell and Thayer. The car will be here in fifteen minutes, which leaves me enough time to have a glass of wine.

Standing in front of the window, a long, low whistle fills the air behind me. Turning around, I find both Lowell and Thayer in the doorway wearing custom tuxedos. Damn, I love a man in a tuxedo. Two men in a tuxedo? I'm tempted to stay home.

"You look gorgeous," Thayer drawls. With his new cane in hand, he slowly walks over to give me a kiss.

"Thanks, handsome," I reply, squatting down to fix my shoe.

"Umm, Kate, I wouldn't bend over in that dress," he murmurs when I stand. With a hungry look in his eyes, his fingers lightly caress the tops of my breasts, which are falling out of the bustier.

"Oops," I squeak, tucking them back in. Both men groan.

Lowell steps forward. "I'm not going to be able to get that sight out of my mind for a while. Simply stunning." Winking, he reaches out and slips a finger into my cleavage, using the bustier as leverage to pull me forward and give me one of his deliciously restrained kisses.

A ping alerts us to the car service's arrival. Grabbing my black velvet cape and clutch, we head out to the large SUV waiting in the driveway. I settle in the back seat between Lowell and Thayer.

Shaw and Lev booked a hotel room for us tonight, so they'll meet us at the entrance to the ballroom.

My fingers convey my nervousness with their restless movement. Catching Lowell's eyes, I notice he's staring at my hands and frowning. I know I'm fidgeting, but I can't help it. His long fingers reach out and pull my hand into his. Clasping it to him, he stares out at the window. A moment later, I feel Thayer take my other hand, and my nerves settle.

Arriving at the ball, Lowell steps out first, then helps both me and Thayer out of the vehicle. Entering the hotel, we head toward the coat check first. I notice the hotel is crowded with spectacularly dressed women and men. This is definitely THE event of the year.

After handing over our coats, we stroll toward the ballroom until we find Lev and Shaw.

"Damn, sweetheart. You look good enough to eat," Lev exclaims, swooping down to pull me in for a full-body hug. After giving me a sweet kiss on the lips, he hands me to Shaw.

"He's right. You look incredible," Shaw murmurs, leaning down to place his own kiss on my lips.

Stepping back to study all four of them, I fan myself dramatically. "I'm a lucky woman to have four incredibly handsome men as my escorts. Let me get a picture with all of you in it, then we'll get someone to take one of all of us." After snapping a few pictures, we finally get into the ballroom and to our table.

The first part of the event is dinner, followed by a silent auction for charity. I bid secretly on a few items for their Christmas. I win one out of three, but I'm still ecstatic. Tucking the details into my clutch, I head back to the table.

Setting my purse down on the table, I turn to Lowell. "Let's dance." His green eyes sparkle and he quickly stands and smoothly twirls me onto the dance floor.

While we dance, I notice we're getting a lot of puzzled looks, and I start to worry. When people get that expression on their face, they're usually trying to work out why I look so familiar. I stumble.

Lowell glances down in surprise. "Are you okay, love?" Seeing my white face, he pulls me off the dance floor. "What is it? Are you sick?"

"What? I... No, I'm fine. I need to go to the ladies room. Please excuse me. I'll meet you back at the table." Without waiting for a reply, I grab my clutch and walk away, leaving him standing there, watching me.

Splashing cold water on my face, I try to get my nerves under control. This is the first big event I've attended since the shooting, and all I can think about is what will happen if someone recognizes me. People tend to be extreme in their reactions, and I don't want to ruin our first evening out together. Taking a few deep breaths, I exhale slowly and get myself under control. Dabbing my face, I square my shoulders and step out into the hallway.

A lady nearby stops when she sees me. I tense.

"Excuse me," she calls out.

"Yes?" Maybe she's searching for someone.

"Are you with Thayer Bradford tonight?"

My shoulders relax. "Yes, I am." Oh, great, an ex-whatever of Thayer's. I almost snort at Thayer's type. A buxom brunette with a painted-on dress dripping in diamonds.

"Such a shame what happened to him. What that man could do with his... equipment, if you get what I mean," she quips. "Tell me. Is everything back to normal with him?"

"His 'equipment' works very well," I snap. "In fact, I'm exhausted from last night. I would tell you about it, but honestly, it doesn't matter because he's off the market. Now, if you will excuse me."

"What about Shaw or that hunky Lev?" she blurts out as I start to step around her.

Speechless, I stare at her. Fury rises, but I push it down. After all, I can appreciate their attractiveness, just not her drooling over them.

"Let's be clear, shall we?" I say slowly, wanting to make sure she hears every word. "They're mine. Thayer, Lev, Lowell, and Shaw. Off the market. Permanently. I'm claiming them. All of them. Go tell your friends. Now, please excuse me."

Her face reddens. "Four men? Isn't that a bit... selfish?"

"Not at all. You should try it. Women deserve to be this happy," I urge her with a smug look of satisfaction on my face. It's her turn to be speechless as I turn to walk away.

I stop. All four of my men are standing behind me, grinning. Along with about two dozen other people. Mortified, I walk into Shaw's arms and hide my face.

"I'm sorry, Shaw," I apologize. "I hope you're not upset."

His shoulders are shaking with laughter. "We're the envy of every man here tonight. You just loudly claimed us to be yours and permanently off the market. They should be so lucky." His voice is husky.

"Personally, I'm ecstatic that you defended my cock so vigorously," Thayer's voice is full of glee as he tells me.

I raise my head and wince. "Can you please keep your voice down?"

"Sweetheart, you just made me the happiest man alive. Don't back down now." Lev gives me a swift kiss while I'm still in Shaw's arms.

Glancing at Lowell, I notice the stern expression on his face. "What is it?"

"Why were you so nervous tonight? I... We thought it was because you didn't want to be seen with all of us, but that doesn't appear to be the case. What is it?" he questions me.

Sighing, I realize how it must have appeared. "I love all of us being together." I dart a glance at the people and shiver. "Part of me can't help worrying someone will recognize me. In an event this large, I was afraid if it happened, they would cause a big scene and ruin the evening. For the last few years, I've avoided big events."

They all converse silently, and I just cross my arms and wait.

Lowell pushes his glasses up on his nose and stares down at me. "I'm sorry, love. We didn't realize because we were caught up in our own fears. We never attended events with Vanessa because she didn't want anyone to know we were all together. When you said yes to the event, but then showed signs of nervousness, we thought it might be too much of a public statement. We were trying to figure out how to make this easier on you."

Stepping over to him, I squeeze him tight, then turn to all of them. "I love you. All of you. I don't care what others think. You're mine, and I'm not letting you go." And with a decisive nod, I look at Shaw. "If you still want me, I'd love to move to the ranch. I miss you all too much during the week."

Shaw's voice is filled with gravel when he agrees. "You're it for us too. We love you, more than we thought it possible to love someone, and we already have your room ready. We've just been waiting for you to say yes."

Feeling lighter, I laugh. "Speaking of rooms... didn't someone say we had a hotel room tonight? Let's take this celebration somewhere a bit more private, shall we?"

After all the heartache and violence from the past, I've finally found my salvation with the men of my dreams, and they've found theirs with me. I want to pinch myself some days, but if this is a dream, I don't want to wake up. Instead, I hold tight to them and to their love. And they hold tight right back.

EPILOGUE

KATE

Pride fills me when I look at the new building in front of me. The Chester Michaels Cancer Center named after my grandpa. He would be so proud. The state-of-the-art cancer research center is a place where doctors can come and learn the latest treatments from world-renown oncologists, gaining the knowledge necessary to fight against the insidious disease.

Because of Thayer's actions, I thought long and hard about practicing oncology again, but in the end, I felt this was a better way to help. Something that fits the person I am today. Anyone could have made the mistake I did. Lack of knowledge isn't a crime, but it costs lives. Finding a way to get critical information into the hands of oncologists across the northeast will save hundreds of people, and appropriately, I used the last of the money from Collin to set it up.

Thayer slings an arm around me. "I'm so proud of you. This is going to be an incredible facility. If doctors know where they can easily get information without having to dig through journals and studies, it will help them to quickly and confidently provide the best treatment for their cancer patients."

We both look over at Paula's granddaughter. A year and a half later, she's still here and in remission.

"I'm going to miss you," he murmurs sadly.

Seeing Thayer every day at work and home put a lot of strain on our relationship. Besides, he was right. Oncology is my calling, not general medicine. Running this center will be a challenge, but I'm looking forward to it. "I think it's time you had your practice back. Although, I hear the hospital needs an ER doctor."

He laughs, but I see the interest spark in his eyes.

Lev comes up and hugs me. "This is amazing. I overheard several of the doctors already talking about the first seminar."

They should be. The lecturer is one of the top five oncologists in the world with his own R&D program, and I'm excited to offer someone of his caliber a platform to showcase his knowledge. "Thanks. He's extremely cutting edge, and I think he'll have a lot of new information to share."

Shaw bends down to kiss me. "Congratulations."

Lowell says nothing, only stares at me with narrowed eyes.

I swallow nervously, wondering if he's guessed my secret.

Lev glances at Thayer, then back to me. "Christmas will be here in a few months. Our second one. Thayer's rehabilitation is finished. What do you think about going to Paris? That should give you enough time to get the center up and running, right? Plus, it's easier for us all to get away during the holidays."

"Paris sounds incredible, but unfortunately, I'll be too pregnant to fly at Christmas," I say nonchalantly.

Silence.

Lowell smiles. "I knew something was up. Your body looks… lush." His eyes are on my breasts as he bends down to give me a wild, utterly undisciplined kiss that tells me how happy he is to hear my news.

Shaw stares at me, a stunned expression on his face. "When are you due?"

"January," I reply, glancing up at him. "Are you happy about it?"

His lips curve. "I'm so damn happy." He cups my face. "Girl or boy, I don't give a damn."

Lev sweeps me into his arms. "I'm thrilled. In fact, I'd like at least several more." His kiss is full of happiness.

I look over at Thayer. Silent tears are rolling down his face. "I've always wanted to be a dad, and I'll be a good one too. Not like my father, I promise."

Leaning into his arms, I stretch up and kiss him. "You're going to be a fantastic dad. All of you." I look at the four men around me. This is going to be one lucky kid. I look around and spot my mother talking to Hank Guthrie, a slight blush on her face. *Hmm.* Maybe there is a way to get her to move here.

THANK YOU!

Thank you for reading! This was the first book I ever wrote. I decided to give it some additional editing love and a couple more chapters. I'd love to hear your thoughts. Whether it's "give me more," or "I want to see a book with…" reviews help me write the next story. Please consider leaving one for this book.

*If you find an error, email me at Stellabrie@stellabrie.com.

*Playlists for all my books can be found on YouTube @authorstellabrie

*Pirating can have severe consequences, preventing authors from creating new stories. Please don't read pirated copies.

AWESOME PEOPLE

To my readers, friends, and fans! Thanks for all the wonderful words of encouragement, friendship, and love for my books! And for participating in my shenanigans and all the other weird things I post. You guys rock! I couldn't do it without you!!!

My awesome beta readers. They catch so many big and little things, help me with names, show me such amazing friendship, encouragement, and excitement, and they can't even share it with anyone! My books are a thousand times better because of their feedback. Thank you, Nia, Bianca, Iliana, Melissa, Rachel, Sandi, and Debbie for everything!

My ARC team who gives me so much support and enthusiasm even though I drop things on them at the last minute. Ooh, look, cover reveal! Book's launching in a week! Seriously, I appreciate all of you!!

My biggest supporters—my husband and my mom. I'm so lucky to have you both! Love you!

And always… a special thanks to all the wonderful authors in the writing community who support each other day in and out. Writing would be a lonely and weird world without you. It would be me and my characters sitting around chatting (drinking) while we plot the next book. Your friendship and support mean a lot to me!

ABOUT THE AUTHOR

Stella Brie lives outside of Nashville, TN, with her husband. After mentioning her desire to write a book a million times to her husband, he challenged her to sit down one day and write a paragraph. Instead, she wrote her first book, *My Salvation*.

She traded in her career in digital marketing, working on big brands, for this wildly creative one. Armed with a notebook crammed full of ideas, she's constantly thinking about bold heroines, sexy men, and HEAs. Whether it's a paranormal book full of creatures and magic or a contemporary romance full of heat and drama, she's dreaming about bringing her books to life.

Latest News and Updates:
Facebook Group: Stella's Stalkers
Instagram: @stellabrie_author
TikTok: @stellabrie_author
REAM: Coming Soon!
Website: Stellabrie.com - Exclusive sneak peeks, cover reveals, giveaways, and more!

BOOKS BY STELLA BRIE

URBAN FANTASY WHY CHOOSE

KILLIAN BLADE SERIES
The Rowan (1)

The Rowan's Stone (2)

The Rowan's Destiny (3)

Wicked Savior - Lucifer's story (MF Romance) - (3.5)

The Light Falls (4) - Meri's story

The Dark Rises (5) - Meri's story

CONTEMPORARY WHY CHOOSE

THE SAVAGES SERIES (Duet)
Savage Traitor (1)

Savage Ruin (2)

Lethal Vengeance (Standalone + Spin-off)

My Salvation (Standalone)